STAR SCOUTS

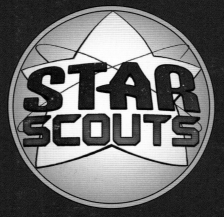

# :01

Fir**st** Second
New York

Copyright © 2017 Mike Lawrence
Published by First Second
First Second is an imprint of Roaring Brook Press,
a division of Holtzbrinck Publishing Holdings Limited Partnership
175 Fifth Avenue, New York, New York 10010

Library of Congress Control Number: 2016938730

ISBN: 978-1-62672-280-4

Our books may be purchased in bulk for promotional, educational,
or business use. Please contact your local bookseller or the Macmillan
Corporate and Premium Sales Department at (800) 221-7945 ext. 5442
or by email at MacmillanSpecialMarkets@macmillan.com.

First edition 2017
Book design by Danielle Ceccolini
Printed in China by Toppan Leefung Printing Ltd., Dongguan City, Guangdong Province

10 9 8 7 6 5 4 3 2 1

Drawn digitally in Photoshop with Kyle T. Webster's digital brushes, inked with a Pentel
Pocket Brush and various Faber-Castell PITT pens on Strathmore 300 series Smooth
Bristol. Colored digitally with Photoshop using Kyle T. Webster's digital brushes. Lettered
with Blambot fonts.

# MIKE LAWRENCE

First Second

New York

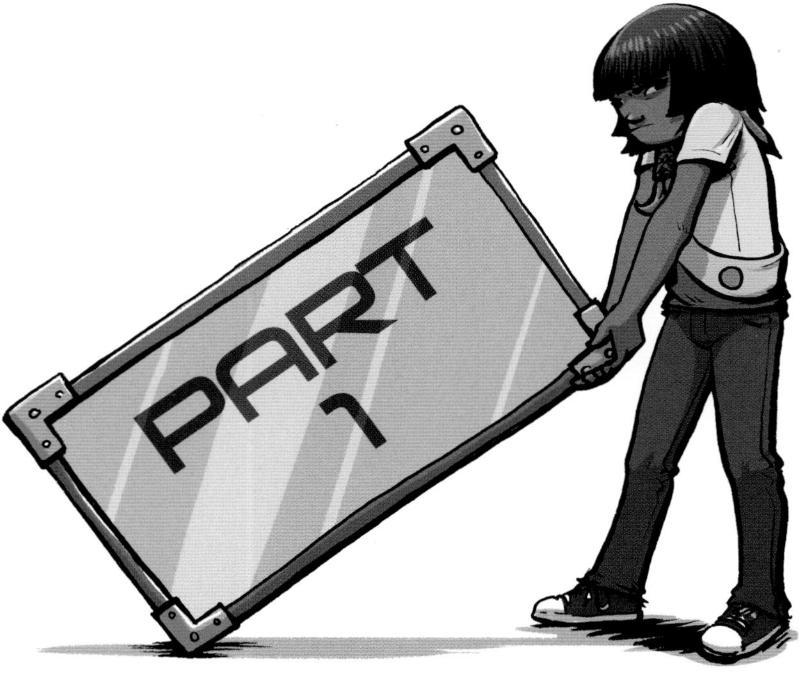
PART
1

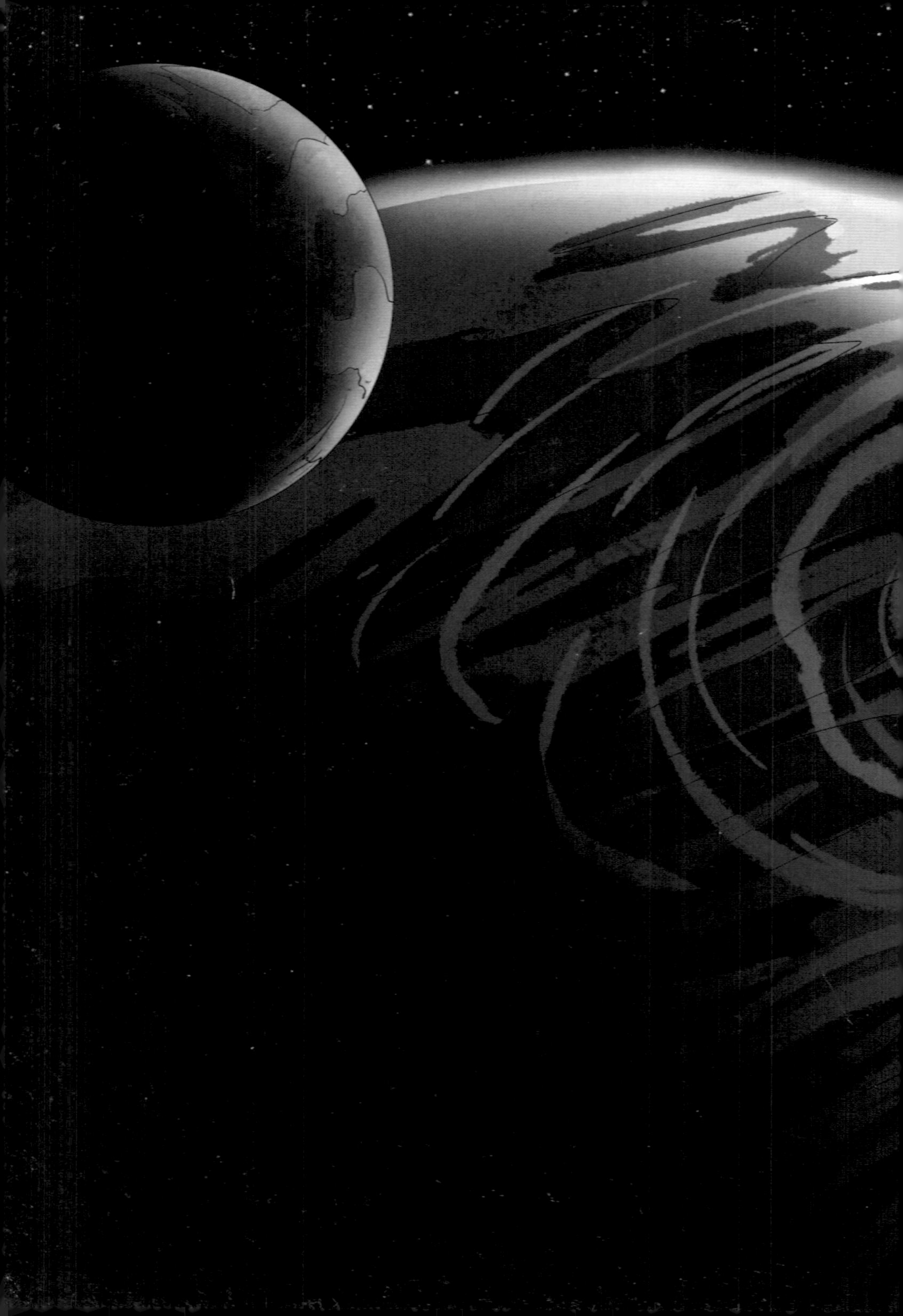

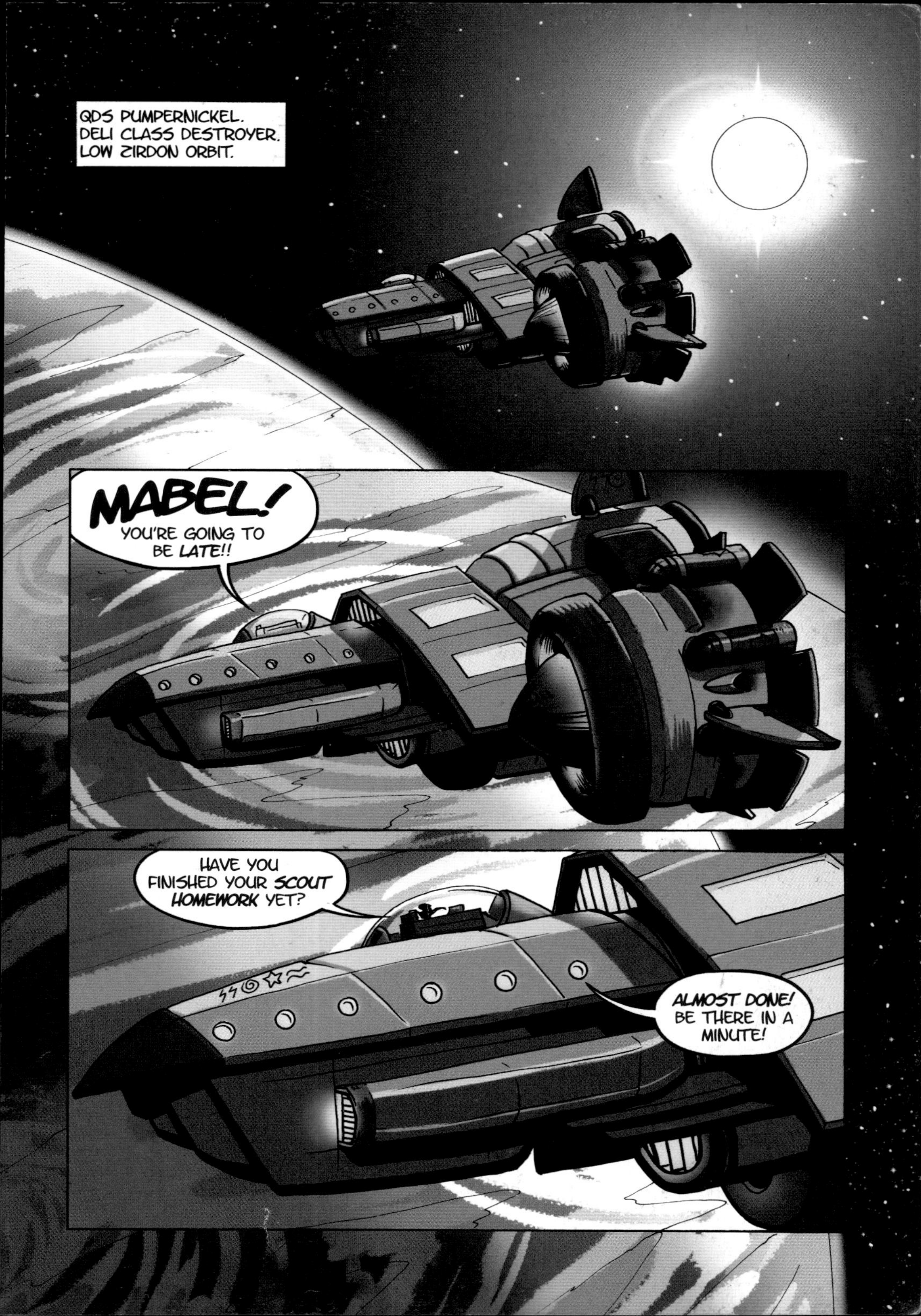
QDS PUMPERNICKEL.
DELI CLASS DESTROYER.
LOW ZIRDON ORBIT.
MABEL! YOU'RE GOING TO BE LATE!!
HAVE YOU FINISHED YOUR SCOUT HOMEWORK YET?
ALMOST DONE! BE THERE IN A MINUTE!

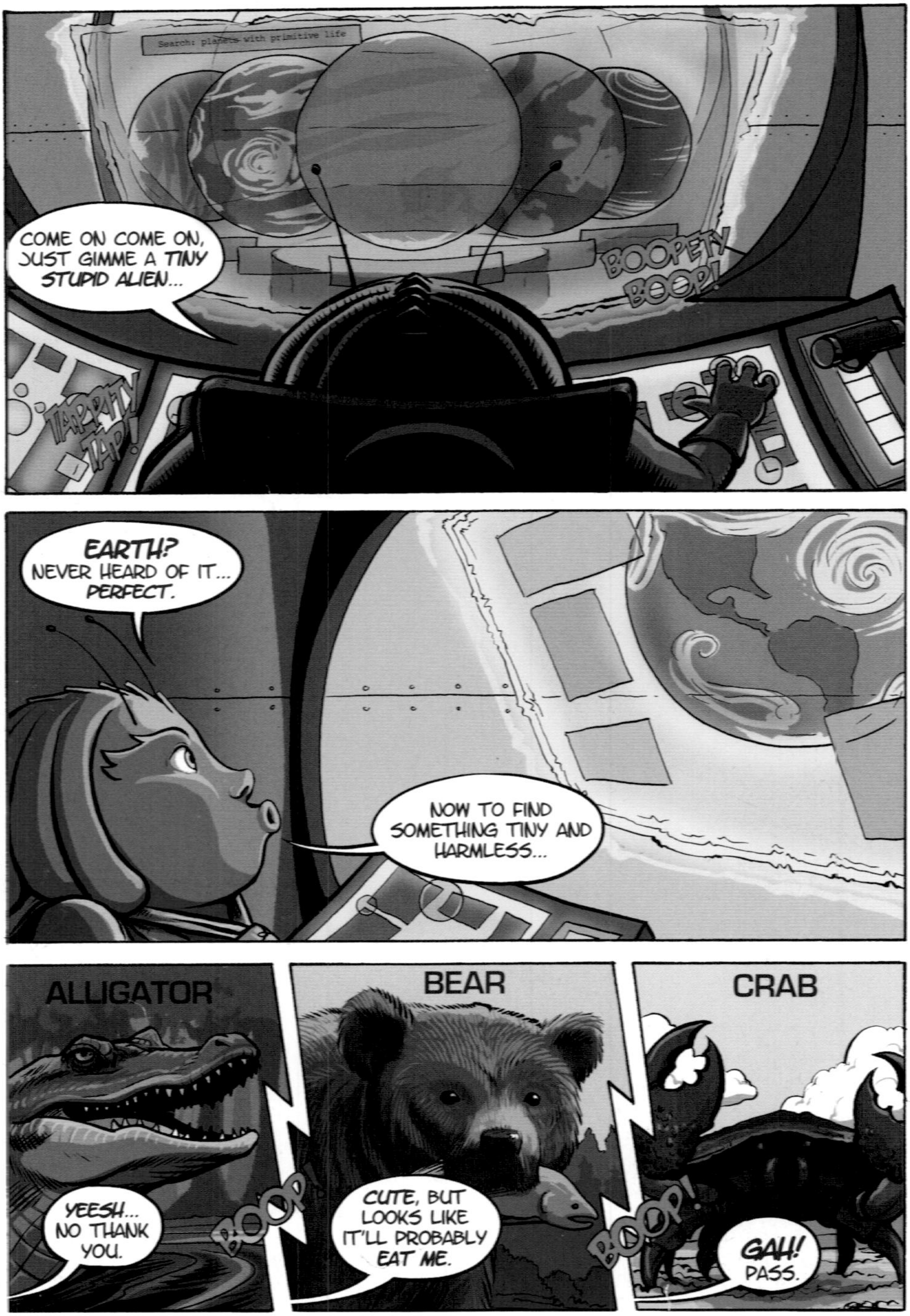
Search: planets with primitive life
COME ON COME ON, JUST GIMME A TINY STUPID ALIEN...
BOOPETY BOOP!
TAPPITY TAP!
EARTH? NEVER HEARD OF IT... PERFECT.
NOW TO FIND SOMETHING TINY AND HARMLESS...
ALLIGATOR
YEESH... NO THANK YOU.
BOOP!
BEAR
CUTE, BUT LOOKS LIKE IT'LL PROBABLY EAT ME.
BOOP!
CRAB
GAH! PASS.

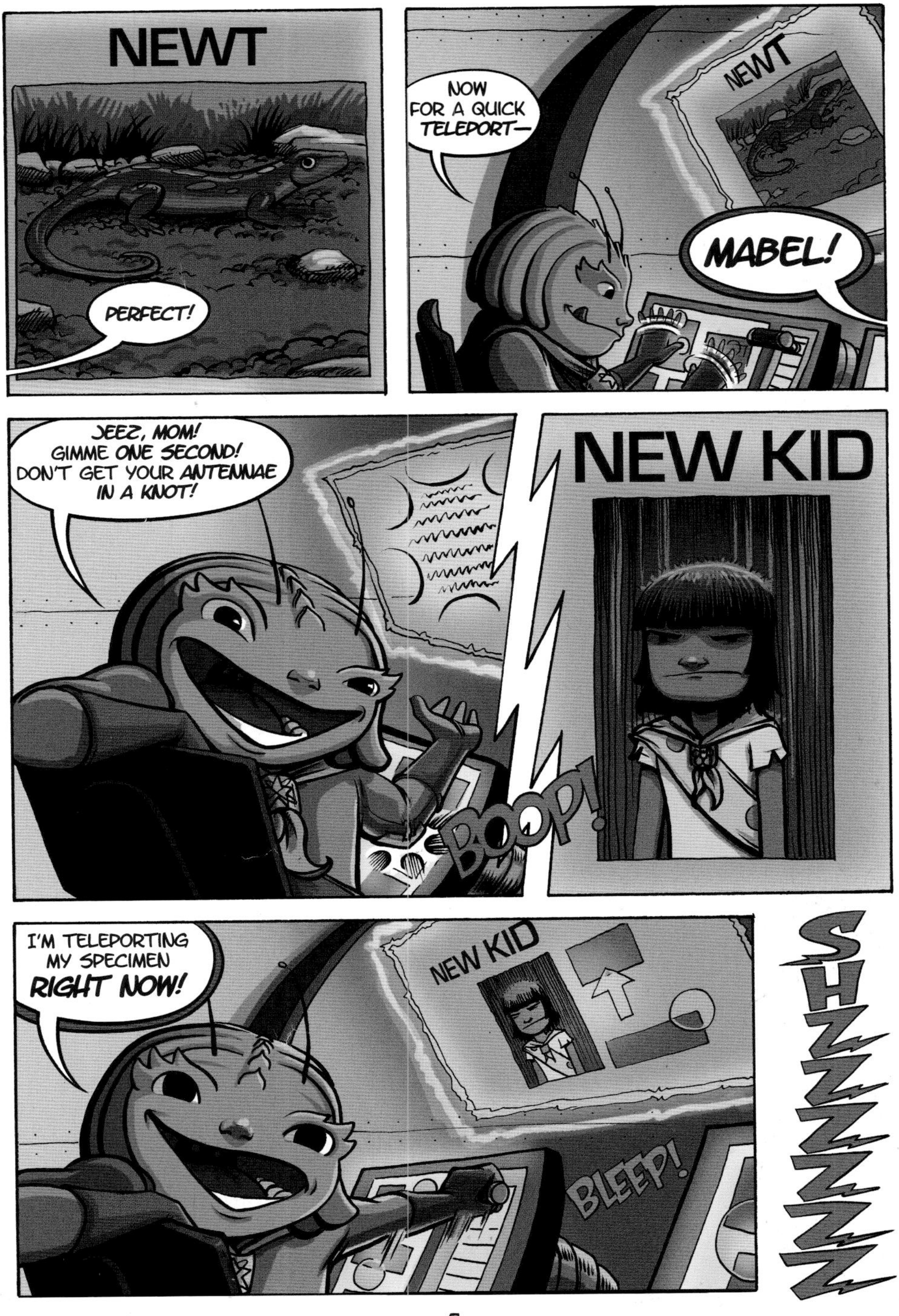
NEWT
PERFECT!
NOW FOR A QUICK TELEPORT—
NEWT
MABEL!
JEEZ, MOM! GIMME ONE SECOND! DON'T GET YOUR ANTENNAE IN A KNOT!
BOOP!
NEW KID
I'M TELEPORTING MY SPECIMEN RIGHT NOW!
NEW KID
BLEEP!
SHZZZZZZ

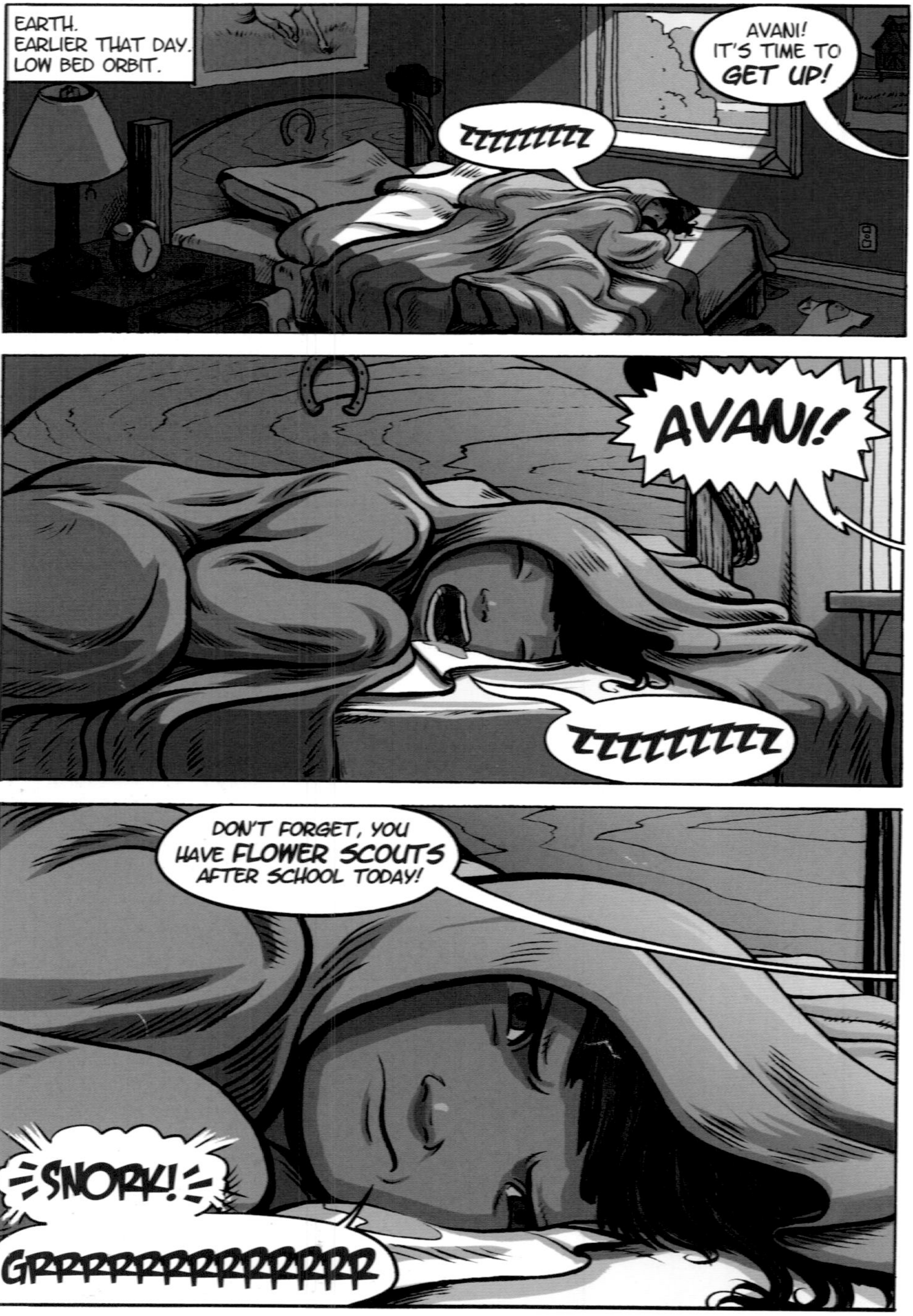
EARTH.
EARLIER THAT DAY.
LOW BED ORBIT.
AVANI! IT'S TIME TO GET UP!
ZZZZZZZZZ
AVANI!
ZZZZZZZZZZ
DON'T FORGET, YOU HAVE FLOWER SCOUTS AFTER SCHOOL TODAY!
SNORK!
GRRRRRRRRRRRRRR

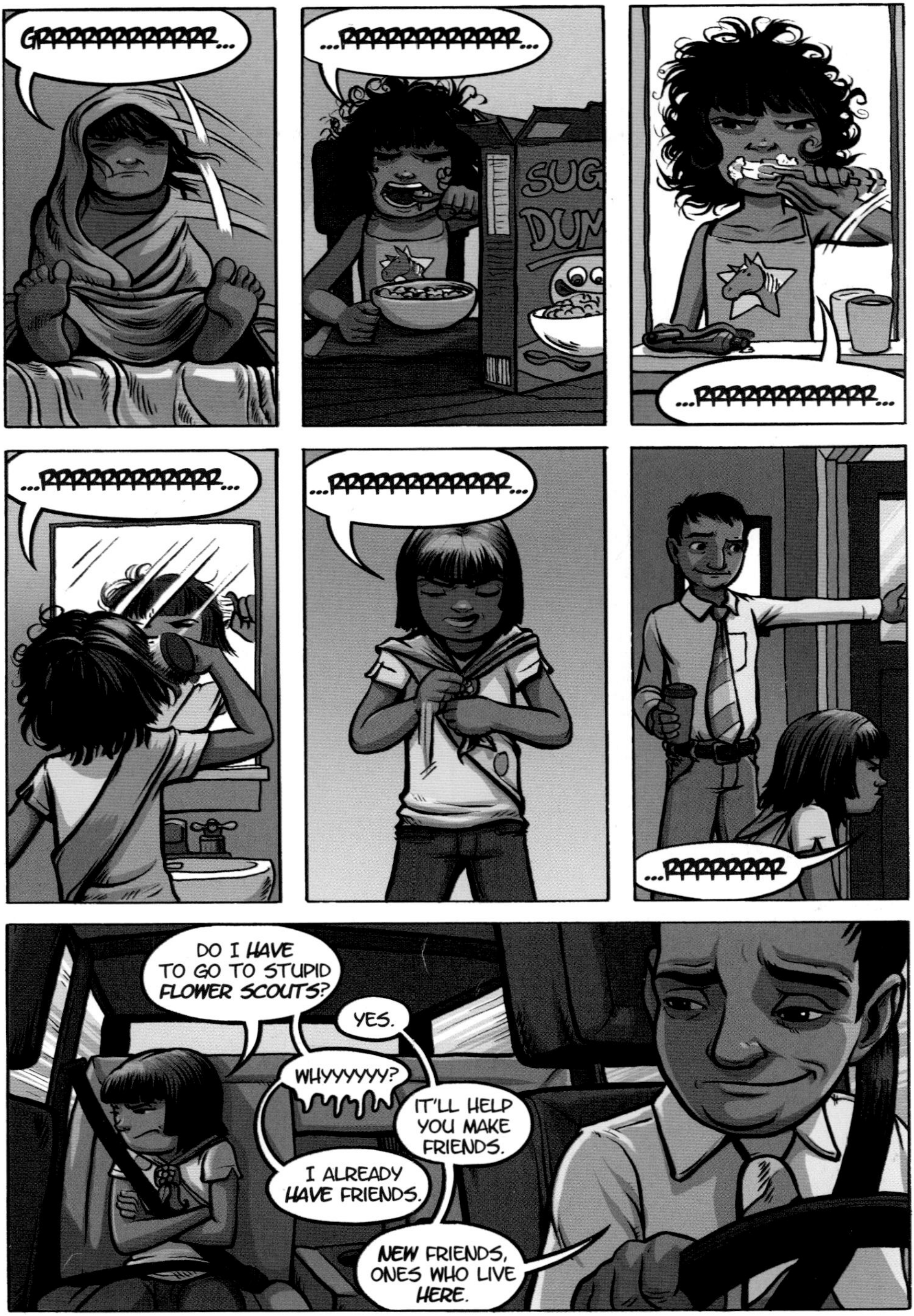
GRRRRRRRRRRRRR...
...RRRRRRRRRRRRR...
SUG DUM
...RRRRRRRRRRRRR...
...RRRRRRRRRRRRR...
...RRRRRRRRRRRRR...
...RRRRRRRR
DO I HAVE TO GO TO STUPID FLOWER SCOUTS?
YES.
WHYYYYYY?
IT'LL HELP YOU MAKE FRIENDS.
I ALREADY HAVE FRIENDS.
NEW FRIENDS, ONES WHO LIVE HERE.

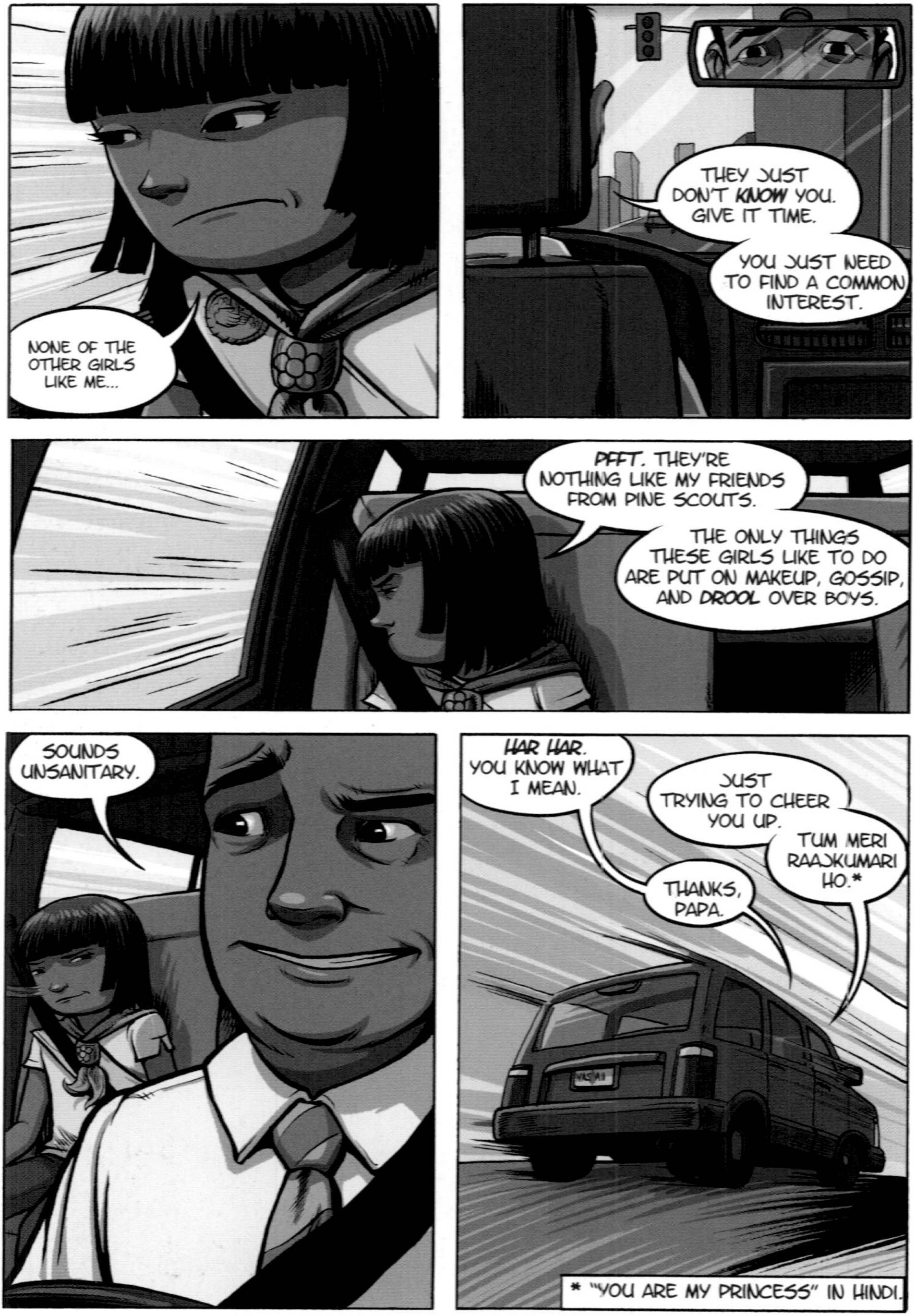
NONE OF THE OTHER GIRLS LIKE ME...
THEY JUST DON'T KNOW YOU. GIVE IT TIME.
YOU JUST NEED TO FIND A COMMON INTEREST.
PFFT. THEY'RE NOTHING LIKE MY FRIENDS FROM PINE SCOUTS.
THE ONLY THINGS THESE GIRLS LIKE TO DO ARE PUT ON MAKEUP, GOSSIP, AND DROOL OVER BOYS.
SOUNDS UNSANITARY.
HAR HAR. YOU KNOW WHAT I MEAN.
JUST TRYING TO CHEER YOU UP.
TUM MERI RAAJKUMARI HO.*
THANKS, PAPA.
* "YOU ARE MY PRINCESS" IN HINDI.

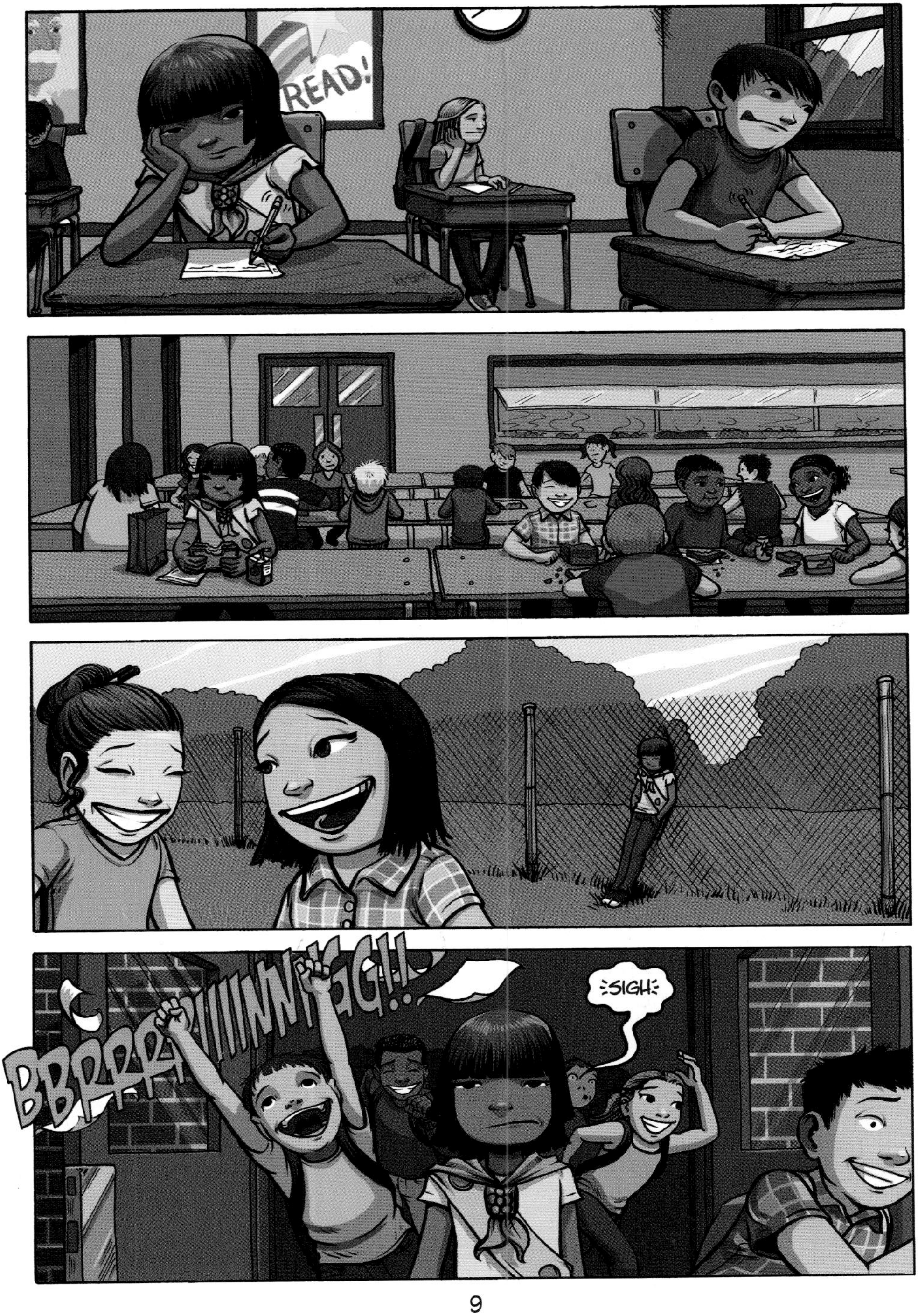
READ!
BBRRRIIIIINNNGG!!
SIGH

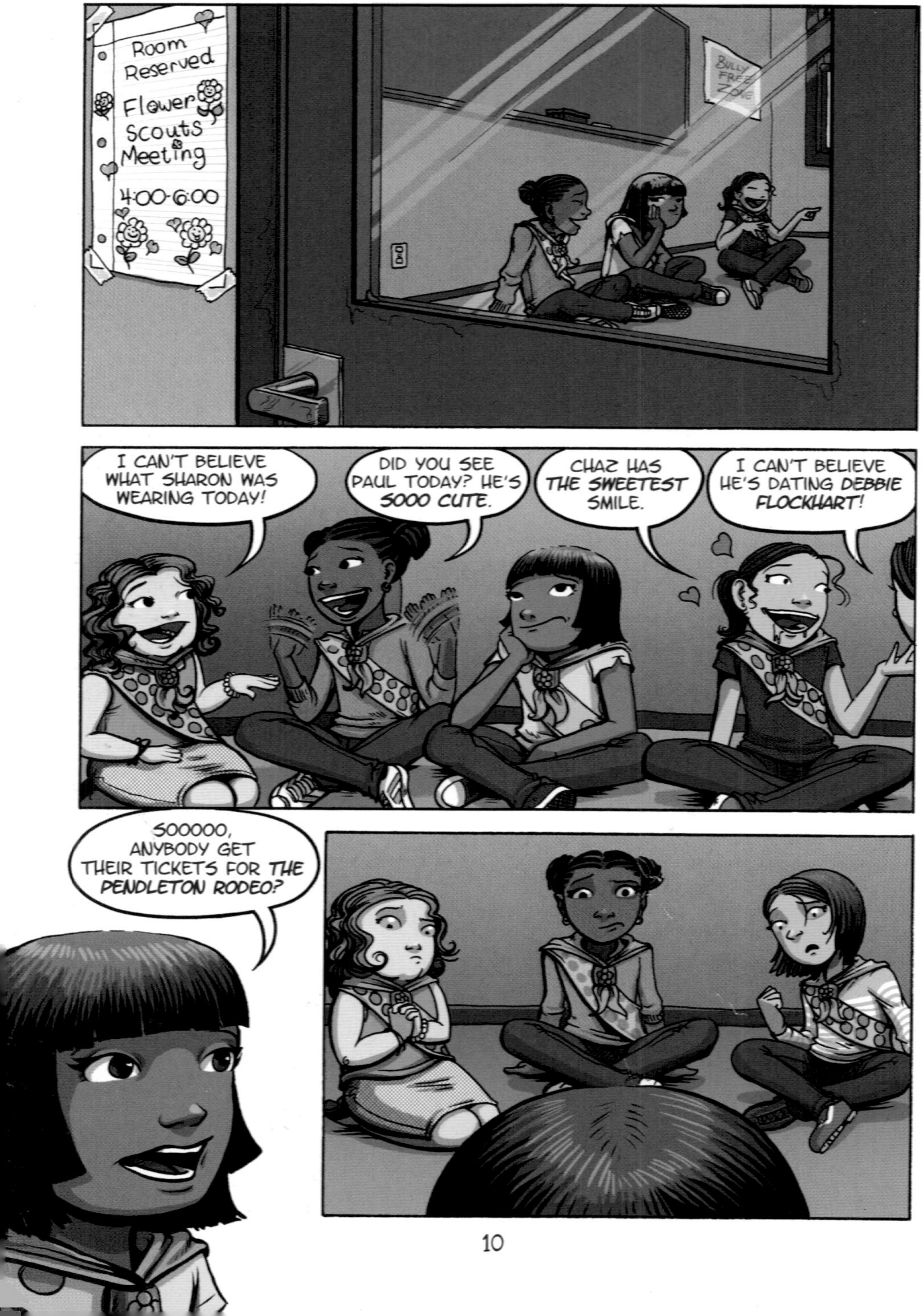
Room Reserved
Flower Scouts Meeting
4:00-6:00
I CAN'T BELIEVE WHAT SHARON WAS WEARING TODAY!
DID YOU SEE PAUL TODAY? HE'S **SOOO CUTE**.
CHAZ HAS **THE SWEETEST** SMILE.
I CAN'T BELIEVE HE'S DATING **DEBBIE FLOCKHART**!
SOOOOO, ANYBODY GET THEIR TICKETS FOR **THE PENDLETON RODEO?**

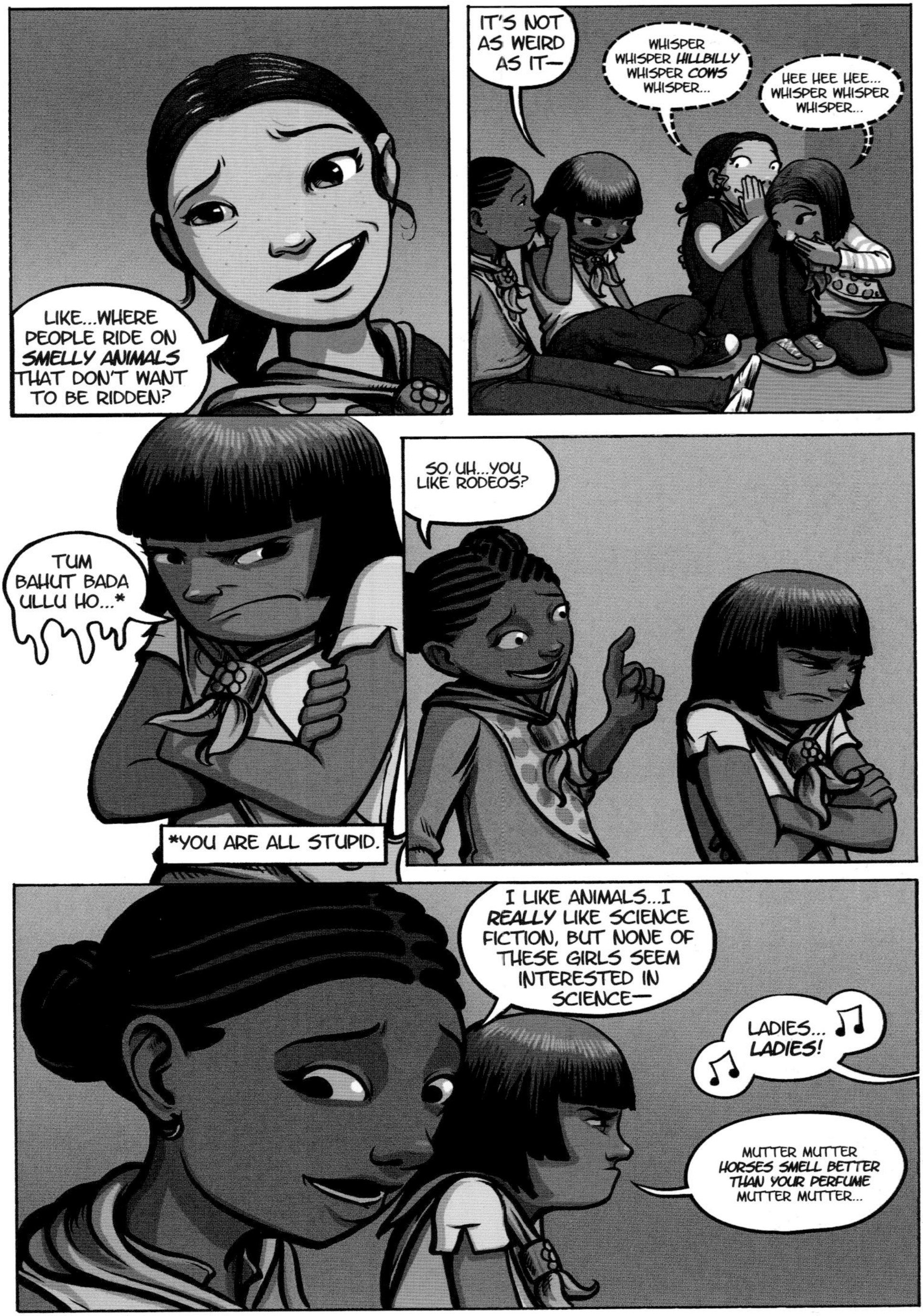
LIKE...WHERE PEOPLE RIDE ON SMELLY ANIMALS THAT DON'T WANT TO BE RIDDEN?
IT'S NOT AS WEIRD AS IT—
WHISPER WHISPER HILLBILLY WHISPER COWS WHISPER...
HEE HEE HEE... WHISPER WHISPER WHISPER...
TUM BAHUT BADA ULLU HO...*
*YOU ARE ALL STUPID.
SO, UH...YOU LIKE RODEOS?
I LIKE ANIMALS...I REALLY LIKE SCIENCE FICTION, BUT NONE OF THESE GIRLS SEEM INTERESTED IN SCIENCE—
LADIES... LADIES!
MUTTER MUTTER HORSES SMELL BETTER THAN YOUR PERFUME MUTTER MUTTER...

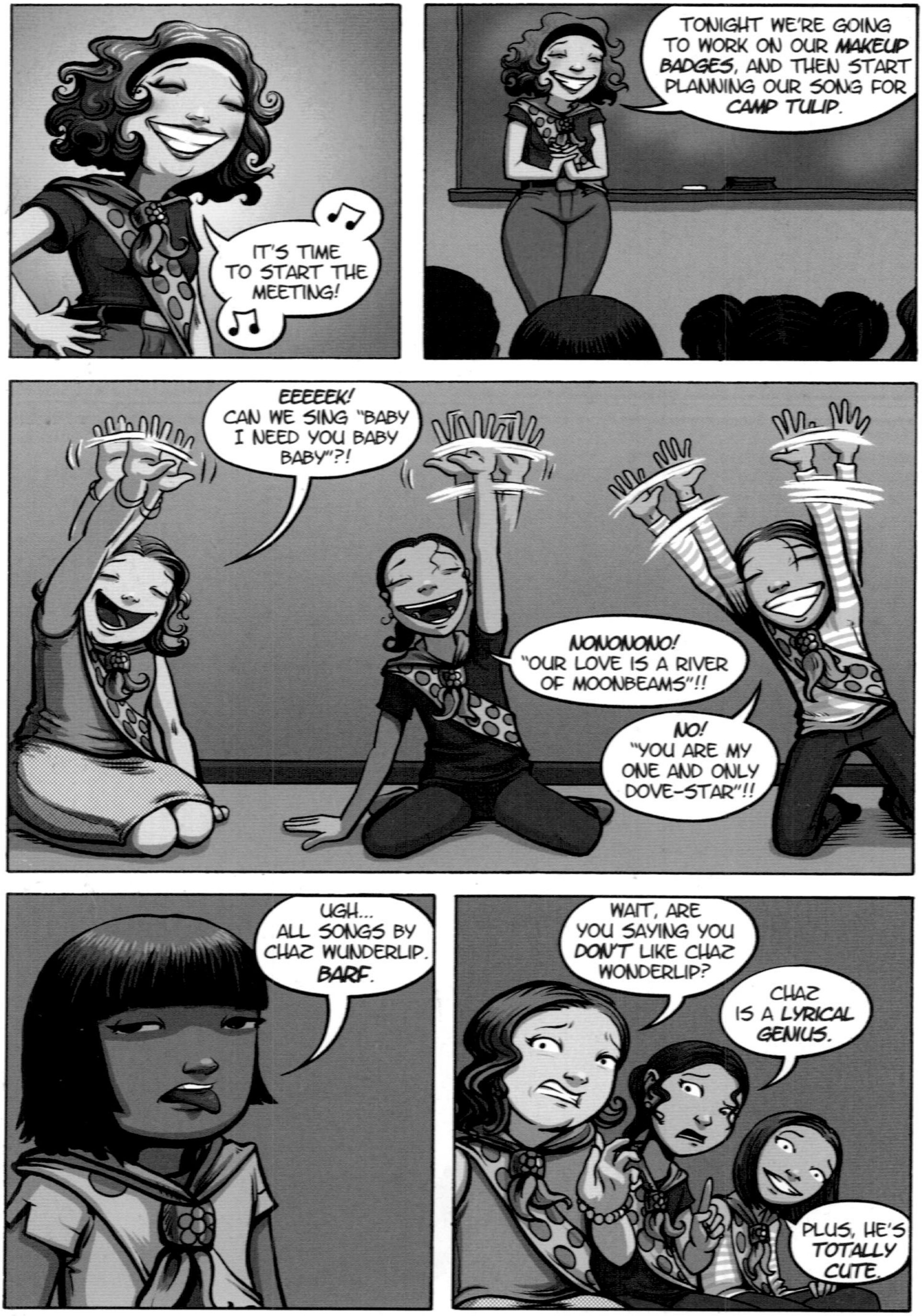
IT'S TIME TO START THE MEETING!
TONIGHT WE'RE GOING TO WORK ON OUR MAKEUP BADGES, AND THEN START PLANNING OUR SONG FOR CAMP TULIP.
EEEEEK! CAN WE SING "BABY I NEED YOU BABY BABY"?!
NONONONO! "OUR LOVE IS A RIVER OF MOONBEAMS"!!
NO! "YOU ARE MY ONE AND ONLY DOVE-STAR"!!
UGH... ALL SONGS BY CHAZ WUNDERLIP. BARF.
WAIT, ARE YOU SAYING YOU DON'T LIKE CHAZ WONDERLIP?
CHAZ IS A LYRICAL GENIUS.
PLUS, HE'S TOTALLY CUTE.

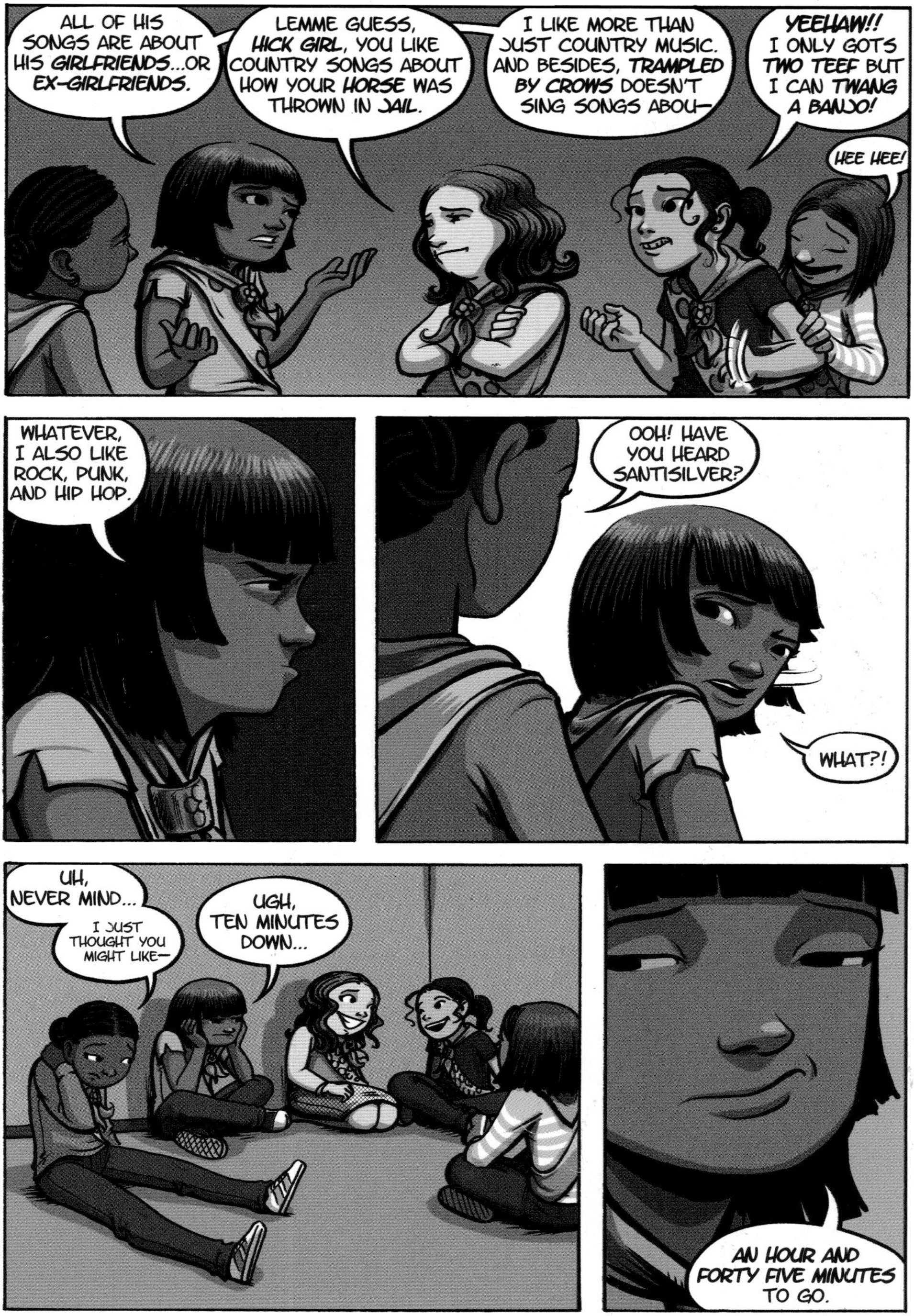
ALL OF HIS SONGS ARE ABOUT HIS GIRLFRIENDS...OR EX-GIRLFRIENDS.
LEMME GUESS, HICK GIRL, YOU LIKE COUNTRY SONGS ABOUT HOW YOUR HORSE WAS THROWN IN JAIL.
I LIKE MORE THAN JUST COUNTRY MUSIC. AND BESIDES, TRAMPLED BY CROWS DOESN'T SING SONGS ABOU—
YEEHAW!! I ONLY GOTS TWO TEEF BUT I CAN TWANG A BANJO!
HEE HEE!
WHATEVER, I ALSO LIKE ROCK, PUNK, AND HIP HOP.
OOH! HAVE YOU HEARD SANTISILVER?
WHAT?!
UH, NEVER MIND...
I JUST THOUGHT YOU MIGHT LIKE—
UGH, TEN MINUTES DOWN...
AN HOUR AND FORTY FIVE MINUTES TO GO.

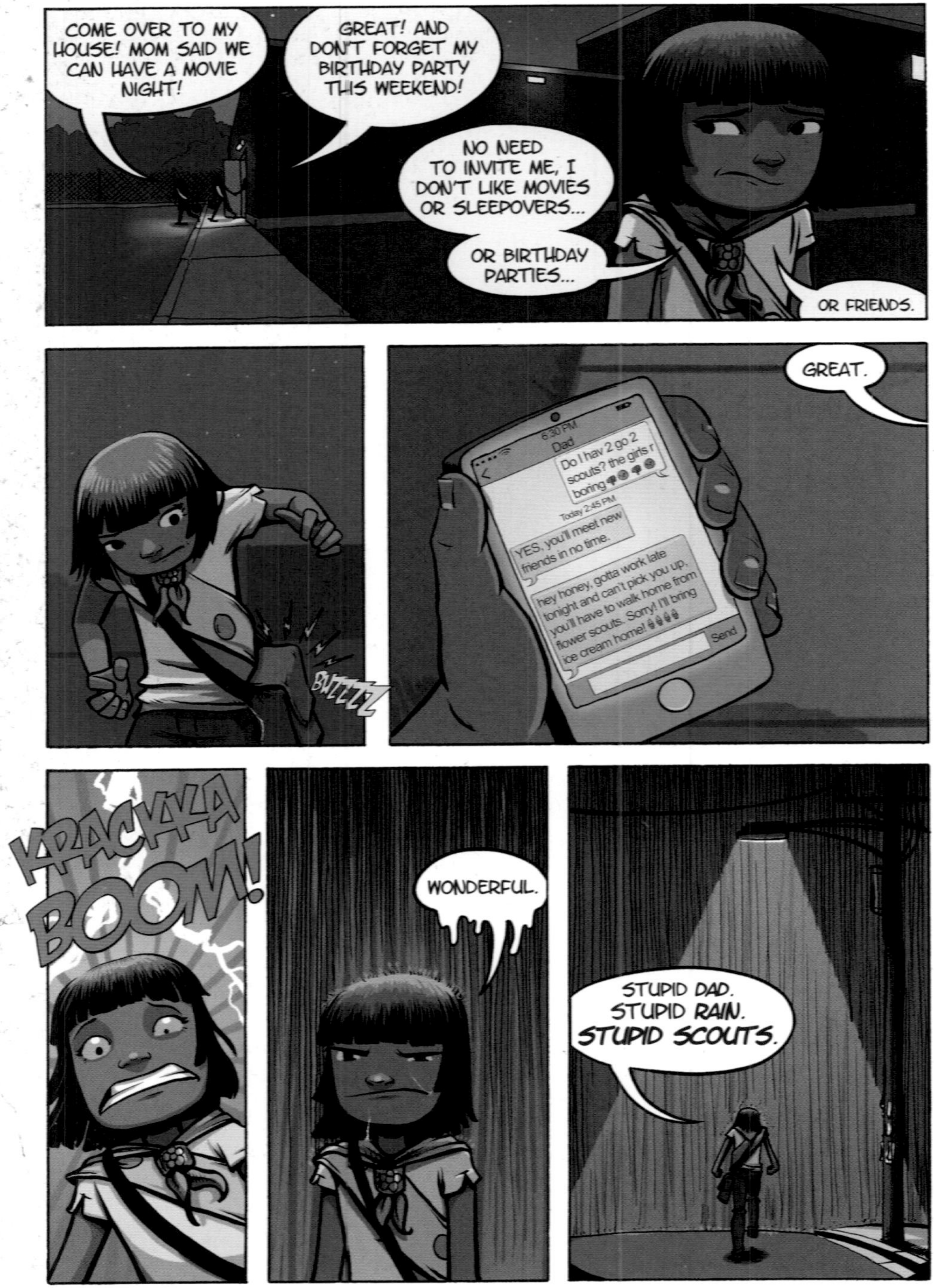
COME OVER TO MY HOUSE! MOM SAID WE CAN HAVE A MOVIE NIGHT!
GREAT! AND DON'T FORGET MY BIRTHDAY PARTY THIS WEEKEND!
NO NEED TO INVITE ME, I DON'T LIKE MOVIES OR SLEEPOVERS...
OR BIRTHDAY PARTIES...
OR FRIENDS.
BWZZZZ
GREAT.
6:30 PM
Dad
Do I hav 2 go 2 scouts? the girls r boring
Today 2:45 PM
YES, you'll meet new friends in no time.
hey honey, gotta work late tonight and can't pick you up, you'll have to walk home from flower scouts. Sorry! I'll bring ice cream home!
Send
KRACKKA BOOM!
WONDERFUL.
STUPID DAD.
STUPID RAIN.
STUPID SCOUTS.

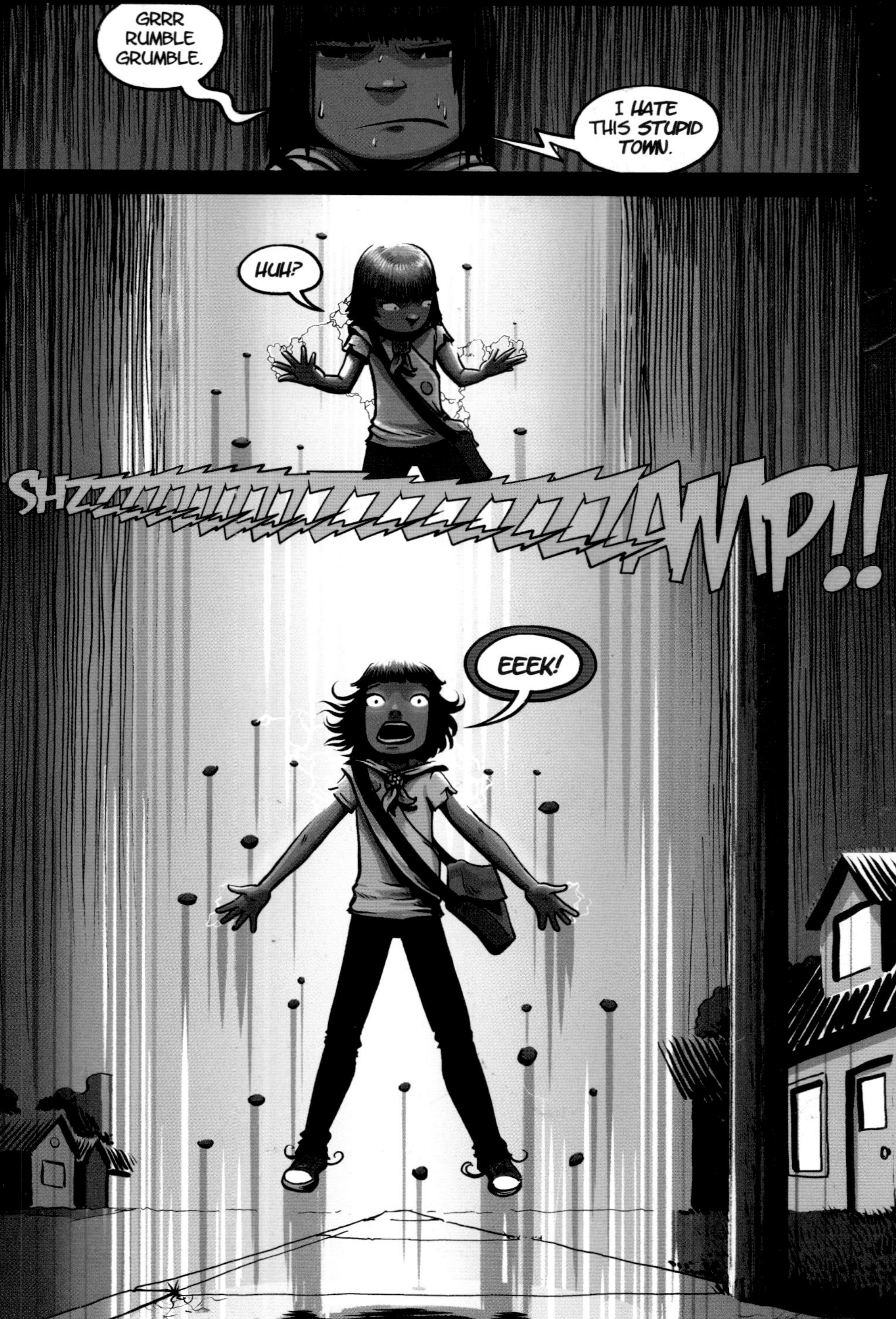
GRRR RUMBLE GRUMBLE.
I HATE THIS STUPID TOWN.
HUH?
SHZZZZZZZZZZZZZZZZZZAMP!!
EEEK!

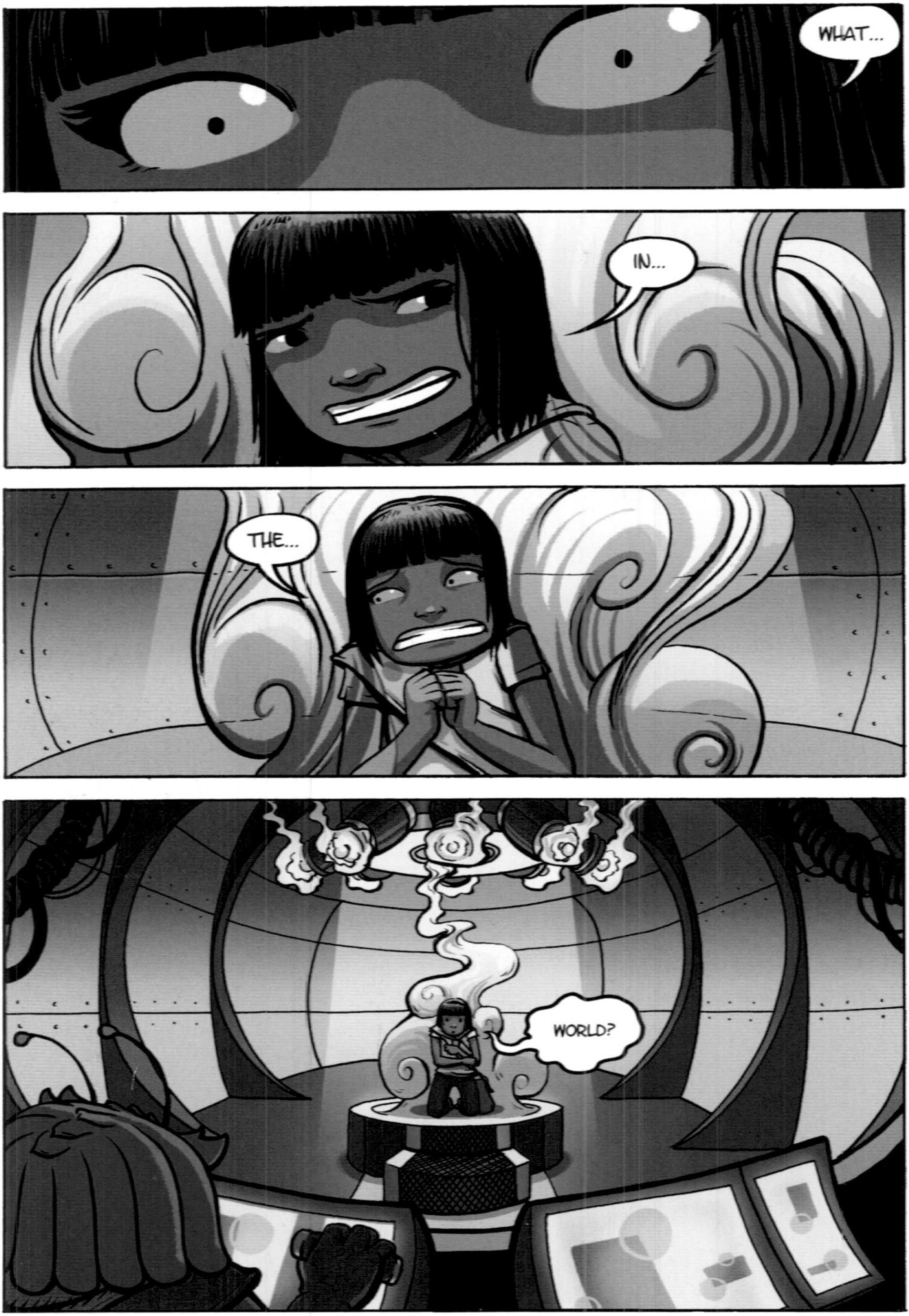
WHAT...
IN...
THE...
WORLD?

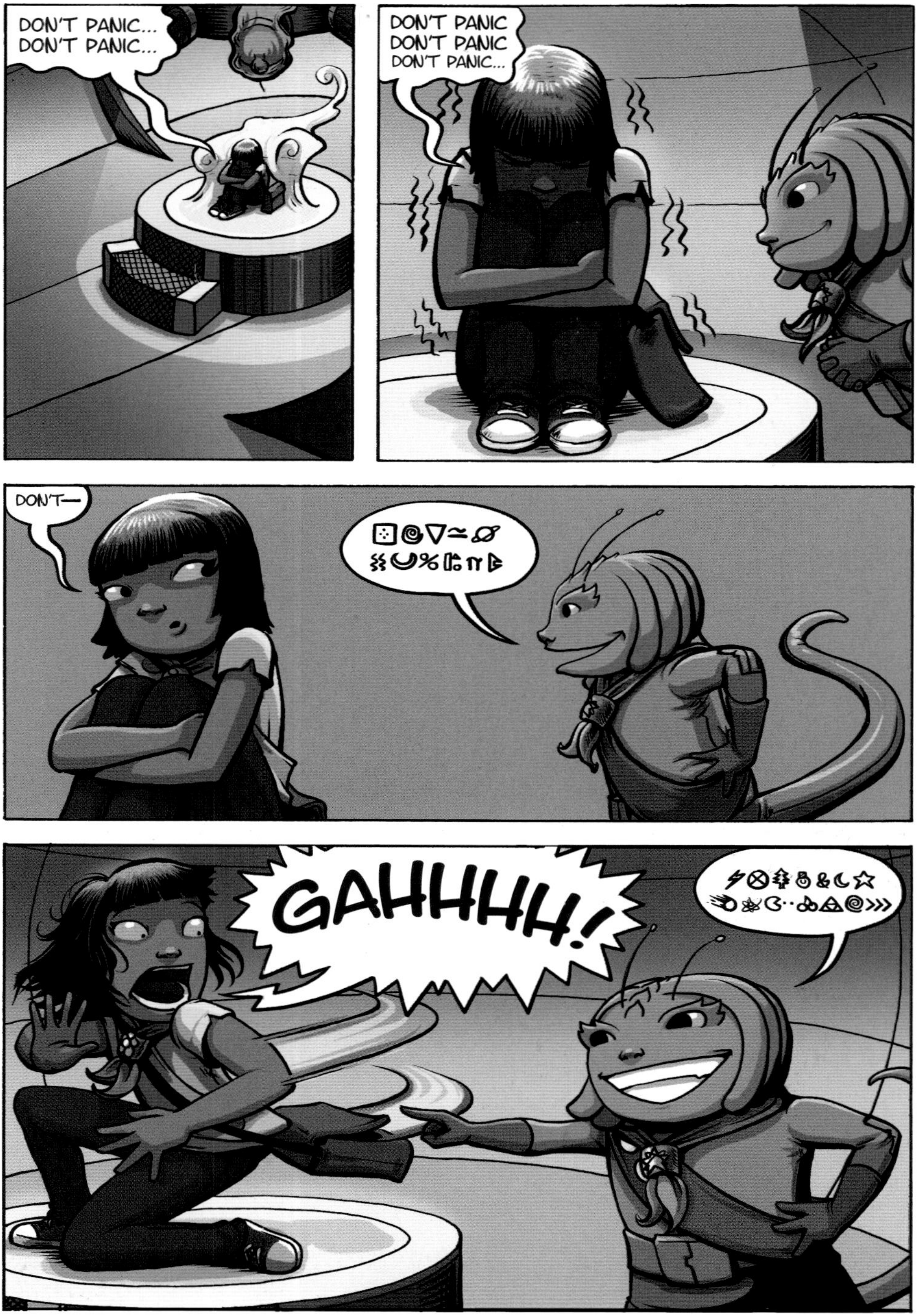
DON'T PANIC...
DON'T PANIC...
DON'T PANIC
DON'T PANIC
DON'T PANIC...
DON'T—
GAHHHH!

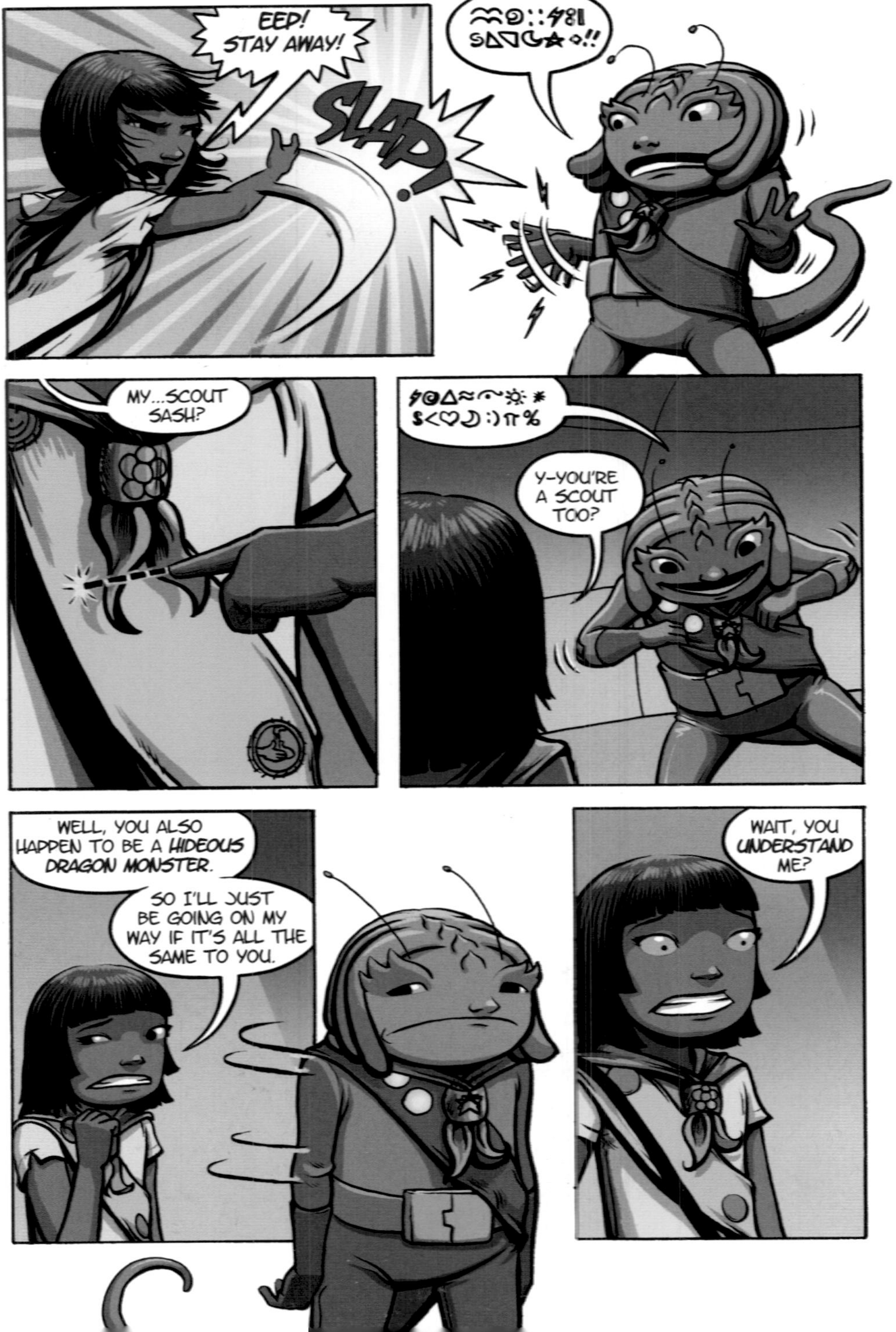
EEP! STAY AWAY!
SLAP!
MY...SCOUT SASH?
Y-YOU'RE A SCOUT TOO?
WELL, YOU ALSO HAPPEN TO BE A HIDEOUS DRAGON MONSTER.
SO I'LL JUST BE GOING ON MY WAY IF IT'S ALL THE SAME TO YOU.
WAIT, YOU UNDERSTAND ME?

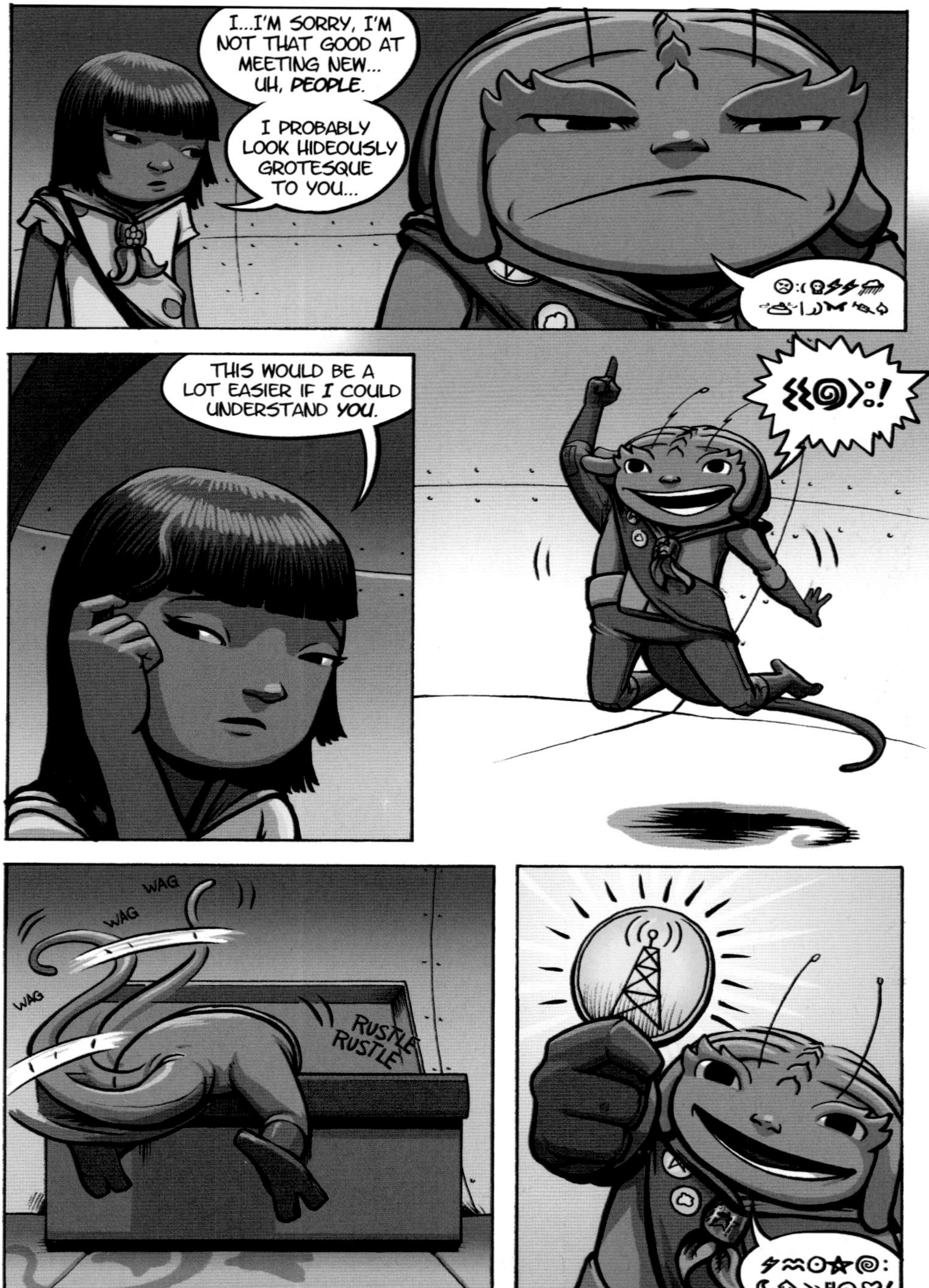
I...I'M SORRY, I'M NOT THAT GOOD AT MEETING NEW... UH, PEOPLE.
I PROBABLY LOOK HIDEOUSLY GROTESQUE TO YOU...
THIS WOULD BE A LOT EASIER IF I COULD UNDERSTAND YOU.
WAG
WAG
WAG
RUSTLE RUSTLE

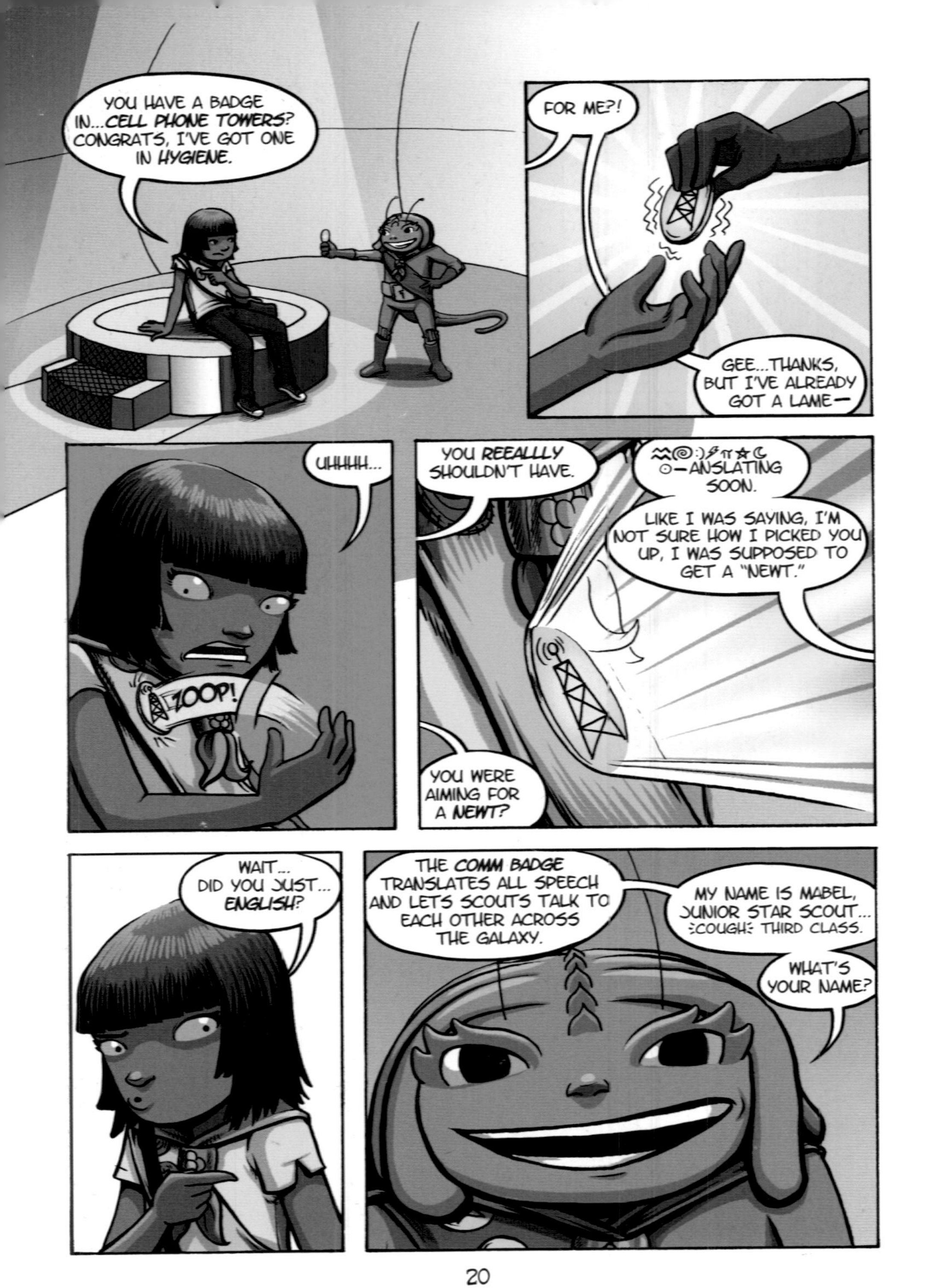
YOU HAVE A BADGE IN...CELL PHONE TOWERS? CONGRATS, I'VE GOT ONE IN HYGIENE.
FOR ME?!
GEE...THANKS, BUT I'VE ALREADY GOT A LAME—
UHHHH...
ZOOP!
YOU REEALLLY SHOULDN'T HAVE.
—ANSLATING SOON.
LIKE I WAS SAYING, I'M NOT SURE HOW I PICKED YOU UP, I WAS SUPPOSED TO GET A "NEWT."
YOU WERE AIMING FOR A NEWT?
WAIT... DID YOU JUST... ENGLISH?
THE COMM BADGE TRANSLATES ALL SPEECH AND LETS SCOUTS TALK TO EACH OTHER ACROSS THE GALAXY.
MY NAME IS MABEL, JUNIOR STAR SCOUT... COUGH THIRD CLASS.
WHAT'S YOUR NAME?

UH... AVANI...AVANI PATEL.
DID YOU SAY MABEL?
SURE DID, I'M NAMED AFTER...
...MABEL THE MASTICATOR! FIRST BATTLE MAIDEN OF QUEEN DEBBIE THE DESTROYER!
AN HONORABLE NAME, AND ONE I HOPE TO LIVE UP TO BY BECOMING THE FIRST GALACTIC SCOUT IN MY FAMILY.
MABEL? DEBBIE? SOUNDS MORE LIKE A BUNCH OF LUNCH LADIES INSTEAD OF A BUNCH OF KNIGHTS.
THESE LUNCH LADIES YOU SPEAK OF MUST BE FIERCE WARRIORS ON EARTH.
BOUND BY BLOOD TO PROTECT THE QUEEN OF YOUR PLANET!

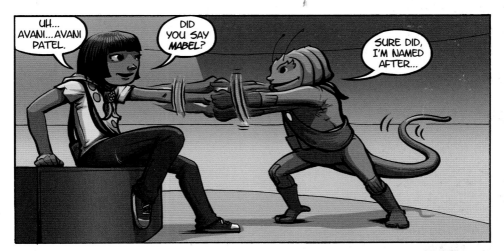

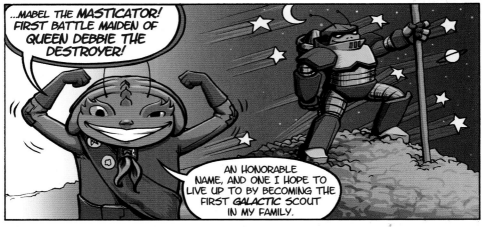

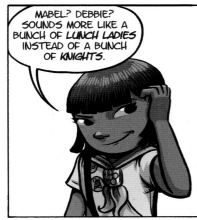

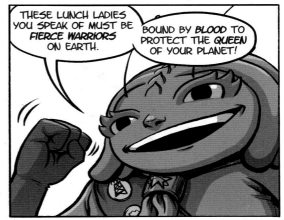

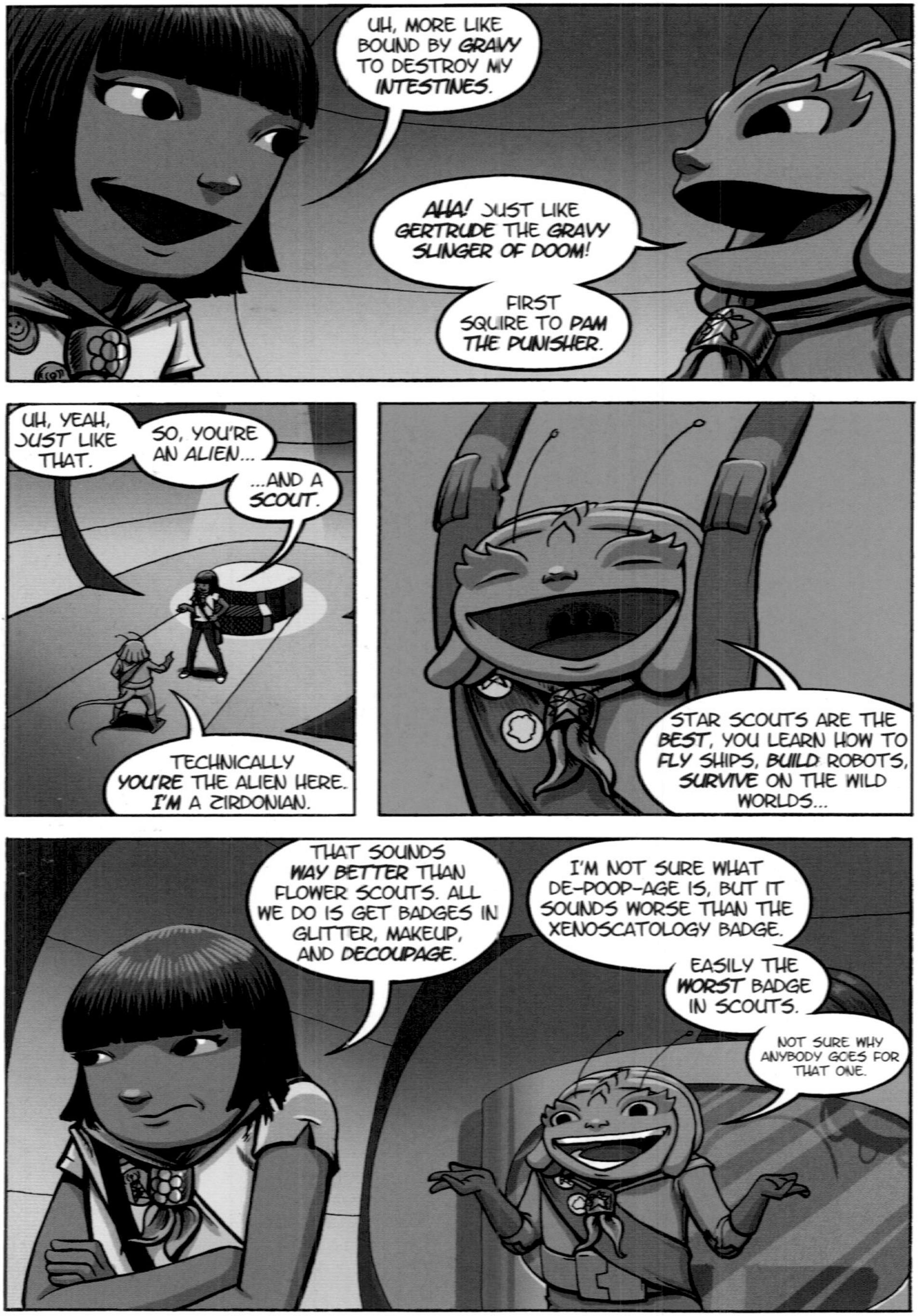

UH, MORE LIKE BOUND BY GRAVY TO DESTROY MY INTESTINES.
AHA! JUST LIKE GERTRUDE THE GRAVY SLINGER OF DOOM!
FIRST SQUIRE TO PAM THE PUNISHER.
UH, YEAH, JUST LIKE THAT.
SO, YOU'RE AN ALIEN...
...AND A SCOUT.
TECHNICALLY YOU'RE THE ALIEN HERE. I'M A ZIRDONIAN.
STAR SCOUTS ARE THE BEST, YOU LEARN HOW TO FLY SHIPS, BUILD ROBOTS, SURVIVE ON THE WILD WORLDS...
THAT SOUNDS WAY BETTER THAN FLOWER SCOUTS. ALL WE DO IS GET BADGES IN GLITTER, MAKEUP, AND DECOUPAGE.
I'M NOT SURE WHAT DE-POOP-AGE IS, BUT IT SOUNDS WORSE THAN THE XENOSCATOLOGY BADGE.
EASILY THE WORST BADGE IN SCOUTS.
NOT SURE WHY ANYBODY GOES FOR THAT ONE.

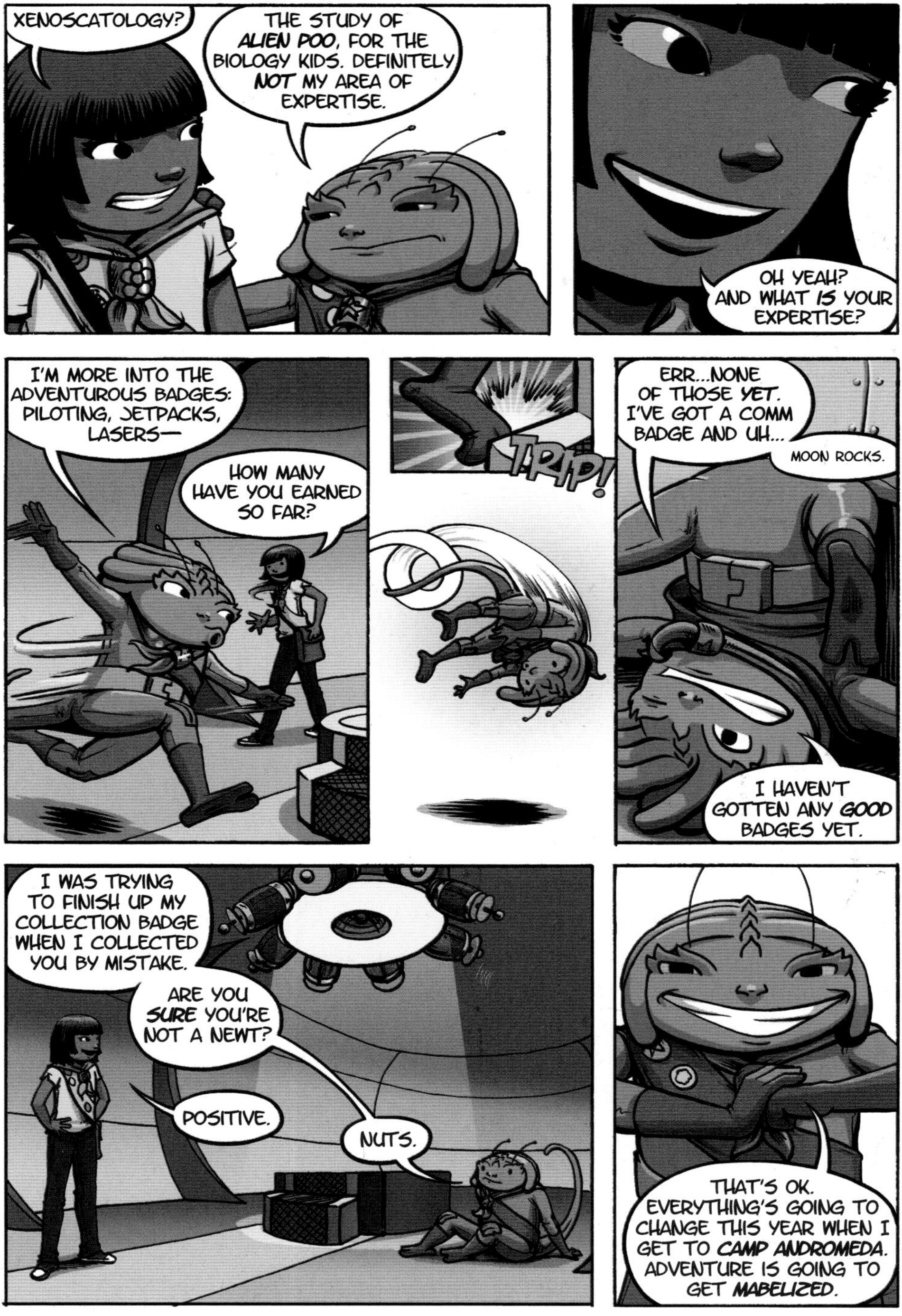
XENOSCATOLOGY?
THE STUDY OF ALIEN POO, FOR THE BIOLOGY KIDS. DEFINITELY NOT MY AREA OF EXPERTISE.
OH YEAH? AND WHAT IS YOUR EXPERTISE?
I'M MORE INTO THE ADVENTUROUS BADGES: PILOTING, JETPACKS, LASERS—
HOW MANY HAVE YOU EARNED SO FAR?
TRIP!
ERR...NONE OF THOSE YET. I'VE GOT A COMM BADGE AND UH...
MOON ROCKS.
I HAVEN'T GOTTEN ANY GOOD BADGES YET.
I WAS TRYING TO FINISH UP MY COLLECTION BADGE WHEN I COLLECTED YOU BY MISTAKE.
ARE YOU SURE YOU'RE NOT A NEWT?
POSITIVE.
NUTS.
THAT'S OK. EVERYTHING'S GOING TO CHANGE THIS YEAR WHEN I GET TO CAMP ANDROMEDA. ADVENTURE IS GOING TO GET MABELIZED.

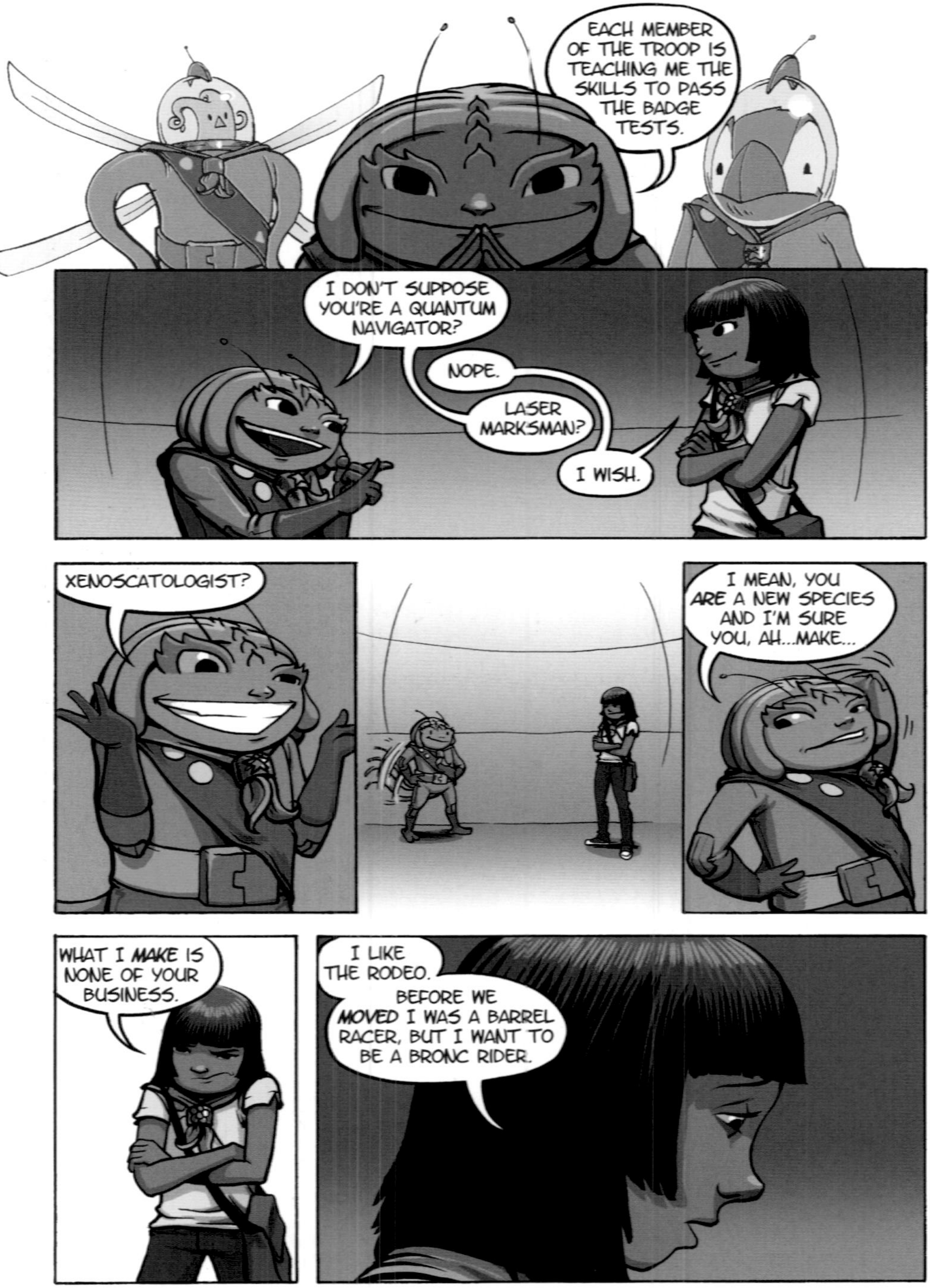
EACH MEMBER OF THE TROOP IS TEACHING ME THE SKILLS TO PASS THE BADGE TESTS.
I DON'T SUPPOSE YOU'RE A QUANTUM NAVIGATOR?
NOPE.
LASER MARKSMAN?
I WISH.
XENOSCATOLOGIST?
I MEAN, YOU *ARE* A NEW SPECIES AND I'M SURE YOU, AH...MAKE...
WHAT I *MAKE* IS NONE OF YOUR BUSINESS.
I LIKE THE RODEO.
BEFORE WE *MOVED* I WAS A BARREL RACER, BUT I WANT TO BE A BRONC RIDER.

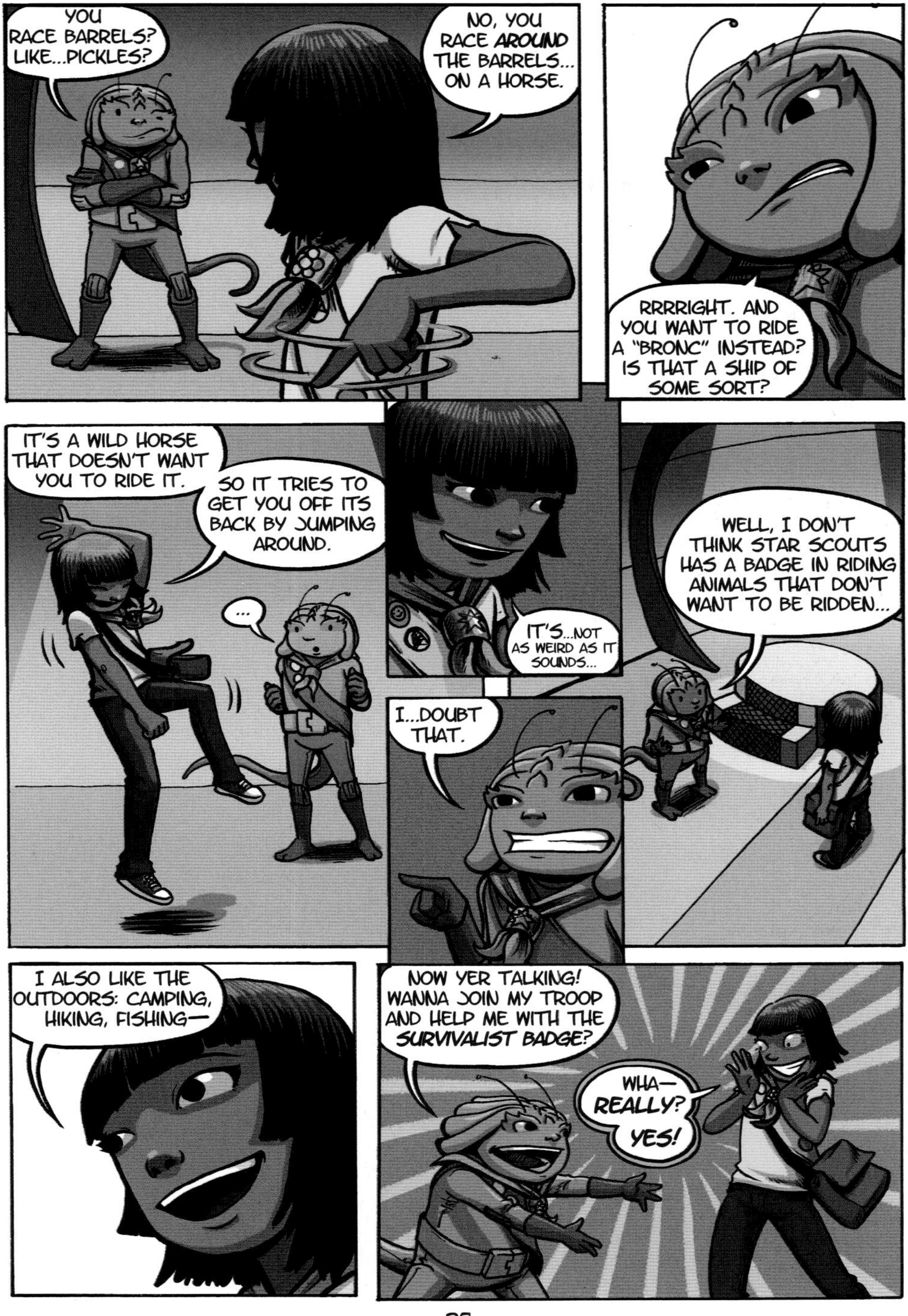
YOU RACE BARRELS? LIKE...PICKLES?
NO, YOU RACE AROUND THE BARRELS... ON A HORSE.
RRRRIGHT. AND YOU WANT TO RIDE A "BRONC" INSTEAD? IS THAT A SHIP OF SOME SORT?
IT'S A WILD HORSE THAT DOESN'T WANT YOU TO RIDE IT.
SO IT TRIES TO GET YOU OFF ITS BACK BY JUMPING AROUND.
...
IT'S...NOT AS WEIRD AS IT SOUNDS...
I...DOUBT THAT.
WELL, I DON'T THINK STAR SCOUTS HAS A BADGE IN RIDING ANIMALS THAT DON'T WANT TO BE RIDDEN...
I ALSO LIKE THE OUTDOORS: CAMPING, HIKING, FISHING—
NOW YER TALKING! WANNA JOIN MY TROOP AND HELP ME WITH THE SURVIVALIST BADGE?
WHA— REALLY? YES!

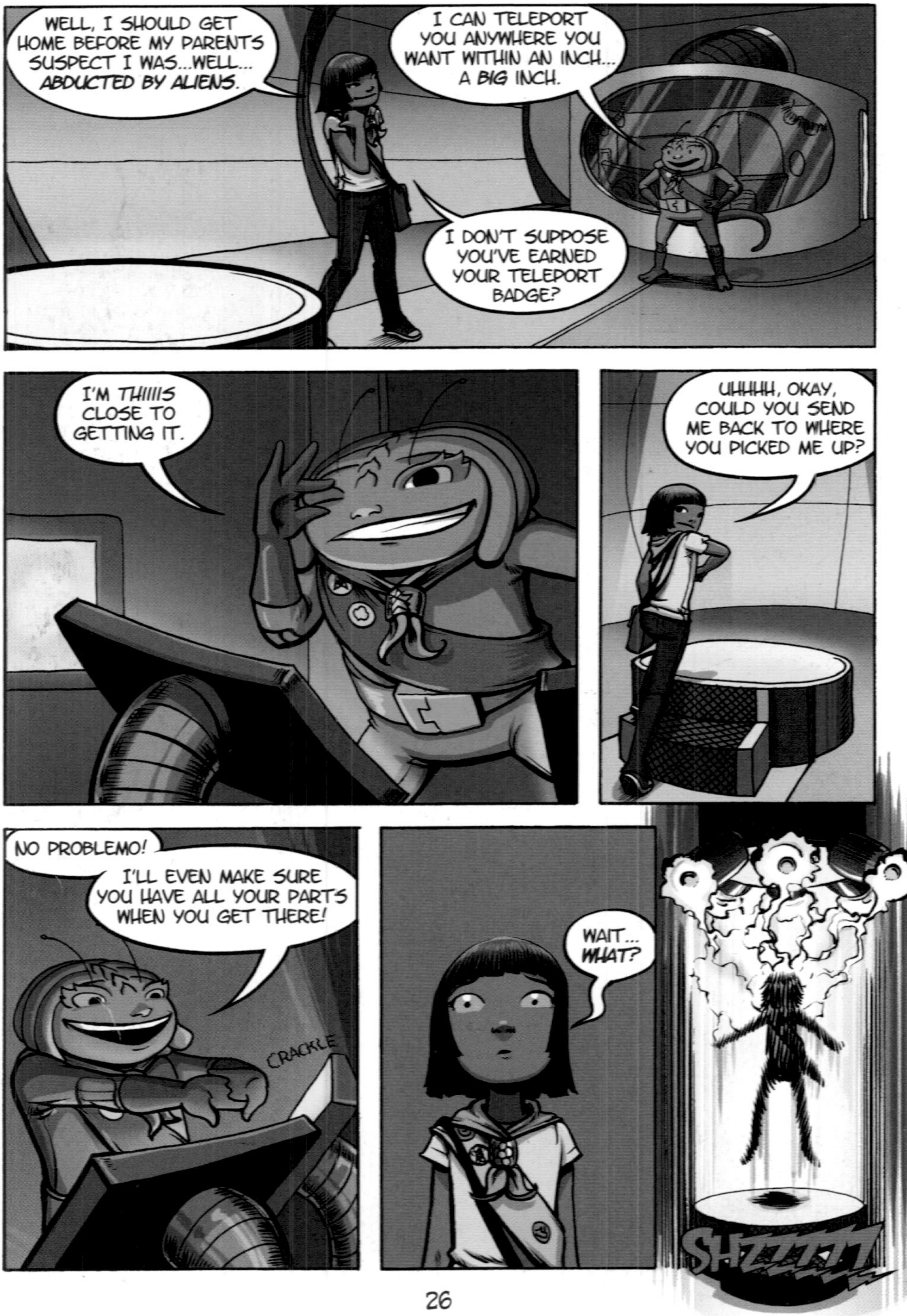
WELL, I SHOULD GET HOME BEFORE MY PARENTS SUSPECT I WAS...WELL... *ABDUCTED BY ALIENS*.
I CAN TELEPORT YOU ANYWHERE YOU WANT WITHIN AN INCH... A *BIG* INCH.
I DON'T SUPPOSE YOU'VE EARNED YOUR TELEPORT BADGE?
I'M THIIIIS CLOSE TO GETTING IT.
UHHHH, OKAY, COULD YOU SEND ME BACK TO WHERE YOU PICKED ME UP?
NO PROBLEMO!
I'LL EVEN MAKE SURE YOU HAVE ALL YOUR PARTS WHEN YOU GET THERE!
CRACKLE
WAIT... *WHAT?*
SHZZZT!

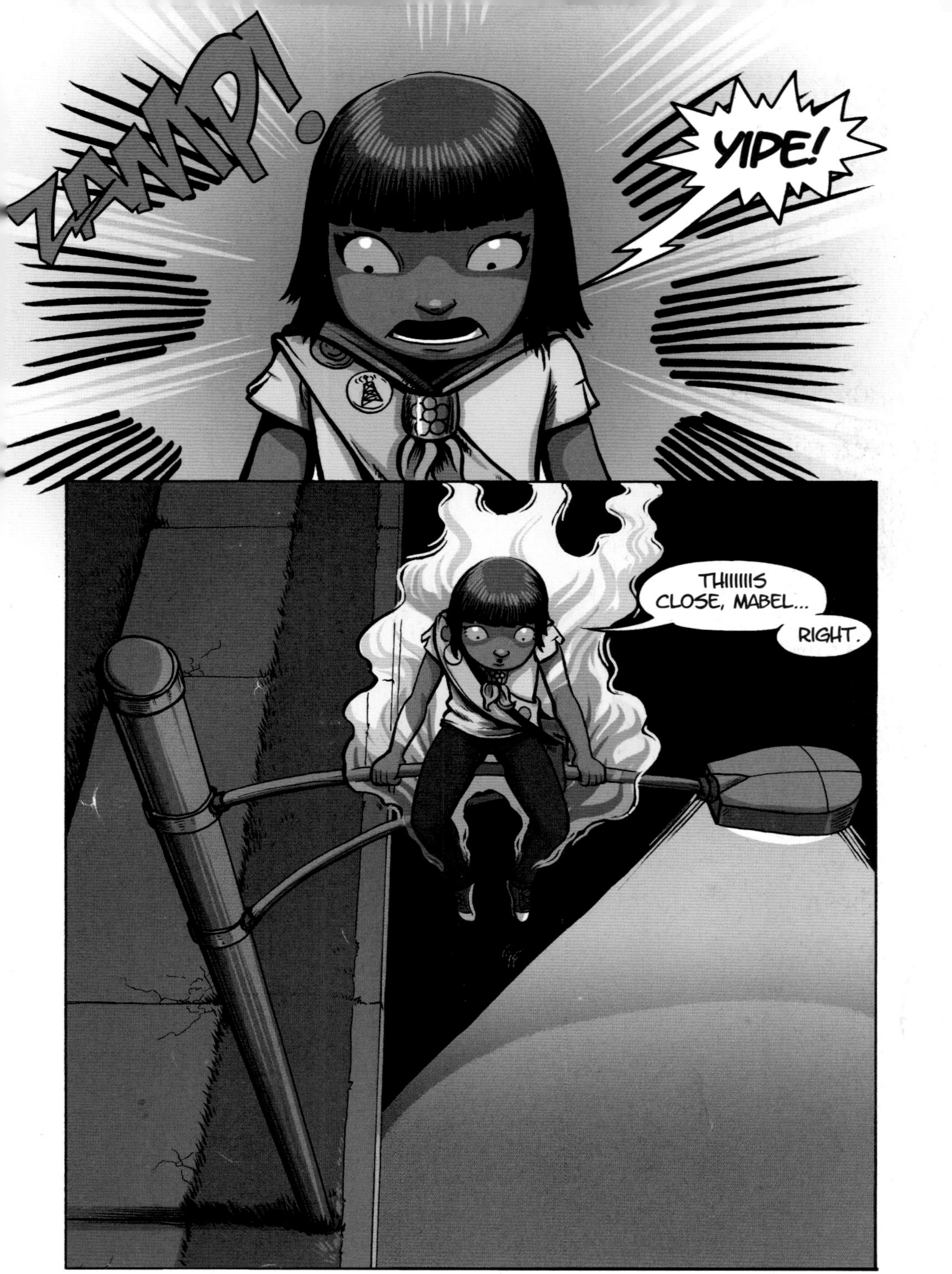
ZAMP!
YIPE!
THIIIIIIS CLOSE, MABEL...
RIGHT.

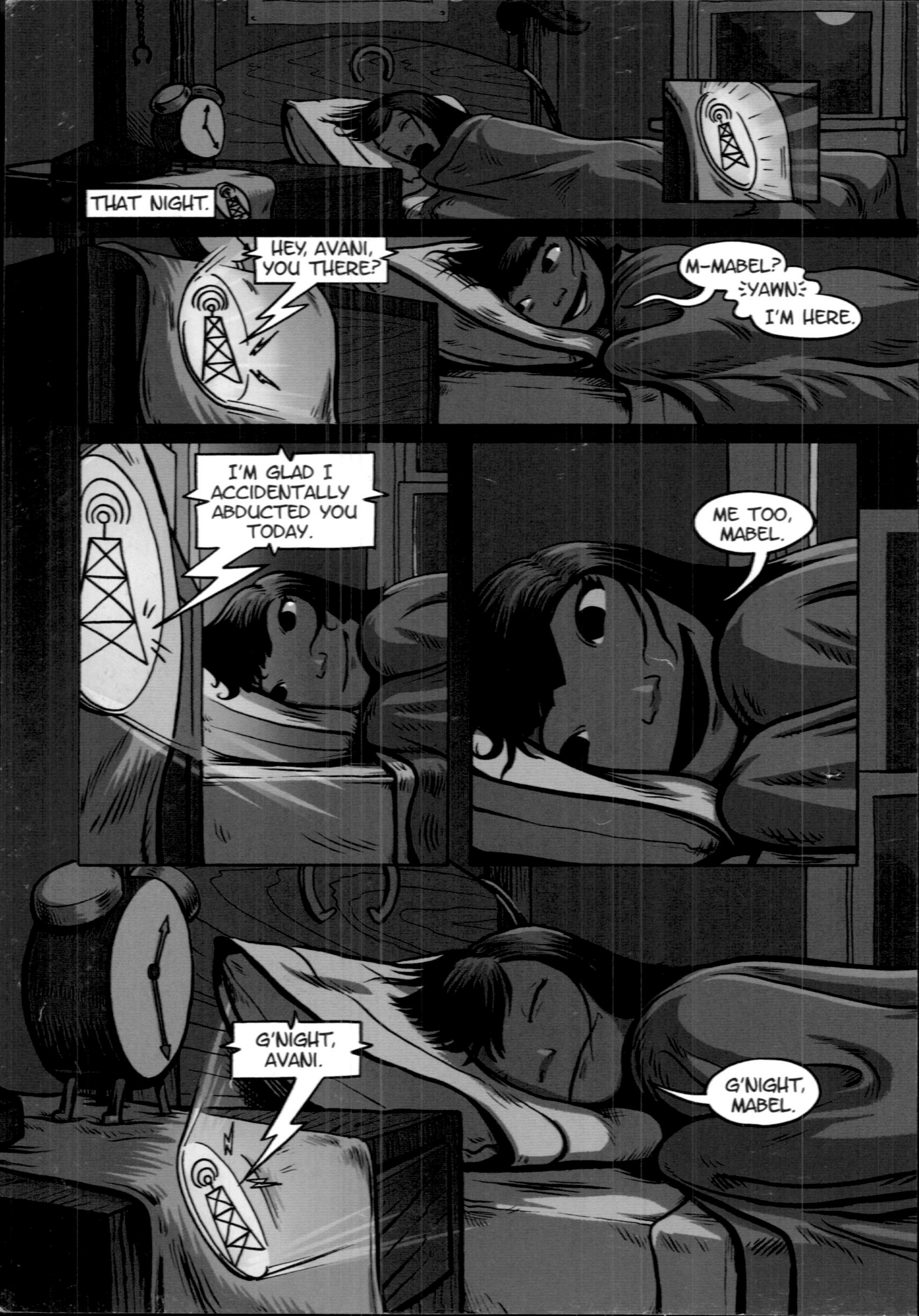
THAT NIGHT.
HEY, AVANI, YOU THERE?
M-MABEL?
YAWN
I'M HERE.
I'M GLAD I ACCIDENTALLY ABDUCTED YOU TODAY.
ME TOO, MABEL.
G'NIGHT, AVANI.
G'NIGHT, MABEL.

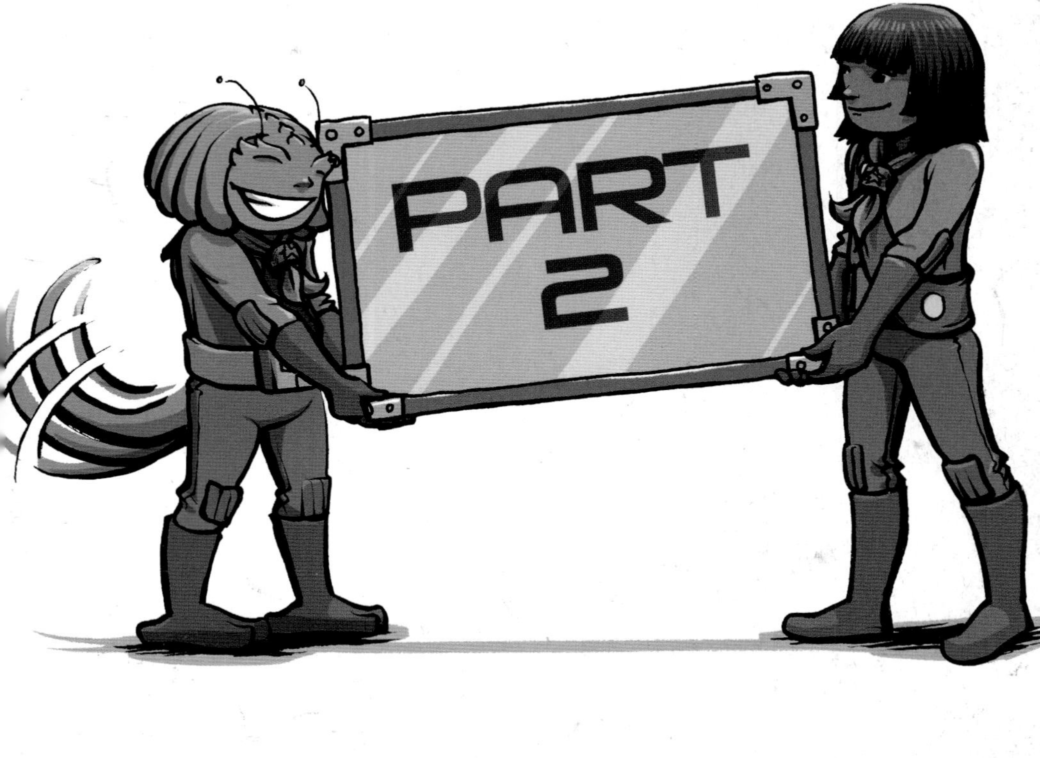
PART
2

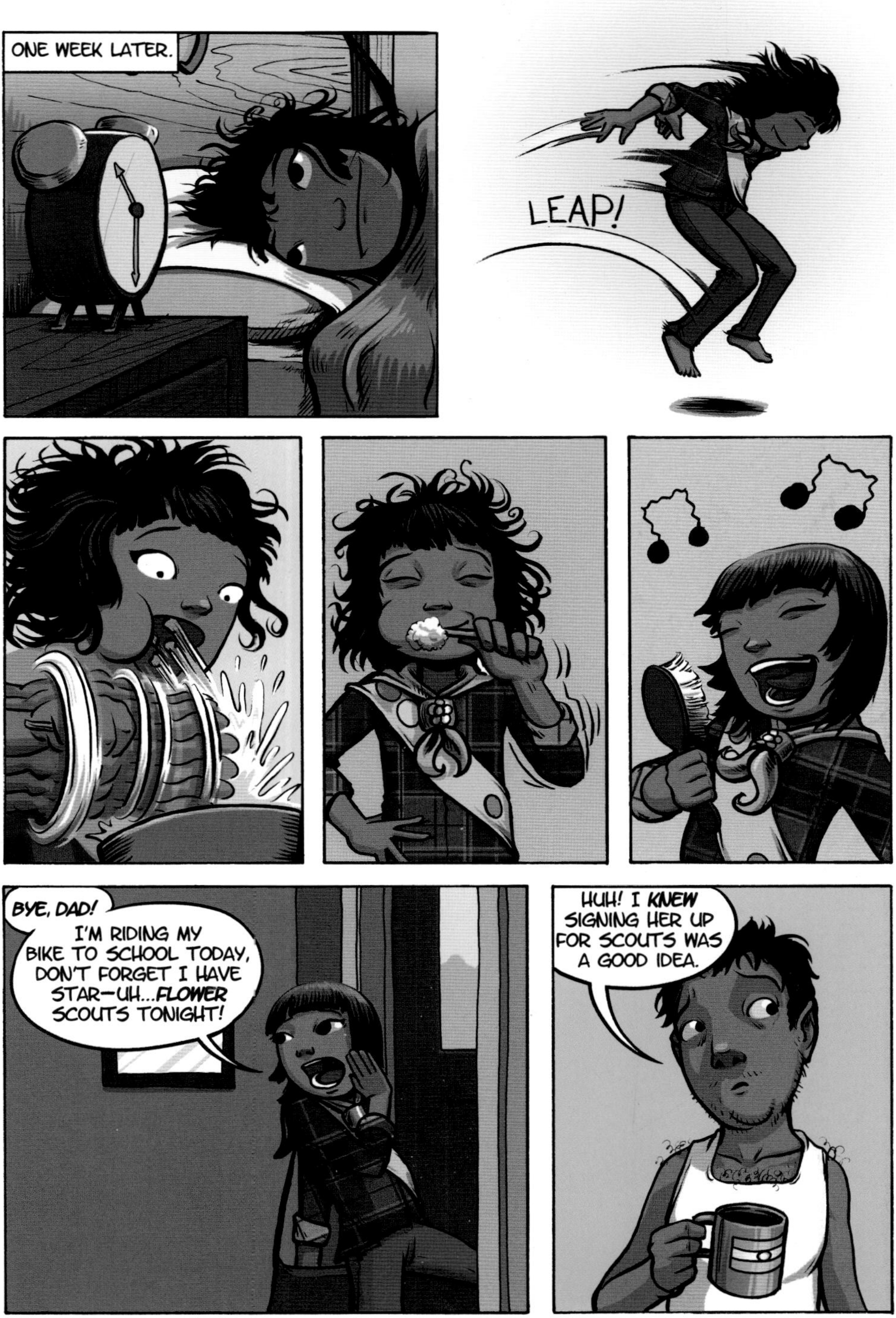
ONE WEEK LATER.
LEAP!
BYE, DAD!
I'M RIDING MY BIKE TO SCHOOL TODAY, DON'T FORGET I HAVE STAR—UH...FLOWER SCOUTS TONIGHT!
HUH! I KNEW SIGNING HER UP FOR SCOUTS WAS A GOOD IDEA.

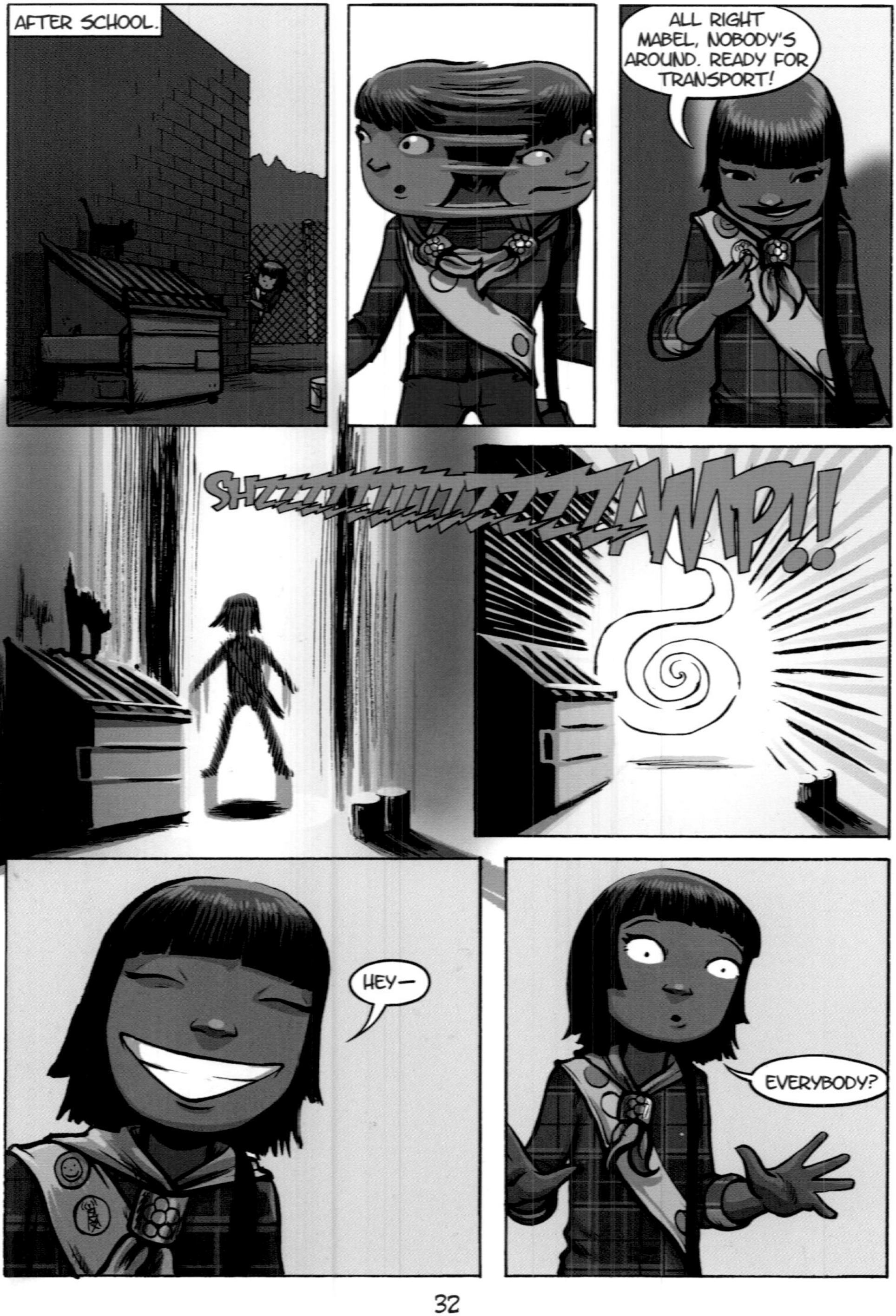
AFTER SCHOOL.
ALL RIGHT MABEL, NOBODY'S AROUND. READY FOR TRANSPORT!
SHZZZZZZZZZZZZZZZZZZZZAMP!!
HEY—
EVERYBODY?

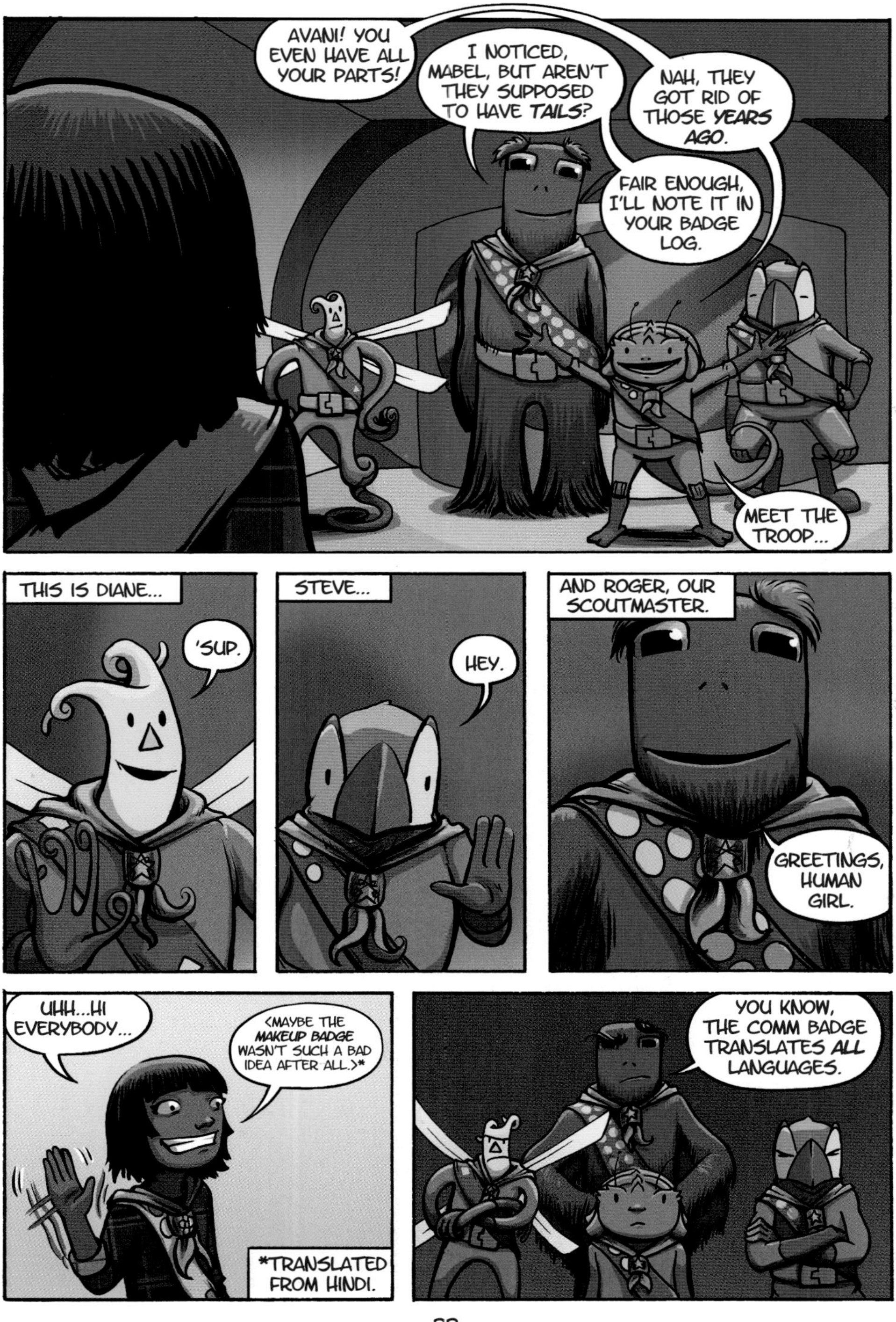
AVANI! YOU EVEN HAVE ALL YOUR PARTS!
I NOTICED, MABEL, BUT AREN'T THEY SUPPOSED TO HAVE TAILS?
NAH, THEY GOT RID OF THOSE YEARS AGO.
FAIR ENOUGH, I'LL NOTE IT IN YOUR BADGE LOG.
MEET THE TROOP...
THIS IS DIANE...
'SUP.
STEVE...
HEY.
AND ROGER, OUR SCOUTMASTER.
GREETINGS, HUMAN GIRL.
UHH...HI EVERYBODY...
<MAYBE THE MAKEUP BADGE WASN'T SUCH A BAD IDEA AFTER ALL.>*
*TRANSLATED FROM HINDI.
YOU KNOW, THE COMM BADGE TRANSLATES ALL LANGUAGES.

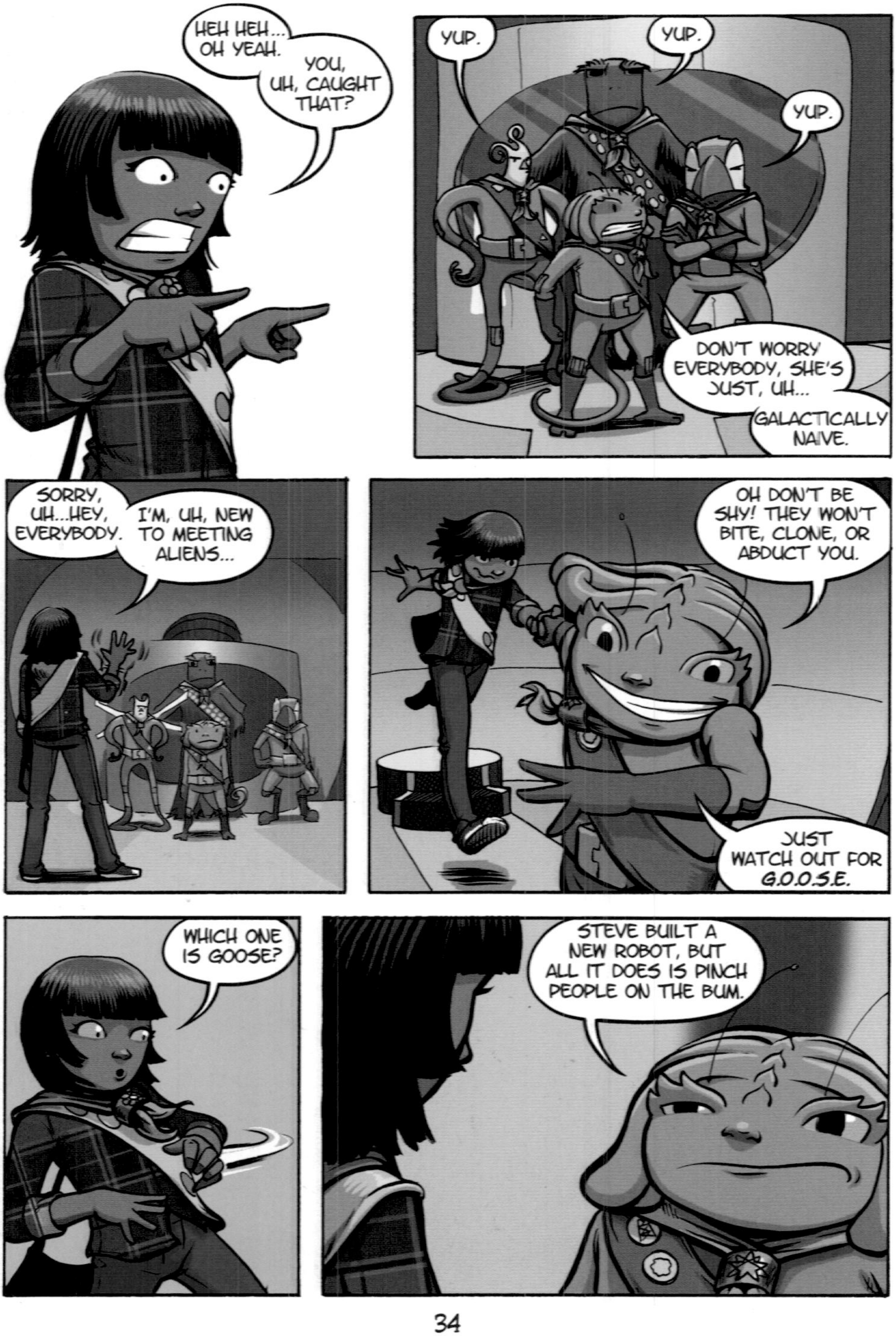
HEH HEH... OH YEAH.
YOU, UH, CAUGHT THAT?
YUP.
YUP.
YUP.
DON'T WORRY EVERYBODY, SHE'S JUST, UH...
GALACTICALLY NAIVE.
SORRY, UH...HEY, EVERYBODY.
I'M, UH, NEW TO MEETING ALIENS...
OH DON'T BE SHY! THEY WON'T BITE, CLONE, OR ABDUCT YOU.
JUST WATCH OUT FOR G.O.O.S.E.
WHICH ONE IS GOOSE?
STEVE BUILT A NEW ROBOT, BUT ALL IT DOES IS PINCH PEOPLE ON THE BUM.

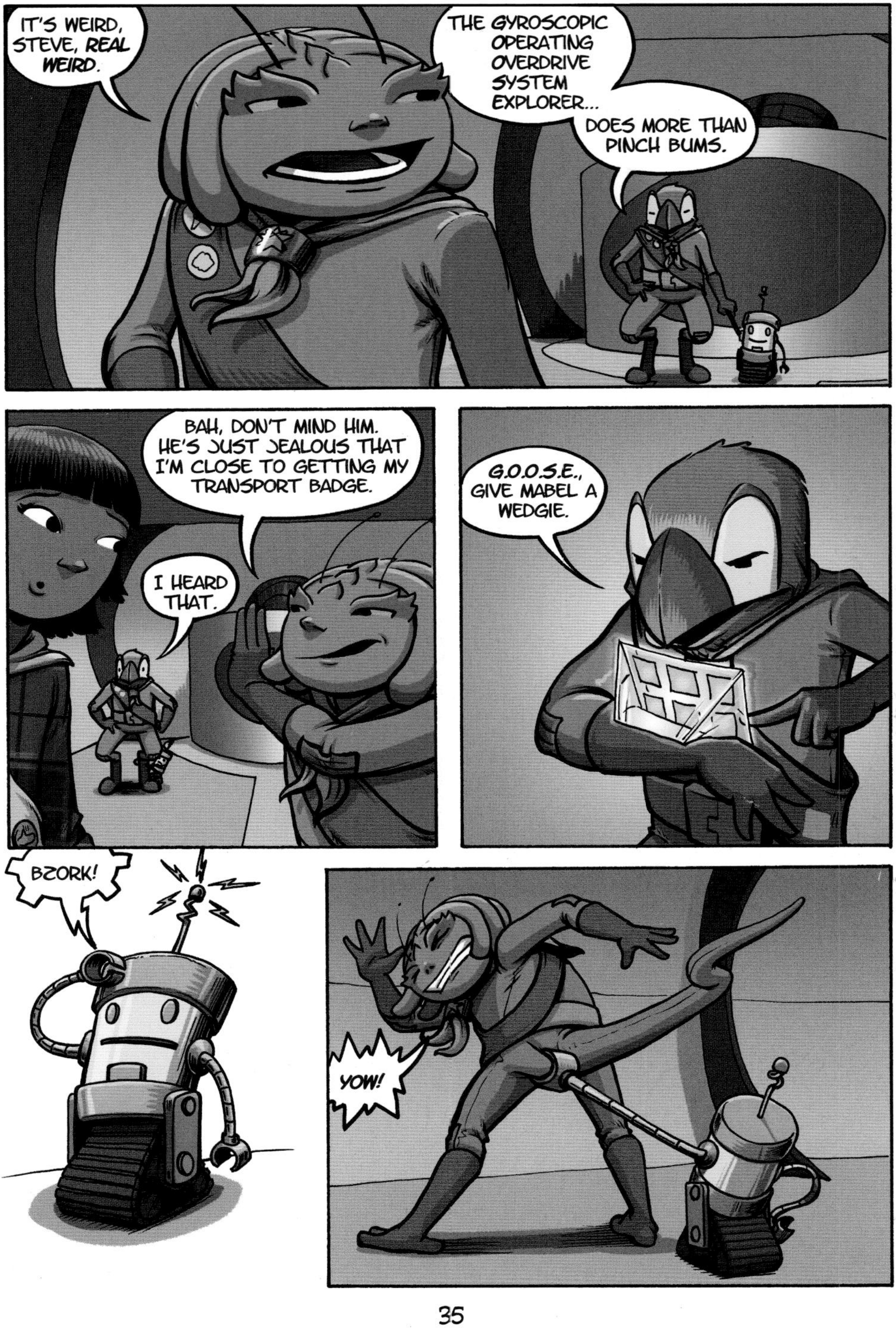
IT'S WEIRD, STEVE, REAL WEIRD.
THE GYROSCOPIC OPERATING OVERDRIVE SYSTEM EXPLORER...
DOES MORE THAN PINCH BUMS.
BAH, DON'T MIND HIM. HE'S JUST JEALOUS THAT I'M CLOSE TO GETTING MY TRANSPORT BADGE.
I HEARD THAT.
G.O.O.S.E., GIVE MABEL A WEDGIE.
BZORK!
YOW!

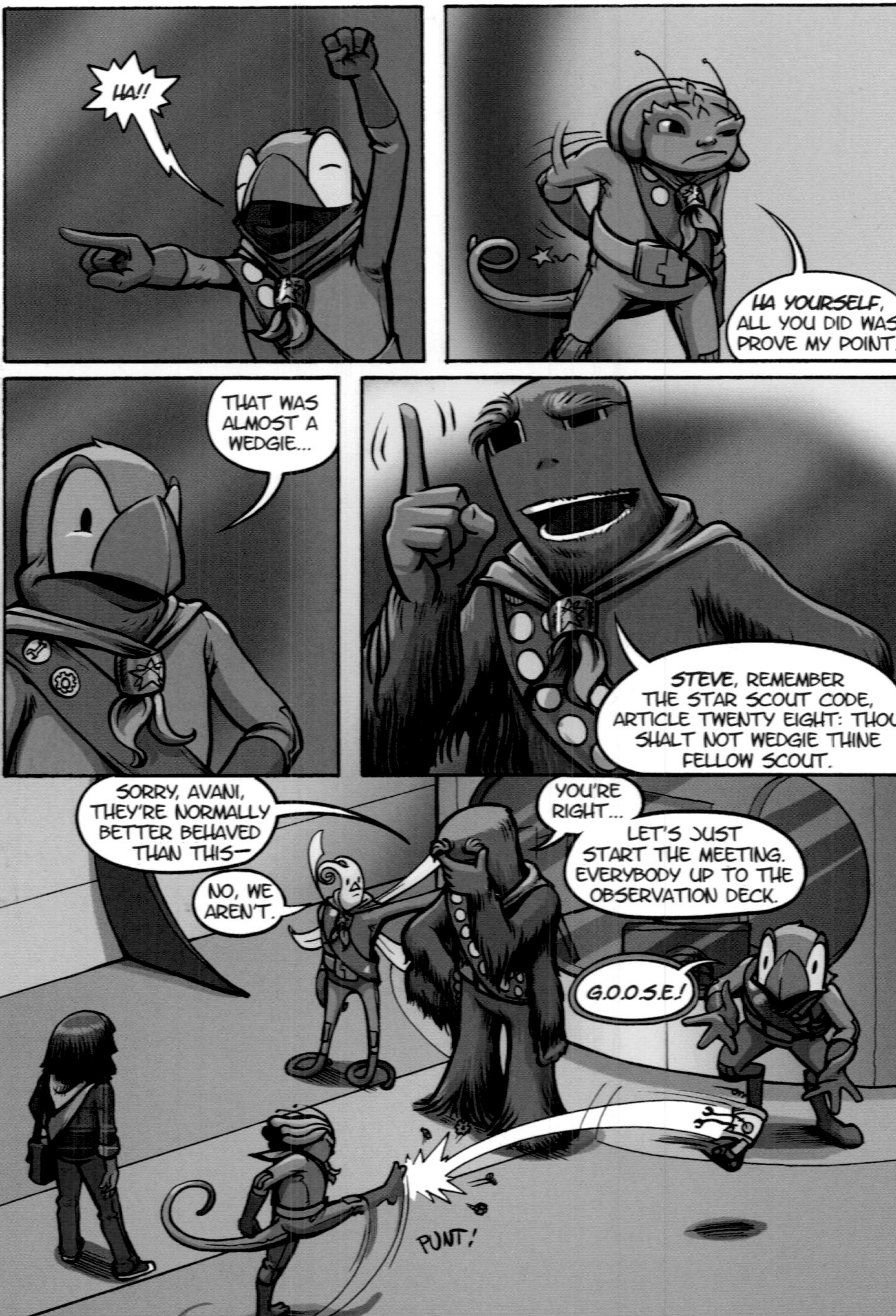
HA!!
HA YOURSELF, ALL YOU DID WAS PROVE MY POINT.
THAT WAS ALMOST A WEDGIE...
STEVE, REMEMBER THE STAR SCOUT CODE, ARTICLE TWENTY EIGHT: THOU SHALT NOT WEDGIE THINE FELLOW SCOUT.
SORRY, AVANI, THEY'RE NORMALLY BETTER BEHAVED THAN THIS—
NO, WE AREN'T.
YOU'RE RIGHT...
LET'S JUST START THE MEETING. EVERYBODY UP TO THE OBSERVATION DECK.
G.O.O.S.E.!
PUNT!

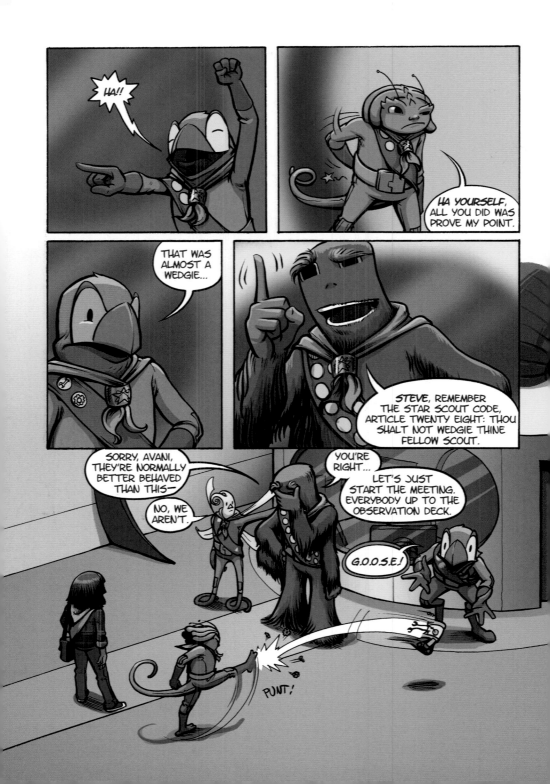

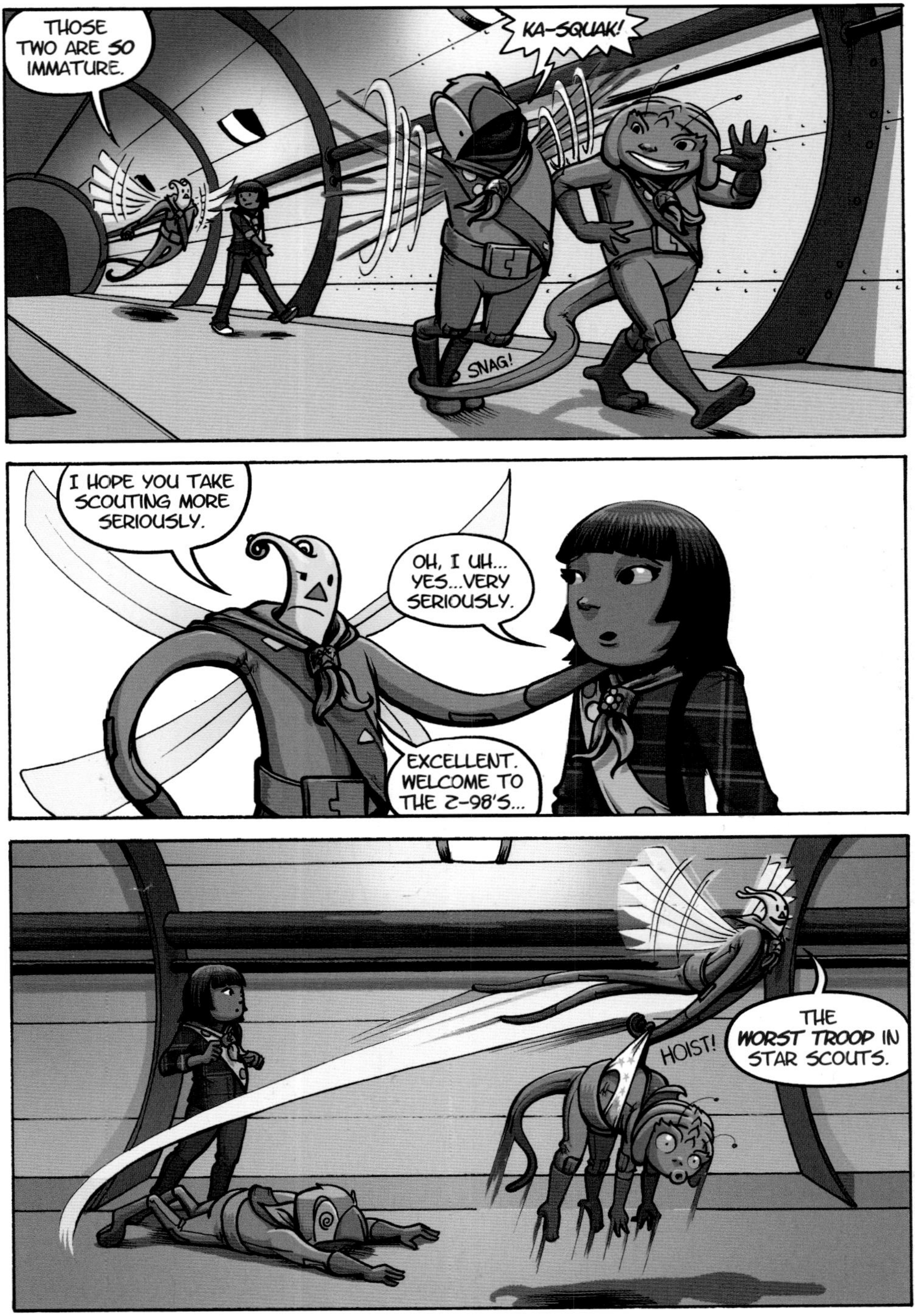
THOSE TWO ARE SO IMMATURE.
KA-SQUAK!
SNAG!
I HOPE YOU TAKE SCOUTING MORE SERIOUSLY.
OH, I UH... YES...VERY SERIOUSLY.
EXCELLENT. WELCOME TO THE Z-98'S...
THE WORST TROOP IN STAR SCOUTS.
HOIST!

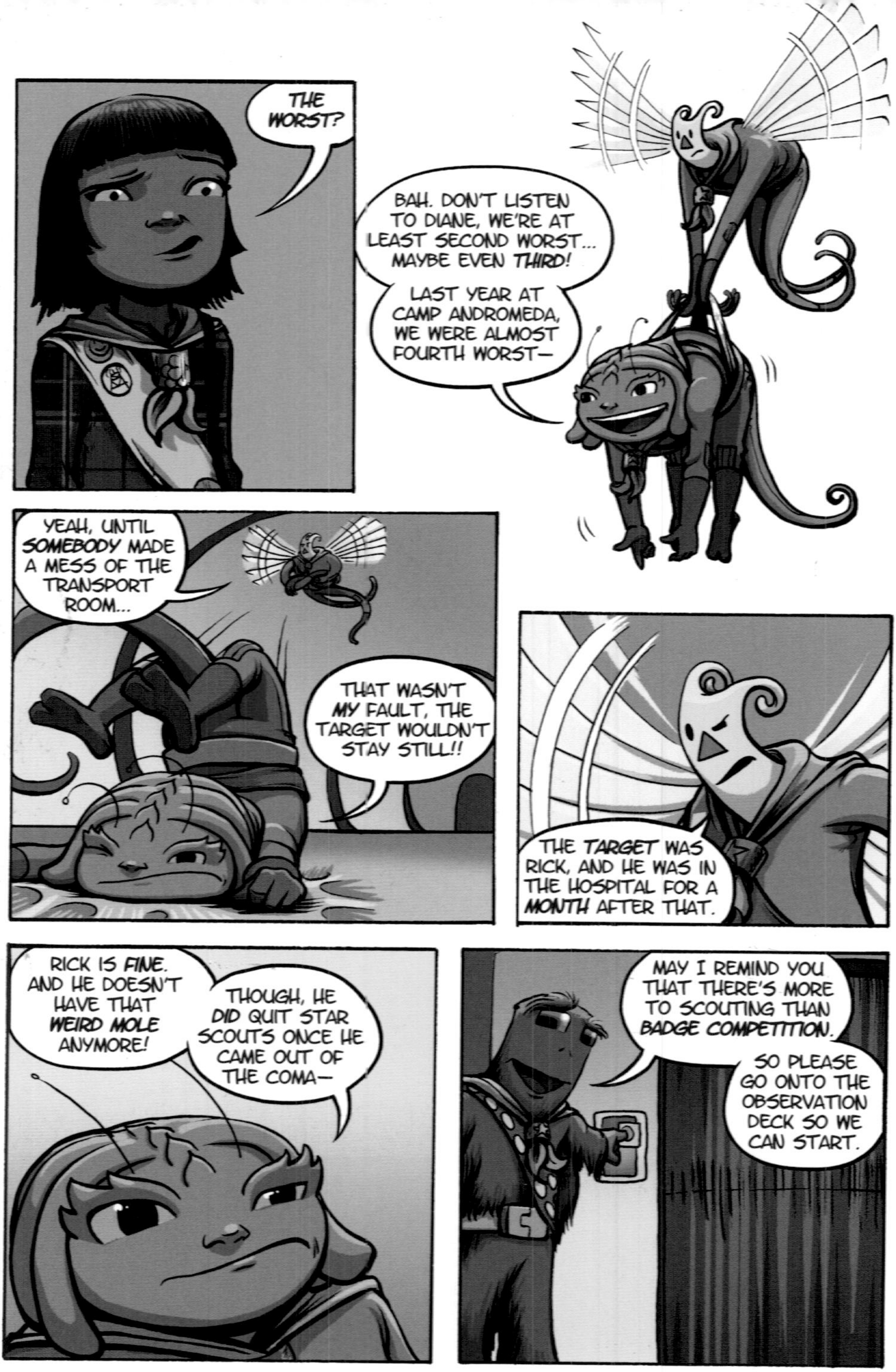
THE WORST?
BAH. DON'T LISTEN TO DIANE, WE'RE AT LEAST SECOND WORST... MAYBE EVEN THIRD!
LAST YEAR AT CAMP ANDROMEDA, WE WERE ALMOST FOURTH WORST—
YEAH, UNTIL SOMEBODY MADE A MESS OF THE TRANSPORT ROOM...
THAT WASN'T MY FAULT, THE TARGET WOULDN'T STAY STILL!!
THE TARGET WAS RICK, AND HE WAS IN THE HOSPITAL FOR A MONTH AFTER THAT.
RICK IS FINE. AND HE DOESN'T HAVE THAT WEIRD MOLE ANYMORE!
THOUGH, HE DID QUIT STAR SCOUTS ONCE HE CAME OUT OF THE COMA—
MAY I REMIND YOU THAT THERE'S MORE TO SCOUTING THAN BADGE COMPETITION.
SO PLEASE GO ONTO THE OBSERVATION DECK SO WE CAN START.

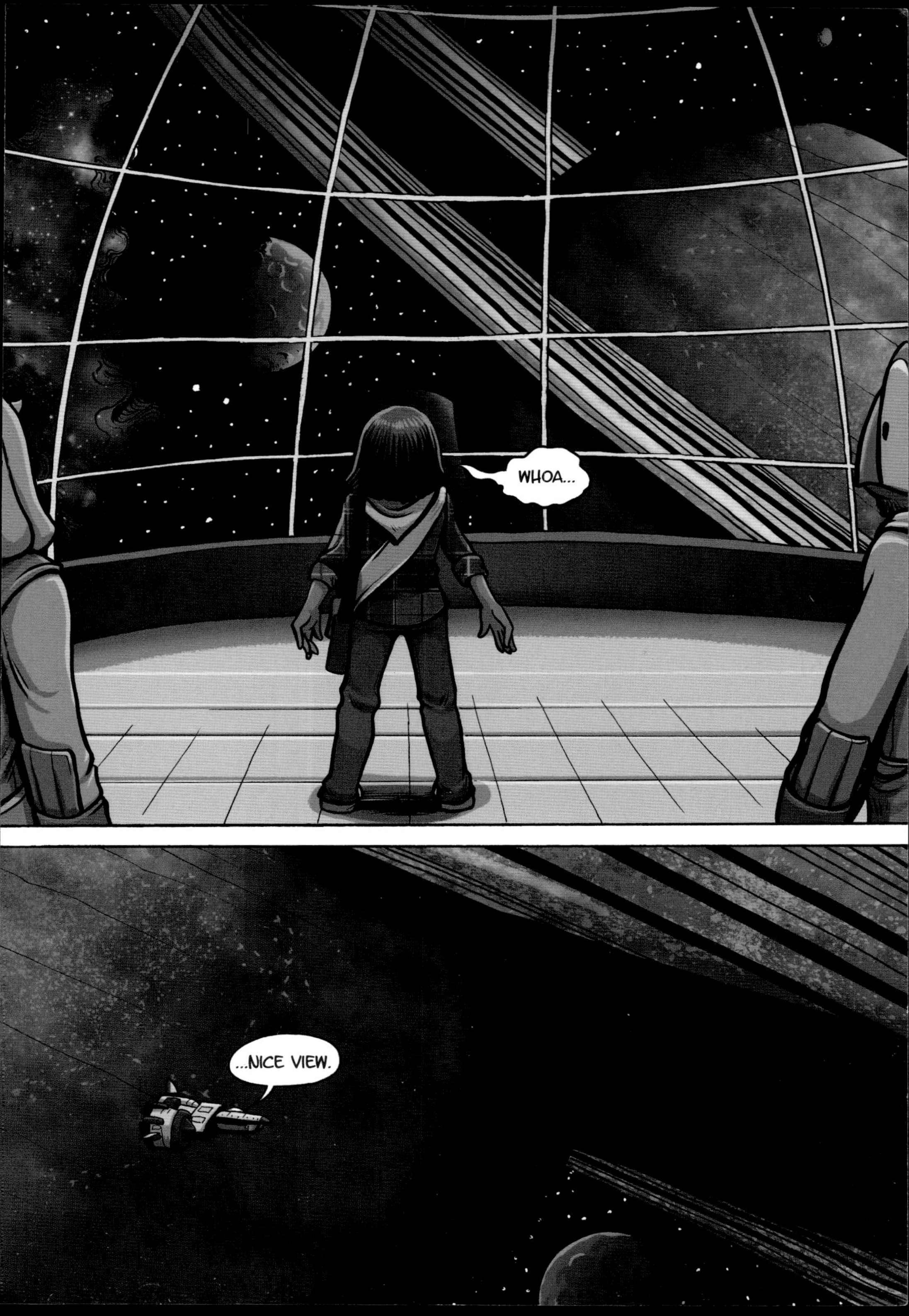
WHOA...
...NICE VIEW.

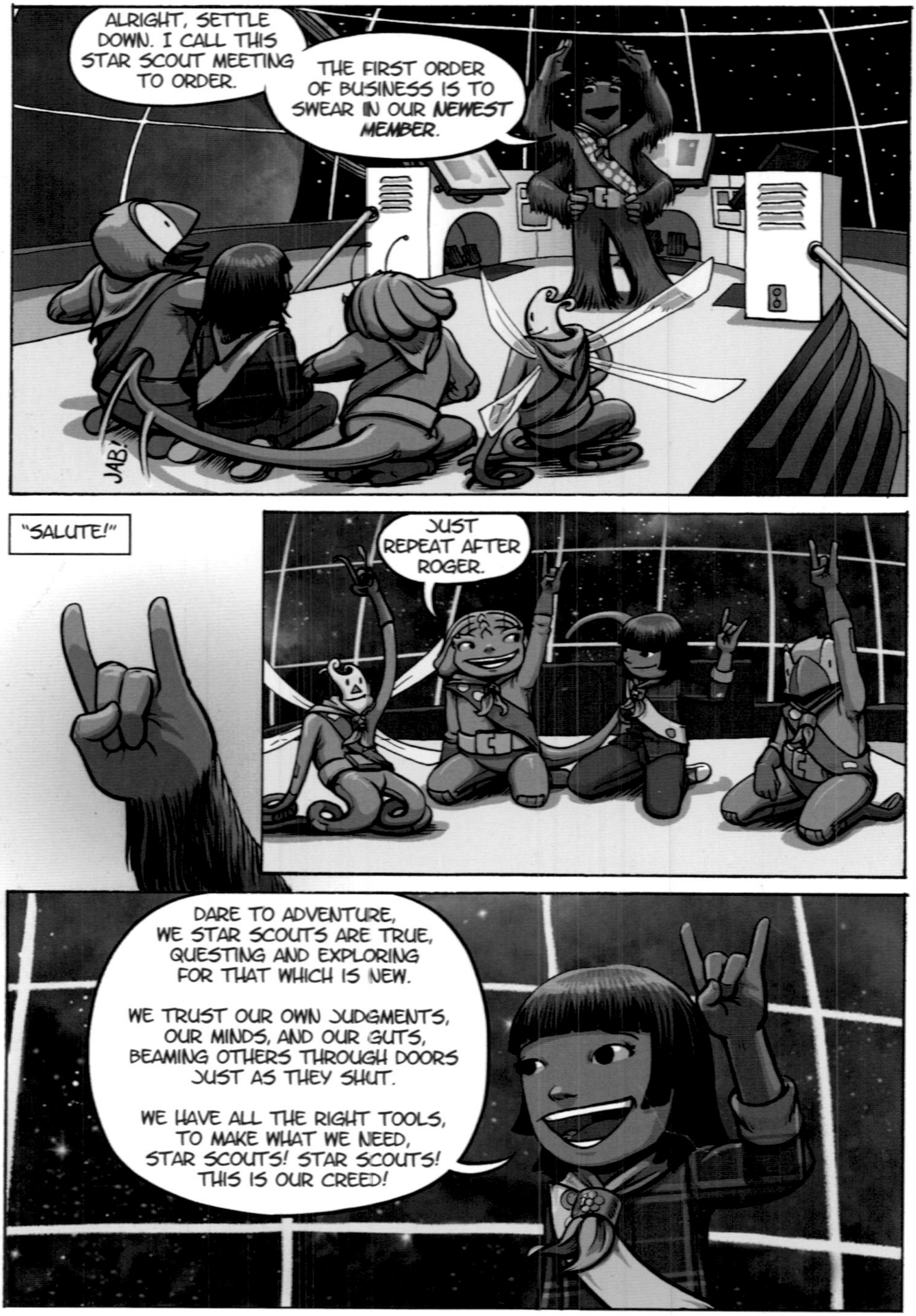
ALRIGHT, SETTLE DOWN. I CALL THIS STAR SCOUT MEETING TO ORDER.
THE FIRST ORDER OF BUSINESS IS TO SWEAR IN OUR *NEWEST MEMBER*.
JAB!
"SALUTE!"
JUST REPEAT AFTER ROGER.
DARE TO ADVENTURE, WE STAR SCOUTS ARE TRUE, QUESTING AND EXPLORING FOR THAT WHICH IS NEW. WE TRUST OUR OWN JUDGMENTS, OUR MINDS, AND OUR GUTS, BEAMING OTHERS THROUGH DOORS JUST AS THEY SHUT. WE HAVE ALL THE RIGHT TOOLS, TO MAKE WHAT WE NEED, STAR SCOUTS! STAR SCOUTS! THIS IS OUR CREED!

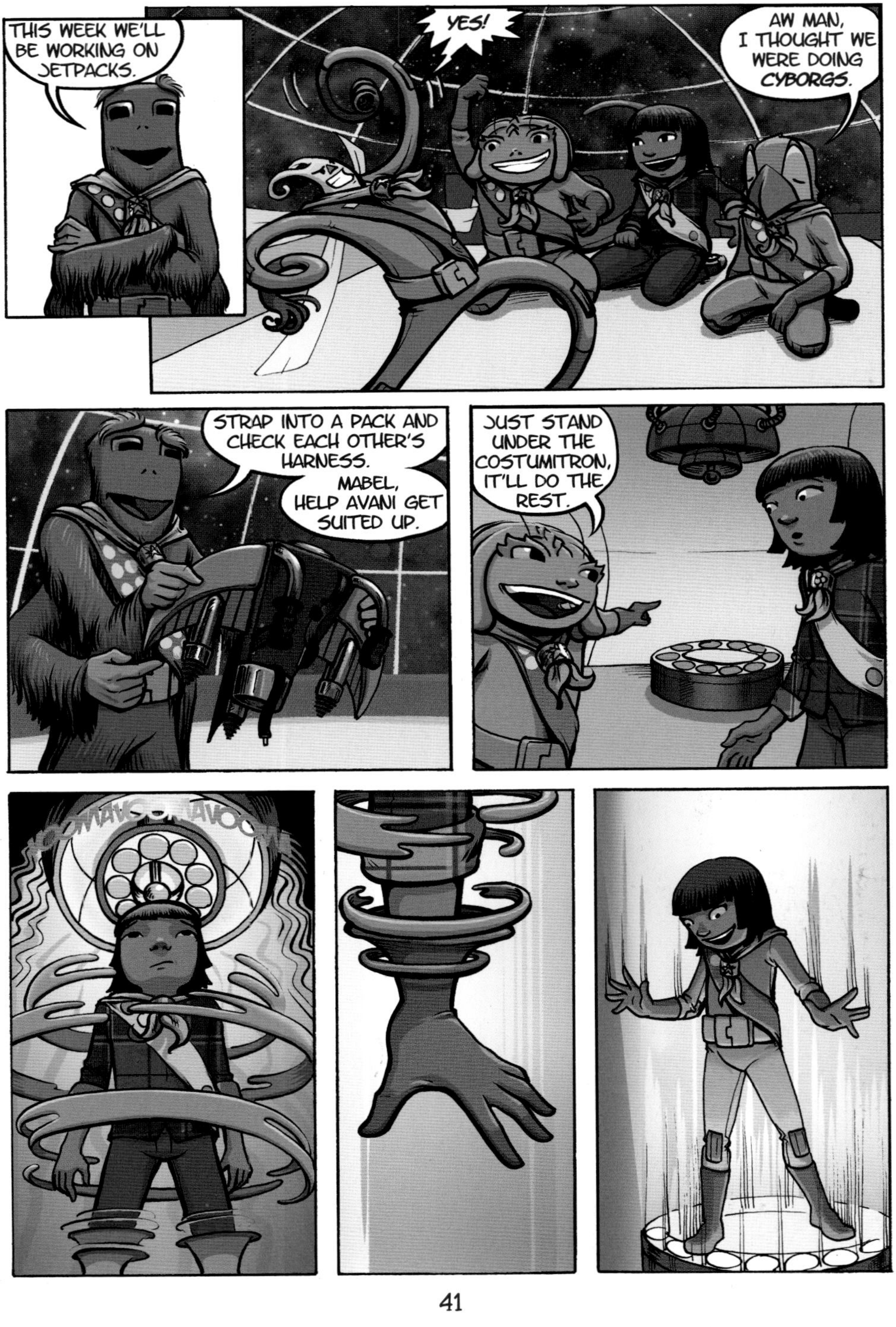
THIS WEEK WE'LL BE WORKING ON JETPACKS.
YES!
AW MAN, I THOUGHT WE WERE DOING *CYBORGS*.
STRAP INTO A PACK AND CHECK EACH OTHER'S HARNESS.
MABEL, HELP AVANI GET SUITED UP.
JUST STAND UNDER THE COSTUMITRON, IT'LL DO THE REST.

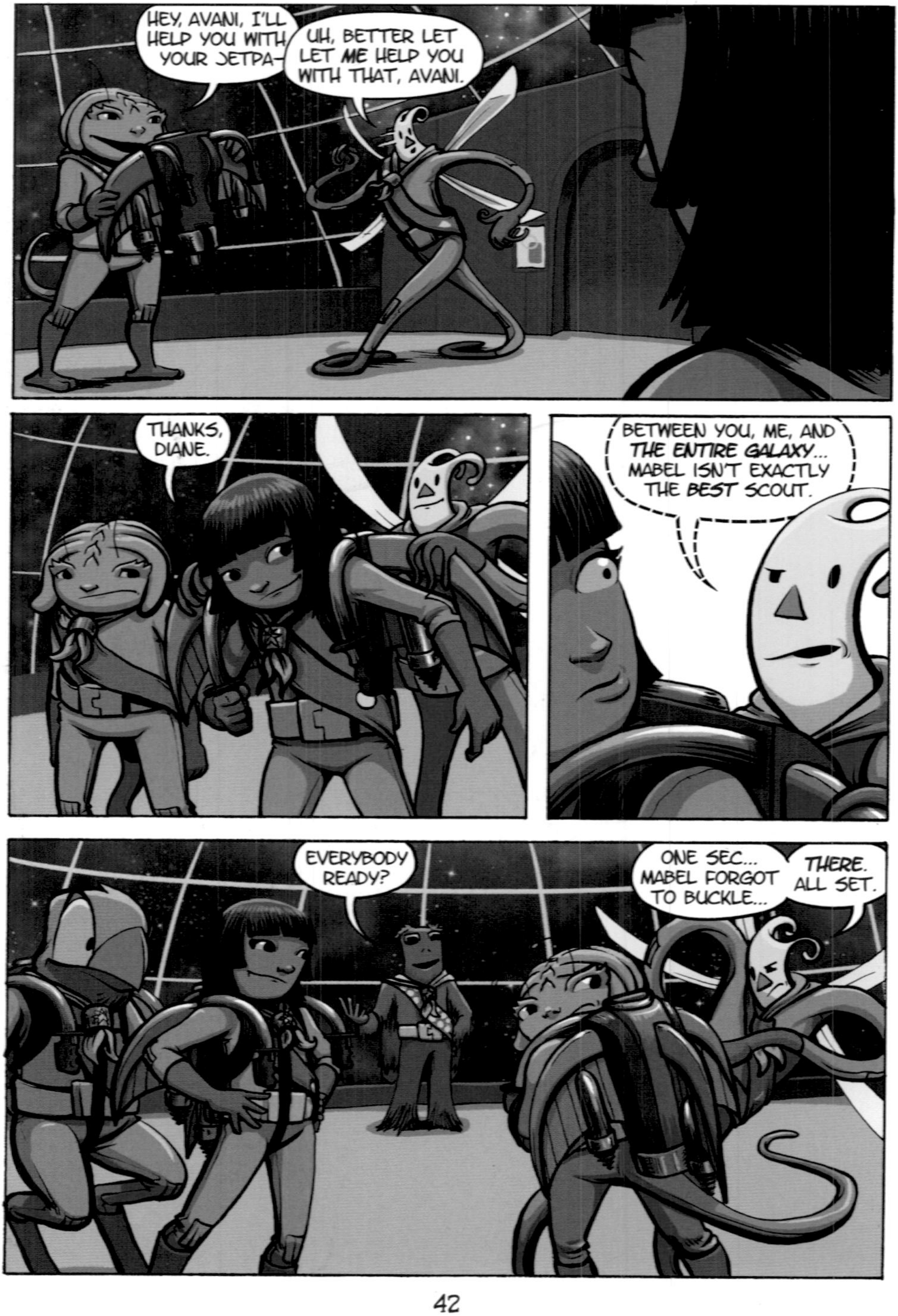
HEY, AVANI, I'LL HELP YOU WITH YOUR JETPA-
UH, BETTER LET LET *ME* HELP YOU WITH THAT, AVANI.
THANKS, DIANE.
BETWEEN YOU, ME, AND *THE ENTIRE GALAXY*... MABEL ISN'T EXACTLY THE *BEST* SCOUT.
EVERYBODY READY?
ONE SEC... MABEL FORGOT TO BUCKLE...
*THERE.* ALL SET.

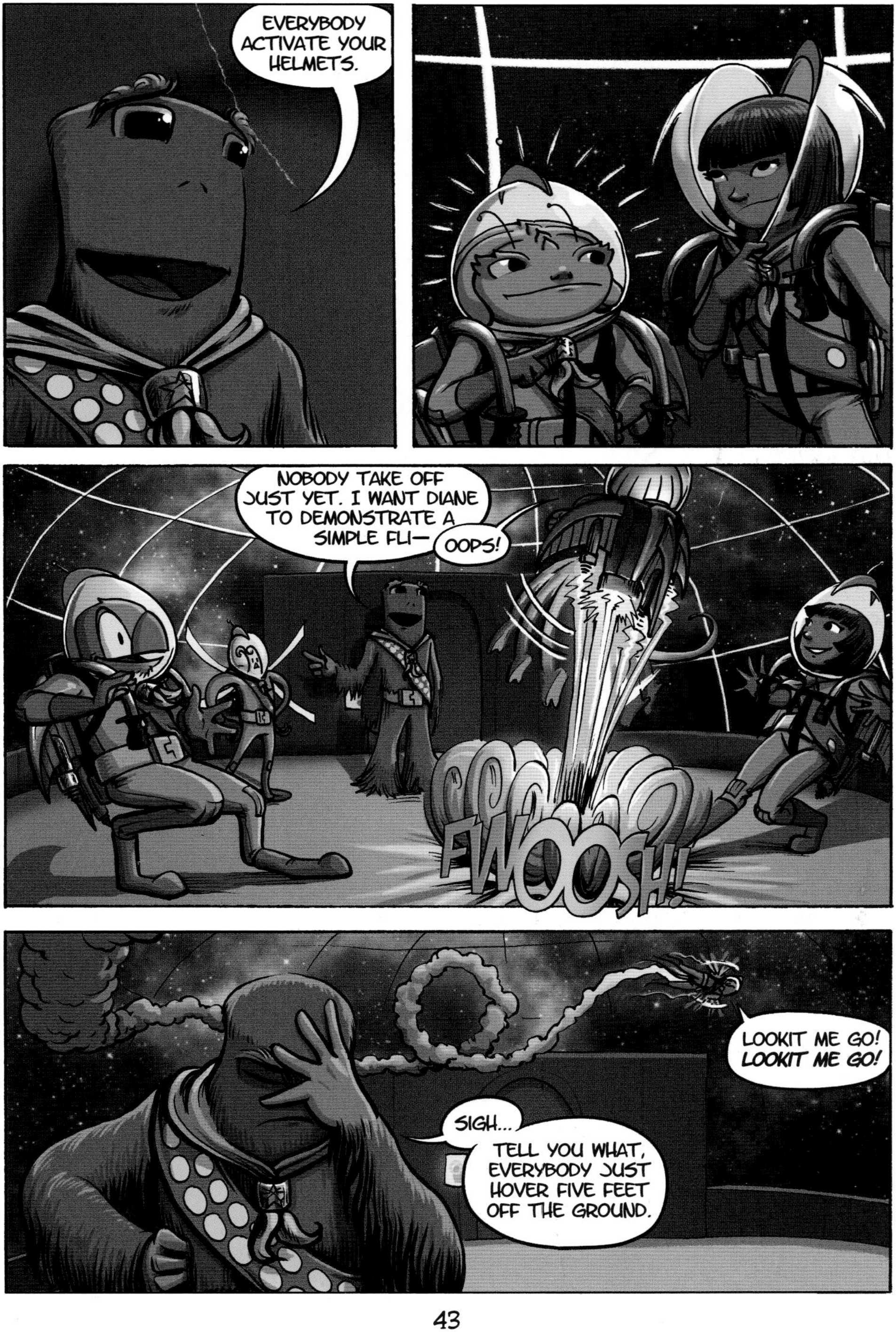
EVERYBODY ACTIVATE YOUR HELMETS.
NOBODY TAKE OFF JUST YET. I WANT DIANE TO DEMONSTRATE A SIMPLE FLI—
OOPS!
FWOOSH!
LOOKIT ME GO! LOOKIT ME GO!
SIGH...
TELL YOU WHAT, EVERYBODY JUST HOVER FIVE FEET OFF THE GROUND.

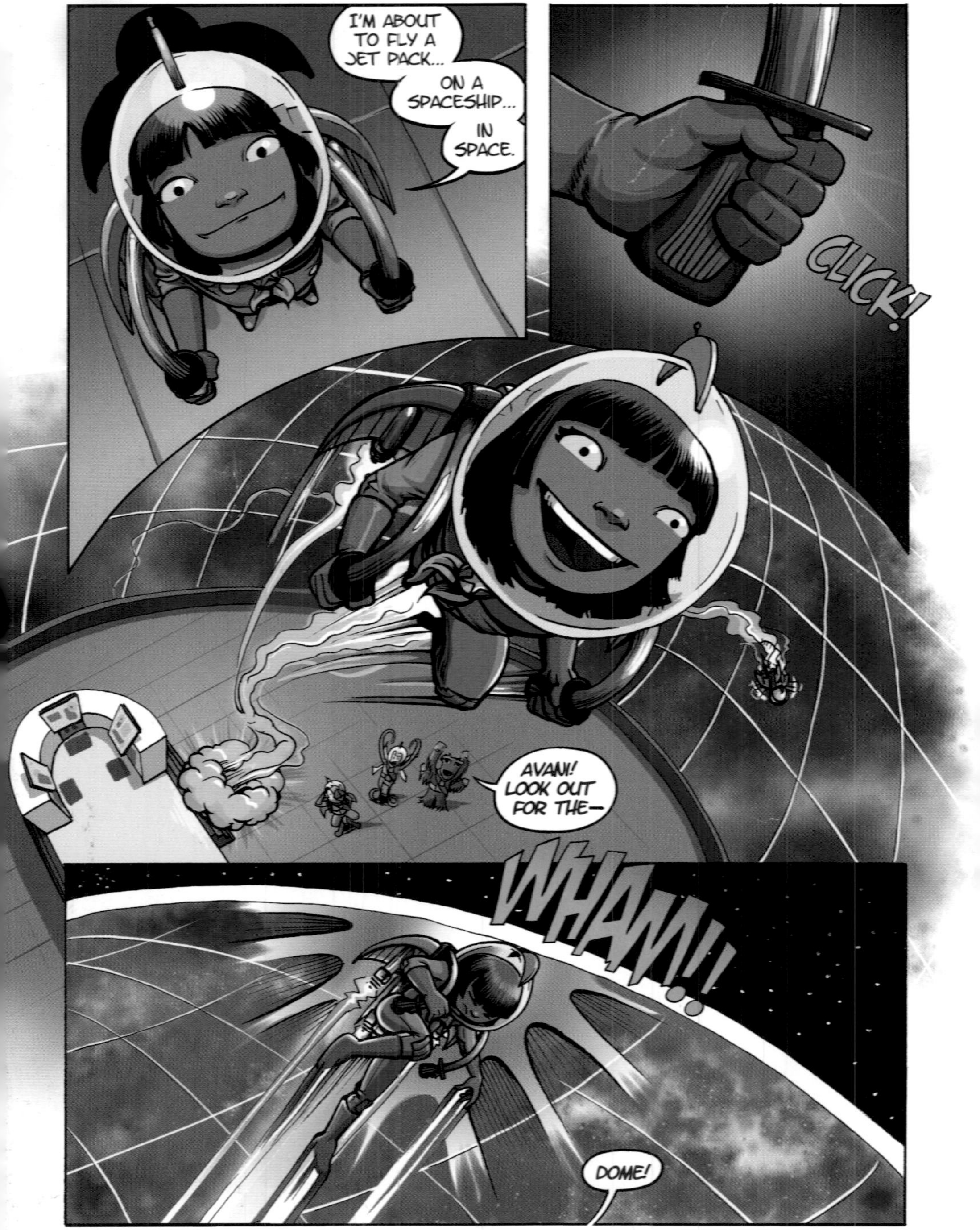
I'M ABOUT TO FLY A JET PACK...
ON A SPACESHIP...
IN SPACE.
CLICK!
AVANI! LOOK OUT FOR THE—
WHAM!!
DOME!

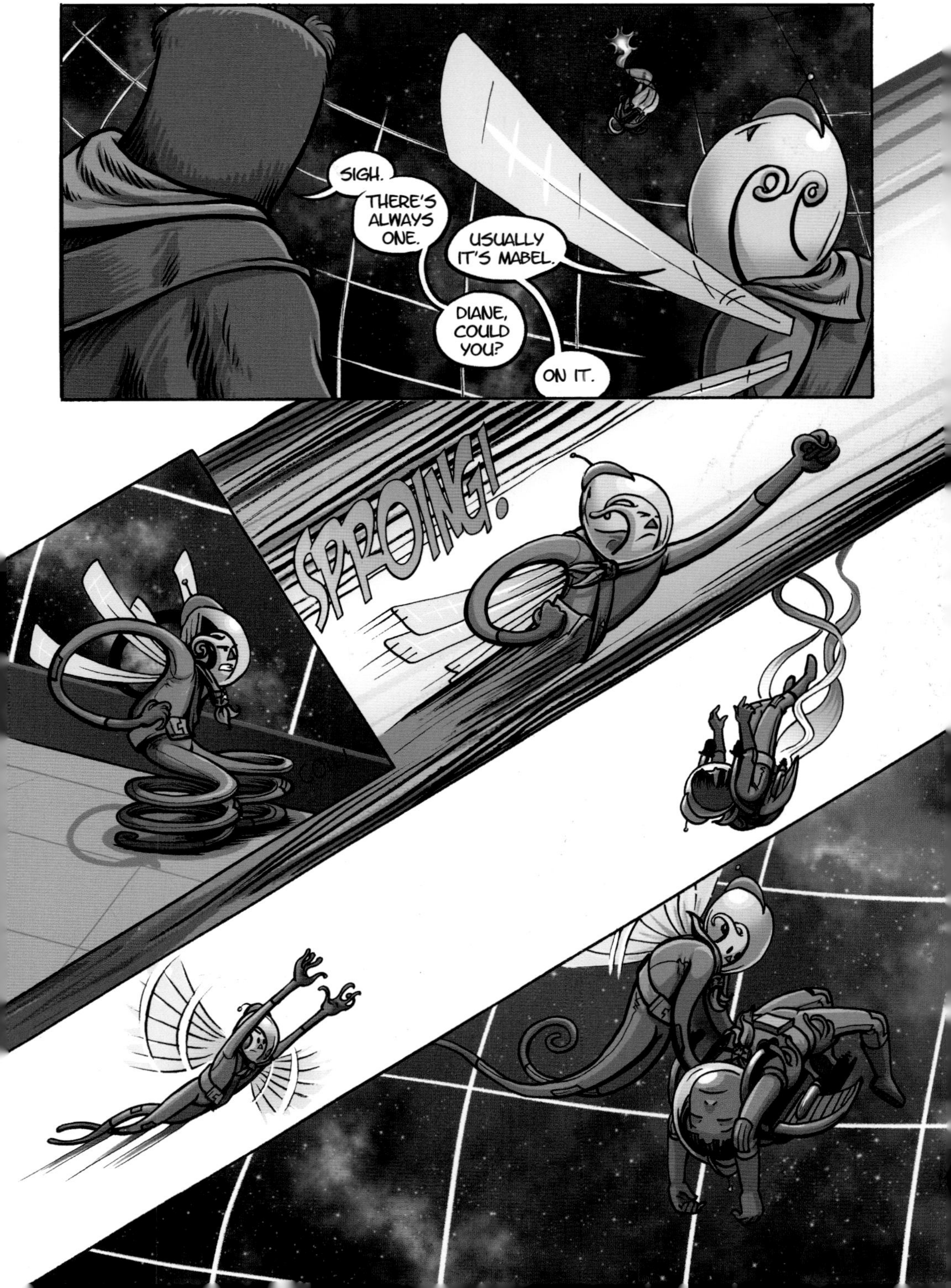
SIGH.
THERE'S ALWAYS ONE.
USUALLY IT'S MABEL.
DIANE, COULD YOU?
ON IT.
SPROING!

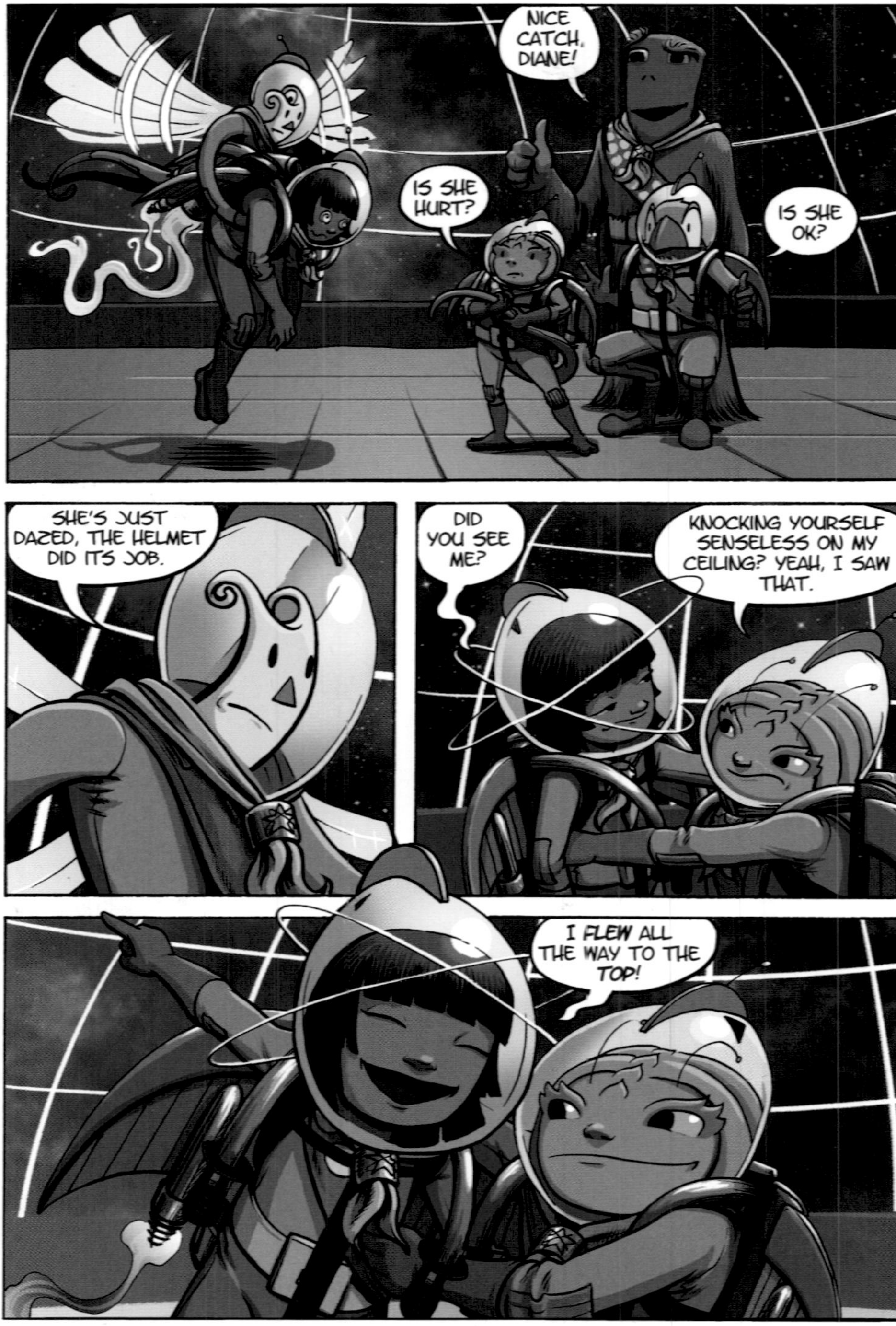
NICE CATCH, DIANE!
IS SHE HURT?
IS SHE OK?
SHE'S JUST DAZED, THE HELMET DID IT'S JOB.
DID YOU SEE ME?
KNOCKING YOURSELF SENSELESS ON MY CEILING? YEAH, I SAW THAT.
I *FLEW* ALL THE WAY TO THE *TOP*!

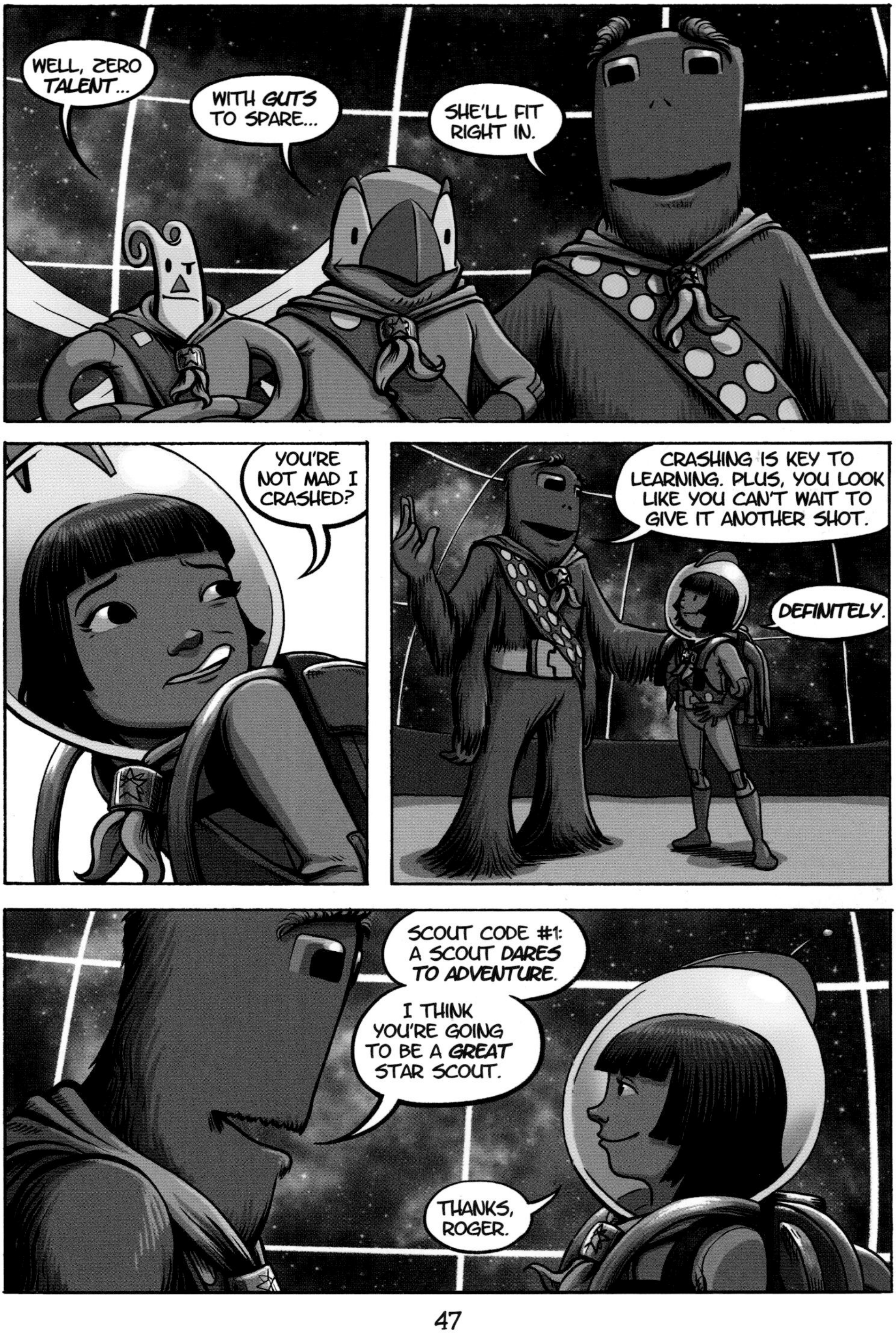
WELL, ZERO TALENT...
WITH GUTS TO SPARE...
SHE'LL FIT RIGHT IN.
YOU'RE NOT MAD I CRASHED?
CRASHING IS KEY TO LEARNING. PLUS, YOU LOOK LIKE YOU CAN'T WAIT TO GIVE IT ANOTHER SHOT.
DEFINITELY.
SCOUT CODE #1: A SCOUT DARES TO ADVENTURE.
I THINK YOU'RE GOING TO BE A GREAT STAR SCOUT.
THANKS, ROGER.

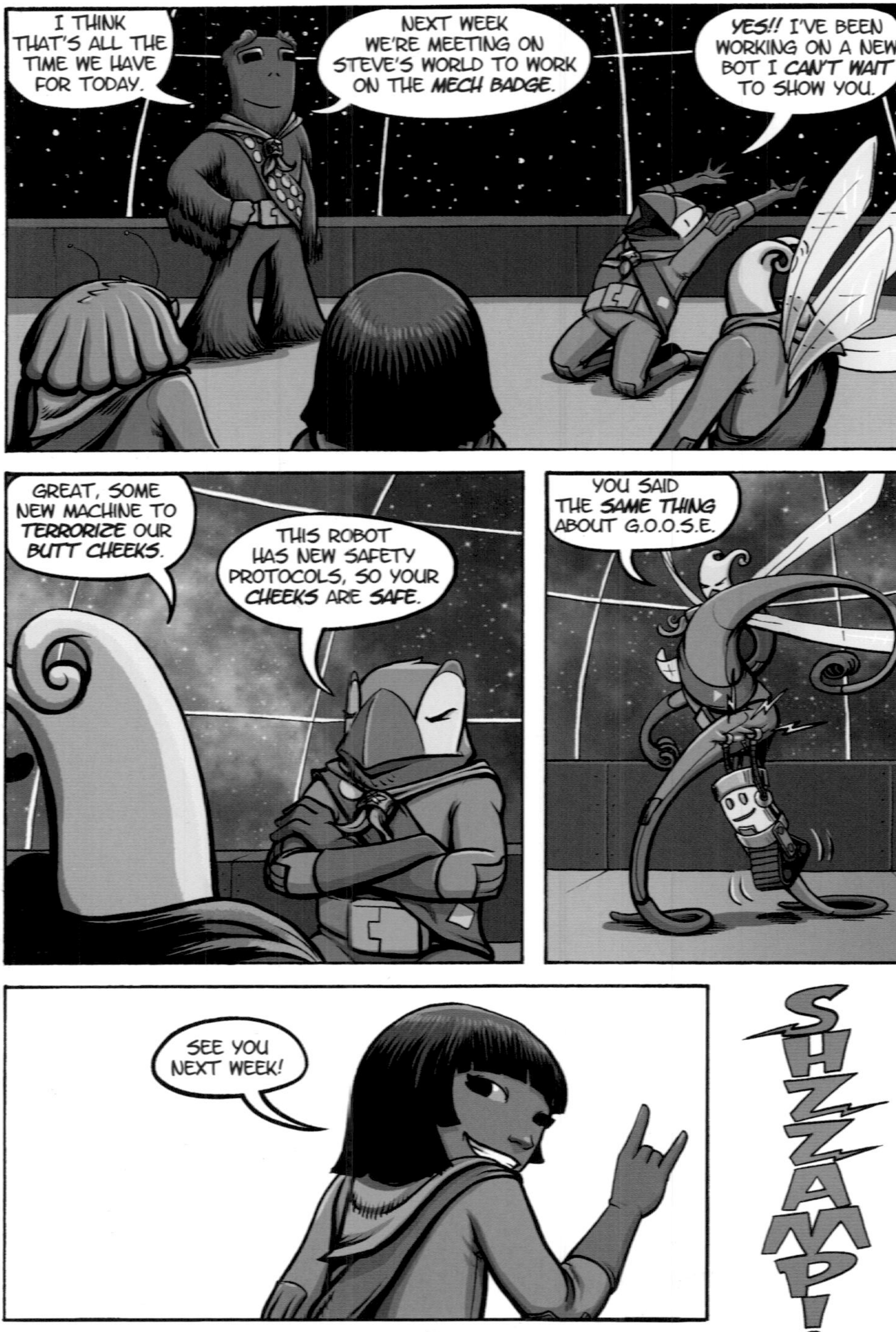

I THINK THAT'S ALL THE TIME WE HAVE FOR TODAY.
NEXT WEEK WE'RE MEETING ON STEVE'S WORLD TO WORK ON THE MECH BADGE.
YES!! I'VE BEEN WORKING ON A NEW BOT I CAN'T WAIT TO SHOW YOU.
GREAT, SOME NEW MACHINE TO TERRORIZE OUR BUTT CHEEKS.
THIS ROBOT HAS NEW SAFETY PROTOCOLS, SO YOUR CHEEKS ARE SAFE.
YOU SAID THE SAME THING ABOUT G.O.O.S.E.
SEE YOU NEXT WEEK!
SHZZAMP!

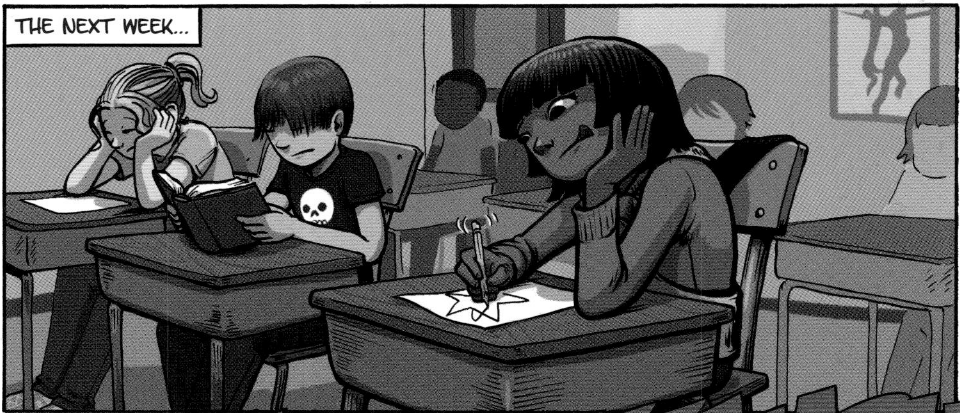
THE NEXT WEEK...

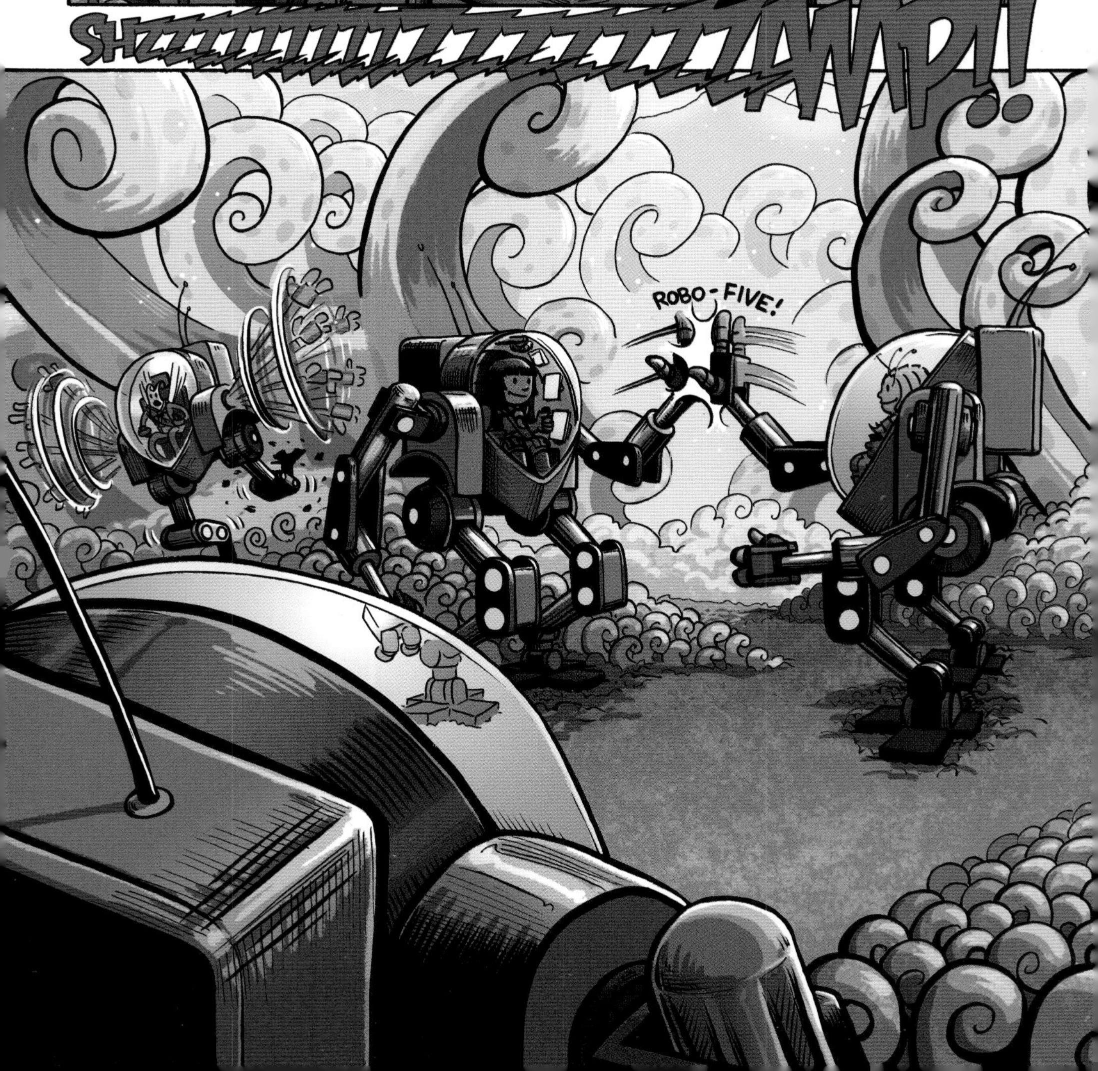
SHZZZZZZZZZZZZZZZZZZZAWP!!
ROBO-FIVE!

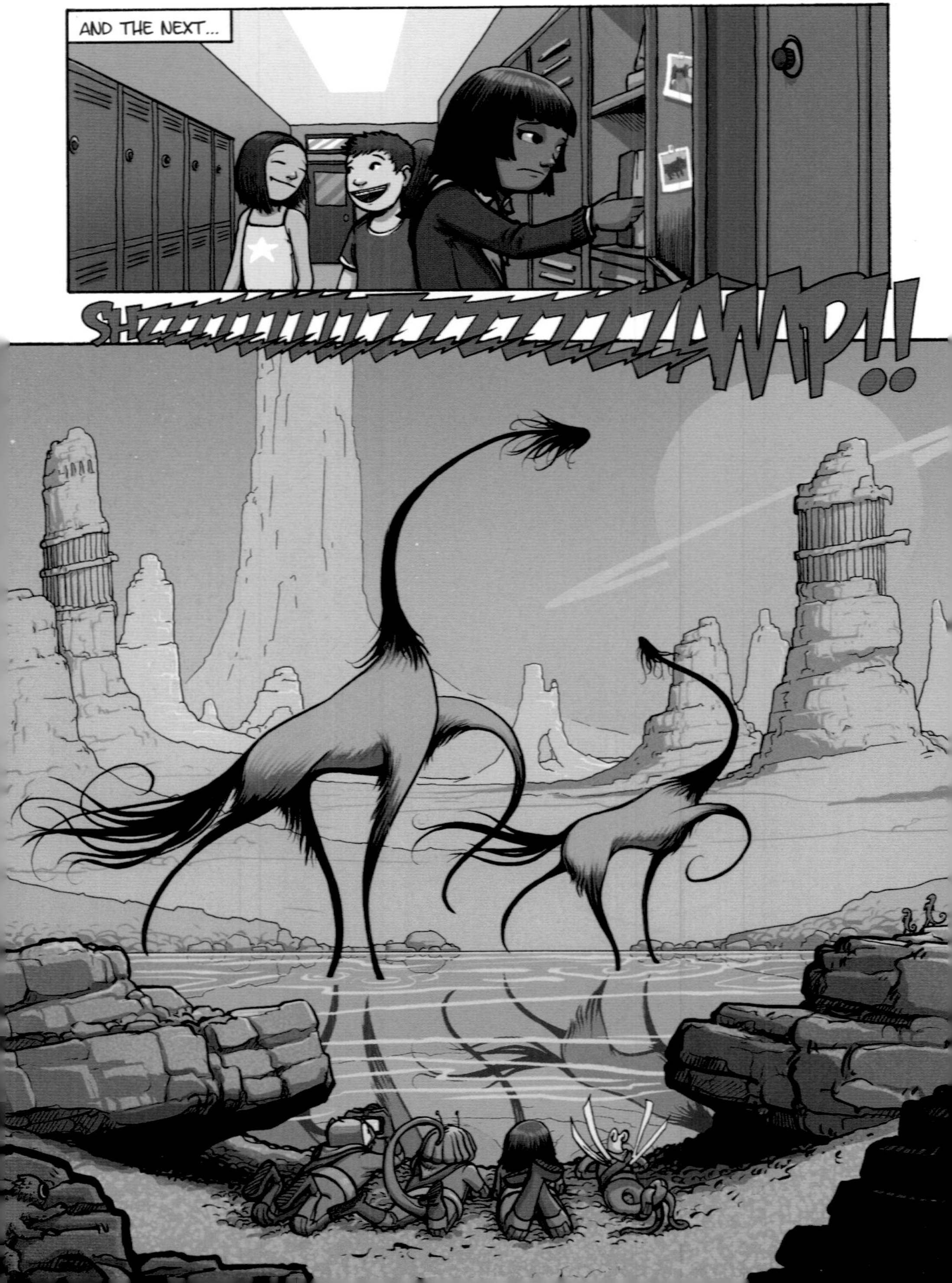
AND THE NEXT...
SHZZZZZZZZZZZZZZZZZZAMP!!

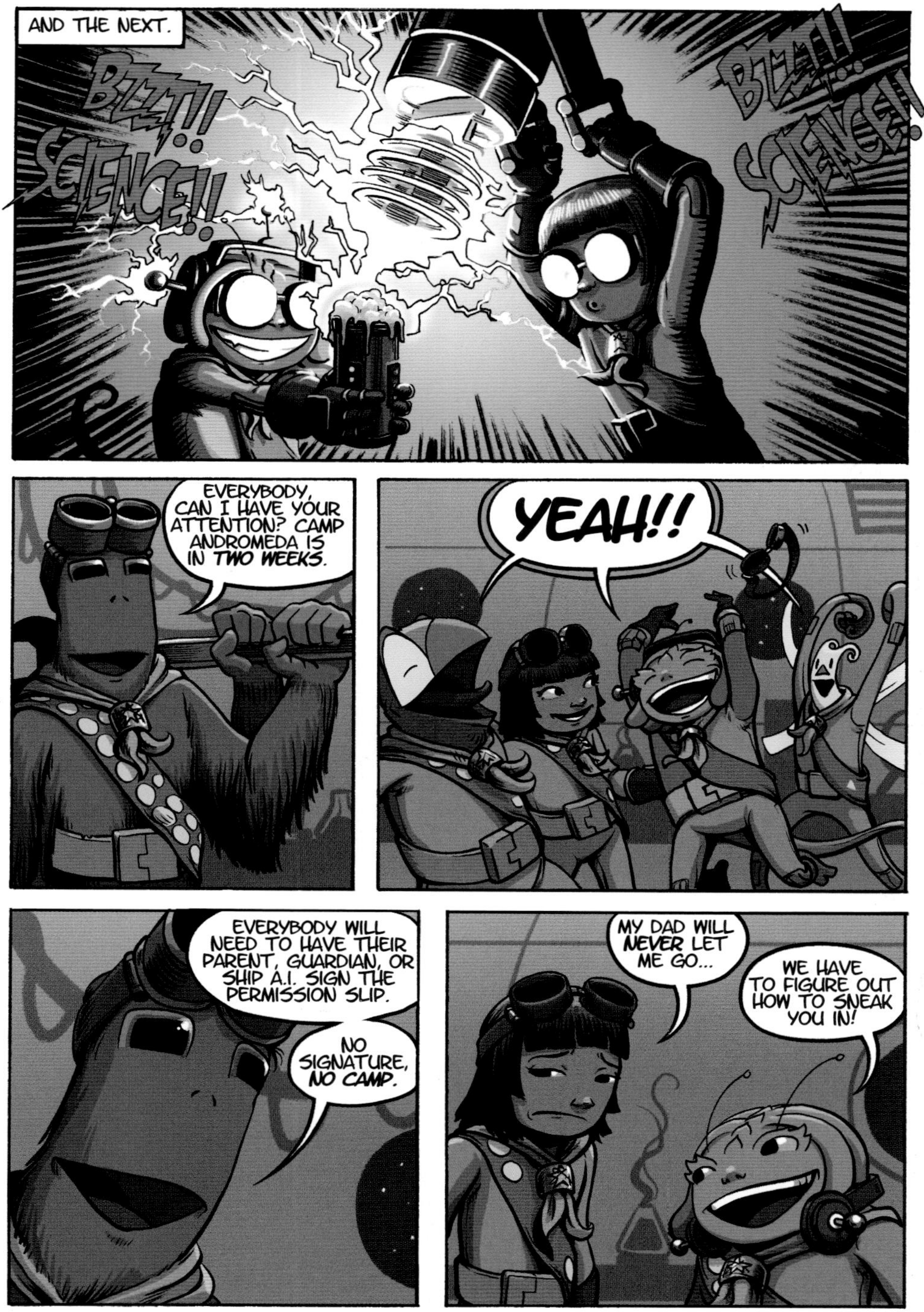
AND THE NEXT.
BZZT!! SCIENCE!!
BZZT!! SCIENCE!!
EVERYBODY, CAN I HAVE YOUR ATTENTION? CAMP ANDROMEDA IS IN TWO WEEKS.
YEAH!!
EVERYBODY WILL NEED TO HAVE THEIR PARENT, GUARDIAN, OR SHIP A.I. SIGN THE PERMISSION SLIP.
NO SIGNATURE, NO CAMP.
MY DAD WILL NEVER LET ME GO...
WE HAVE TO FIGURE OUT HOW TO SNEAK YOU IN!

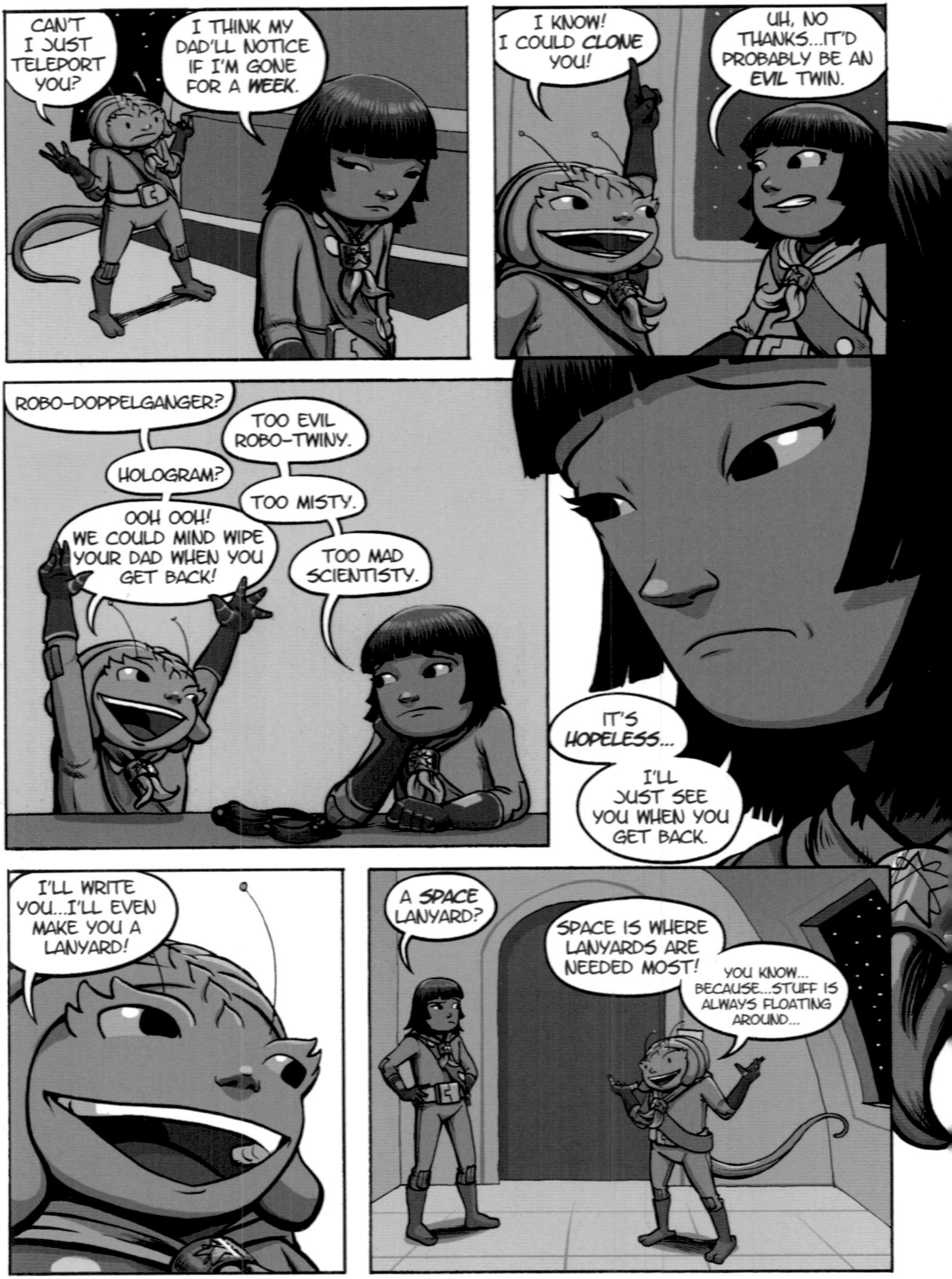

CAN'T I JUST TELEPORT YOU?
I THINK MY DAD'LL NOTICE IF I'M GONE FOR A WEEK.
I KNOW! I COULD CLONE YOU!
UH, NO THANKS...IT'D PROBABLY BE AN EVIL TWIN.
ROBO-DOPPELGANGER?
TOO EVIL ROBO-TWINY.
HOLOGRAM?
TOO MISTY.
OOH OOH! WE COULD MIND WIPE YOUR DAD WHEN YOU GET BACK!
TOO MAD SCIENTISTY.
IT'S HOPELESS...
I'LL JUST SEE YOU WHEN YOU GET BACK.
I'LL WRITE YOU...I'LL EVEN MAKE YOU A LANYARD!
A SPACE LANYARD?
SPACE IS WHERE LANYARDS ARE NEEDED MOST!
YOU KNOW... BECAUSE...STUFF IS ALWAYS FLOATING AROUND...

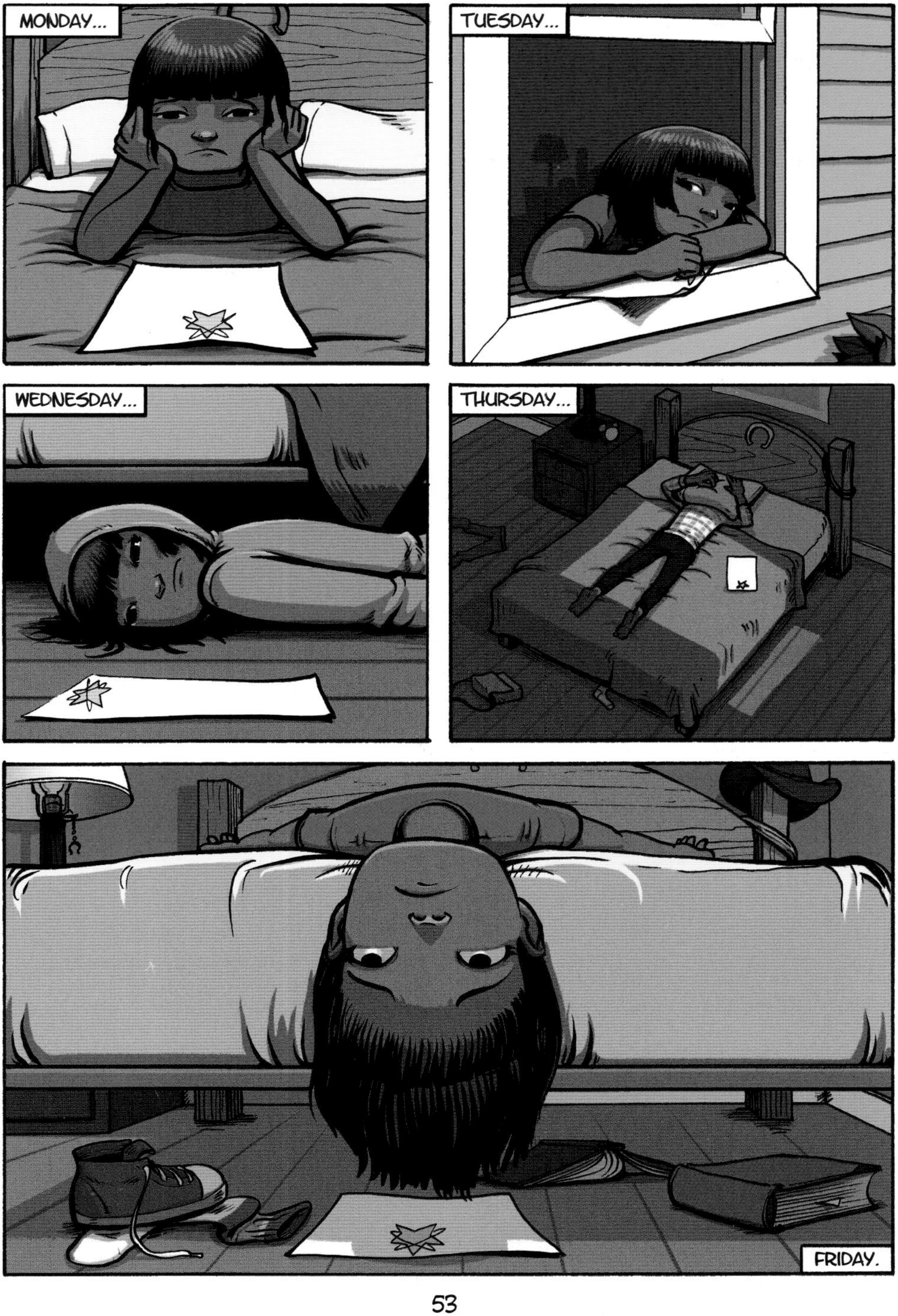
MONDAY...
TUESDAY...
WEDNESDAY...
THURSDAY...
FRIDAY.

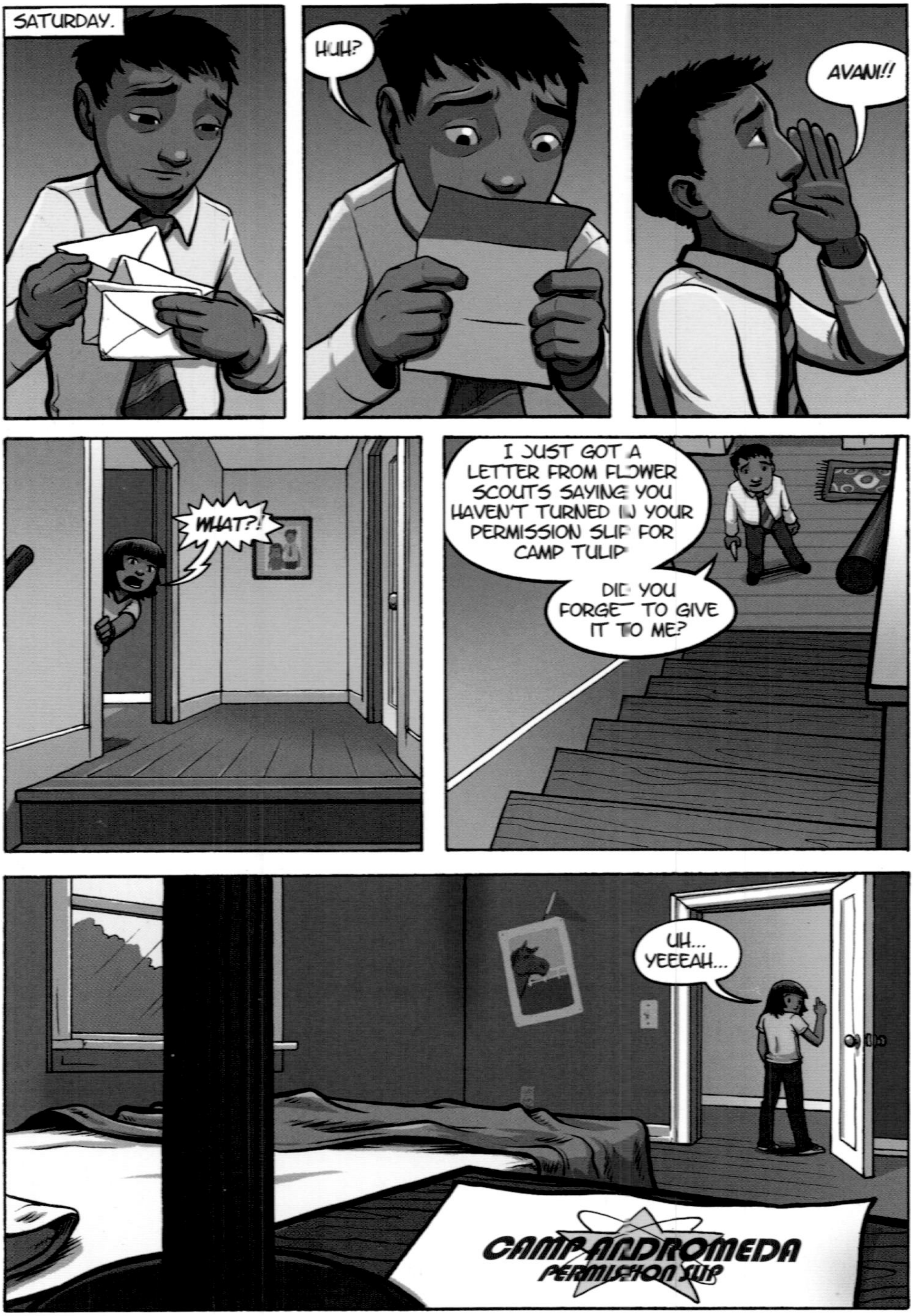
SATURDAY.
HUH?
AVANI!!
WHAT?!
I JUST GOT A LETTER FROM FLOWER SCOUTS SAYING YOU HAVEN'T TURNED IN YOUR PERMISSION SLIP FOR CAMP TULIP!
DID YOU FORGET TO GIVE IT TO ME?
UH... YEEEAH...
CAMP ANDROMEDA
PERMISSION SLIP

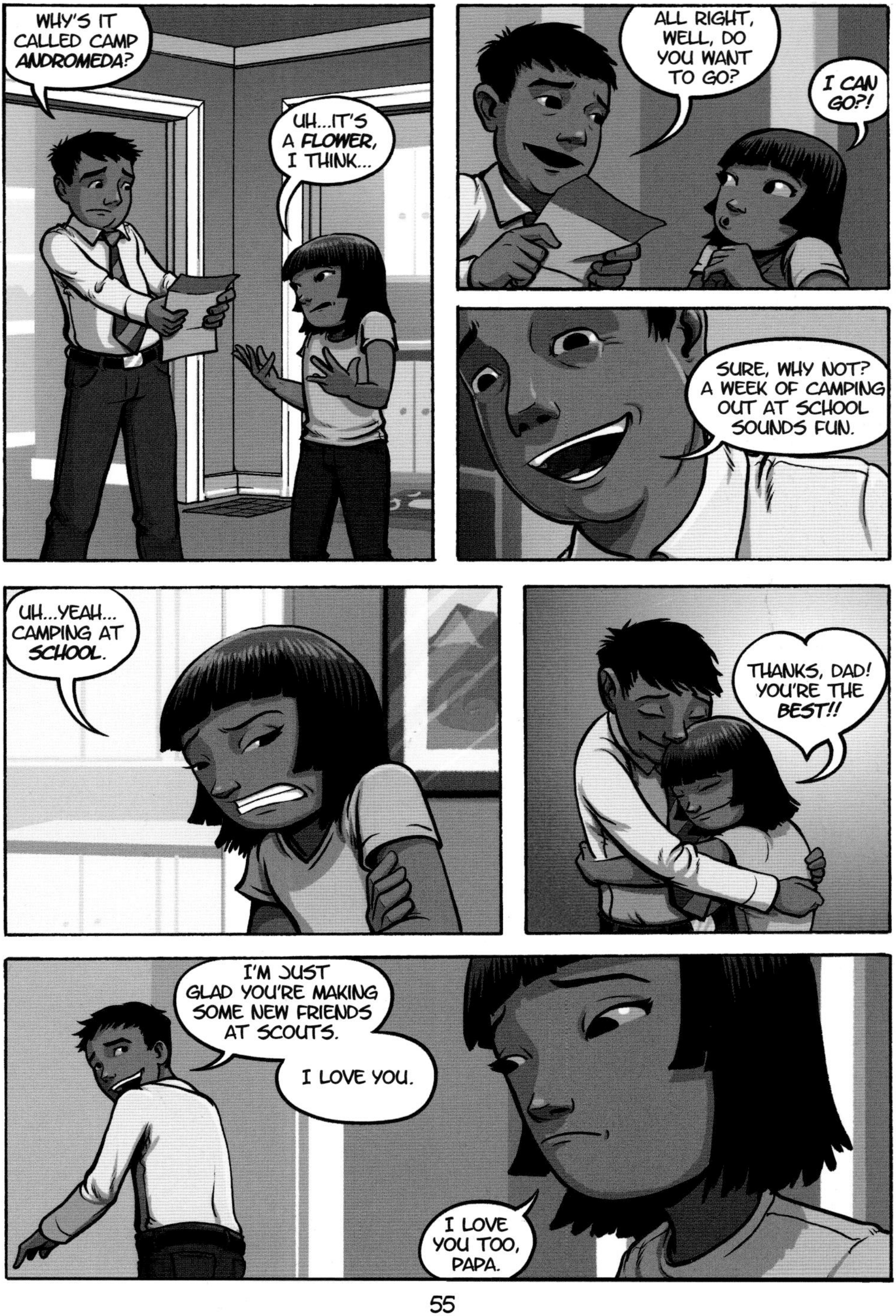
WHY'S IT CALLED CAMP ANDROMEDA?
UH...IT'S A FLOWER, I THINK...
ALL RIGHT, WELL, DO YOU WANT TO GO?
I CAN GO?!
SURE, WHY NOT? A WEEK OF CAMPING OUT AT SCHOOL SOUNDS FUN.
UH...YEAH... CAMPING AT SCHOOL.
THANKS, DAD! YOU'RE THE BEST!!
I'M JUST GLAD YOU'RE MAKING SOME NEW FRIENDS AT SCOUTS.
I LOVE YOU.
I LOVE YOU TOO, PAPA.

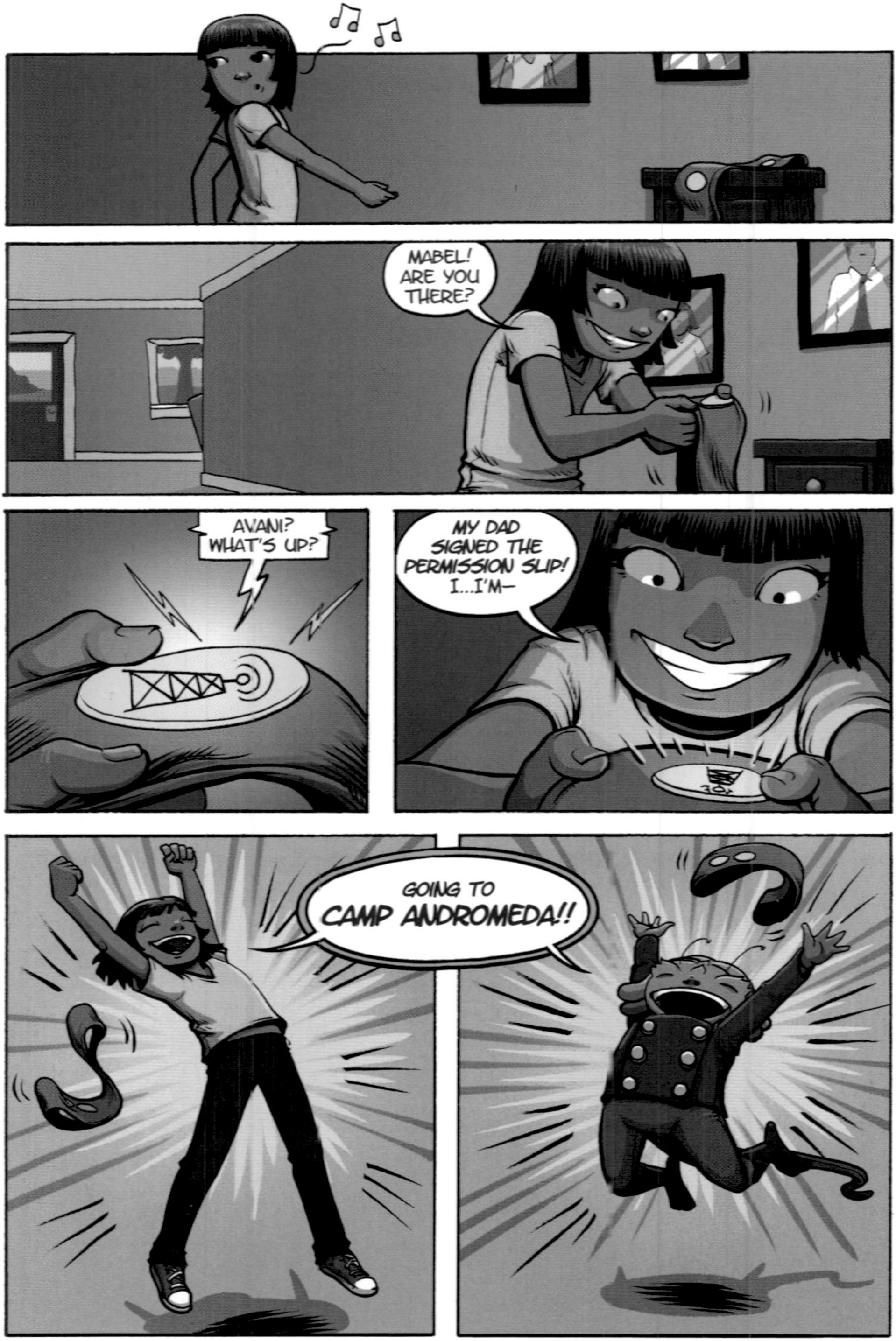

MABEL! ARE YOU THERE?
AVANI? WHAT'S UP?
MY DAD SIGNED THE PERMISSION SLIP! I...I'M–
GOING TO CAMP ANDROMEDA!!

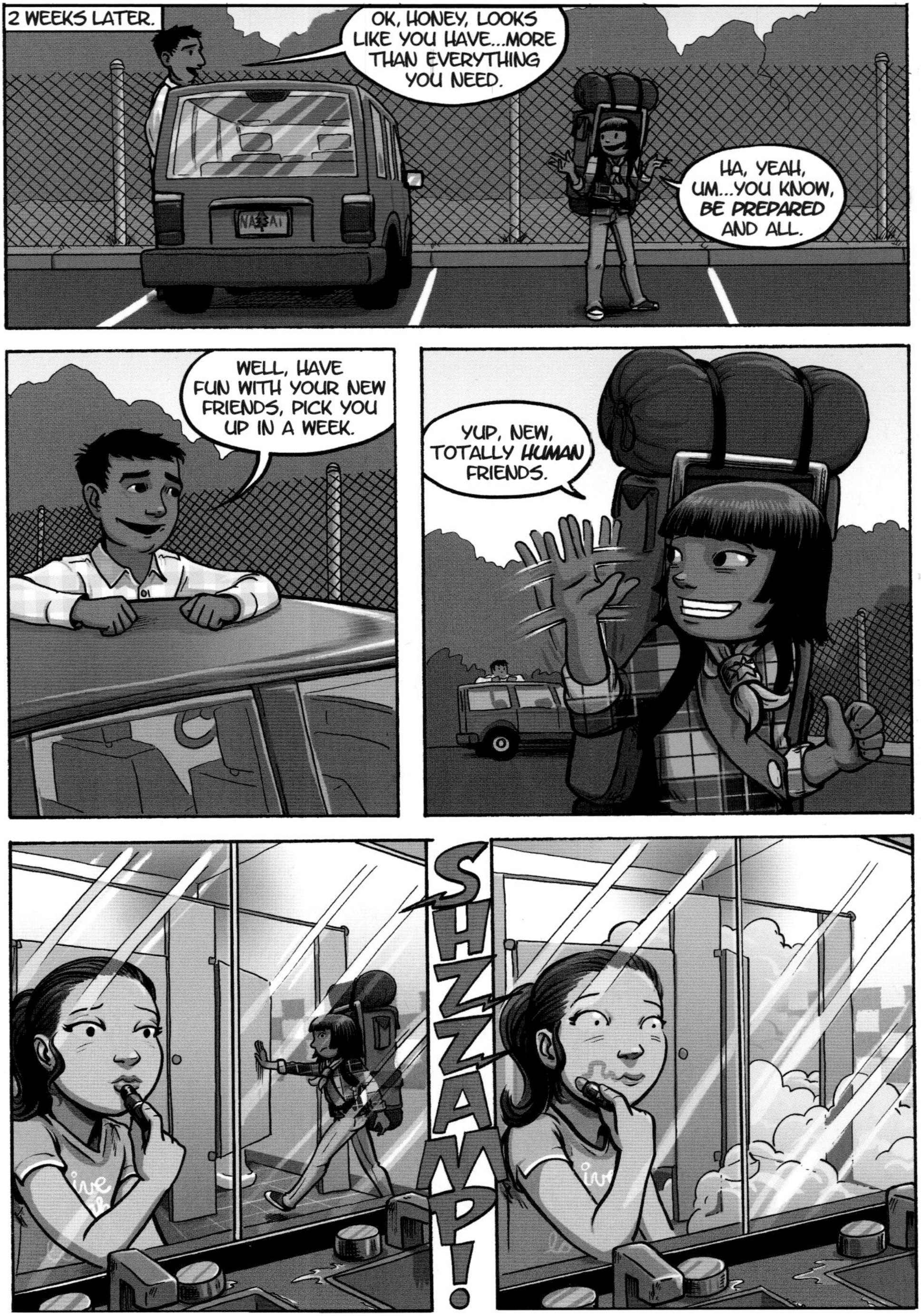
2 WEEKS LATER.
OK, HONEY, LOOKS LIKE YOU HAVE...MORE THAN EVERYTHING YOU NEED.
HA, YEAH, UM...YOU KNOW, BE PREPARED AND ALL.
WELL, HAVE FUN WITH YOUR NEW FRIENDS, PICK YOU UP IN A WEEK.
YUP, NEW, TOTALLY HUMAN FRIENDS.
SHZZAMP!

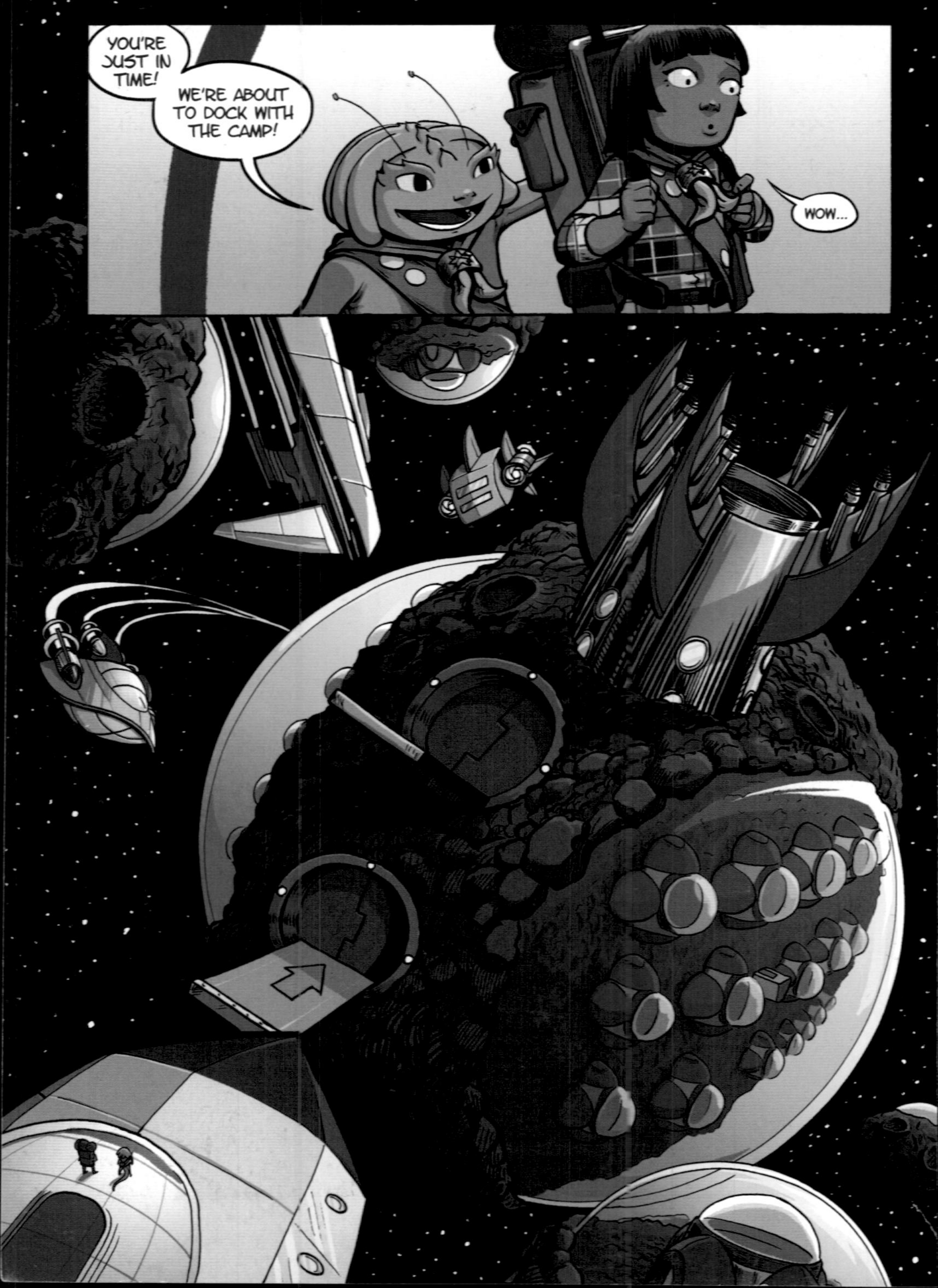
YOU'RE JUST IN TIME!
WE'RE ABOUT TO DOCK WITH THE CAMP!
WOW...

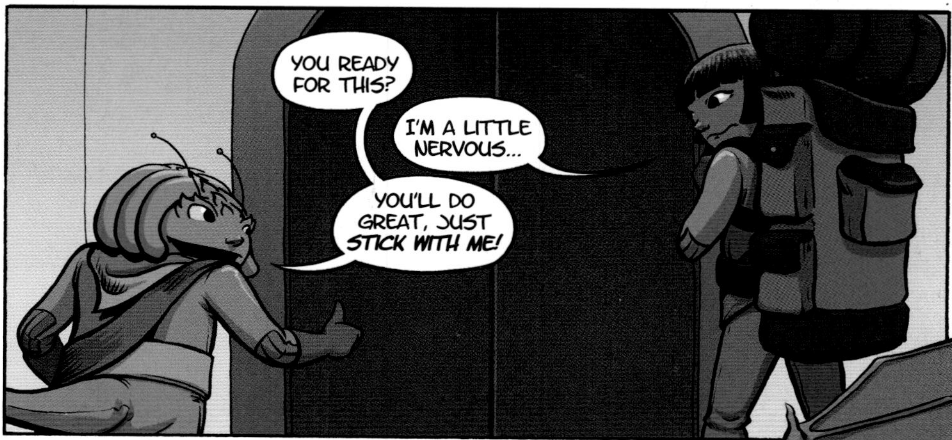
YOU READY FOR THIS?
I'M A LITTLE NERVOUS...
YOU'LL DO GREAT, JUST STICK WITH ME!

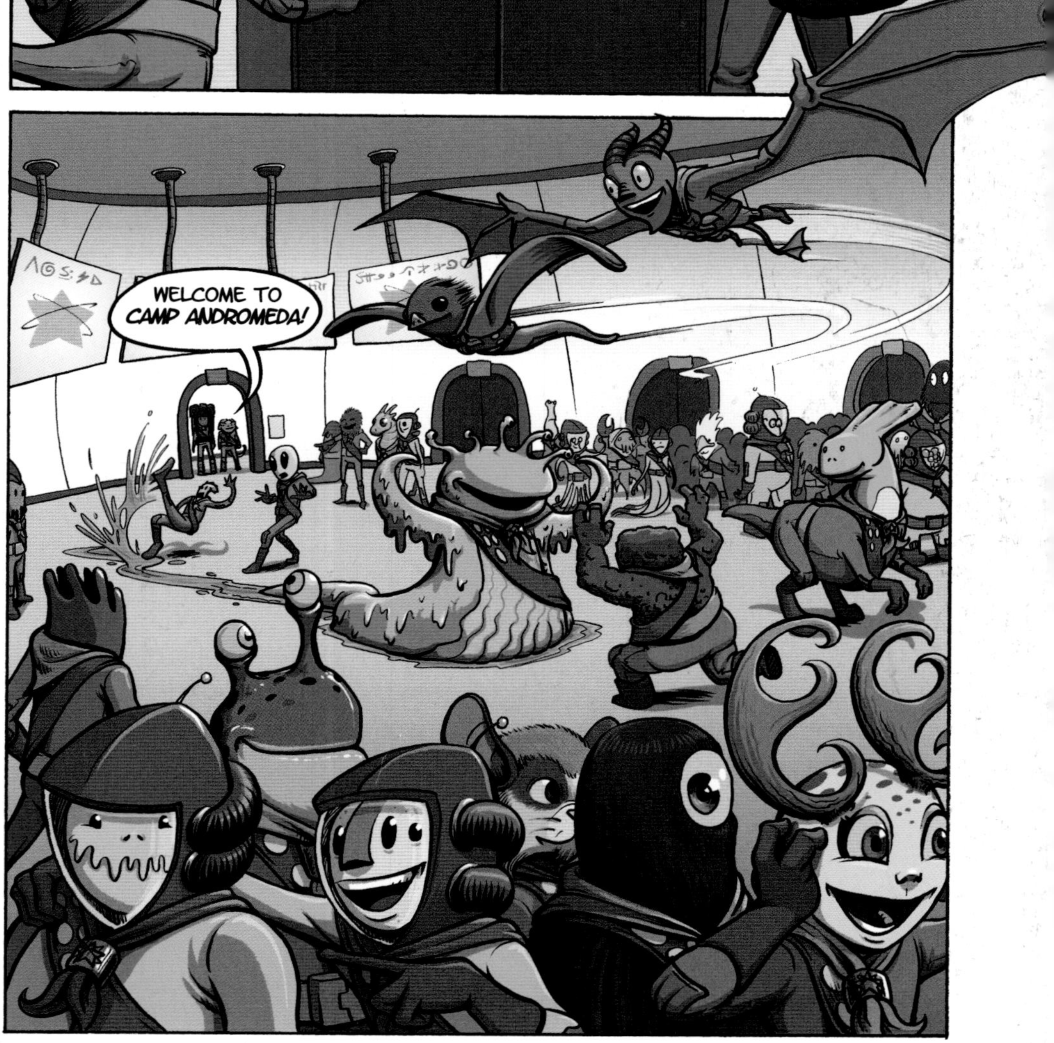
WELCOME TO CAMP ANDROMEDA!

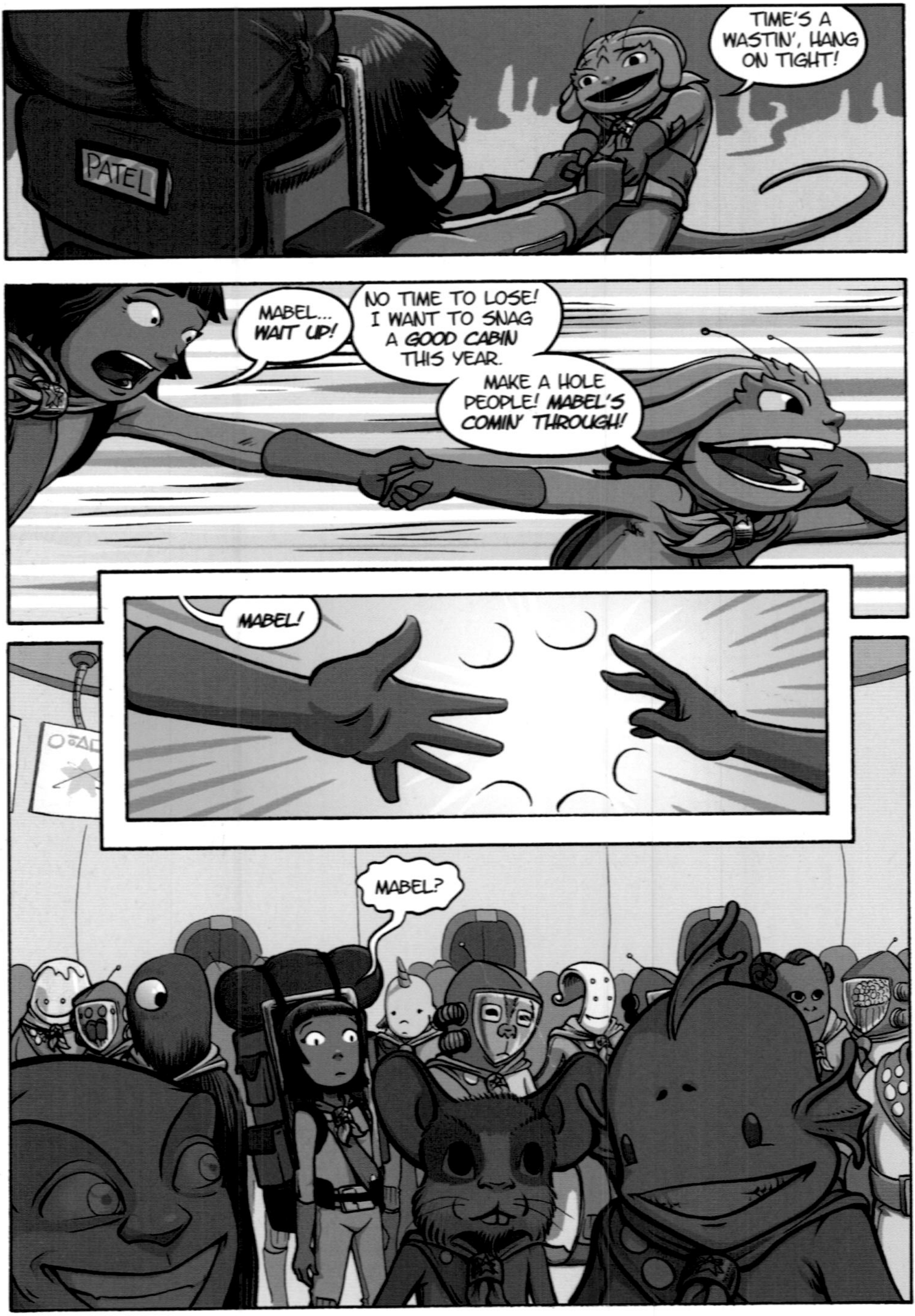

PATEL
TIME'S A WASTIN', HANG ON TIGHT!
MABEL... WAIT UP!
NO TIME TO LOSE! I WANT TO SNAG A GOOD CABIN THIS YEAR.
MAKE A HOLE PEOPLE! MABEL'S COMIN' THROUGH!
MABEL!
MABEL?

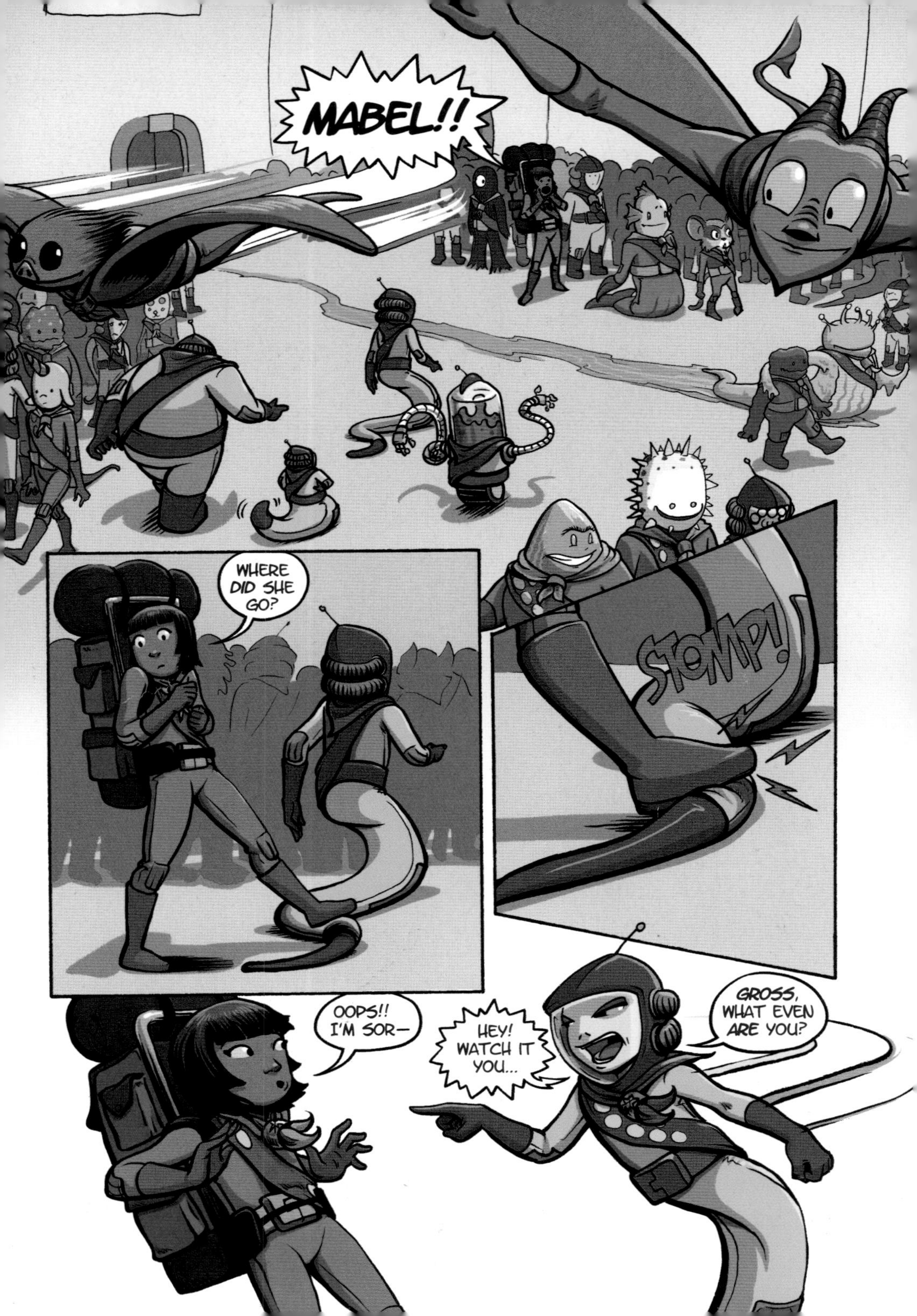
MABEL!!
WHERE DID SHE GO?
STOMP!
OOPS!! I'M SOR—
HEY! WATCH IT YOU...
GROSS, WHAT EVEN ARE YOU?

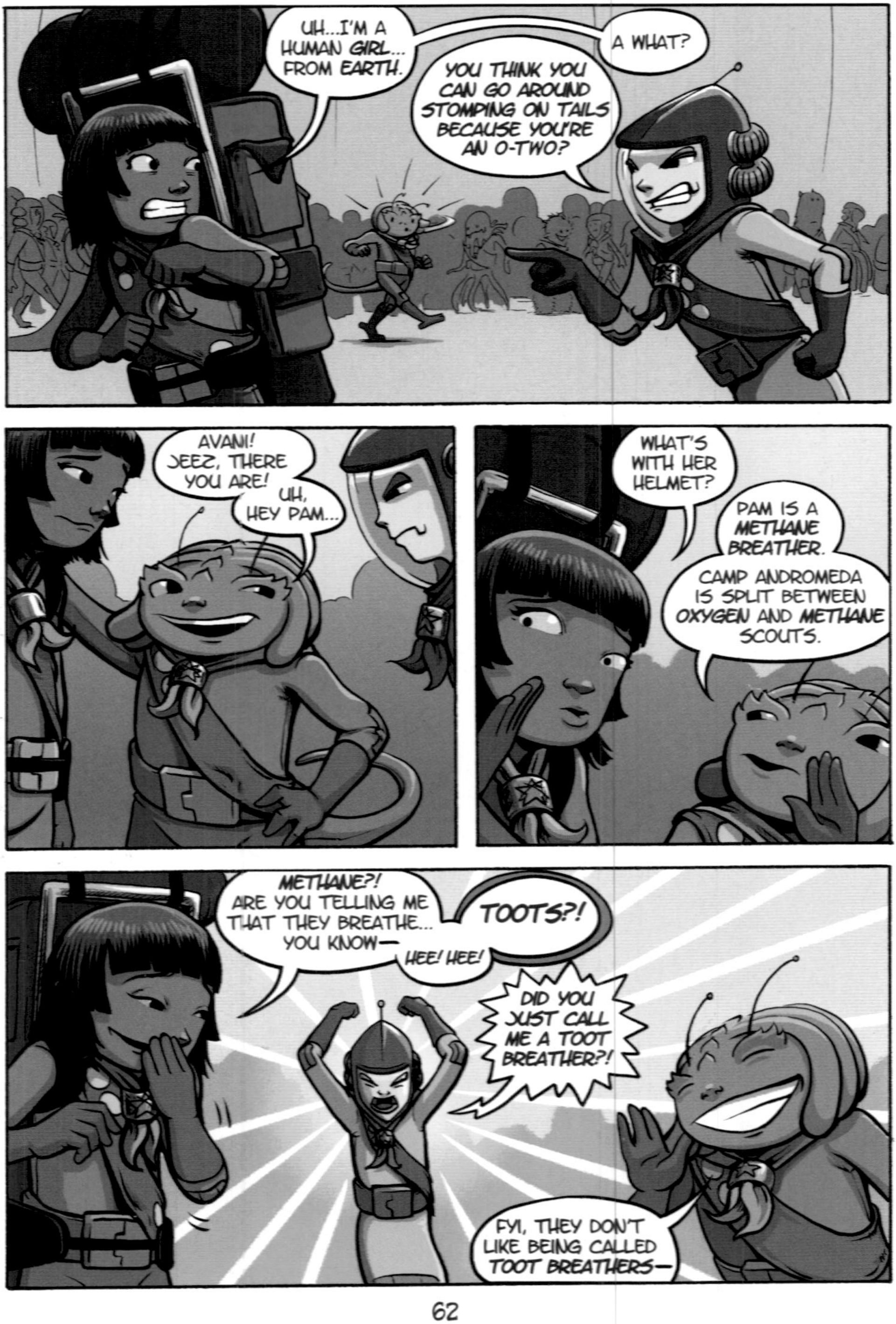
UH...I'M A HUMAN GIRL... FROM EARTH.
A WHAT?
YOU THINK YOU CAN GO AROUND STOMPING ON TAILS BECAUSE YOU'RE AN O-TWO?
AVANI! JEEZ, THERE YOU ARE!
UH, HEY PAM...
WHAT'S WITH HER HELMET?
PAM IS A METHANE BREATHER.
CAMP ANDROMEDA IS SPLIT BETWEEN OXYGEN AND METHANE SCOUTS.
METHANE?! ARE YOU TELLING ME THAT THEY BREATHE... YOU KNOW—
TOOTS?!
HEE! HEE!
DID YOU JUST CALL ME A TOOT BREATHER?!
FYI, THEY DON'T LIKE BEING CALLED TOOT BREATHERS—

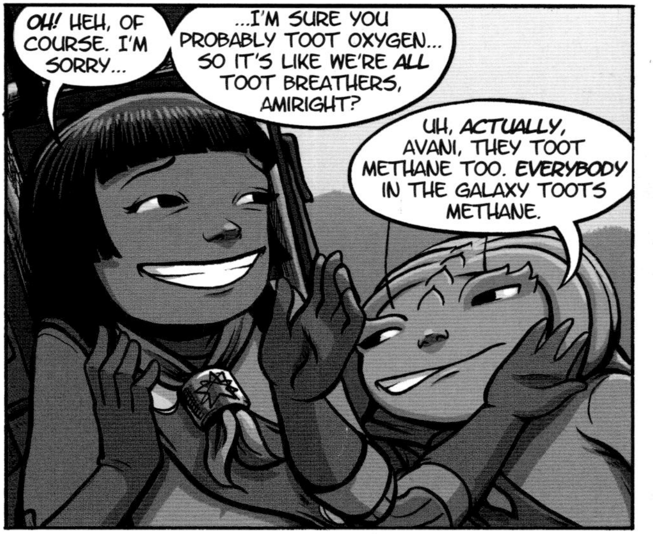
OH! HEH, OF COURSE. I'M SORRY...
...I'M SURE YOU PROBABLY TOOT OXYGEN... SO IT'S LIKE WE'RE ALL TOOT BREATHERS, AMIRIGHT?
UH, ACTUALLY, AVANI, THEY TOOT METHANE TOO. EVERYBODY IN THE GALAXY TOOTS METHANE.

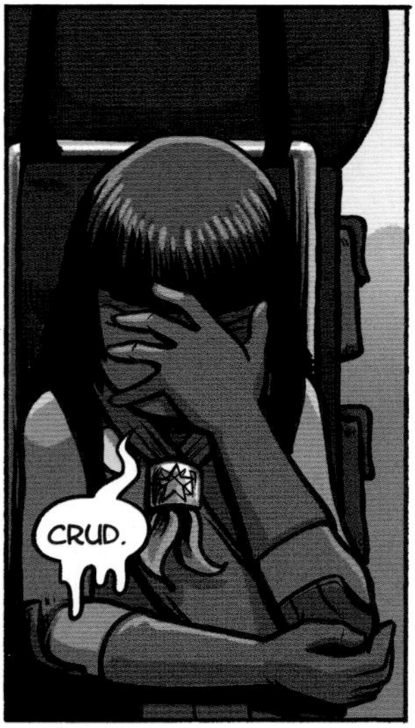
CRUD.

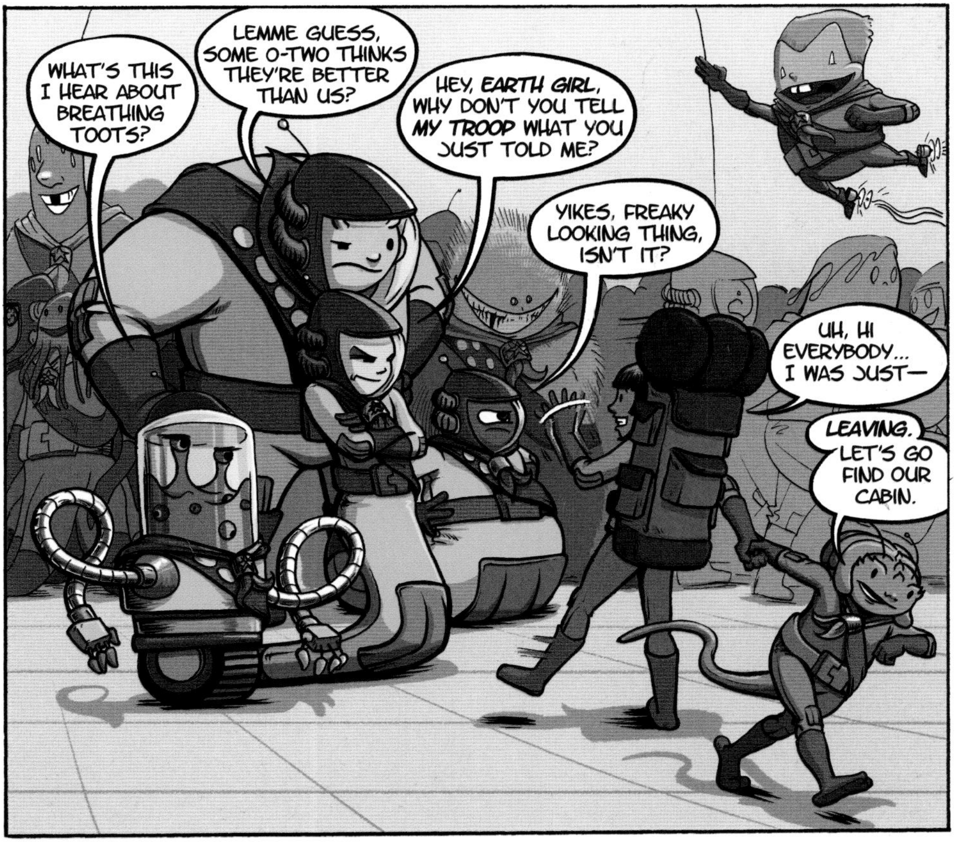
WHAT'S THIS I HEAR ABOUT BREATHING TOOTS?
LEMME GUESS, SOME O-TWO THINKS THEY'RE BETTER THAN US?
HEY, EARTH GIRL, WHY DON'T YOU TELL MY TROOP WHAT YOU JUST TOLD ME?
YIKES, FREAKY LOOKING THING, ISN'T IT?
UH, HI EVERYBODY... I WAS JUST—
LEAVING. LET'S GO FIND OUR CABIN.

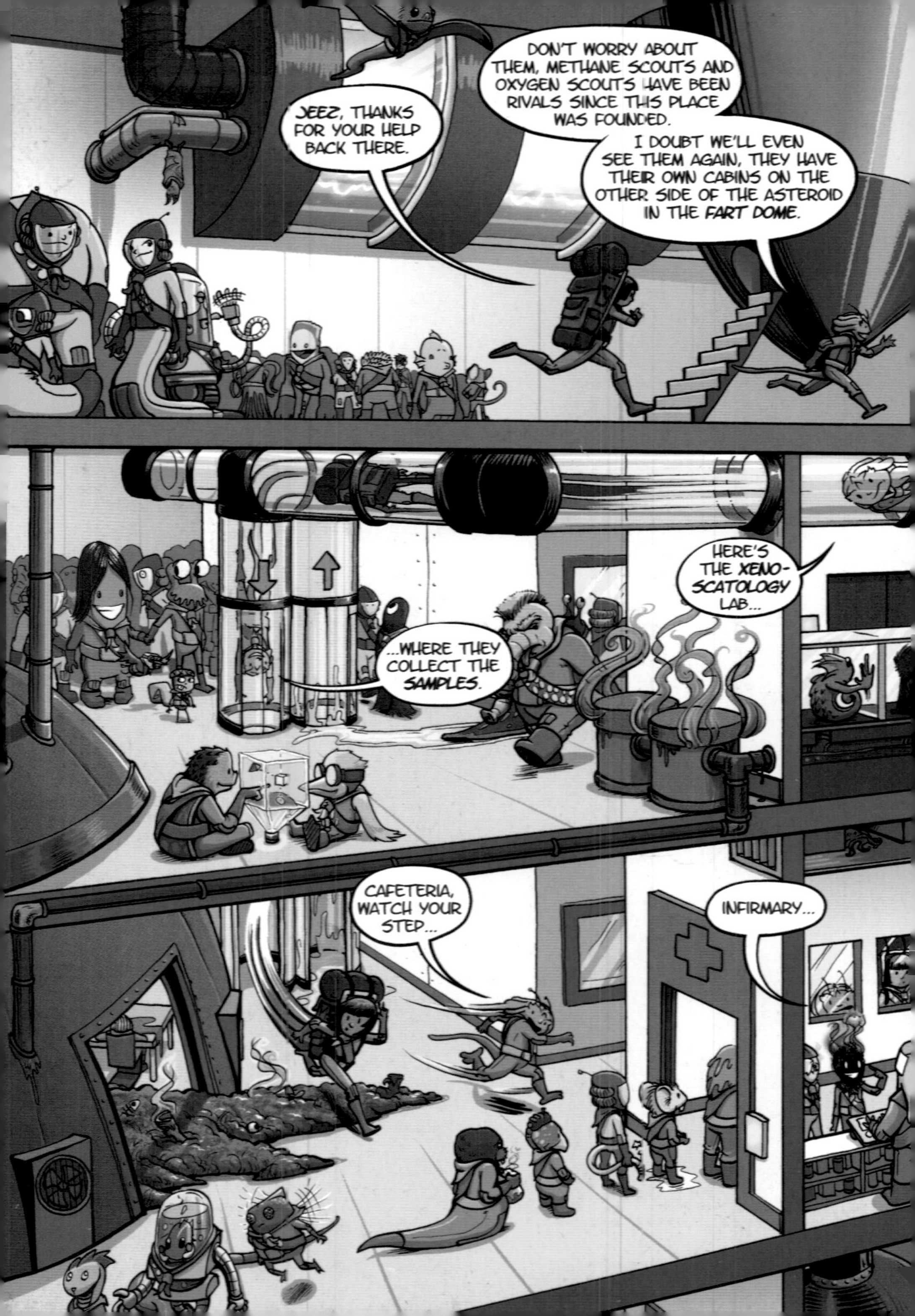

JEEZ, THANKS FOR YOUR HELP BACK THERE.
DON'T WORRY ABOUT THEM, METHANE SCOUTS AND OXYGEN SCOUTS HAVE BEEN RIVALS SINCE THIS PLACE WAS FOUNDED.
I DOUBT WE'LL EVEN SEE THEM AGAIN, THEY HAVE THEIR OWN CABINS ON THE OTHER SIDE OF THE ASTEROID IN THE *FART DOME*.
HERE'S THE **XENO-SCATOLOGY** LAB...
...WHERE THEY COLLECT THE ***SAMPLES***.
CAFETERIA, WATCH YOUR STEP...
INFIRMARY...

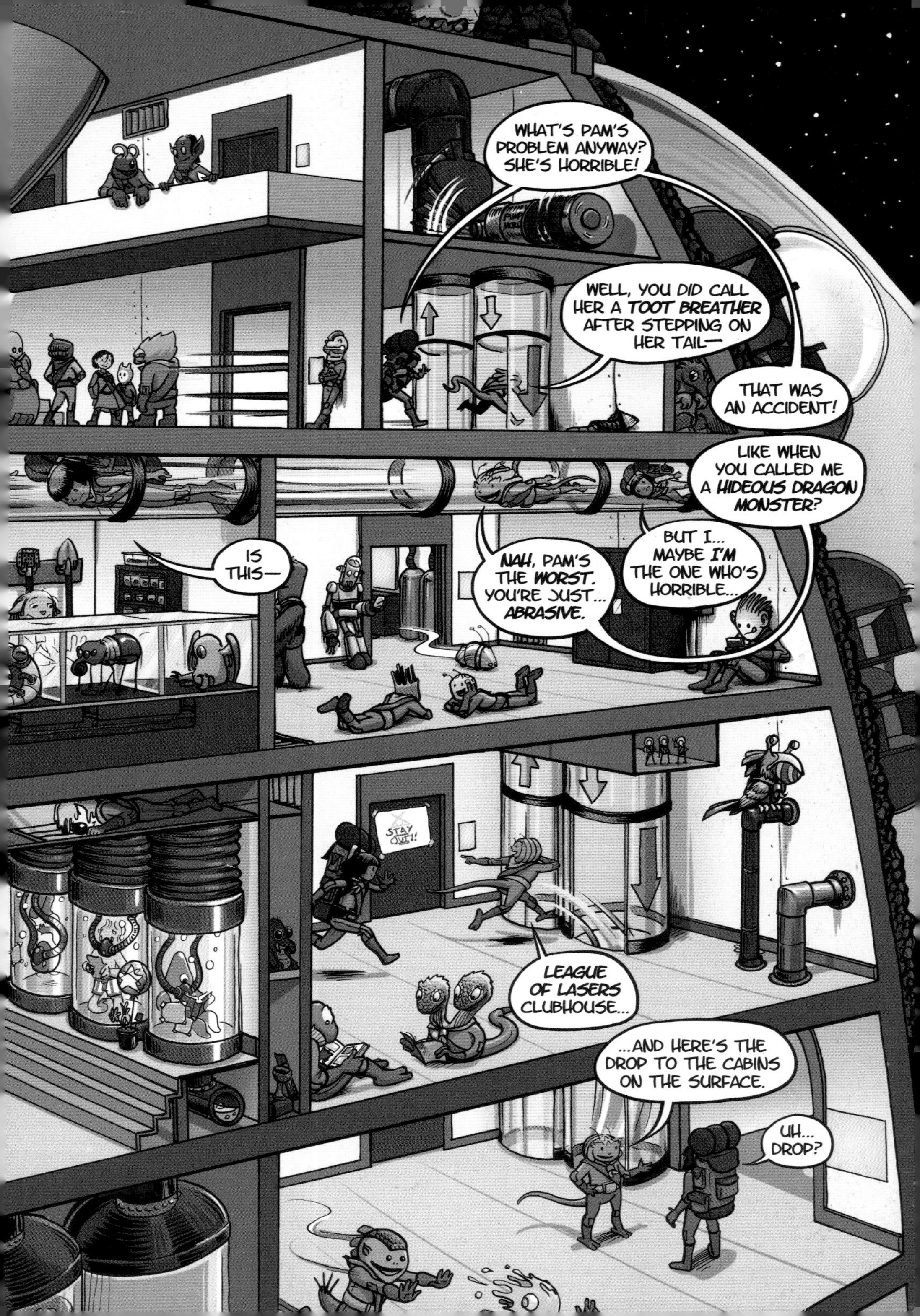
WHAT'S PAM'S PROBLEM ANYWAY? SHE'S HORRIBLE!
WELL, YOU DID CALL HER A TOOT BREATHER AFTER STEPPING ON HER TAIL—
THAT WAS AN ACCIDENT!
LIKE WHEN YOU CALLED ME A HIDEOUS DRAGON MONSTER?
BUT I... MAYBE I'M THE ONE WHO'S HORRIBLE...
NAH, PAM'S THE WORST. YOU'RE JUST... ABRASIVE.
IS THIS—
STAY OUT!!
LEAGUE OF LASERS CLUBHOUSE...
...AND HERE'S THE DROP TO THE CABINS ON THE SURFACE.
UH... DROP?

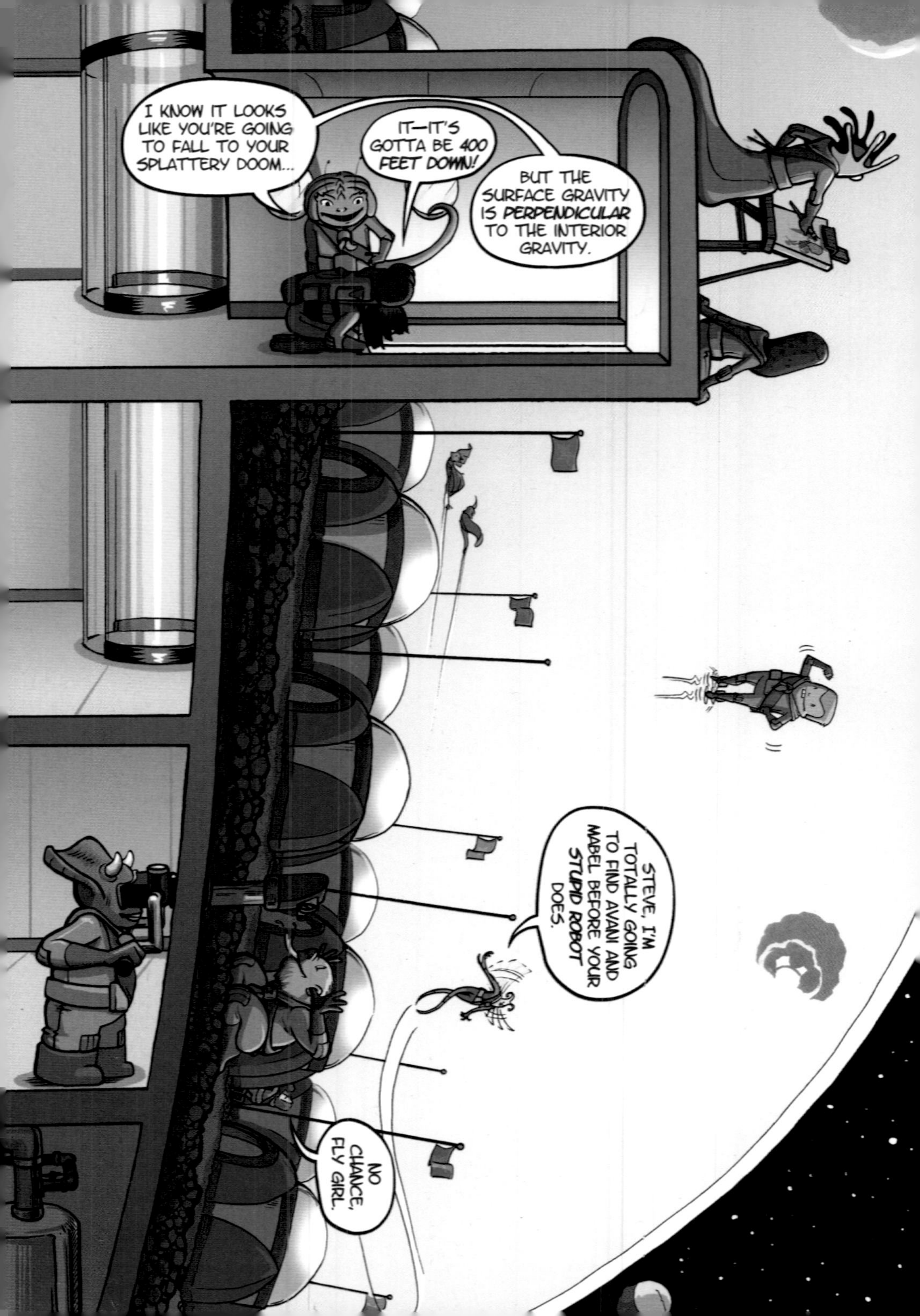
I KNOW IT LOOKS LIKE YOU'RE GOING TO FALL TO YOUR SPLATTERY DOOM...
IT—IT'S GOTTA BE 400 *FEET DOWN!*
BUT THE SURFACE GRAVITY IS **PERPENDICULAR** TO THE INTERIOR GRAVITY.
STEVE, I'M TOTALLY GOING TO FIND AVANI AND MABEL BEFORE YOUR *STUPID ROBOT* DOES.
NO CHANCE, FLY GIRL.

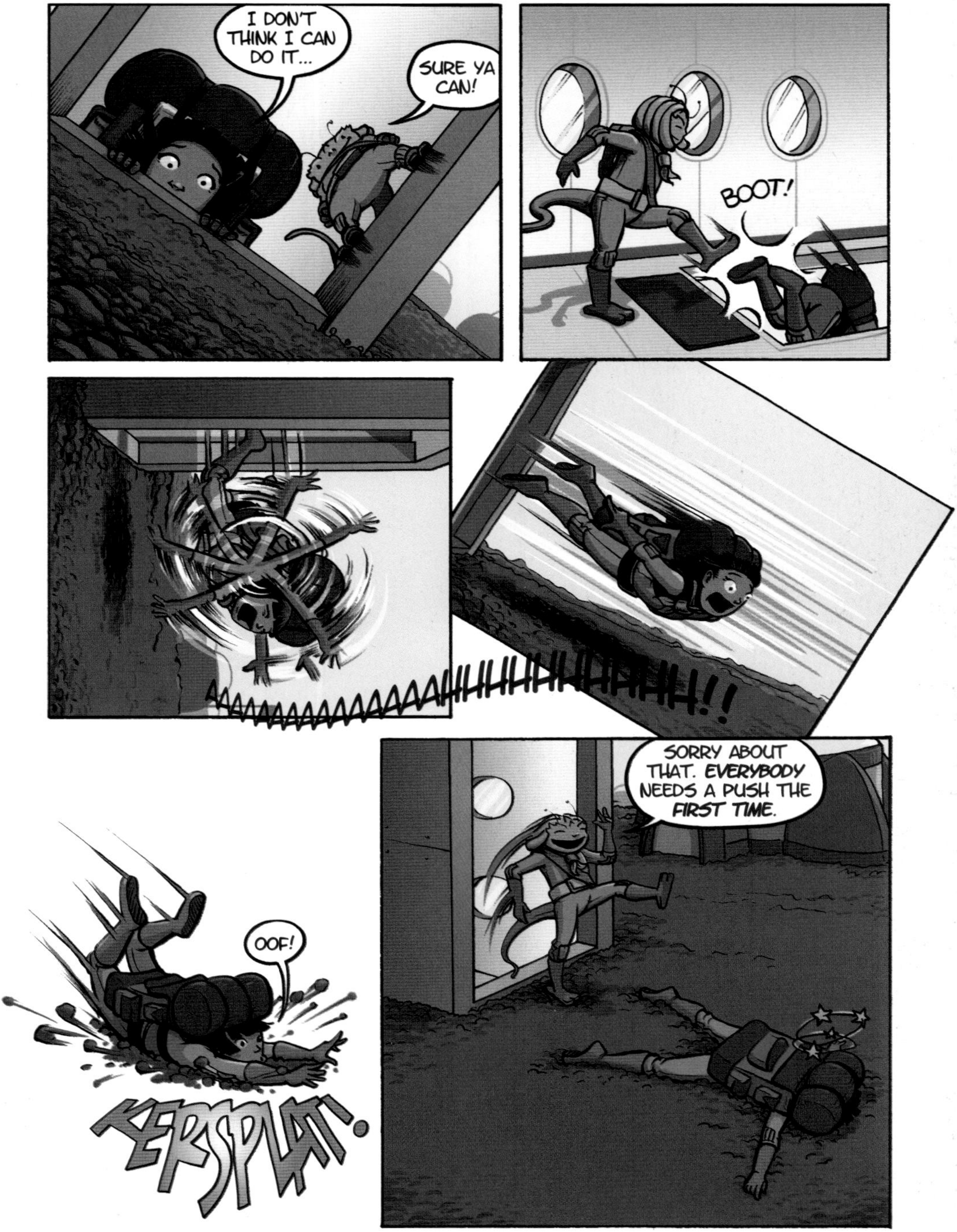

I DON'T THINK I CAN DO IT...
SURE YA CAN!
BOOT!
AAAAAAAAAAAAAAAAAHHHHHHHHHHHH!!
OOF!
KERSPLAT!
SORRY ABOUT THAT. EVERYBODY NEEDS A PUSH THE FIRST TIME.

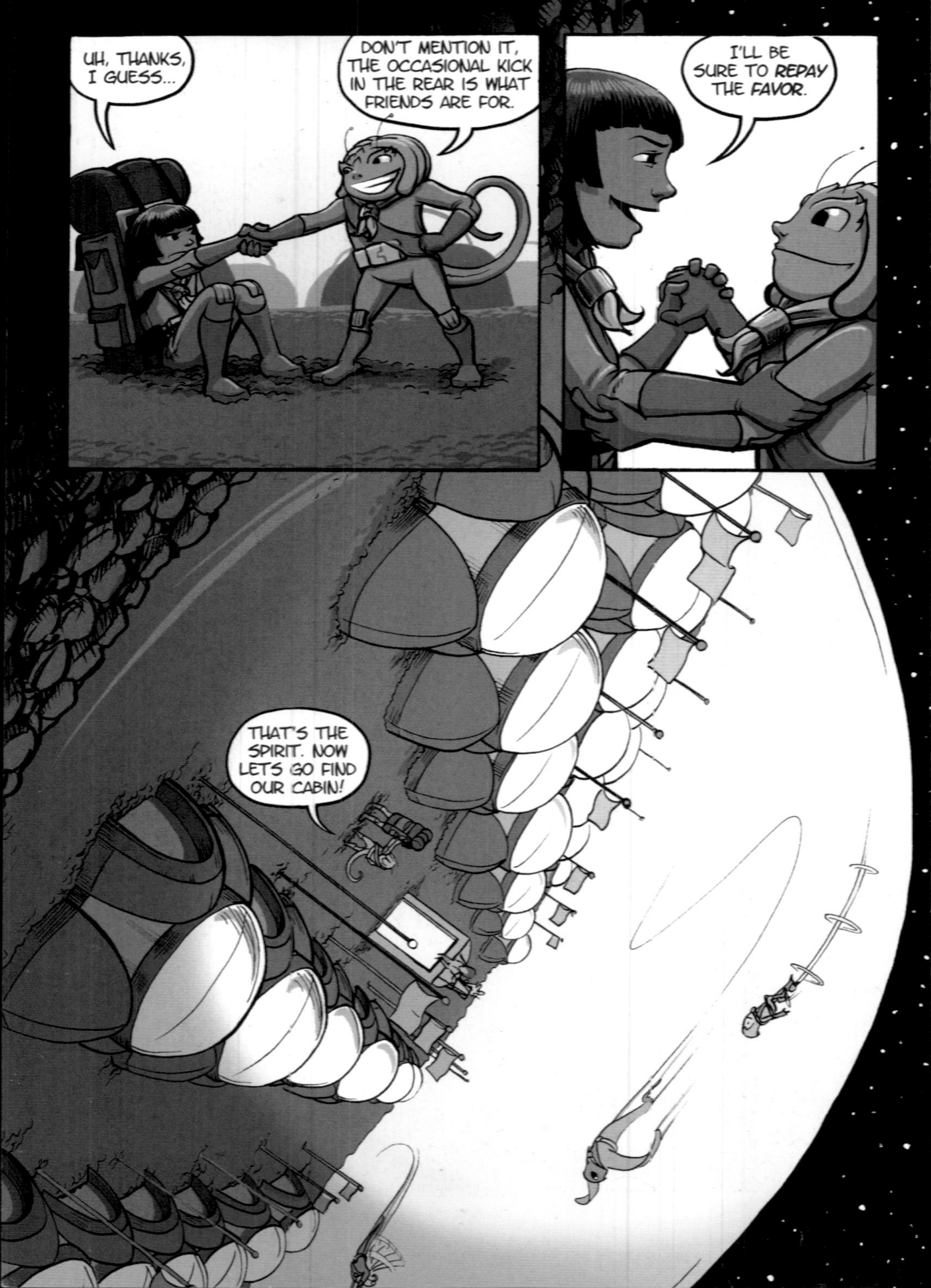
UH, THANKS, I GUESS...
DON'T MENTION IT, THE OCCASIONAL KICK IN THE REAR IS WHAT FRIENDS ARE FOR.
I'LL BE SURE TO REPAY THE FAVOR.
THAT'S THE SPIRIT. NOW LET'S GO FIND OUR CABIN!

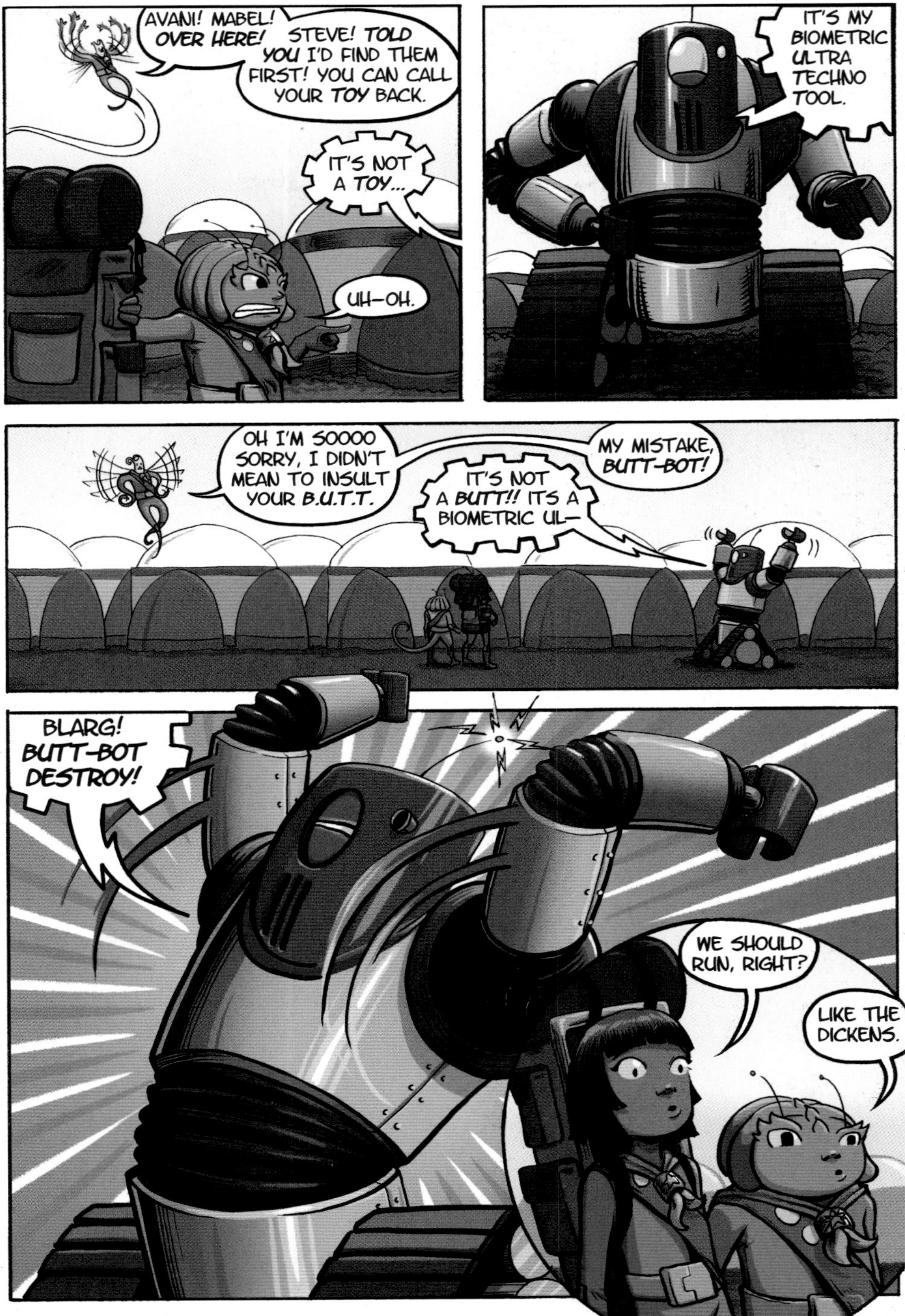
AVANI! MABEL! OVER HERE!
STEVE! TOLD YOU I'D FIND THEM FIRST! YOU CAN CALL YOUR TOY BACK.
IT'S NOT A TOY...
UH-OH.
IT'S MY BIOMETRIC ULTRA TECHNO TOOL.
OH I'M SOOOO SORRY, I DIDN'T MEAN TO INSULT YOUR B.U.T.T.
MY MISTAKE, BUTT-BOT!
IT'S NOT A BUTT!! ITS A BIOMETRIC UL-
BLARG! BUTT-BOT DESTROY!
WE SHOULD RUN, RIGHT?
LIKE THE DICKENS.

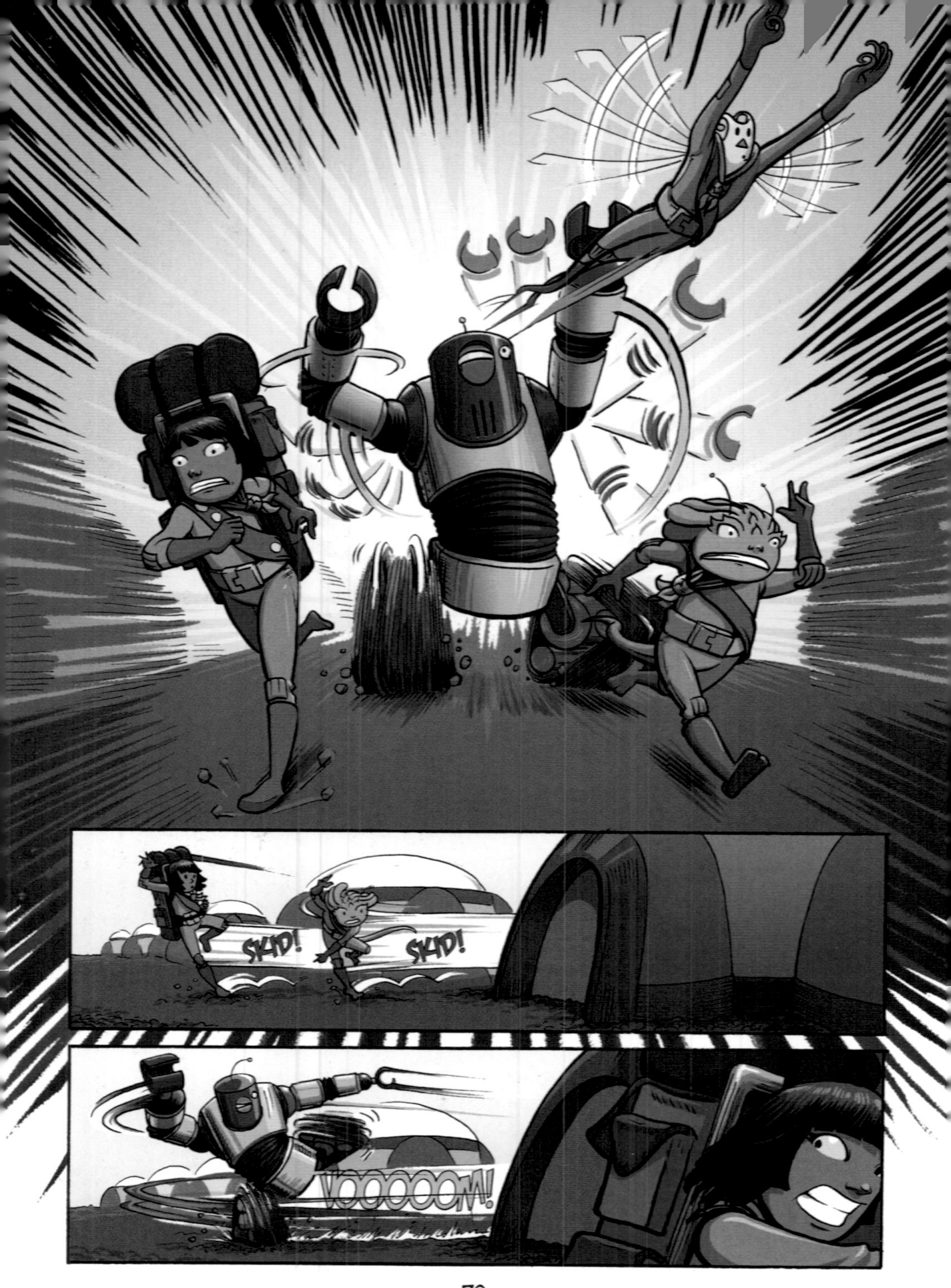
SKID!
SKID!
VOOOOOOM!

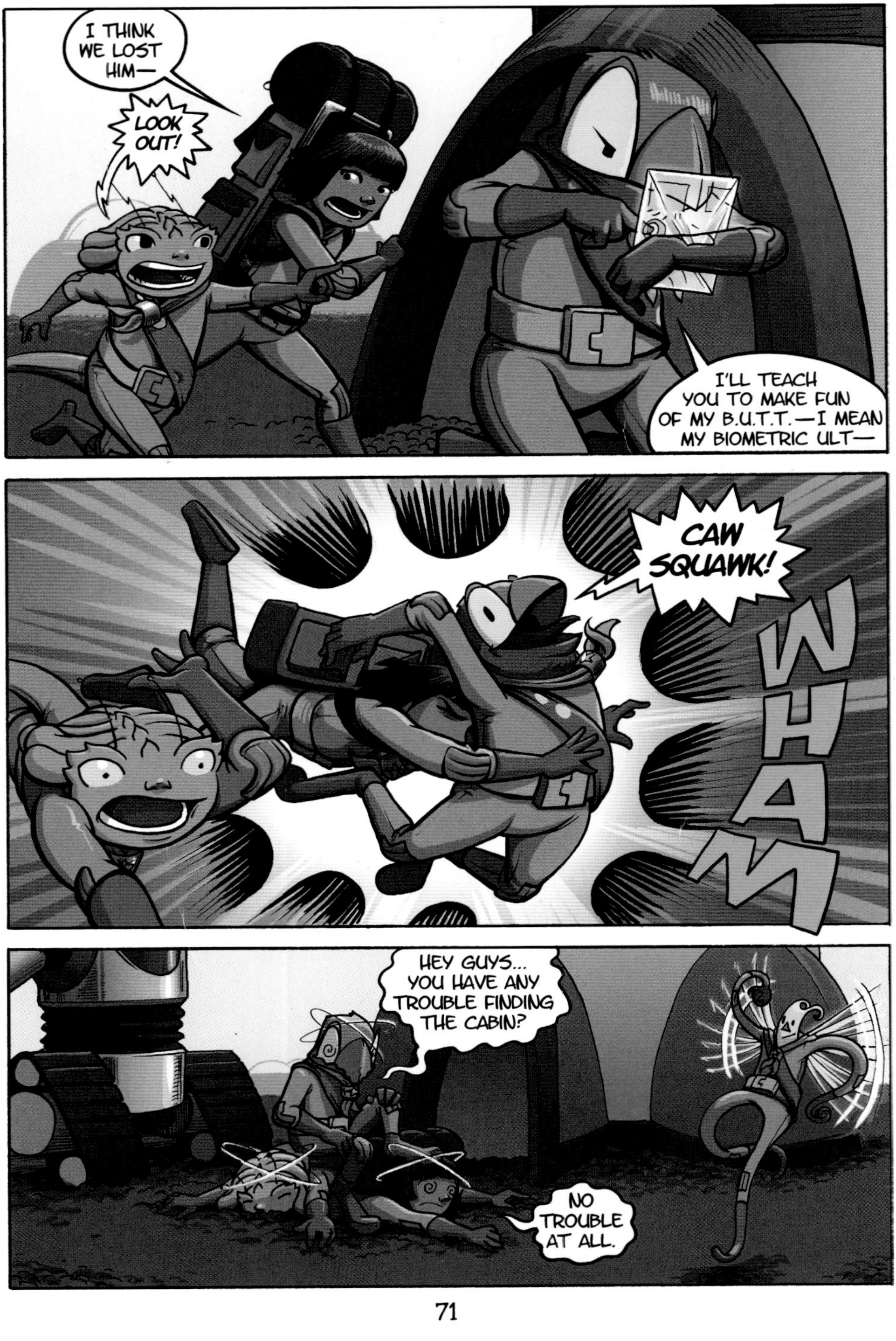

I THINK WE LOST HIM—
LOOK OUT!
I'LL TEACH YOU TO MAKE FUN OF MY B.U.T.T.—I MEAN MY BIOMETRIC ULT—
CAW SQUAWK!
WHAM
HEY GUYS... YOU HAVE ANY TROUBLE FINDING THE CABIN?
NO TROUBLE AT ALL.

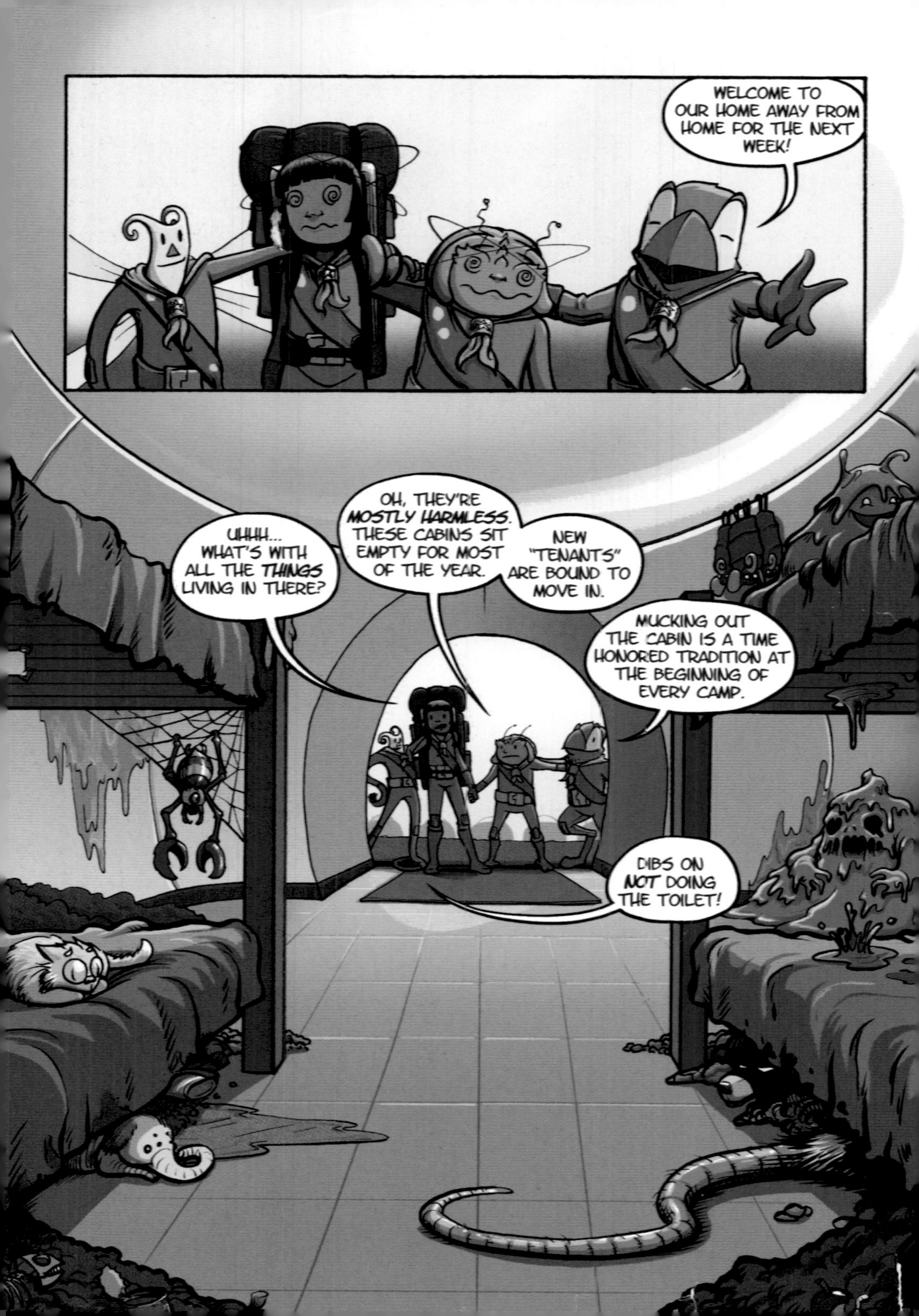
WELCOME TO OUR HOME AWAY FROM HOME FOR THE NEXT WEEK!
UHHH... WHAT'S WITH ALL THE *THINGS* LIVING IN THERE?
OH, THEY'RE ***MOSTLY HARMLESS***. THESE CABINS SIT EMPTY FOR MOST OF THE YEAR.
NEW "TENANTS" ARE BOUND TO MOVE IN.
MUCKING OUT THE CABIN IS A TIME HONORED TRADITION AT THE BEGINNING OF EVERY CAMP.
DIBS ON ***NOT*** DOING THE TOILET!

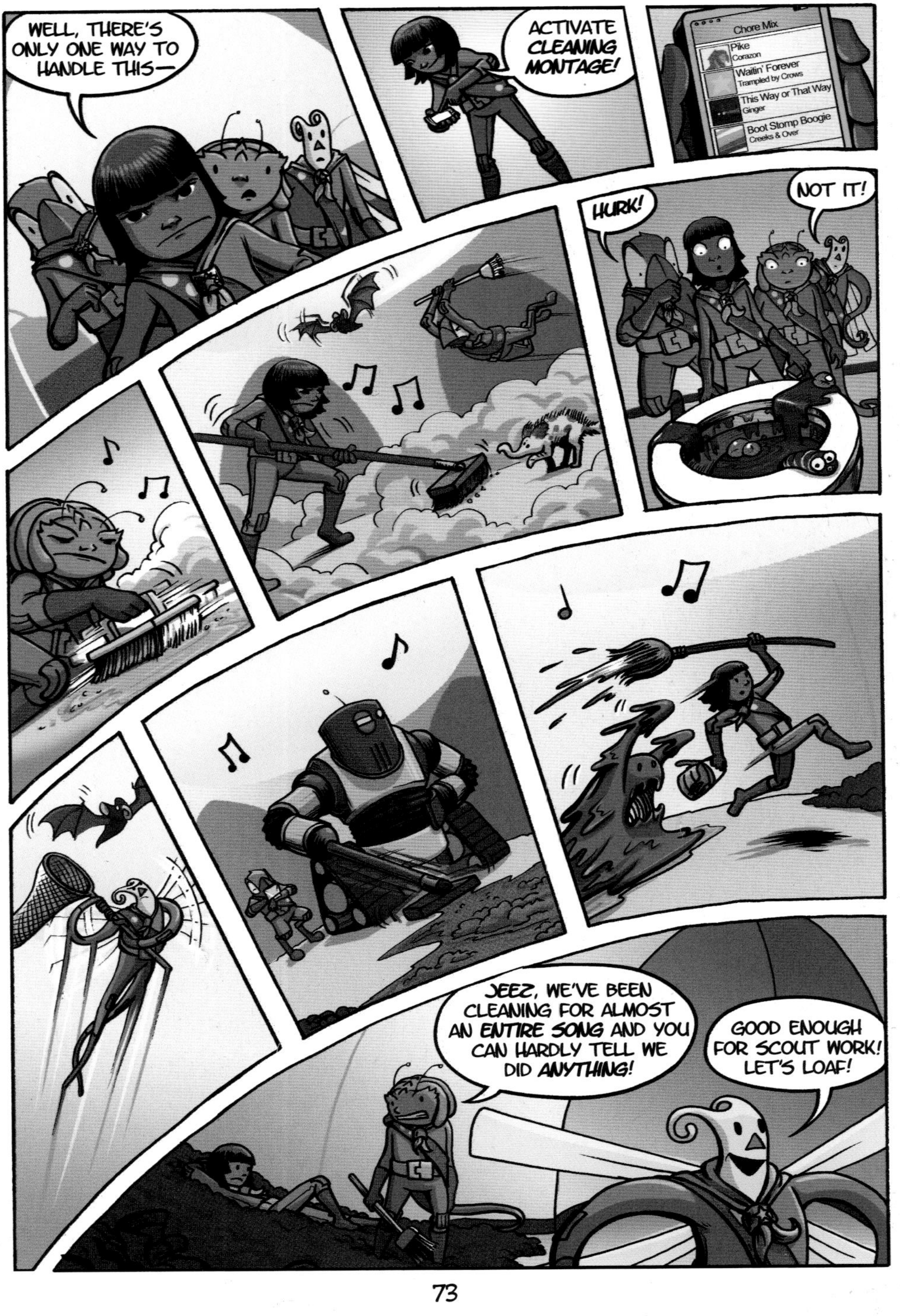

WELL, THERE'S ONLY ONE WAY TO HANDLE THIS—
ACTIVATE CLEANING MONTAGE!
Chore Mix
Pike
Corazon
Waitin' Forever
Trampled by Crows
This Way or That Way
Ginger
Boot Stomp Boogie
Creeks & Over
HURK!
NOT IT!
JEEZ, WE'VE BEEN CLEANING FOR ALMOST AN ENTIRE SONG AND YOU CAN HARDLY TELL WE DID ANYTHING!
GOOD ENOUGH FOR SCOUT WORK! LET'S LOAF!

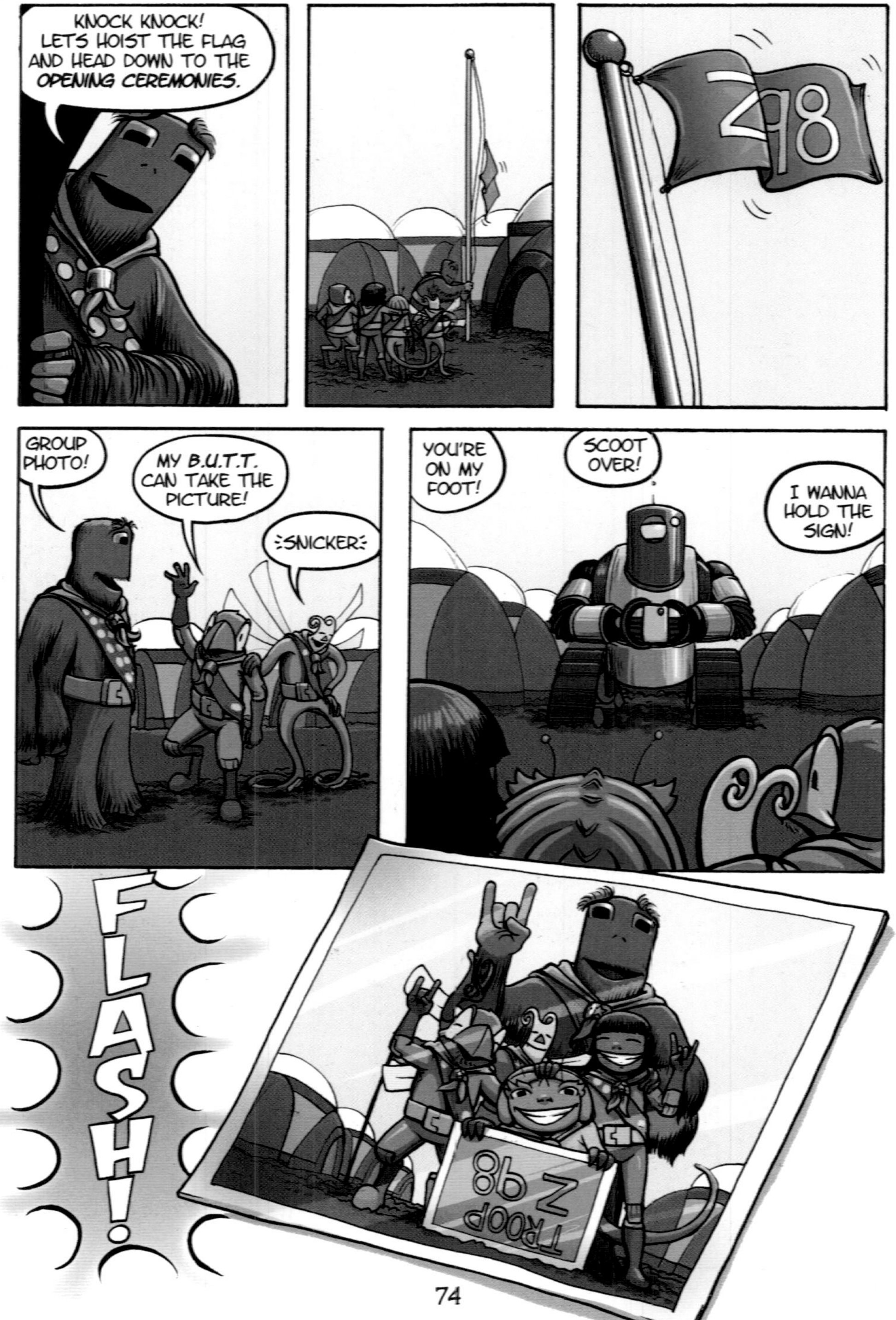
KNOCK KNOCK! LET'S HOIST THE FLAG AND HEAD DOWN TO THE OPENING CEREMONIES.
Z98
GROUP PHOTO!
MY B.U.T.T. CAN TAKE THE PICTURE!
SNICKER
YOU'RE ON MY FOOT!
SCOOT OVER!
I WANNA HOLD THE SIGN!
FLASH!
TROOP Z 98

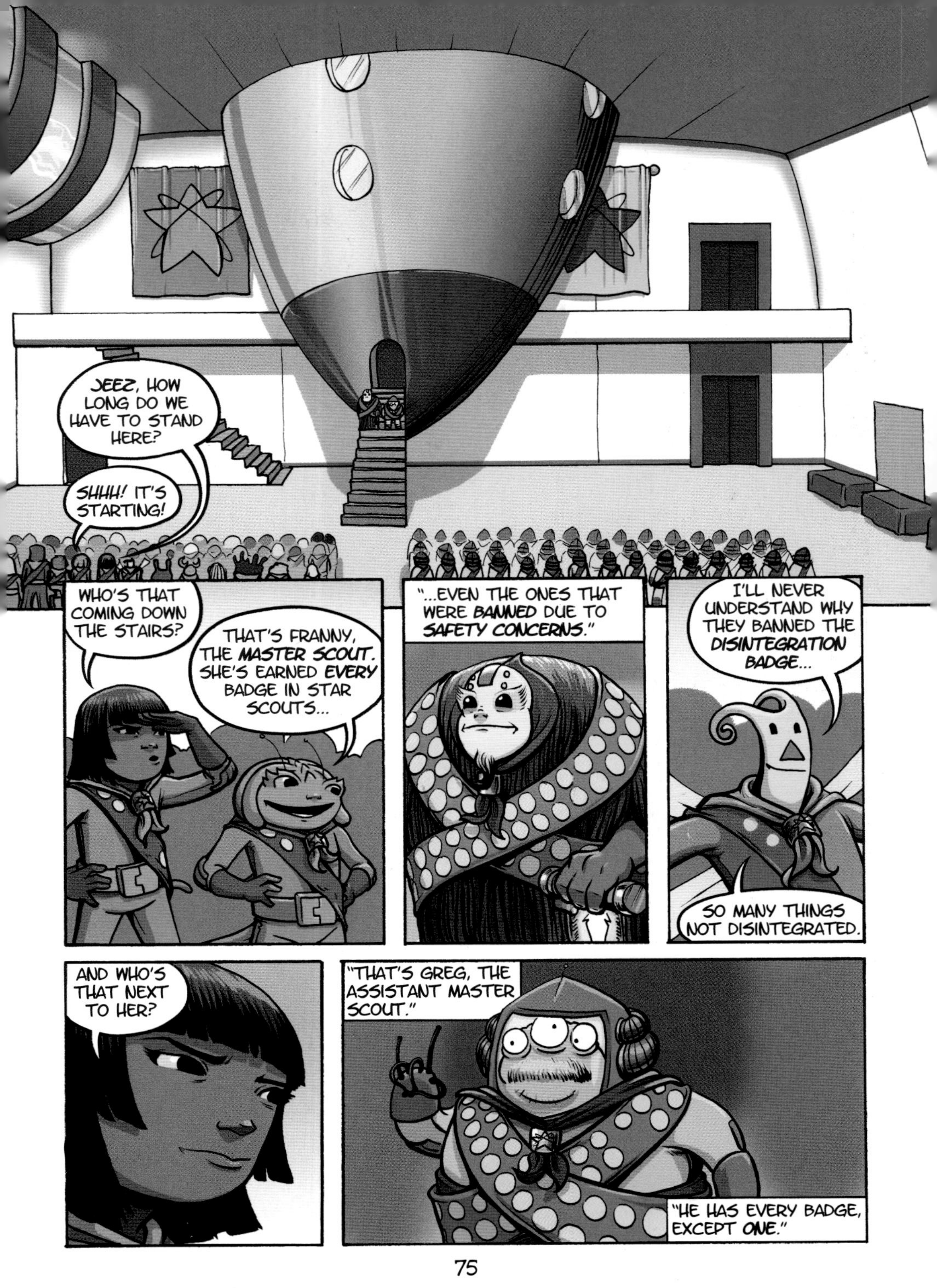
JEEZ, HOW LONG DO WE HAVE TO STAND HERE?
SHHH! IT'S STARTING!
WHO'S THAT COMING DOWN THE STAIRS?
THAT'S FRANNY, THE **MASTER SCOUT**. SHE'S EARNED **EVERY** BADGE IN STAR SCOUTS...
"...EVEN THE ONES THAT WERE **BANNED** DUE TO **SAFETY CONCERNS**."
I'LL NEVER UNDERSTAND WHY THEY BANNED THE **DISINTEGRATION BADGE**...
SO MANY THINGS NOT DISINTEGRATED.
AND WHO'S THAT NEXT TO HER?
"THAT'S GREG, THE ASSISTANT MASTER SCOUT."
"HE HAS EVERY BADGE, EXCEPT **ONE**."

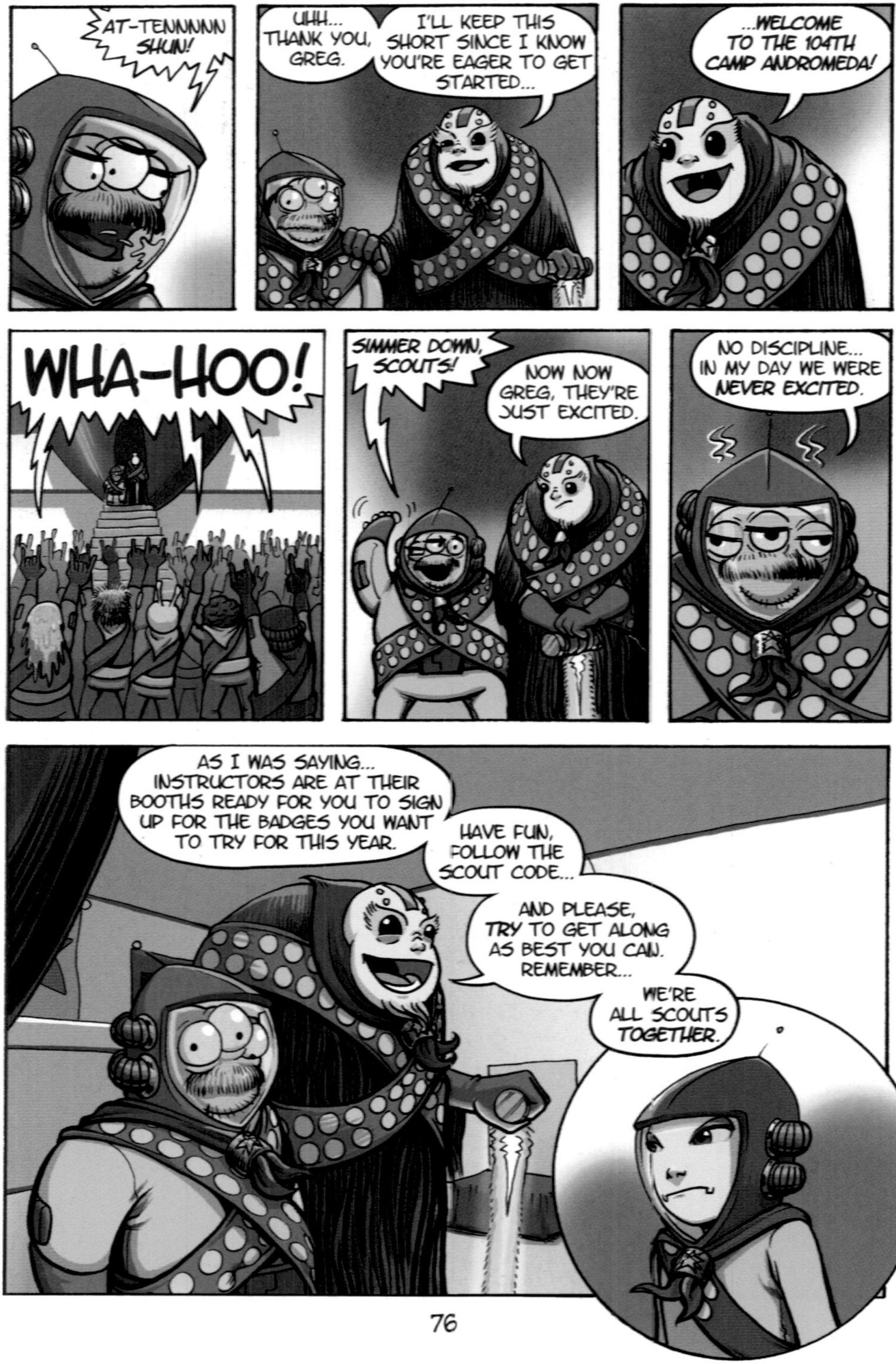
AT-TENNNNN SHUN!
UHH... THANK YOU, GREG.
I'LL KEEP THIS SHORT SINCE I KNOW YOU'RE EAGER TO GET STARTED...
...WELCOME TO THE 104TH CAMP ANDROMEDA!
WHA-HOO!
SIMMER DOWN, SCOUTS!
NOW NOW GREG, THEY'RE JUST EXCITED.
NO DISCIPLINE... IN MY DAY WE WERE NEVER EXCITED.
AS I WAS SAYING... INSTRUCTORS ARE AT THEIR BOOTHS READY FOR YOU TO SIGN UP FOR THE BADGES YOU WANT TO TRY FOR THIS YEAR.
HAVE FUN, FOLLOW THE SCOUT CODE...
AND PLEASE, TRY TO GET ALONG AS BEST YOU CAN. REMEMBER...
WE'RE ALL SCOUTS TOGETHER.

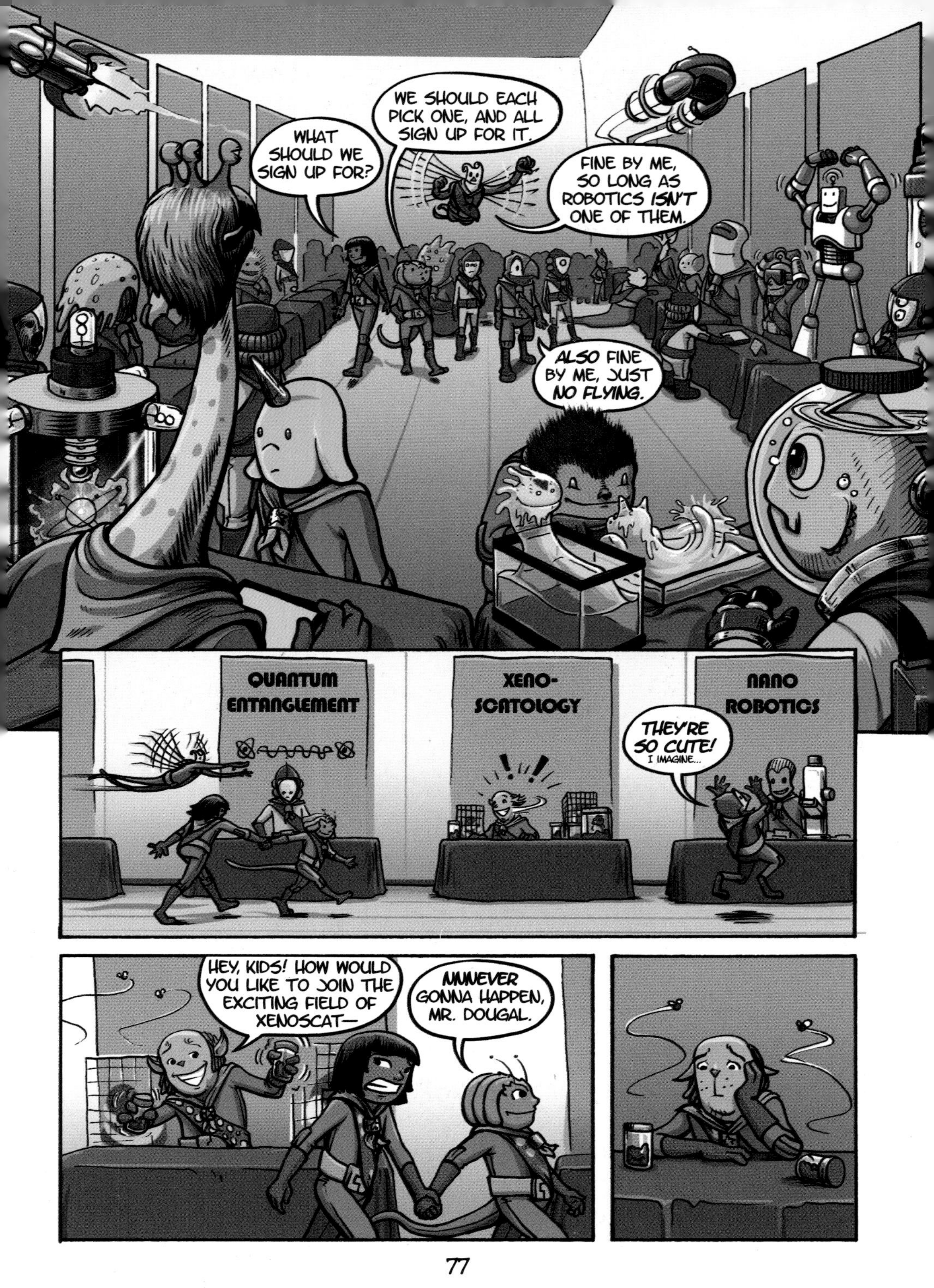
WHAT SHOULD WE SIGN UP FOR?
WE SHOULD EACH PICK ONE, AND ALL SIGN UP FOR IT.
FINE BY ME, SO LONG AS ROBOTICS ISN'T ONE OF THEM.
ALSO FINE BY ME, JUST NO FLYING.
QUANTUM ENTANGLEMENT
XENO-SCATOLOGY
NANO ROBOTICS
THEY'RE SO CUTE! I IMAGINE...
HEY, KIDS! HOW WOULD YOU LIKE TO JOIN THE EXCITING FIELD OF XENOSCAT—
NNNEVER GONNA HAPPEN, MR. DOUGAL.

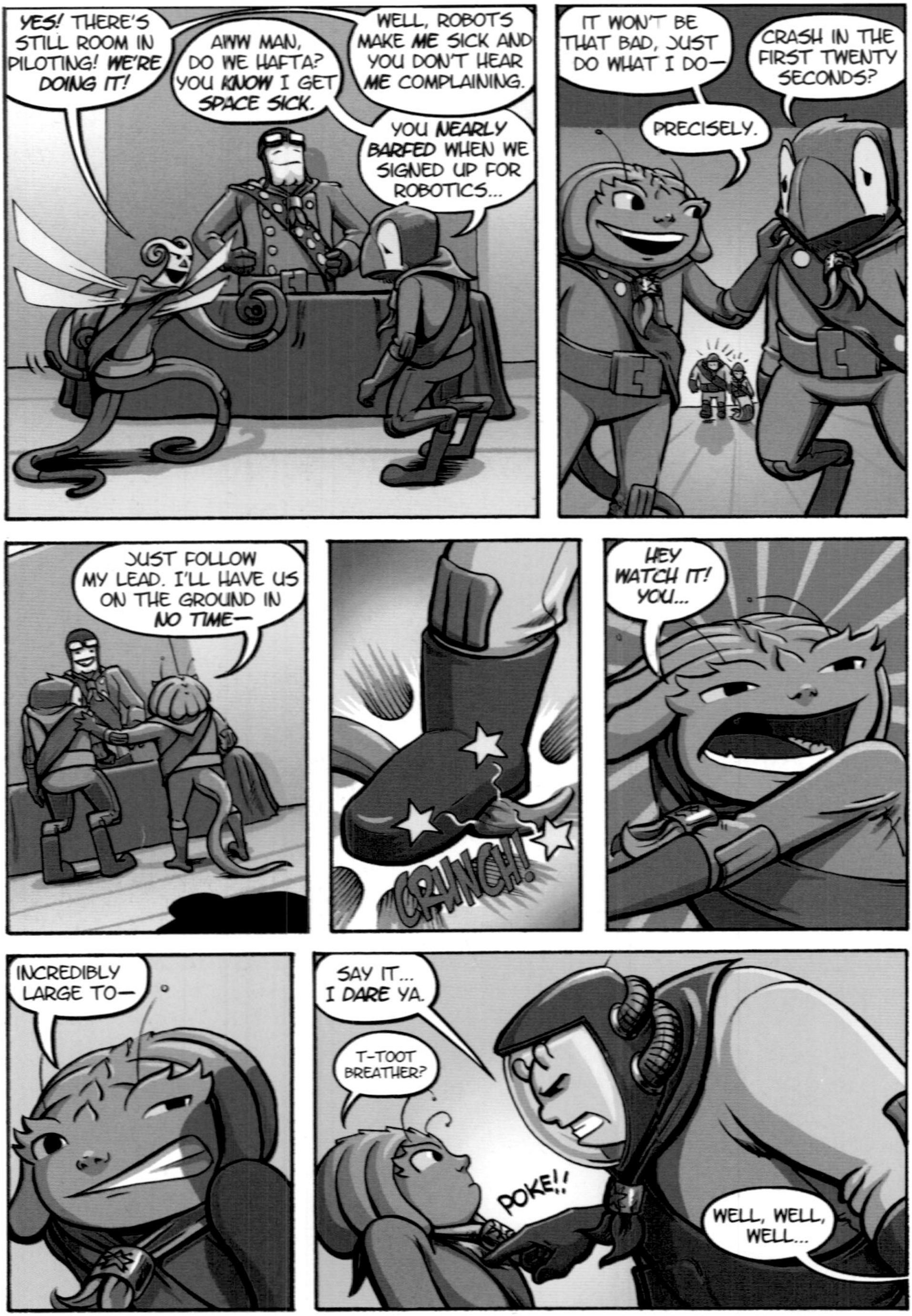
YES! THERE'S STILL ROOM IN PILOTING! WE'RE DOING IT!
AWW MAN, DO WE HAFTA? YOU KNOW I GET SPACE SICK.
WELL, ROBOTS MAKE ME SICK AND YOU DON'T HEAR ME COMPLAINING.
YOU NEARLY BARFED WHEN WE SIGNED UP FOR ROBOTICS...
IT WON'T BE THAT BAD, JUST DO WHAT I DO—
CRASH IN THE FIRST TWENTY SECONDS?
PRECISELY.
JUST FOLLOW MY LEAD. I'LL HAVE US ON THE GROUND IN NO TIME—
CRUNCH!
HEY WATCH IT! YOU...
INCREDIBLY LARGE TO—
SAY IT... I DARE YA.
T-TOOT BREATHER?
POKE!!
WELL, WELL, WELL...

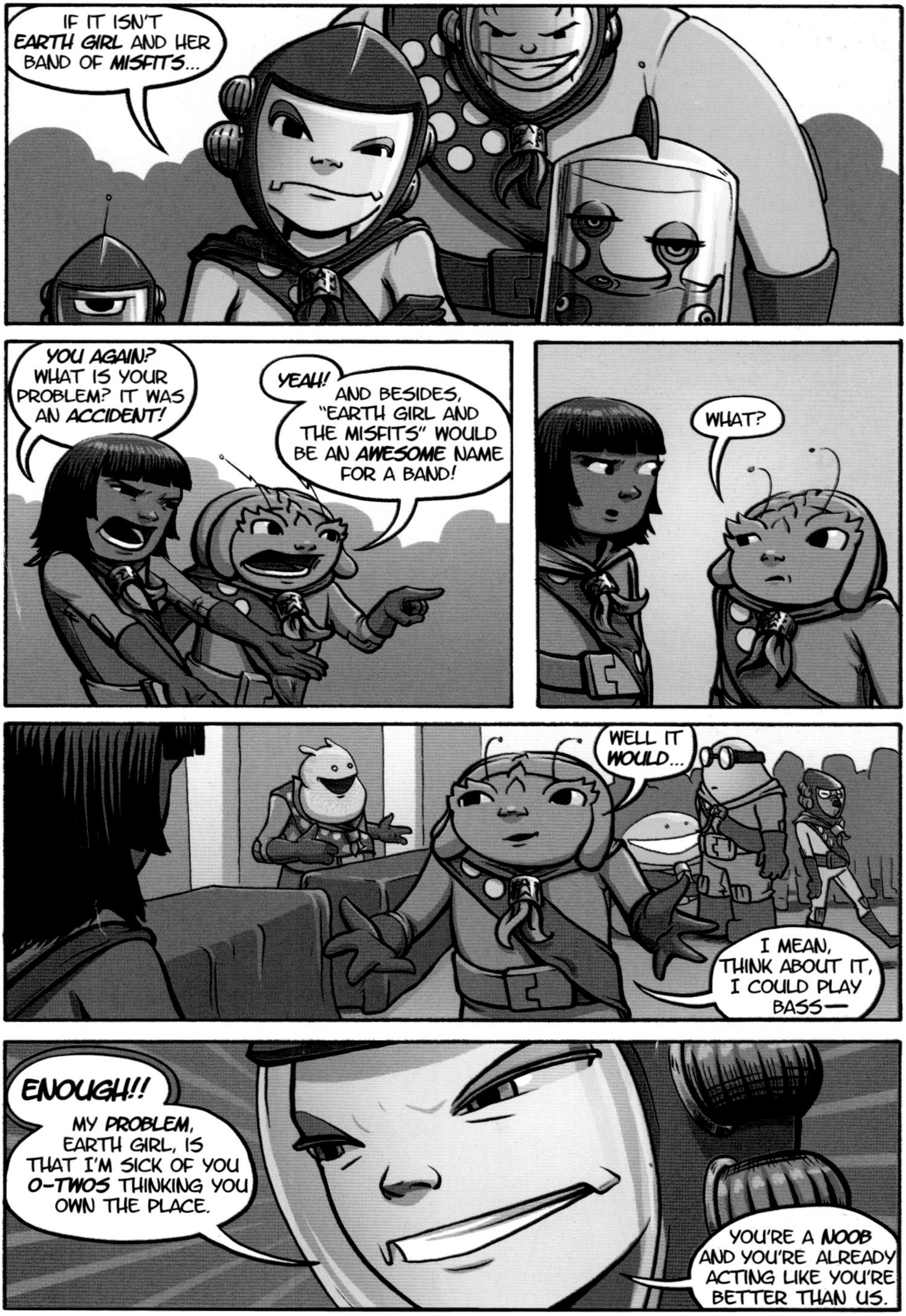
IF IT ISN'T EARTH GIRL AND HER BAND OF MISFITS...
YOU AGAIN? WHAT IS YOUR PROBLEM? IT WAS AN ACCIDENT!
YEAH!
AND BESIDES, "EARTH GIRL AND THE MISFITS" WOULD BE AN AWESOME NAME FOR A BAND!
WHAT?
WELL IT WOULD...
I MEAN, THINK ABOUT IT, I COULD PLAY BASS—
ENOUGH!!
MY PROBLEM, EARTH GIRL, IS THAT I'M SICK OF YOU O-TWOS THINKING YOU OWN THE PLACE.
YOU'RE A NOOB AND YOU'RE ALREADY ACTING LIKE YOU'RE BETTER THAN US.

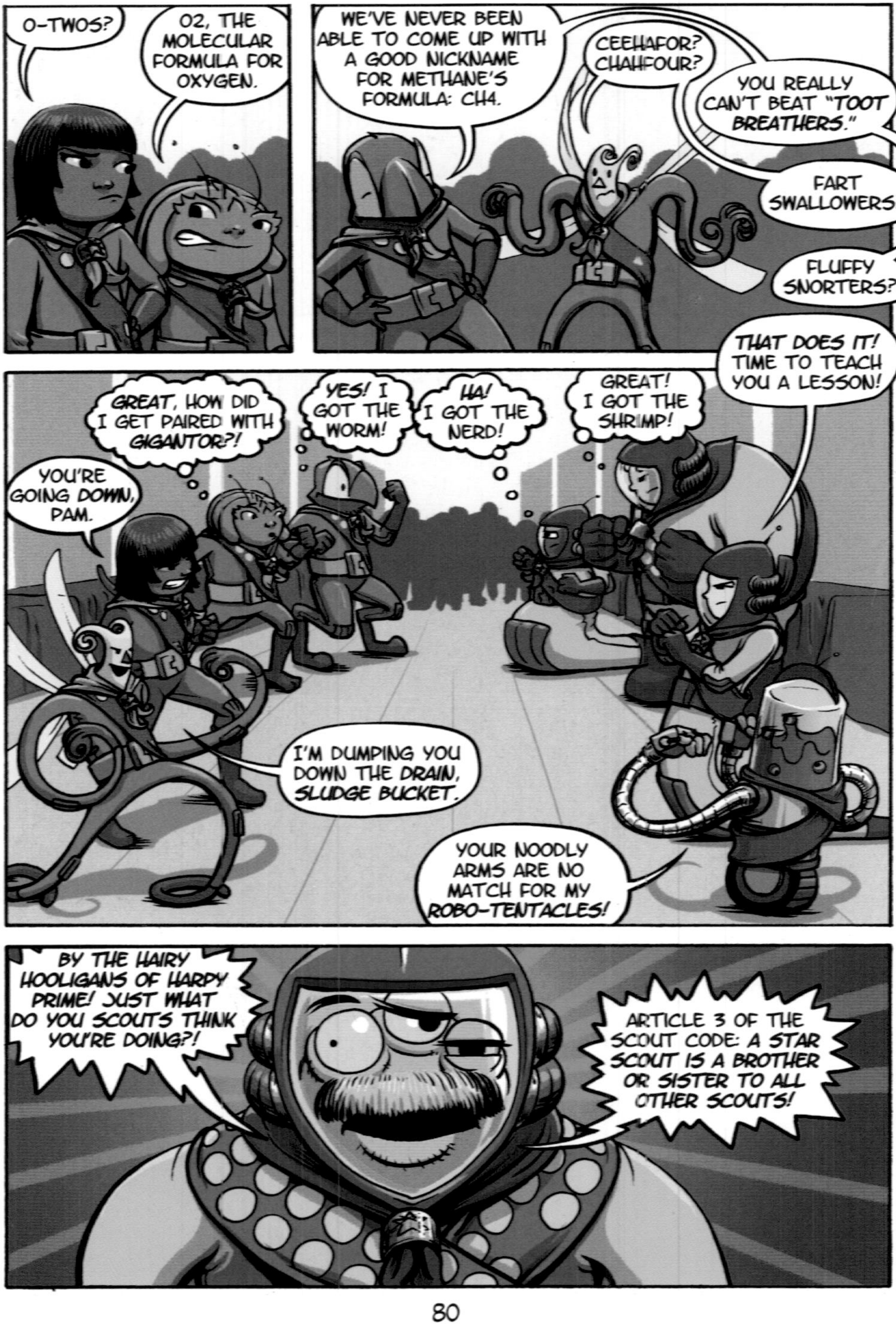
O-TWOS?
O2, THE MOLECULAR FORMULA FOR OXYGEN.
WE'VE NEVER BEEN ABLE TO COME UP WITH A GOOD NICKNAME FOR METHANE'S FORMULA: CH4.
CEEHAFOR? CHAHFOUR?
YOU REALLY CAN'T BEAT "TOOT BREATHERS."
FART SWALLOWERS?
FLUFFY SNORTERS?
THAT DOES IT! TIME TO TEACH YOU A LESSON!
GREAT, HOW DID I GET PAIRED WITH GIGANTOR?!
YES! I GOT THE WORM!
HA! I GOT THE NERD!
GREAT! I GOT THE SHRIMP!
YOU'RE GOING DOWN, PAM.
I'M DUMPING YOU DOWN THE DRAIN, SLUDGE BUCKET.
YOUR NOODLY ARMS ARE NO MATCH FOR MY ROBO-TENTACLES!
BY THE HAIRY HOOLIGANS OF HARPY PRIME! JUST WHAT DO YOU SCOUTS THINK YOU'RE DOING?!
ARTICLE 3 OF THE SCOUT CODE: A STAR SCOUT IS A BROTHER OR SISTER TO ALL OTHER SCOUTS!

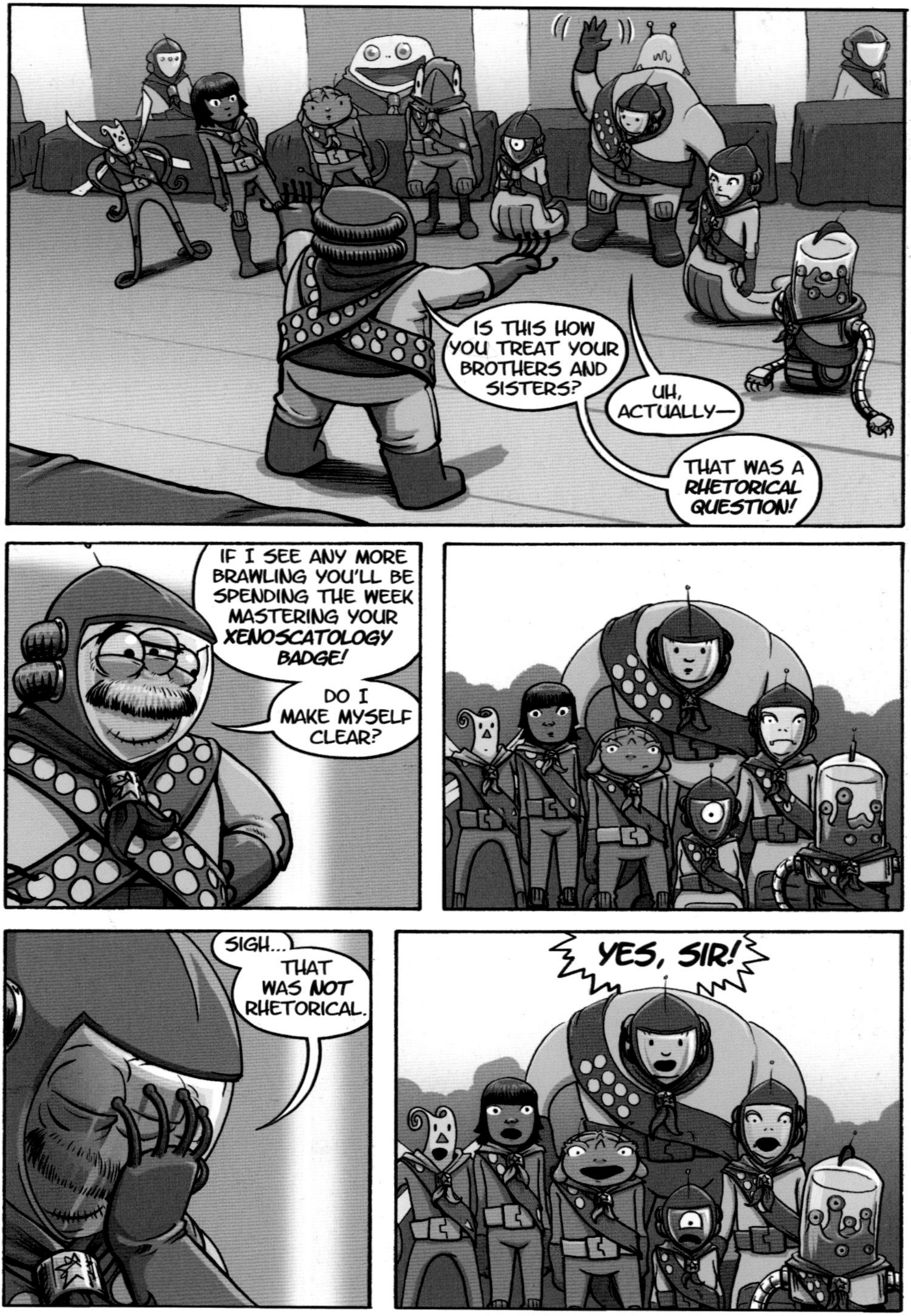
IS THIS HOW YOU TREAT YOUR BROTHERS AND SISTERS?
UH, ACTUALLY—
THAT WAS A RHETORICAL QUESTION!
IF I SEE ANY MORE BRAWLING YOU'LL BE SPENDING THE WEEK MASTERING YOUR XENOSCATOLOGY BADGE!
DO I MAKE MYSELF CLEAR?
SIGH...
THAT WAS NOT RHETORICAL.
YES, SIR!

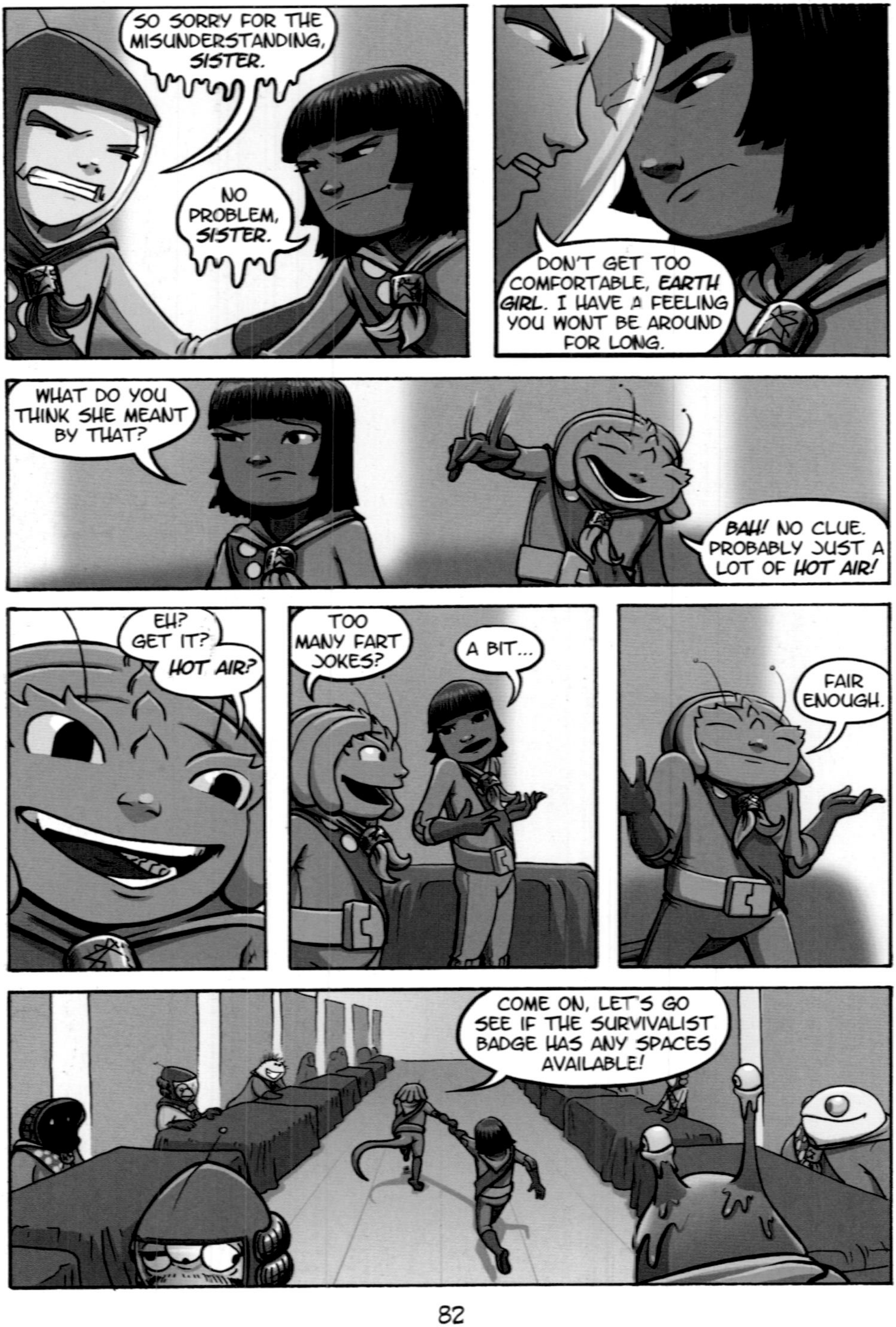
SO SORRY FOR THE MISUNDERSTANDING, SISTER.
NO PROBLEM, SISTER.
DON'T GET TOO COMFORTABLE, EARTH GIRL. I HAVE A FEELING YOU WONT BE AROUND FOR LONG.
WHAT DO YOU THINK SHE MEANT BY THAT?
BAH! NO CLUE. PROBABLY JUST A LOT OF HOT AIR!
EH? GET IT?
HOT AIR?
TOO MANY FART JOKES?
A BIT...
FAIR ENOUGH.
COME ON, LET'S GO SEE IF THE SURVIVALIST BADGE HAS ANY SPACES AVAILABLE!

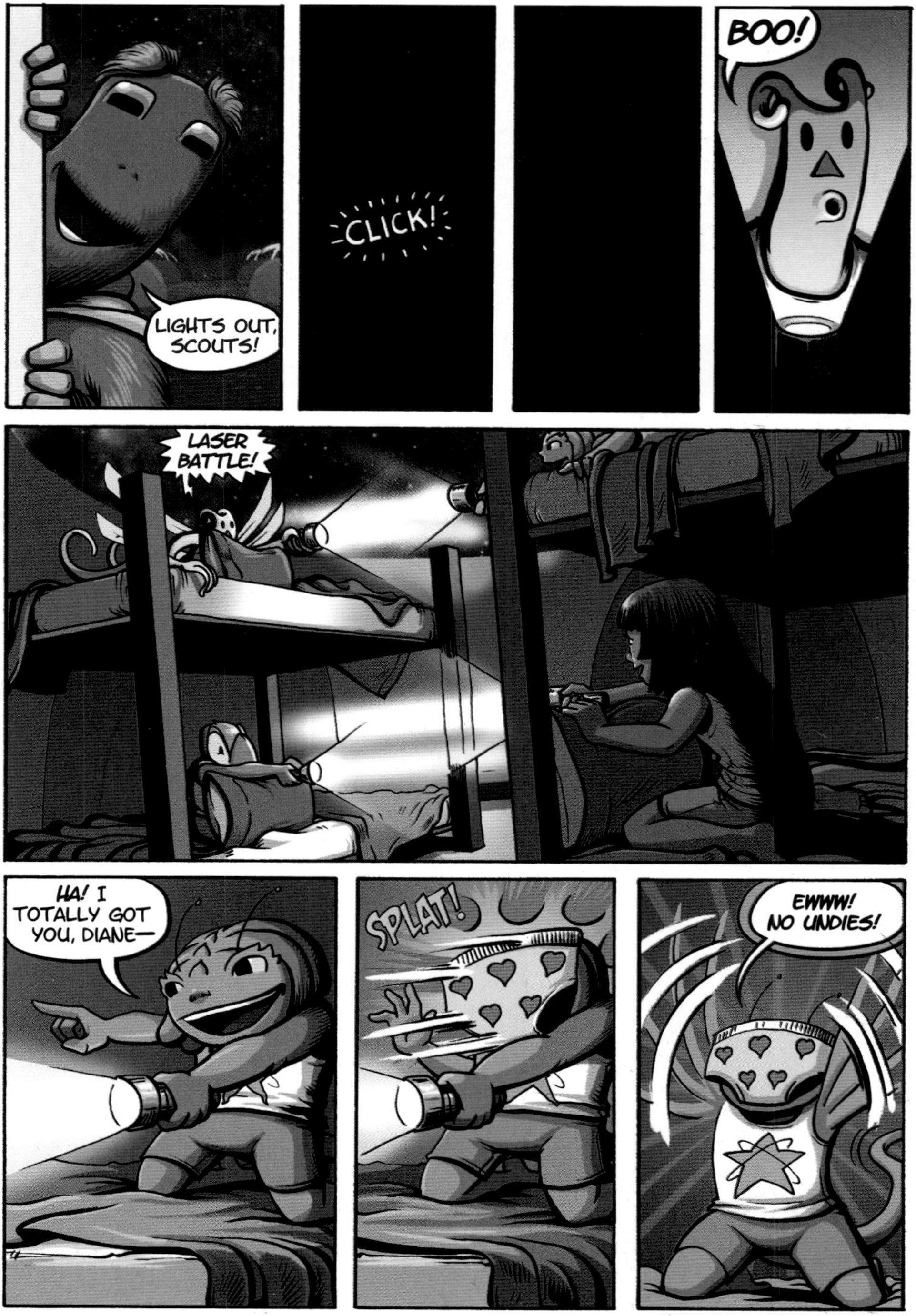
LIGHTS OUT, SCOUTS!
CLICK!
BOO!
LASER BATTLE!
HA! I TOTALLY GOT YOU, DIANE—
SPLAT!
EWWW! NO UNDIES!

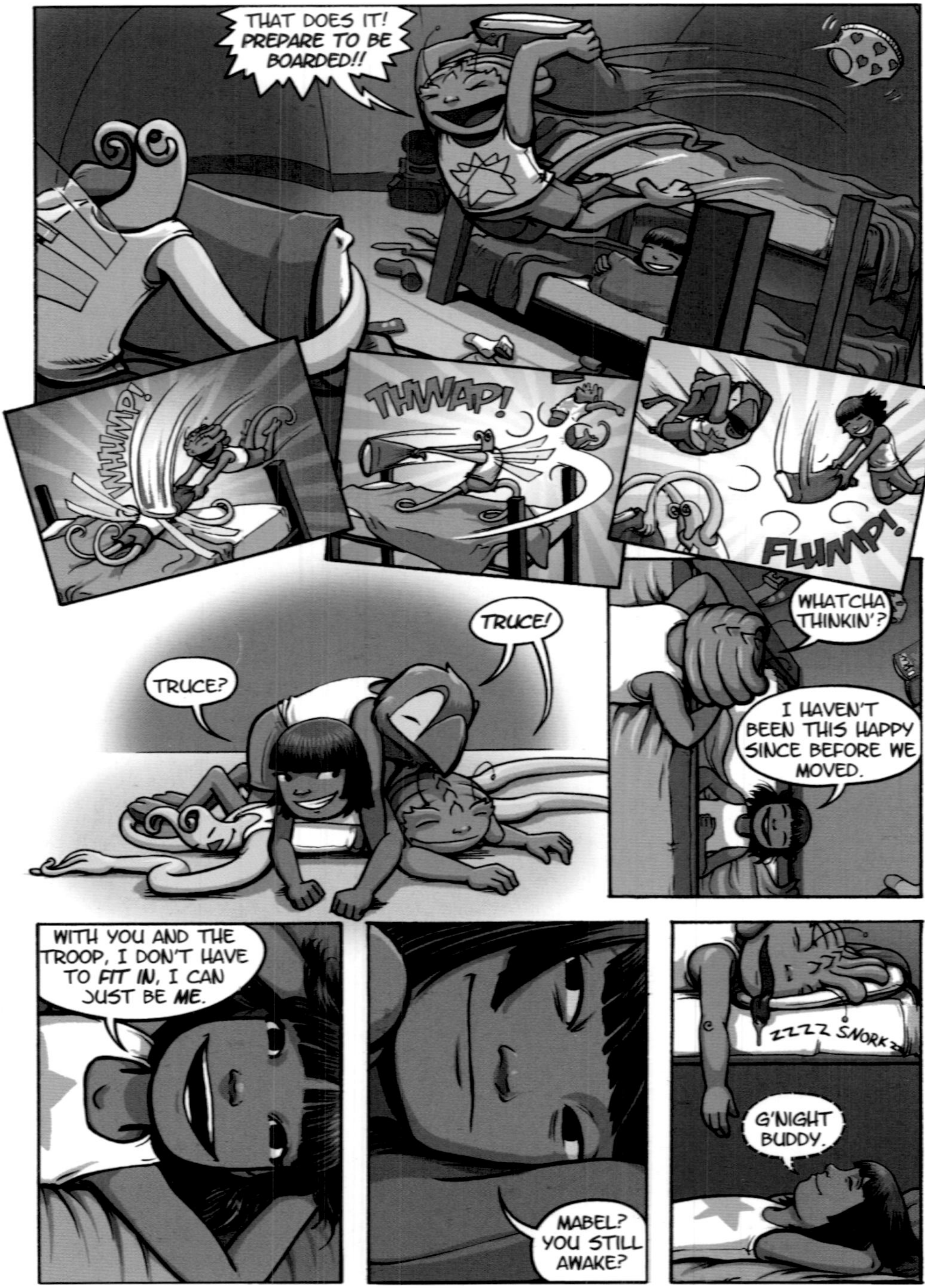
THAT DOES IT! PREPARE TO BE BOARDED!!
WHUMP!
THWAP!
FLUMP!
TRUCE?
TRUCE!
WHATCHA THINKIN'?
I HAVEN'T BEEN THIS HAPPY SINCE BEFORE WE MOVED.
WITH YOU AND THE TROOP, I DON'T HAVE TO FIT IN, I CAN JUST BE ME.
MABEL? YOU STILL AWAKE?
ZZZZ SNORK
G'NIGHT BUDDY.

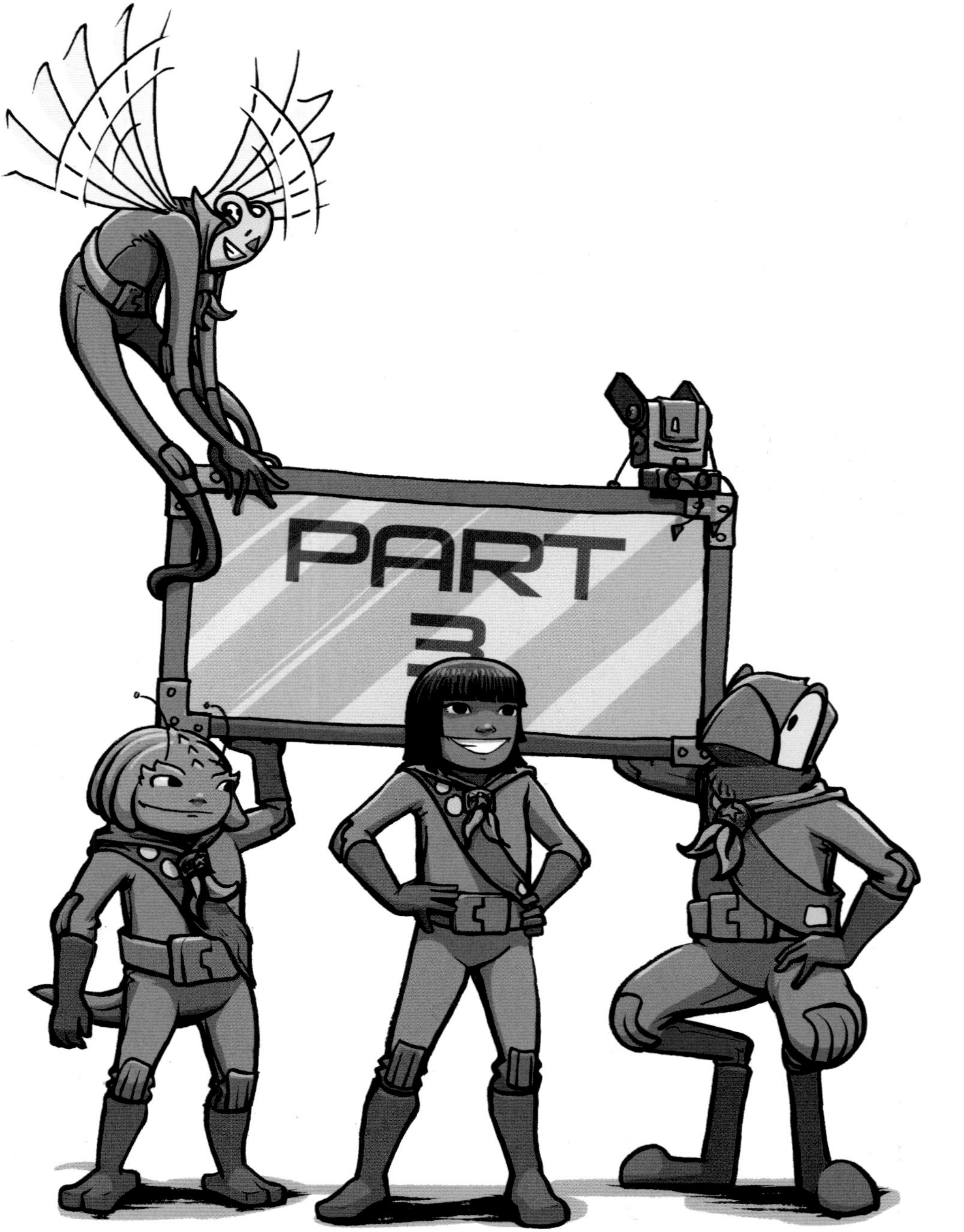
PART
3

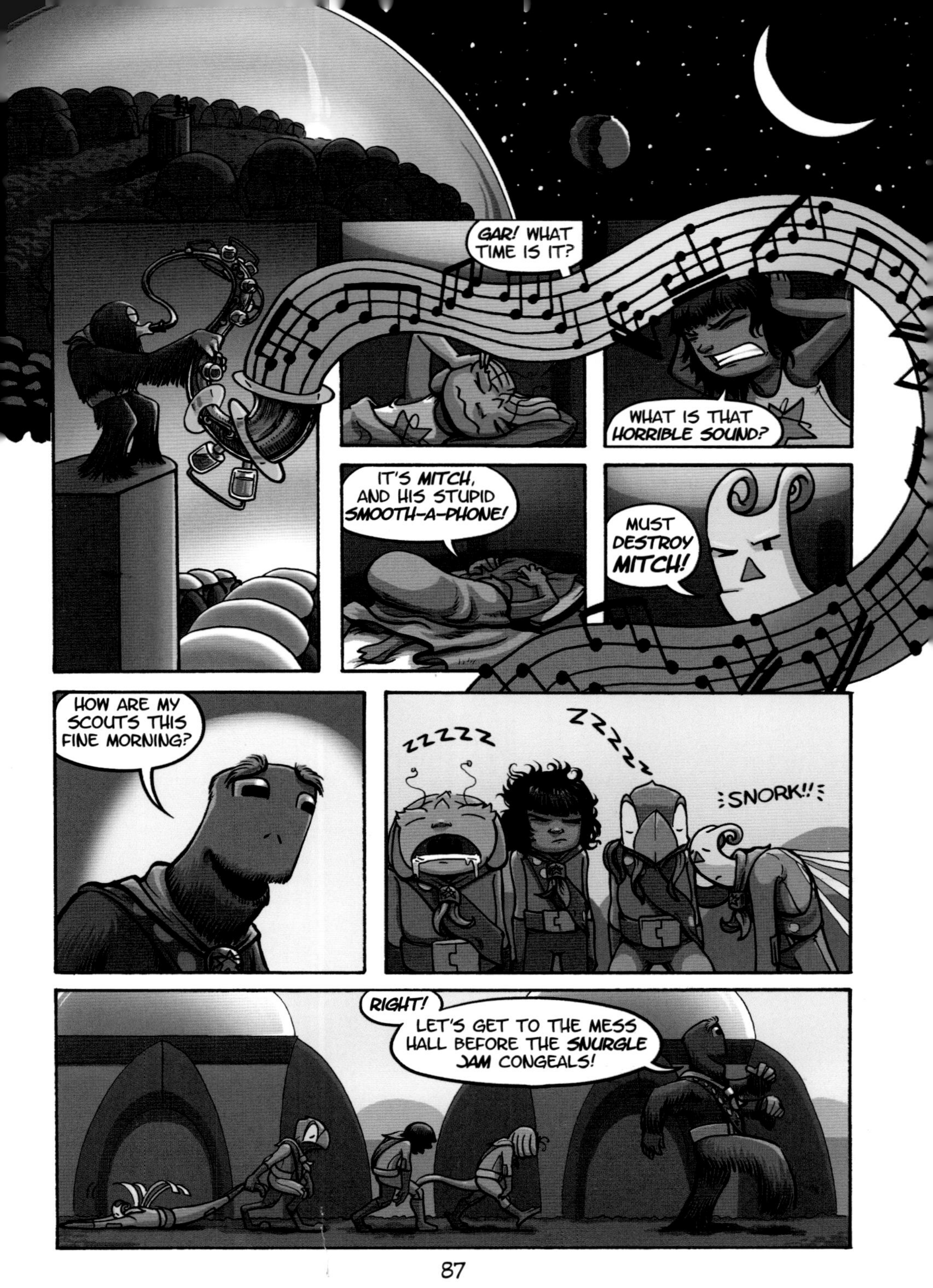
GAR! WHAT TIME IS IT?
WHAT IS THAT HORRIBLE SOUND?
IT'S MITCH, AND HIS STUPID SMOOTH-A-PHONE!
MUST DESTROY MITCH!
HOW ARE MY SCOUTS THIS FINE MORNING?
ZZZZZ
ZZZZZ
SNORK!!
RIGHT!
LET'S GET TO THE MESS HALL BEFORE THE SNURGLE JAM CONGEALS!

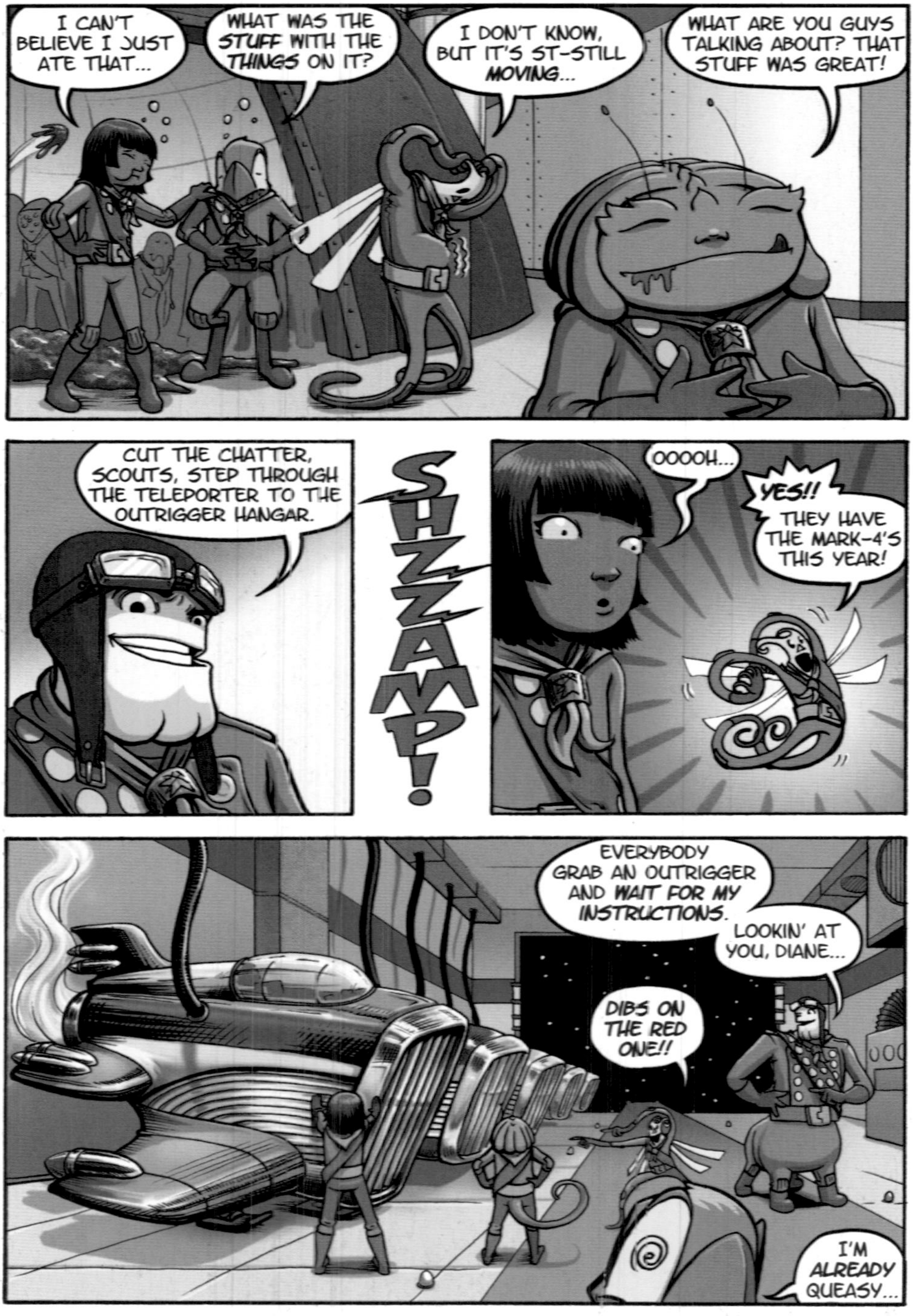
I CAN'T BELIEVE I JUST ATE THAT...
WHAT WAS THE STUFF WITH THE THINGS ON IT?
I DON'T KNOW, BUT IT'S ST-STILL MOVING...
WHAT ARE YOU GUYS TALKING ABOUT? THAT STUFF WAS GREAT!
CUT THE CHATTER, SCOUTS, STEP THROUGH THE TELEPORTER TO THE OUTRIGGER HANGAR.
SHZZAMP!
OOOOH...
YES!! THEY HAVE THE MARK-4'S THIS YEAR!
EVERYBODY GRAB AN OUTRIGGER AND WAIT FOR MY INSTRUCTIONS.
LOOKIN' AT YOU, DIANE...
DIBS ON THE RED ONE!!
I'M ALREADY QUEASY...

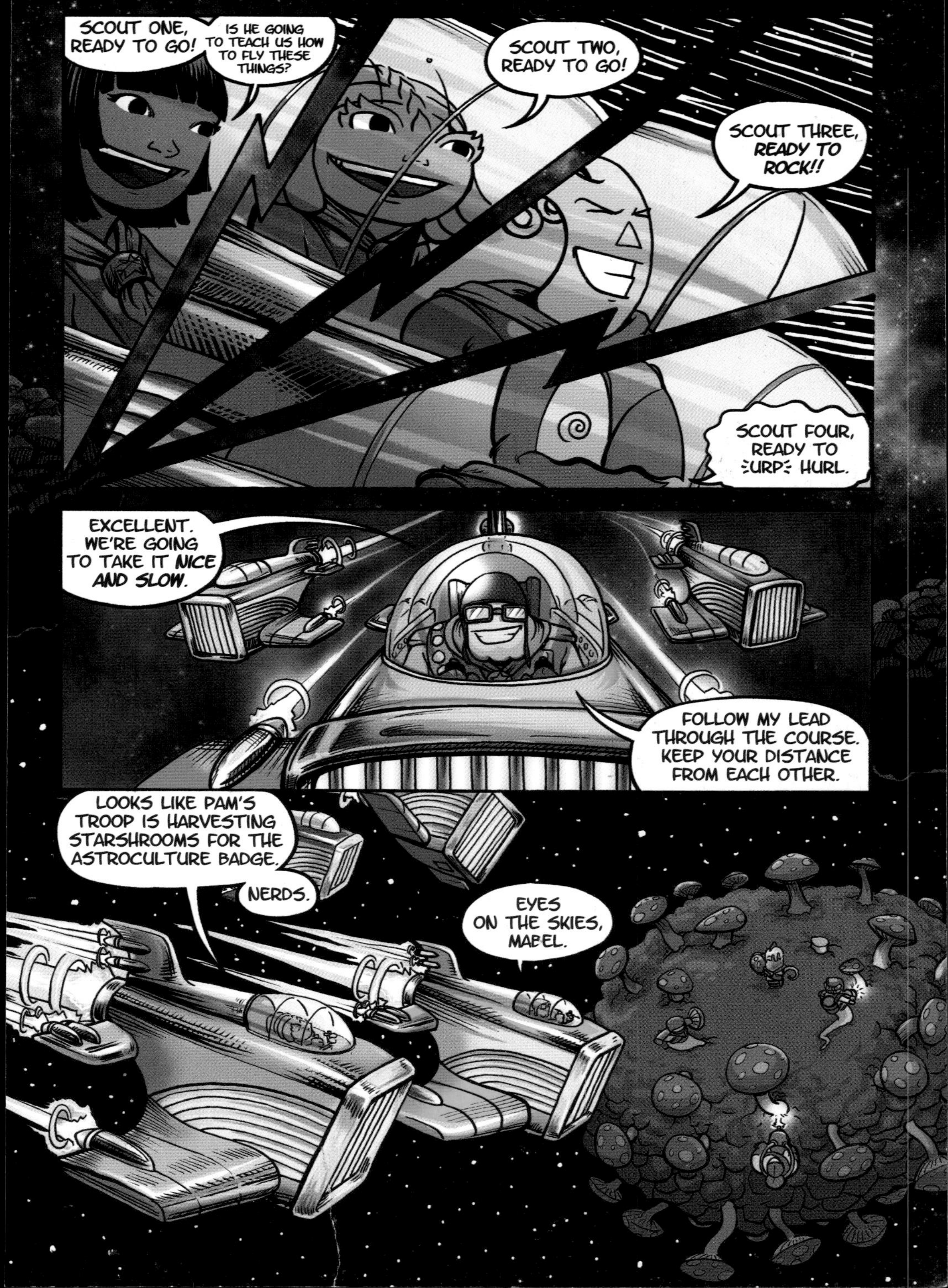
SCOUT ONE, READY TO GO!
IS HE GOING TO TEACH US HOW TO FLY THESE THINGS?
SCOUT TWO, READY TO GO!
SCOUT THREE, READY TO ROCK!!
SCOUT FOUR, READY TO URP HURL.
EXCELLENT. WE'RE GOING TO TAKE IT NICE AND SLOW.
FOLLOW MY LEAD THROUGH THE COURSE. KEEP YOUR DISTANCE FROM EACH OTHER.
LOOKS LIKE PAM'S TROOP IS HARVESTING STARSHROOMS FOR THE ASTROCULTURE BADGE.
NERDS.
EYES ON THE SKIES, MABEL.

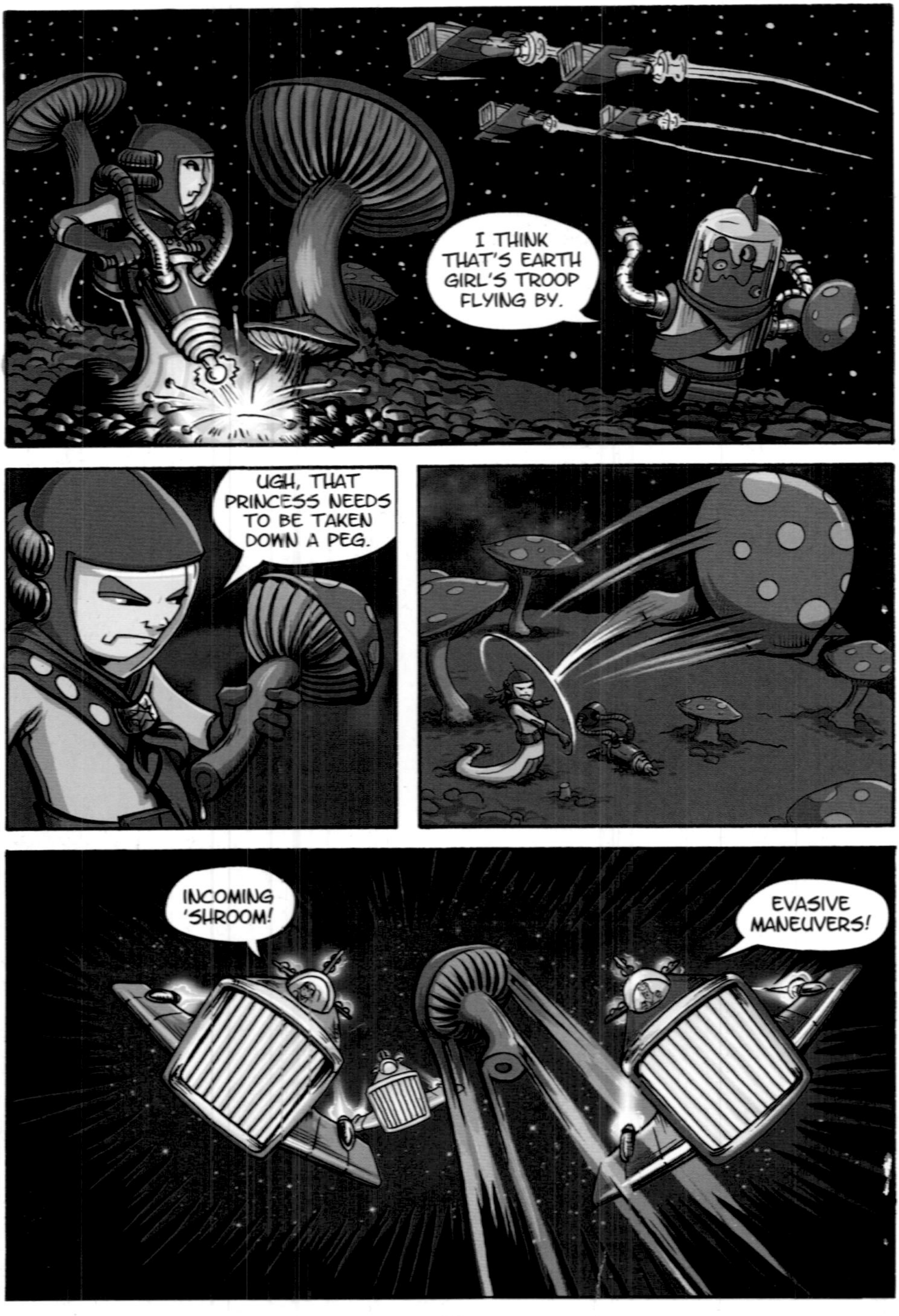
I THINK THAT'S EARTH GIRL'S TROOP FLYING BY.
UGH, THAT PRINCESS NEEDS TO BE TAKEN DOWN A PEG.
INCOMING 'SHROOM!
EVASIVE MANEUVERS!

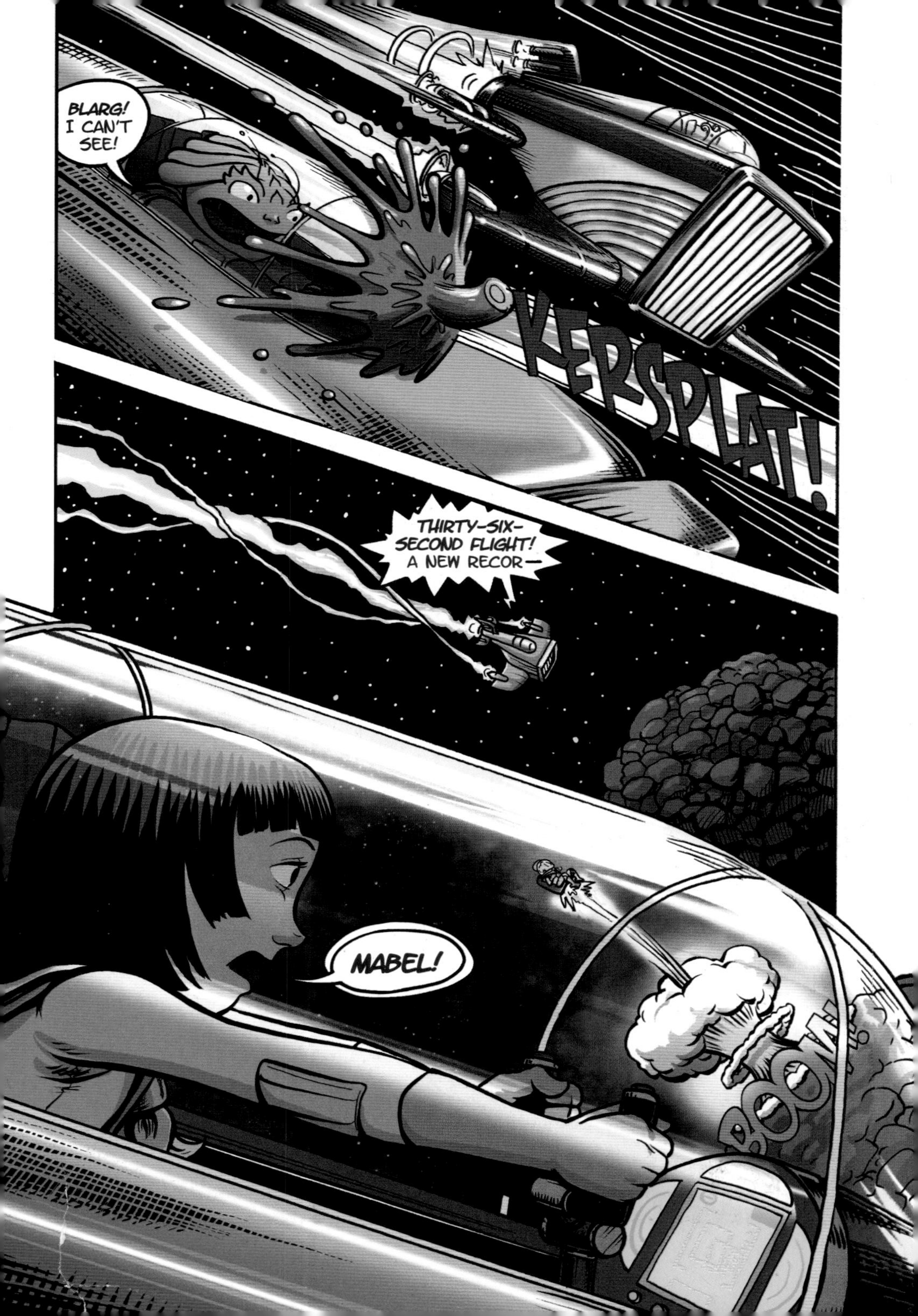
BLARG! I CAN'T SEE!
KERSPLAT!
THIRTY-SIX-SECOND FLIGHT! A NEW RECOR—
MABEL!
BOOM!

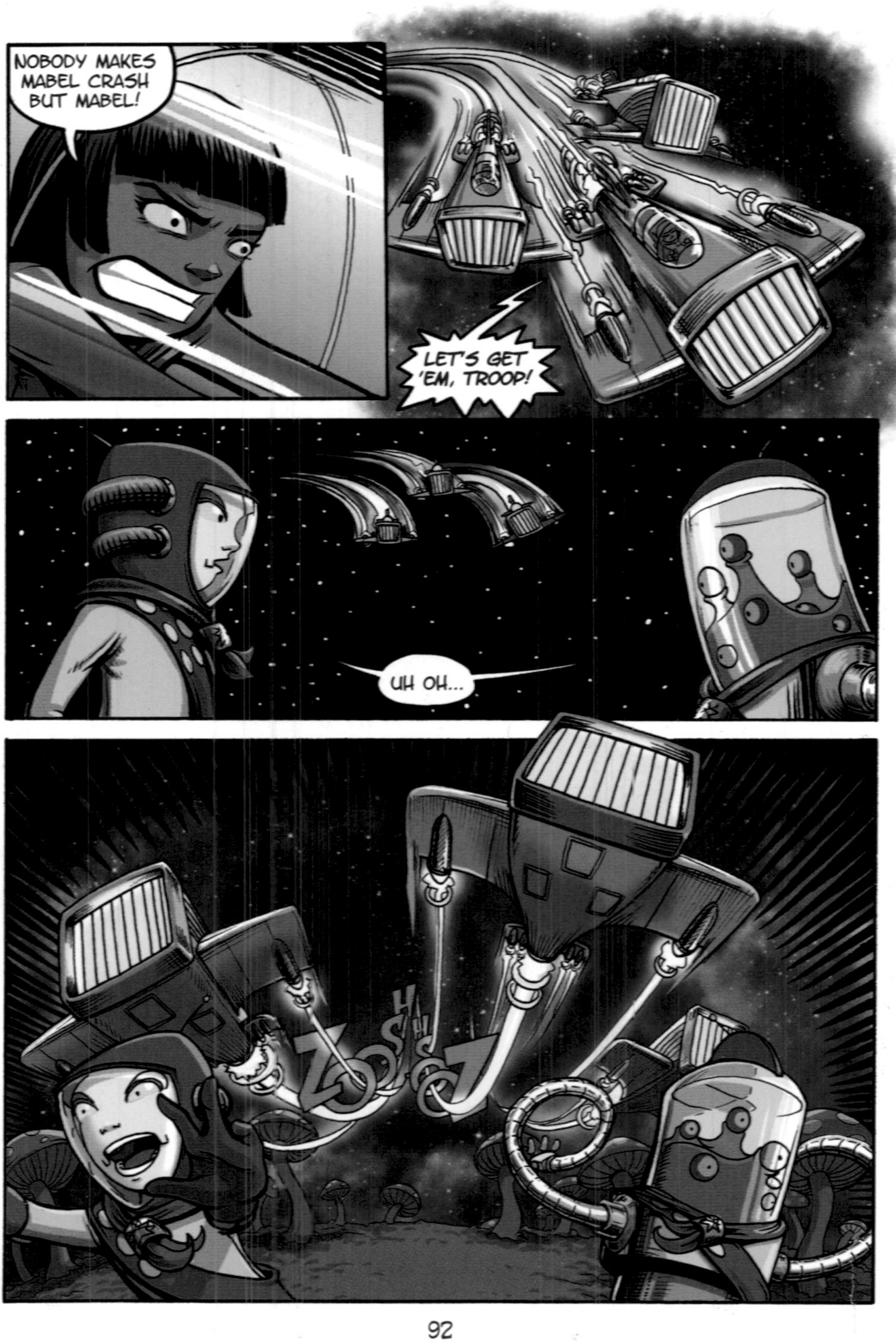
NOBODY MAKES MABEL CRASH BUT MABEL!
LET'S GET 'EM, TROOP!
UH OH...

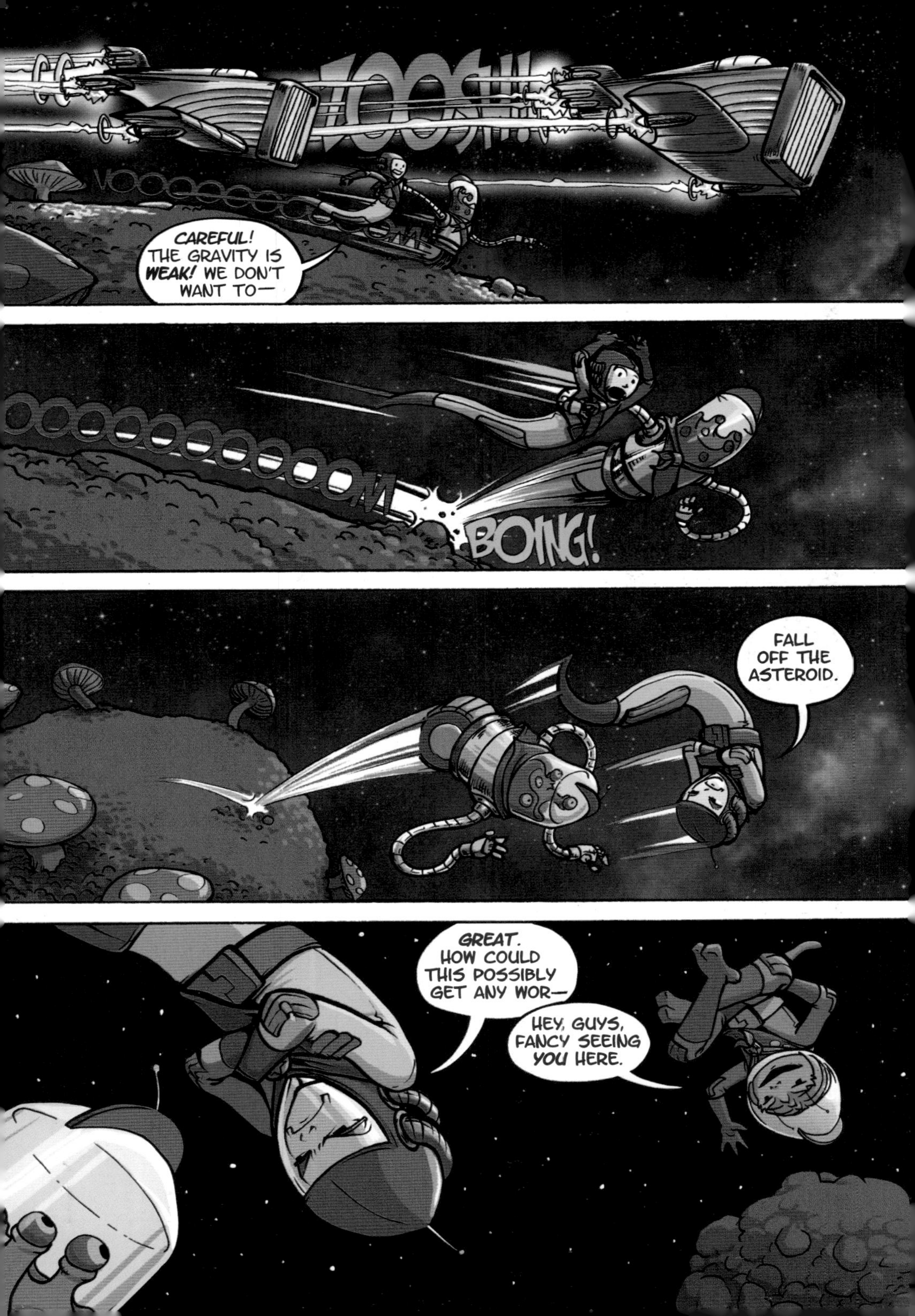
WOOSH!!
VOOOOOOOOOOM
CAREFUL! THE GRAVITY IS WEAK! WE DON'T WANT TO—
OOOOOOOOOOOOM
BOING!
FALL OFF THE ASTEROID.
GREAT. HOW COULD THIS POSSIBLY GET ANY WOR—
HEY, GUYS, FANCY SEEING YOU HERE.

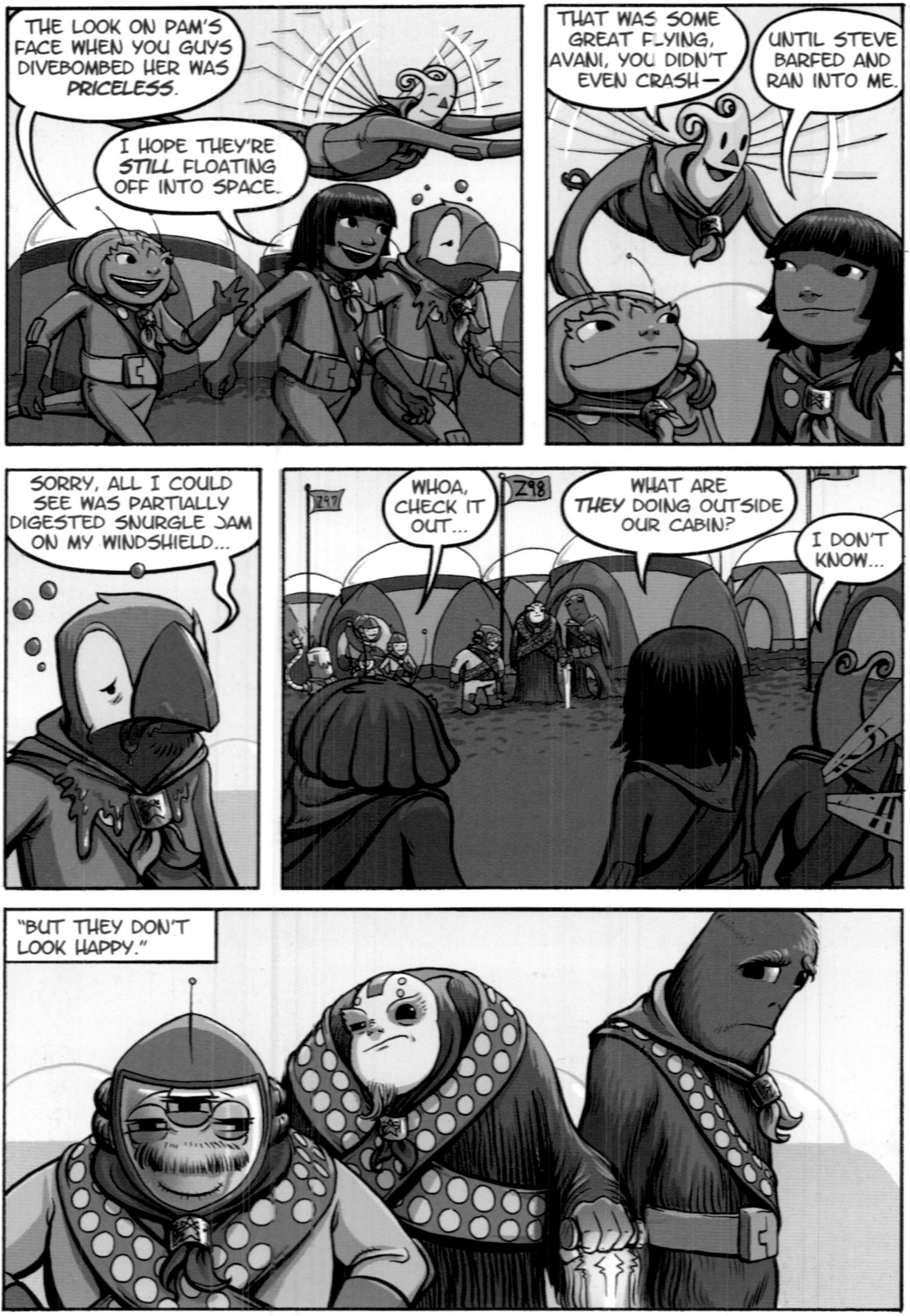
THE LOOK ON PAM'S FACE WHEN YOU GUYS DIVEBOMBED HER WAS *PRICELESS*.
I HOPE THEY'RE *STILL* FLOATING OFF INTO SPACE.
THAT WAS SOME GREAT FLYING, AVANI, YOU DIDN'T EVEN CRASH—
UNTIL STEVE BARFED AND RAN INTO ME.
SORRY, ALL I COULD SEE WAS PARTIALLY DIGESTED SNURGLE JAM ON MY WINDSHIELD...
Z97
WHOA, CHECK IT OUT...
Z98
WHAT ARE *THEY* DOING OUTSIDE OUR CABIN?
I DON'T KNOW...
"BUT THEY DON'T LOOK HAPPY."

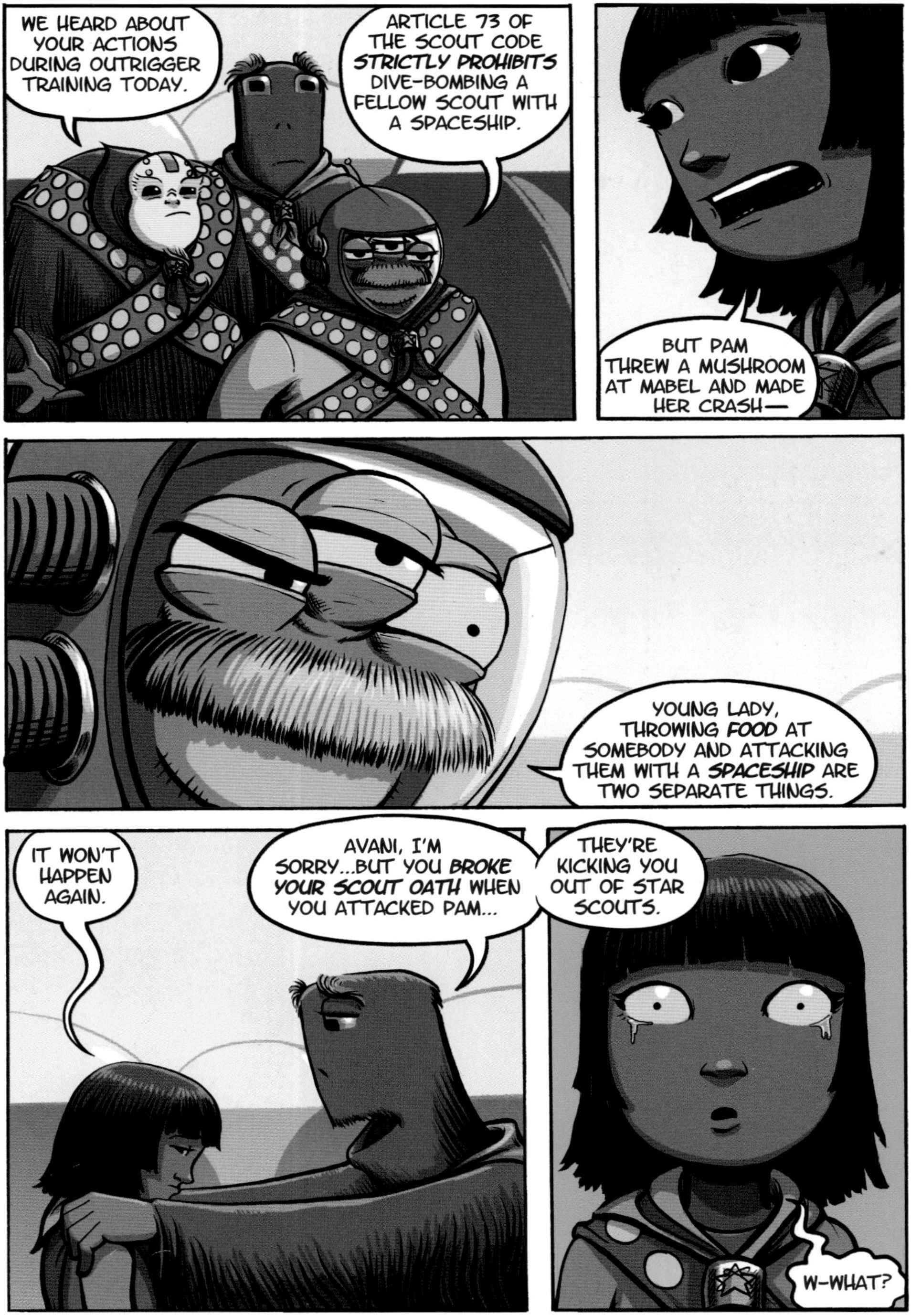
WE HEARD ABOUT YOUR ACTIONS DURING OUTRIGGER TRAINING TODAY.
ARTICLE 73 OF THE SCOUT CODE STRICTLY PROHIBITS DIVE-BOMBING A FELLOW SCOUT WITH A SPACESHIP.
BUT PAM THREW A MUSHROOM AT MABEL AND MADE HER CRASH—
YOUNG LADY, THROWING FOOD AT SOMEBODY AND ATTACKING THEM WITH A SPACESHIP ARE TWO SEPARATE THINGS.
IT WON'T HAPPEN AGAIN.
AVANI, I'M SORRY...BUT YOU BROKE YOUR SCOUT OATH WHEN YOU ATTACKED PAM...
THEY'RE KICKING YOU OUT OF STAR SCOUTS.
W-WHAT?

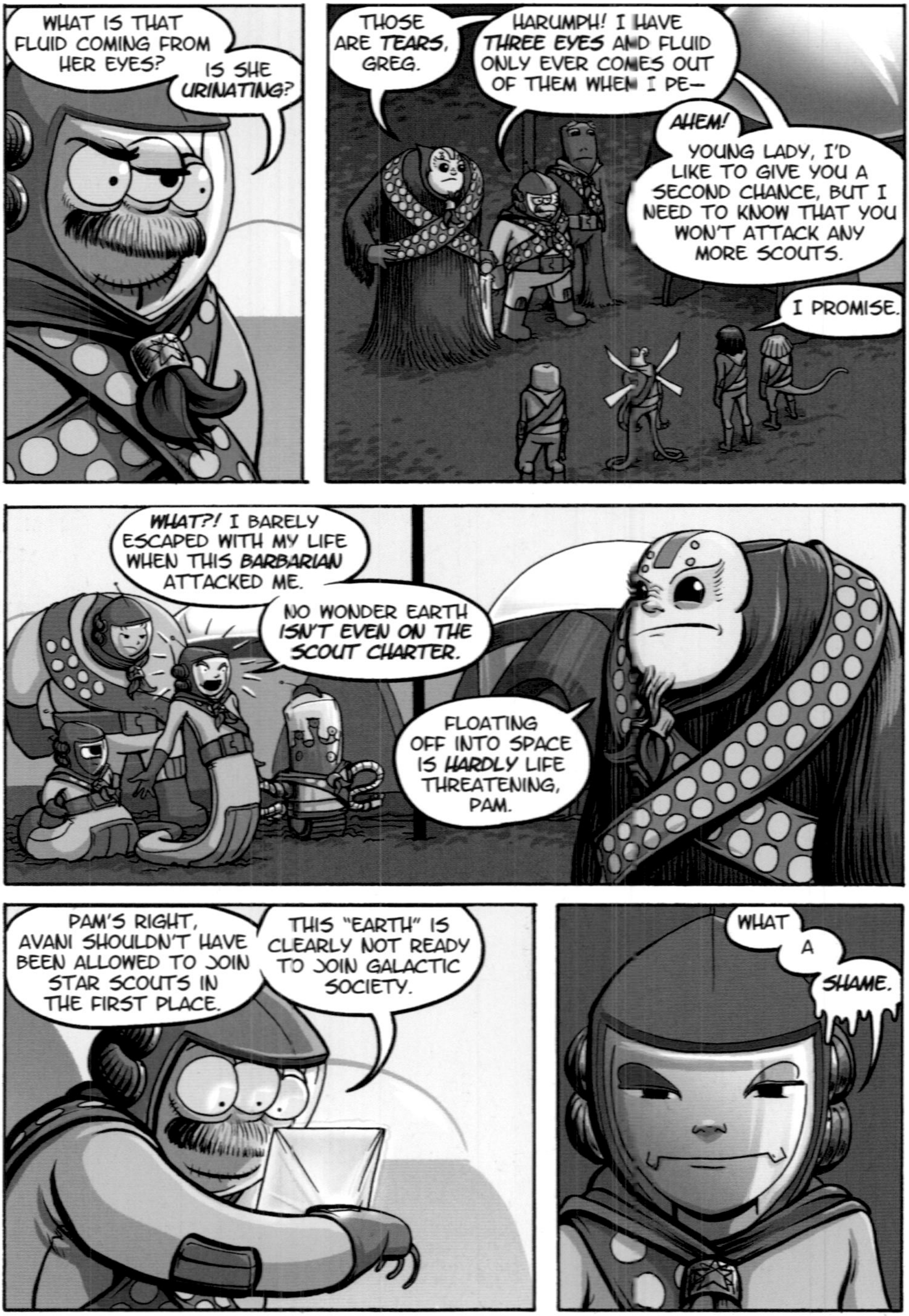
WHAT IS THAT FLUID COMING FROM HER EYES?
IS SHE URINATING?
THOSE ARE TEARS, GREG.
HARUMPH! I HAVE THREE EYES AND FLUID ONLY EVER COMES OUT OF THEM WHEN I PE—
AHEM!
YOUNG LADY, I'D LIKE TO GIVE YOU A SECOND CHANCE, BUT I NEED TO KNOW THAT YOU WON'T ATTACK ANY MORE SCOUTS.
I PROMISE.
WHAT?! I BARELY ESCAPED WITH MY LIFE WHEN THIS BARBARIAN ATTACKED ME.
NO WONDER EARTH ISN'T EVEN ON THE SCOUT CHARTER.
FLOATING OFF INTO SPACE IS HARDLY LIFE THREATENING, PAM.
PAM'S RIGHT, AVANI SHOULDN'T HAVE BEEN ALLOWED TO JOIN STAR SCOUTS IN THE FIRST PLACE.
THIS "EARTH" IS CLEARLY NOT READY TO JOIN GALACTIC SOCIETY.
WHAT A SHAME.

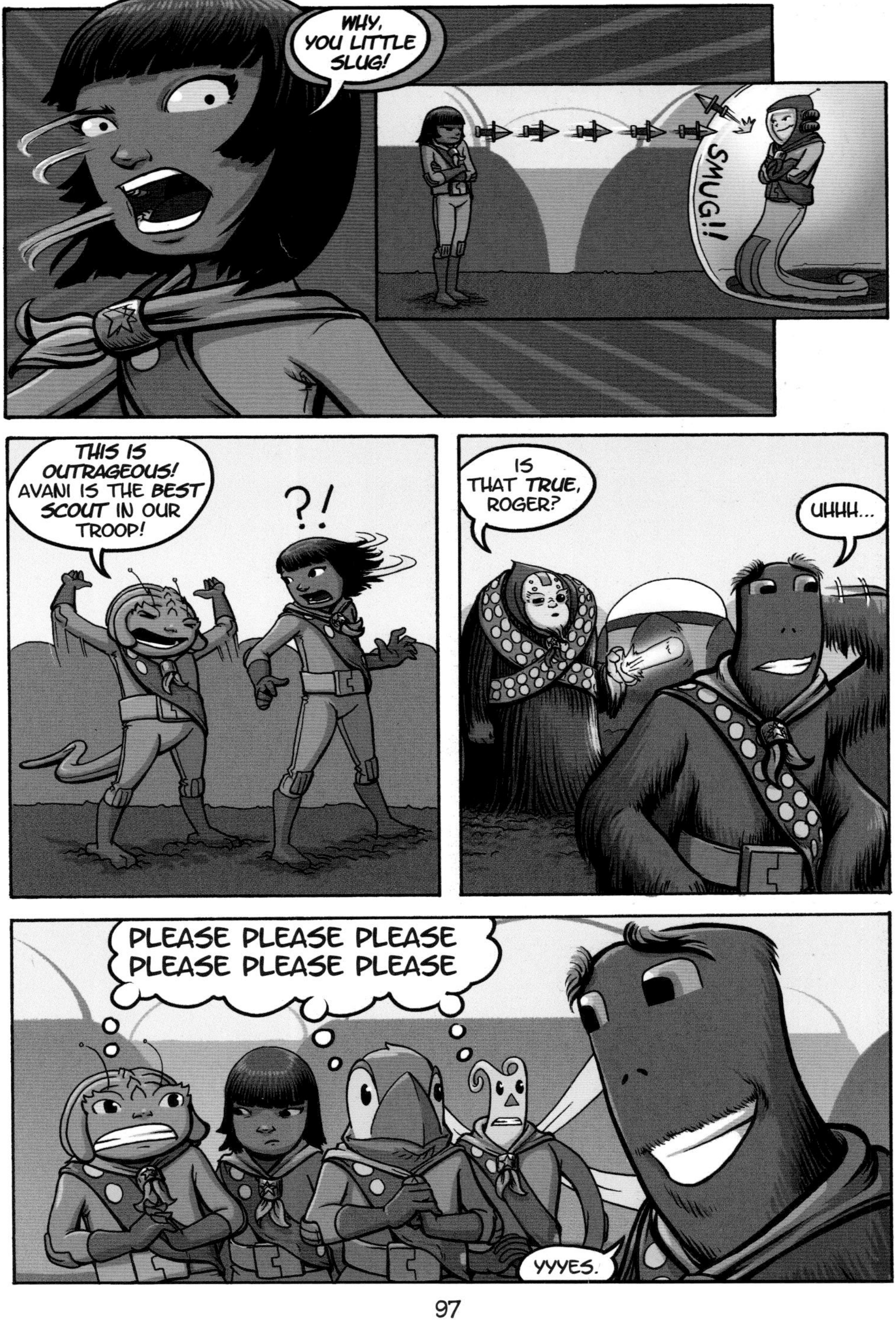
WHY, YOU LITTLE SLUG!
SMUG!!
THIS IS OUTRAGEOUS! AVANI IS THE BEST SCOUT IN OUR TROOP!
?!
IS THAT TRUE, ROGER?
UHHH...
PLEASE PLEASE PLEASE PLEASE PLEASE PLEASE
YYYES.

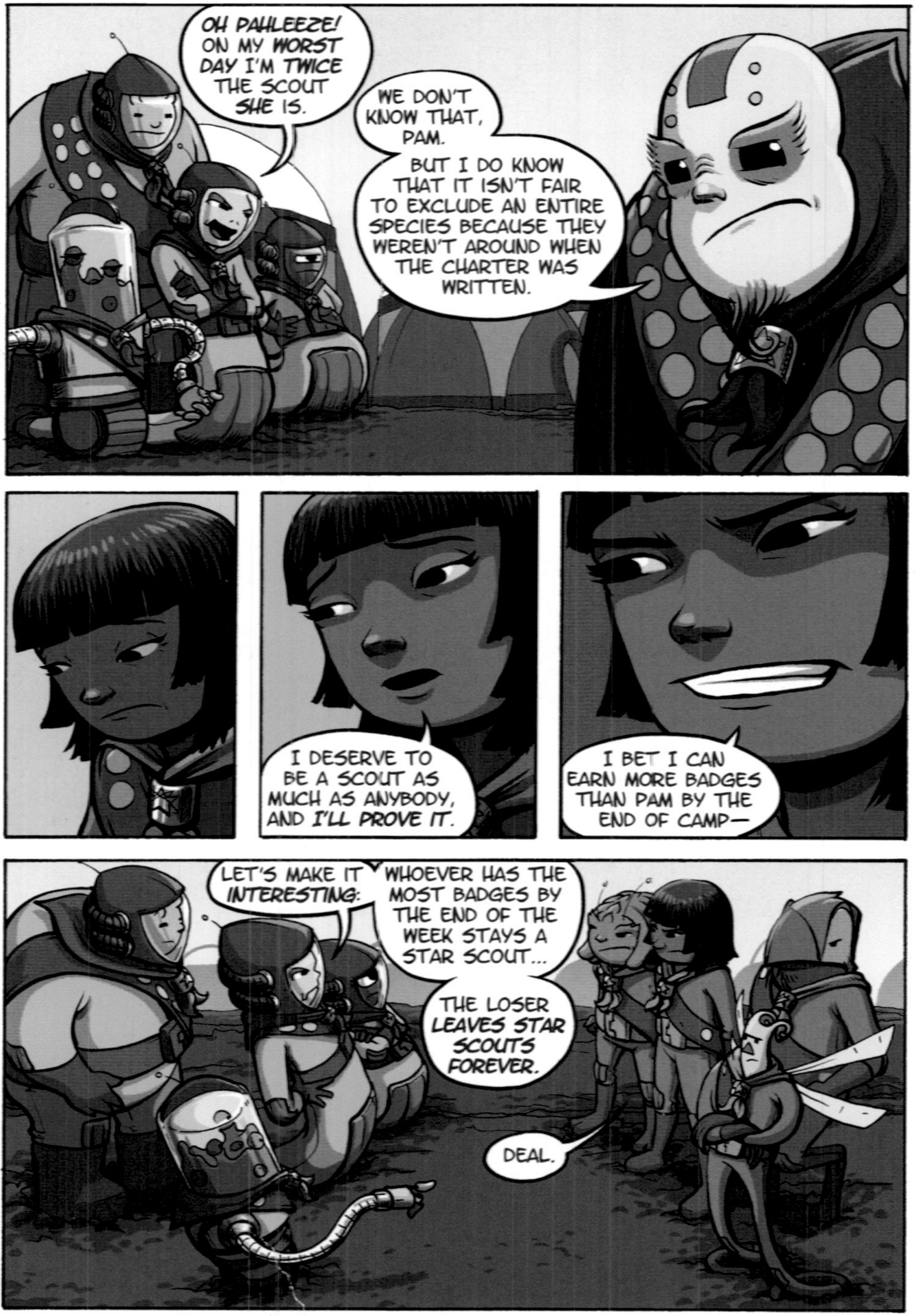

OH PAHLEEZE! ON MY WORST DAY I'M TWICE THE SCOUT SHE IS.
WE DON'T KNOW THAT, PAM.
BUT I DO KNOW THAT IT ISN'T FAIR TO EXCLUDE AN ENTIRE SPECIES BECAUSE THEY WEREN'T AROUND WHEN THE CHARTER WAS WRITTEN.
I DESERVE TO BE A SCOUT AS MUCH AS ANYBODY, AND I'LL PROVE IT.
I BET I CAN EARN MORE BADGES THAN PAM BY THE END OF CAMP—
LET'S MAKE IT INTERESTING:
WHOEVER HAS THE MOST BADGES BY THE END OF THE WEEK STAYS A STAR SCOUT...
THE LOSER LEAVES STAR SCOUTS FOREVER.
DEAL.

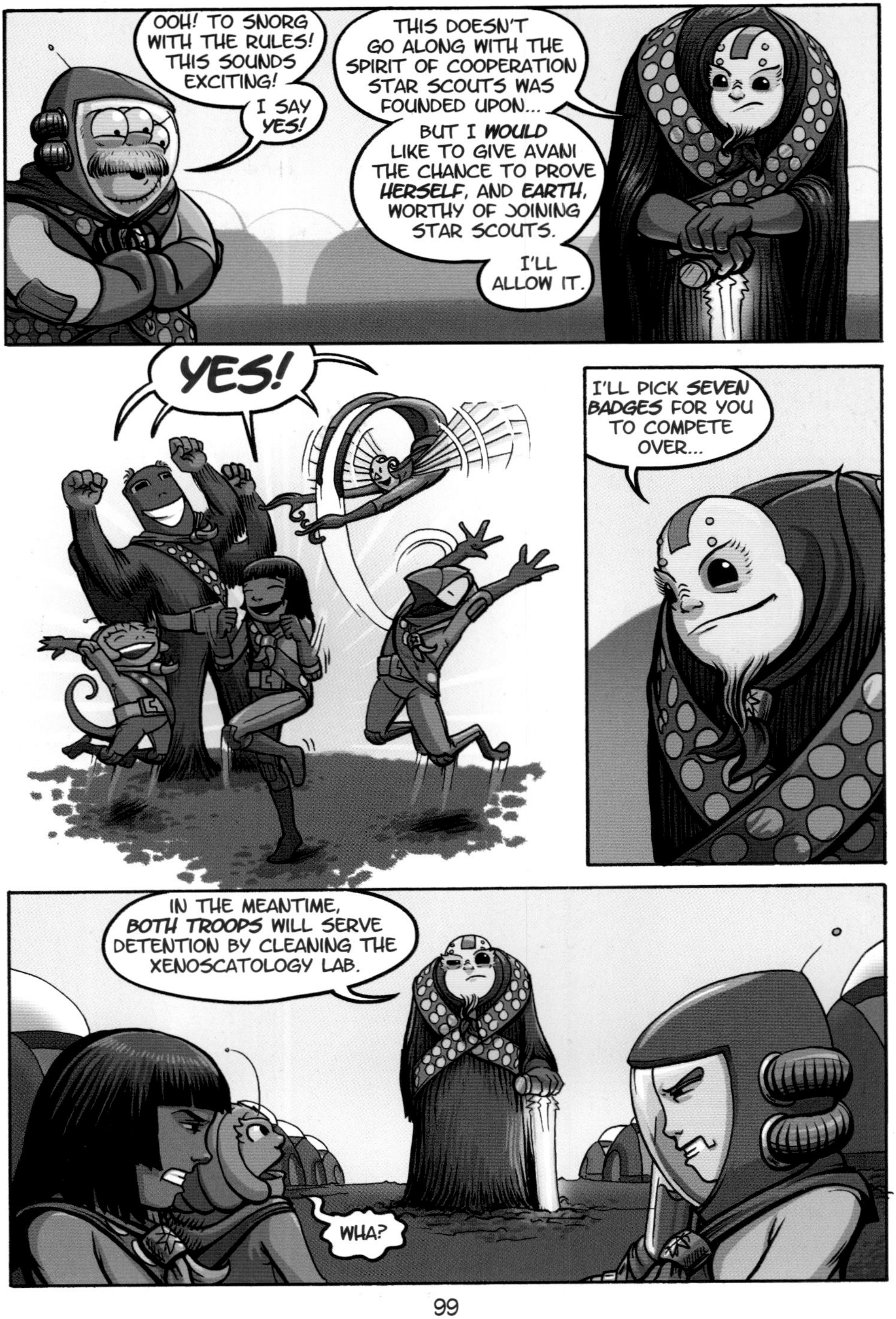

OOH! TO SNORG WITH THE RULES! THIS SOUNDS EXCITING!
I SAY YES!
THIS DOESN'T GO ALONG WITH THE SPIRIT OF COOPERATION STAR SCOUTS WAS FOUNDED UPON...
BUT I WOULD LIKE TO GIVE AVANI THE CHANCE TO PROVE HERSELF, AND EARTH, WORTHY OF JOINING STAR SCOUTS.
I'LL ALLOW IT.
YES!
I'LL PICK SEVEN BADGES FOR YOU TO COMPETE OVER...
IN THE MEANTIME, BOTH TROOPS WILL SERVE DETENTION BY CLEANING THE XENOSCATOLOGY LAB.
WHA?

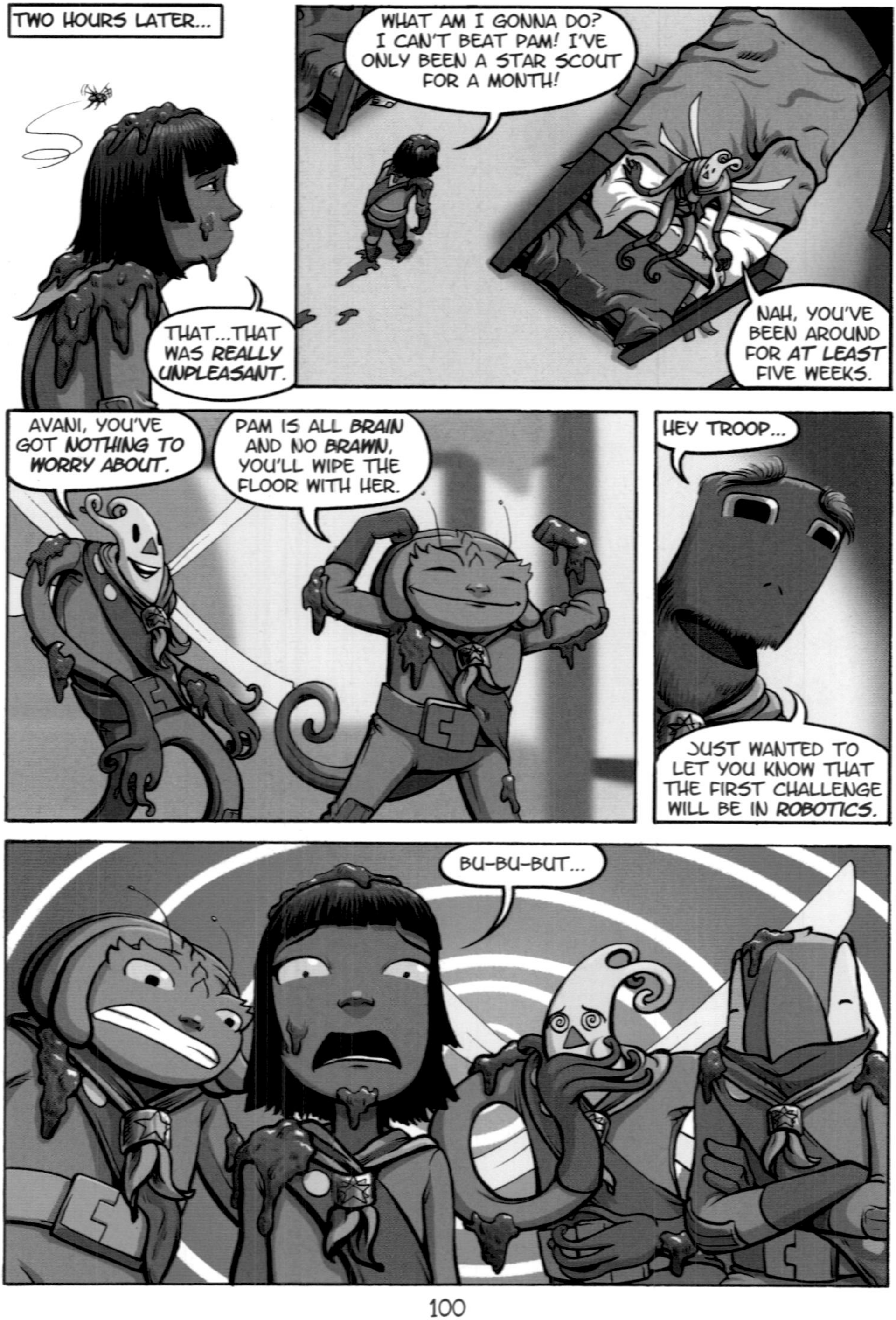
TWO HOURS LATER...
THAT...THAT WAS REALLY UNPLEASANT.
WHAT AM I GONNA DO? I CAN'T BEAT PAM! I'VE ONLY BEEN A STAR SCOUT FOR A MONTH!
NAH, YOU'VE BEEN AROUND FOR AT LEAST FIVE WEEKS.
AVANI, YOU'VE GOT NOTHING TO WORRY ABOUT.
PAM IS ALL BRAIN AND NO BRAWN, YOU'LL WIPE THE FLOOR WITH HER.
HEY TROOP...
JUST WANTED TO LET YOU KNOW THAT THE FIRST CHALLENGE WILL BE IN ROBOTICS.
BU-BU-BUT...

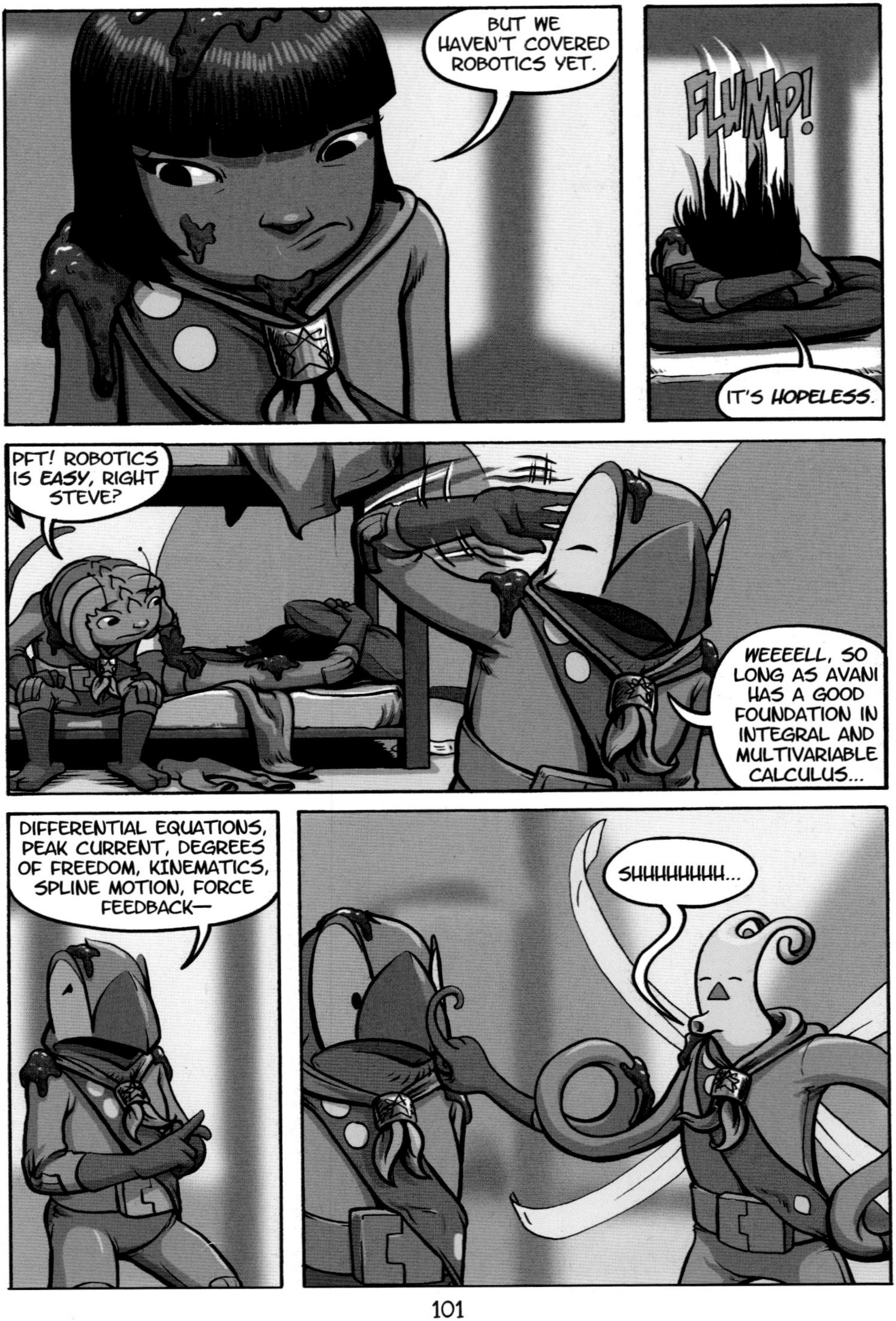
BUT WE HAVEN'T COVERED ROBOTICS YET.
FLUMP!
IT'S HOPELESS.
PFT! ROBOTICS IS EASY, RIGHT STEVE?
WEEEELL, SO LONG AS AVANI HAS A GOOD FOUNDATION IN INTEGRAL AND MULTIVARIABLE CALCULUS...
DIFFERENTIAL EQUATIONS, PEAK CURRENT, DEGREES OF FREEDOM, KINEMATICS, SPLINE MOTION, FORCE FEEDBACK—
SHHHHHHHH...

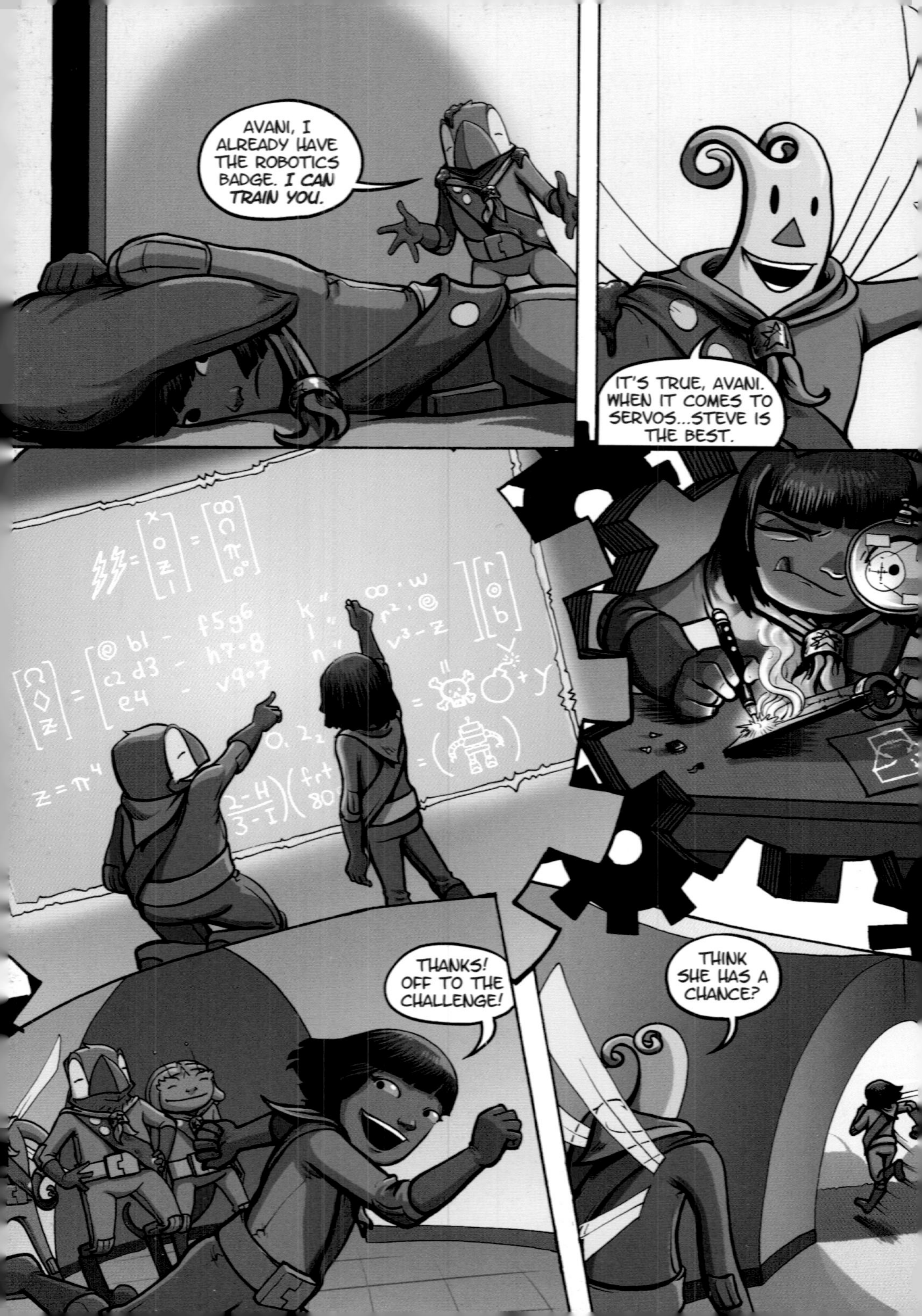
AVANI, I ALREADY HAVE THE ROBOTICS BADGE. *I CAN TRAIN YOU.*
IT'S TRUE, AVANI. WHEN IT COMES TO SERVOS...STEVE IS THE BEST.
THANKS! OFF TO THE CHALLENGE!
THINK SHE HAS A CHANCE?

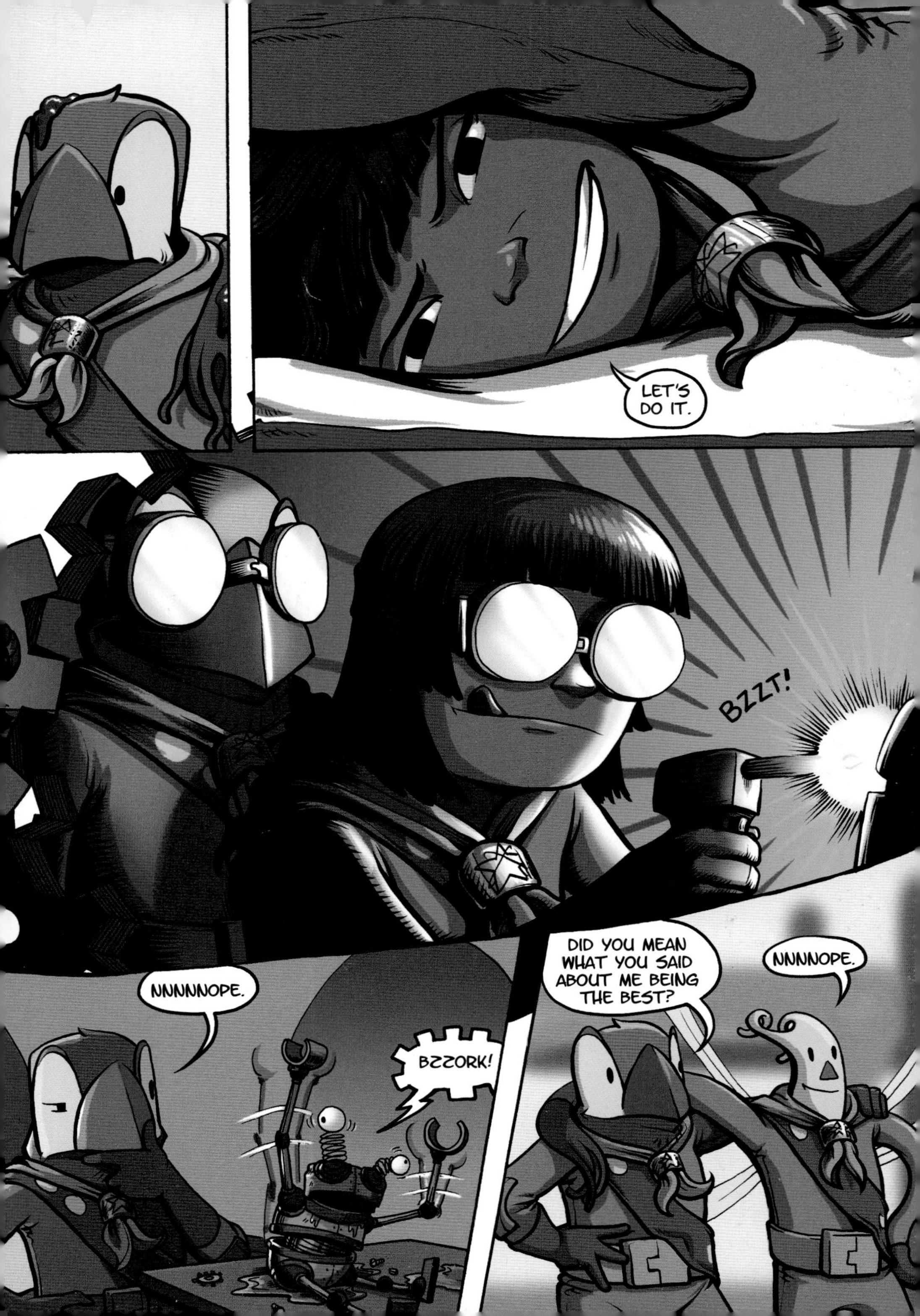
LET'S DO IT.
BZZT!
NNNNNOPE.
BZZORK!
DID YOU MEAN WHAT YOU SAID ABOUT ME BEING THE BEST?
NNNNOPE.

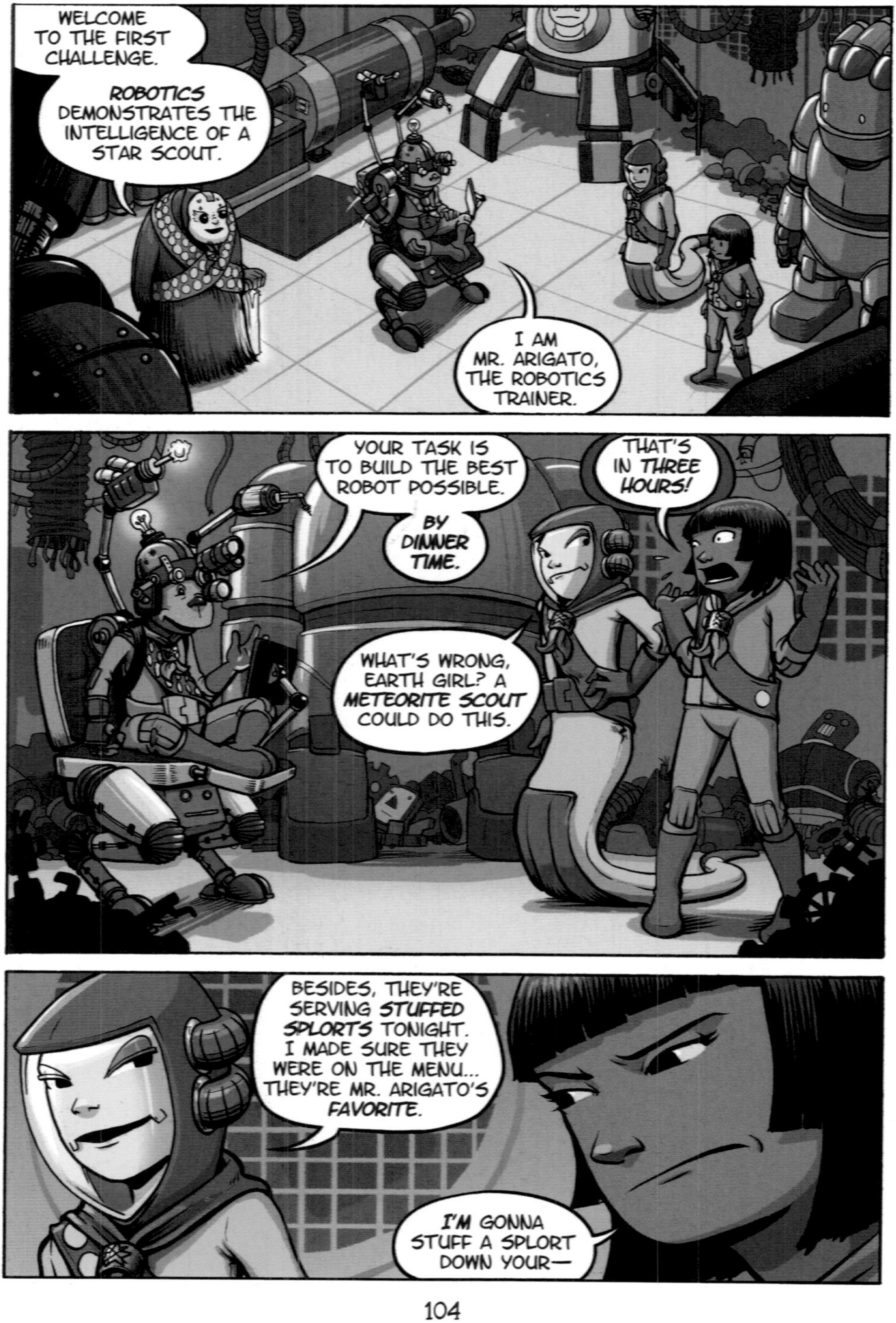
WELCOME TO THE FIRST CHALLENGE.
ROBOTICS DEMONSTRATES THE INTELLIGENCE OF A STAR SCOUT.
I AM MR. ARIGATO, THE ROBOTICS TRAINER.
YOUR TASK IS TO BUILD THE BEST ROBOT POSSIBLE.
BY DINNER TIME.
THAT'S IN THREE HOURS!
WHAT'S WRONG, EARTH GIRL? A METEORITE SCOUT COULD DO THIS.
BESIDES, THEY'RE SERVING STUFFED SPLORTS TONIGHT. I MADE SURE THEY WERE ON THE MENU... THEY'RE MR. ARIGATO'S FAVORITE.
I'M GONNA STUFF A SPLORT DOWN YOUR—

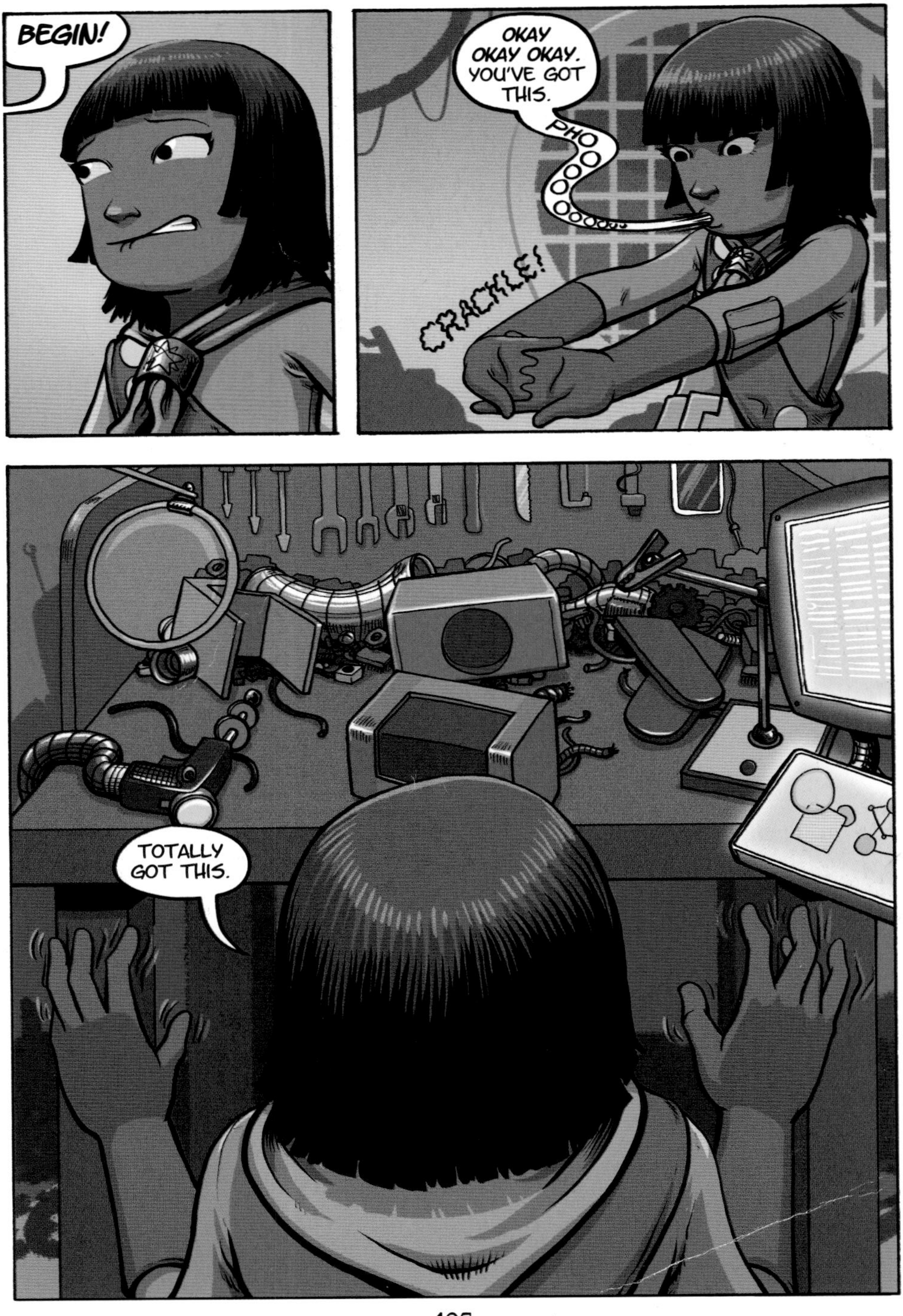
BEGIN!
OKAY OKAY OKAY. YOU'VE GOT THIS.
PHOOOOOOOOOO
CRACKLE!
TOTALLY GOT THIS.

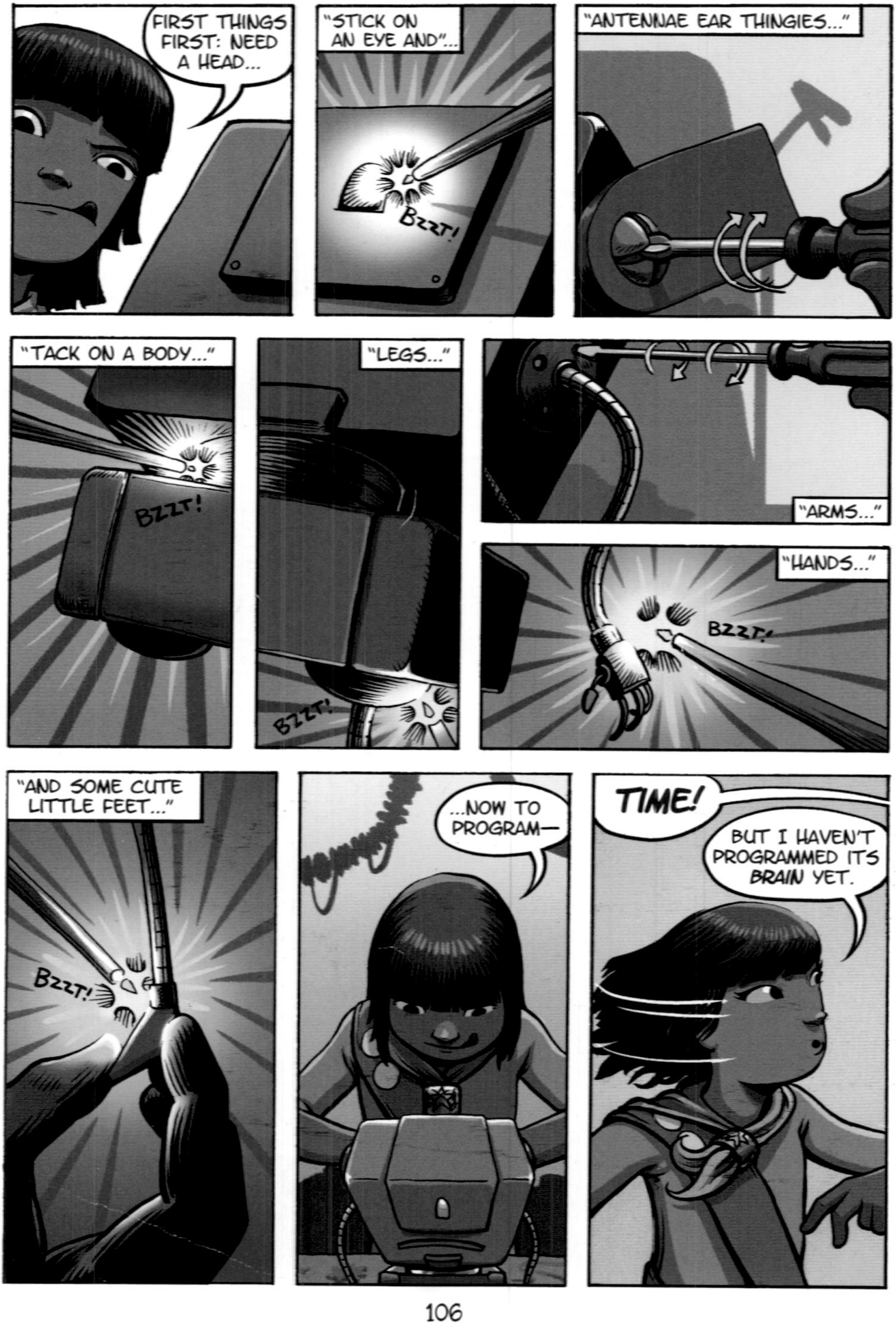
FIRST THINGS FIRST: NEED A HEAD...
"STICK ON AN EYE AND"...
BZZT!
"ANTENNAE EAR THINGIES..."
"TACK ON A BODY..."
BZZT!
"LEGS..."
BZZT!
"ARMS..."
"HANDS..."
BZZT!
"AND SOME CUTE LITTLE FEET..."
BZZT!
...NOW TO PROGRAM—
TIME!
BUT I HAVEN'T PROGRAMMED ITS *BRAIN* YET.

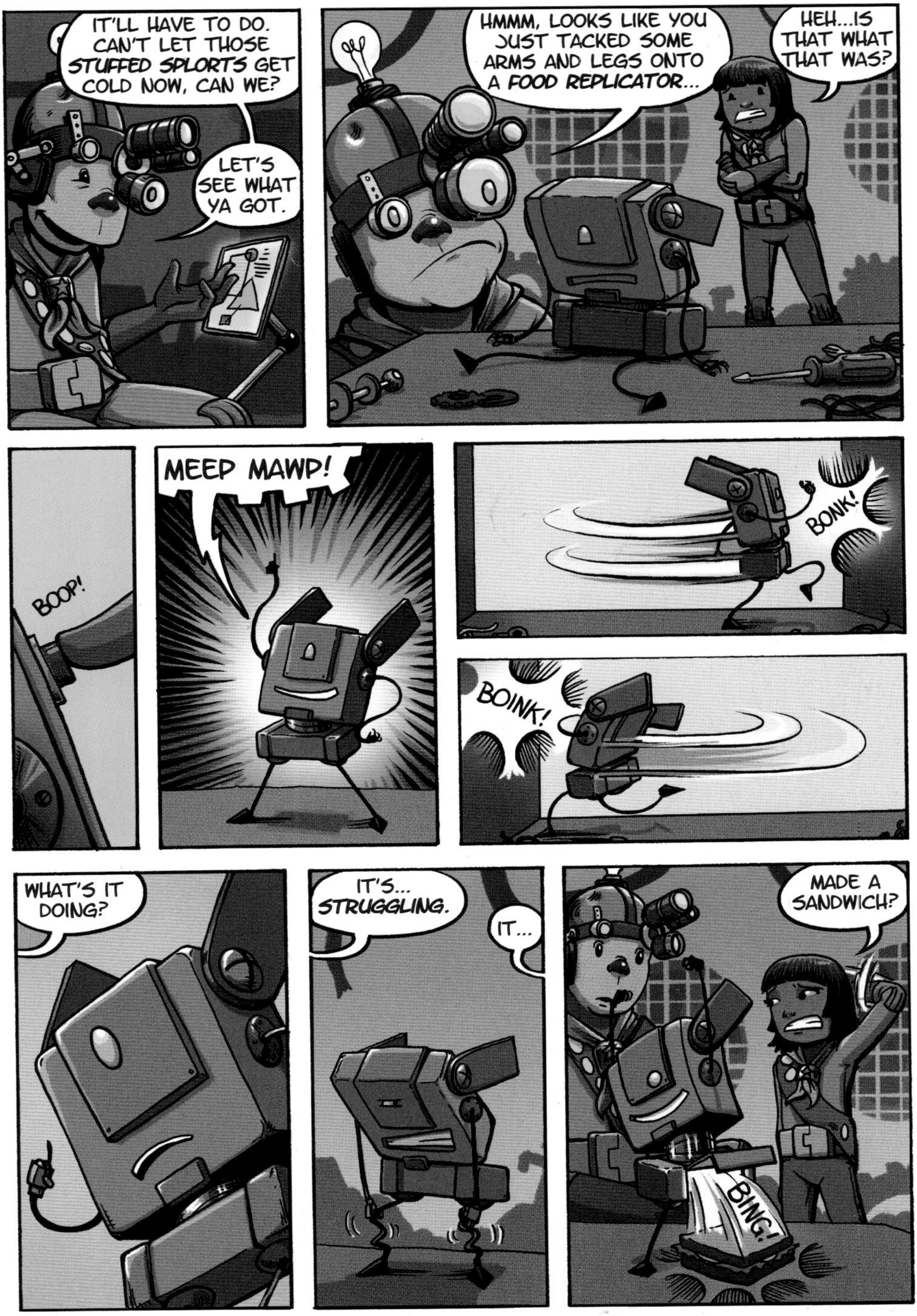
IT'LL HAVE TO DO. CAN'T LET THOSE STUFFED SPLORTS GET COLD NOW, CAN WE?
LET'S SEE WHAT YA GOT.
HMMM, LOOKS LIKE YOU JUST TACKED SOME ARMS AND LEGS ONTO A FOOD REPLICATOR...
HEH...IS THAT WHAT THAT WAS?
BOOP!
MEEP MAWP!
BONK!
BOINK!
WHAT'S IT DOING?
IT'S... STRUGGLING.
IT...
MADE A SANDWICH?
BING!

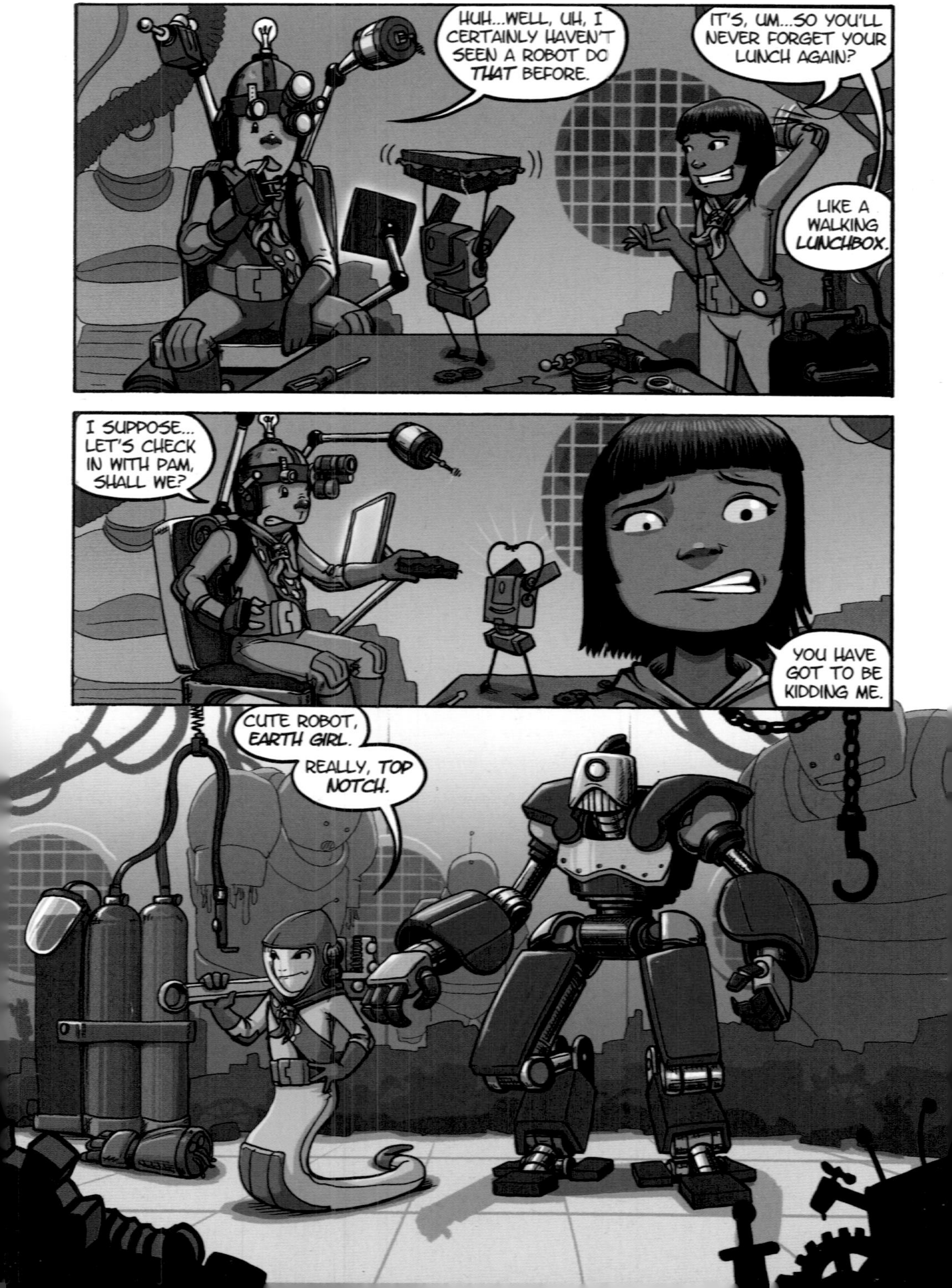
HUH...WELL, UH, I CERTAINLY HAVEN'T SEEN A ROBOT DO *THAT* BEFORE.
IT'S, UM...SO YOU'LL NEVER FORGET YOUR LUNCH AGAIN?
LIKE A WALKING *LUNCHBOX.*
I SUPPOSE... LET'S CHECK IN WITH PAM, SHALL WE?
YOU HAVE GOT TO BE KIDDING ME.
CUTE ROBOT, *EARTH GIRL.*
REALLY, TOP *NOTCH.*

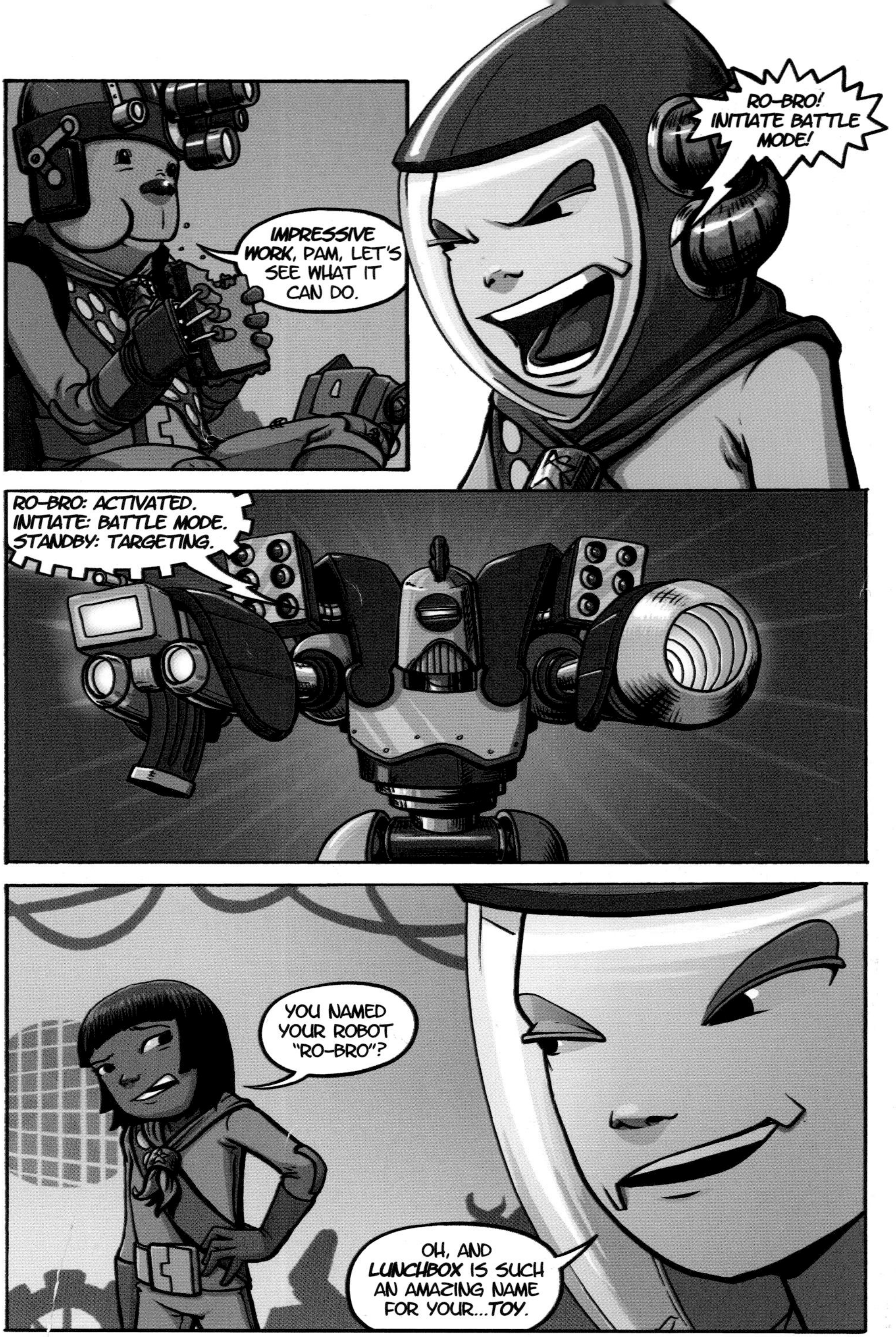
RO-BRO! INITIATE BATTLE MODE!
IMPRESSIVE WORK, PAM, LET'S SEE WHAT IT CAN DO.
RO-BRO: ACTIVATED. INITIATE: BATTLE MODE. STANDBY: TARGETING.
YOU NAMED YOUR ROBOT "RO-BRO"?
OH, AND LUNCHBOX IS SUCH AN AMAZING NAME FOR YOUR...TOY.

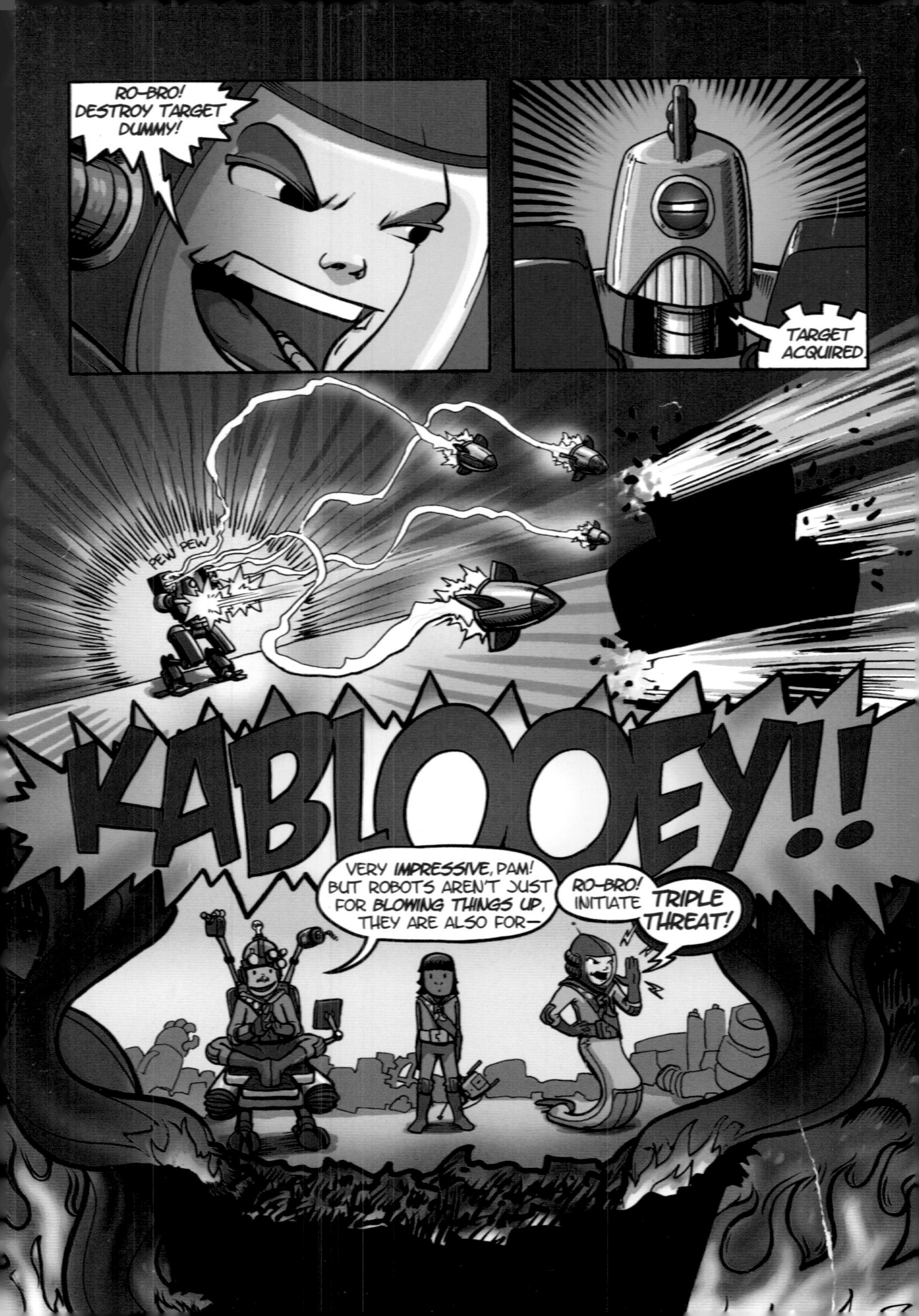
RO-BRO! DESTROY TARGET DUMMY!
TARGET ACQUIRED.
PEW PEW
KABLOOEY!!
VERY IMPRESSIVE, PAM! BUT ROBOTS AREN'T JUST FOR BLOWING THINGS UP, THEY ARE ALSO FOR—
RO-BRO! INITIATE TRIPLE THREAT!

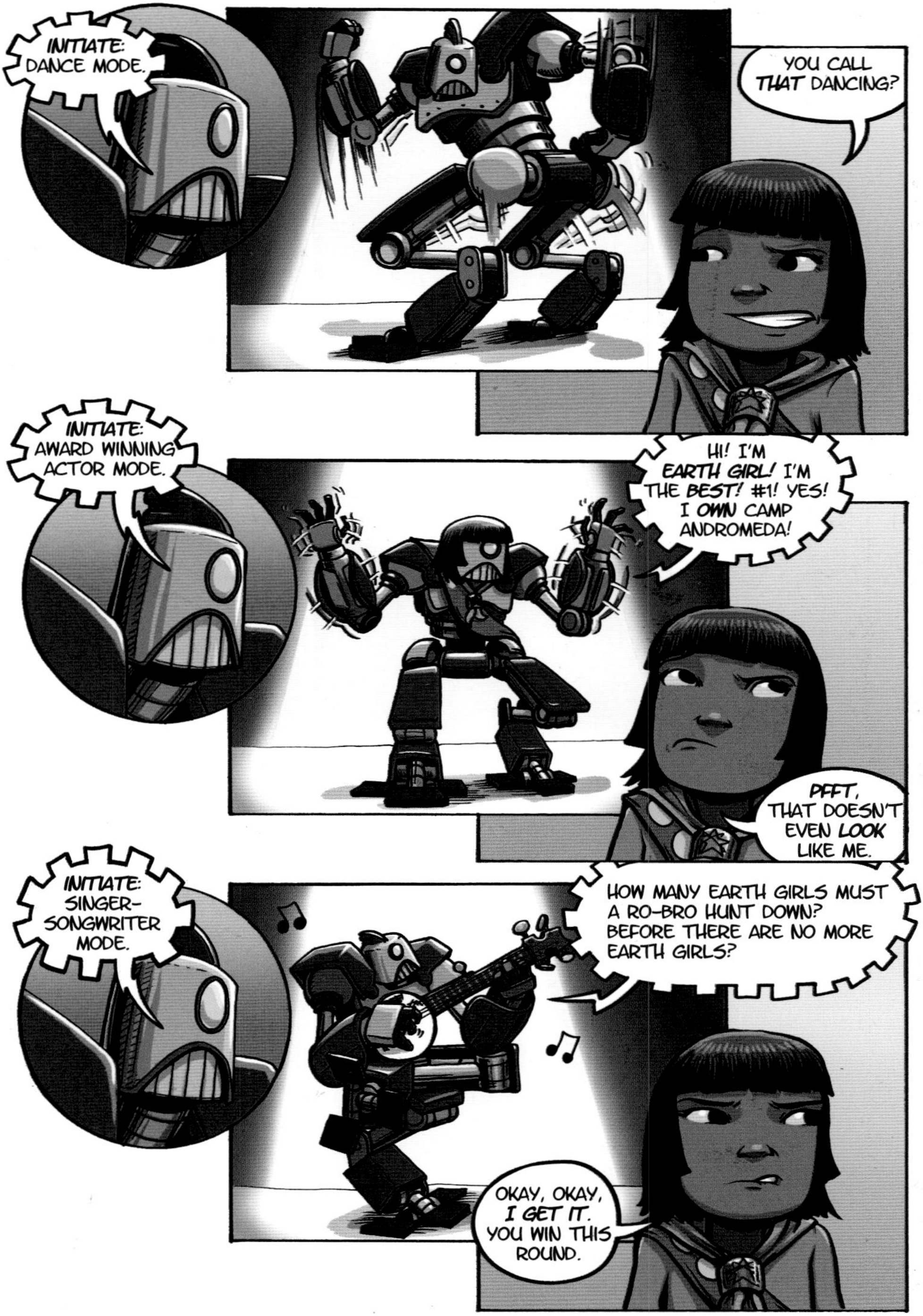
INITIATE: DANCE MODE.
YOU CALL THAT DANCING?
INITIATE: AWARD WINNING ACTOR MODE.
HI! I'M EARTH GIRL! I'M THE BEST! #1! YES! I OWN CAMP ANDROMEDA!
PFFT, THAT DOESN'T EVEN LOOK LIKE ME.
INITIATE: SINGER-SONGWRITER MODE.
HOW MANY EARTH GIRLS MUST A RO-BRO HUNT DOWN? BEFORE THERE ARE NO MORE EARTH GIRLS?
OKAY, OKAY, I GET IT. YOU WIN THIS ROUND.

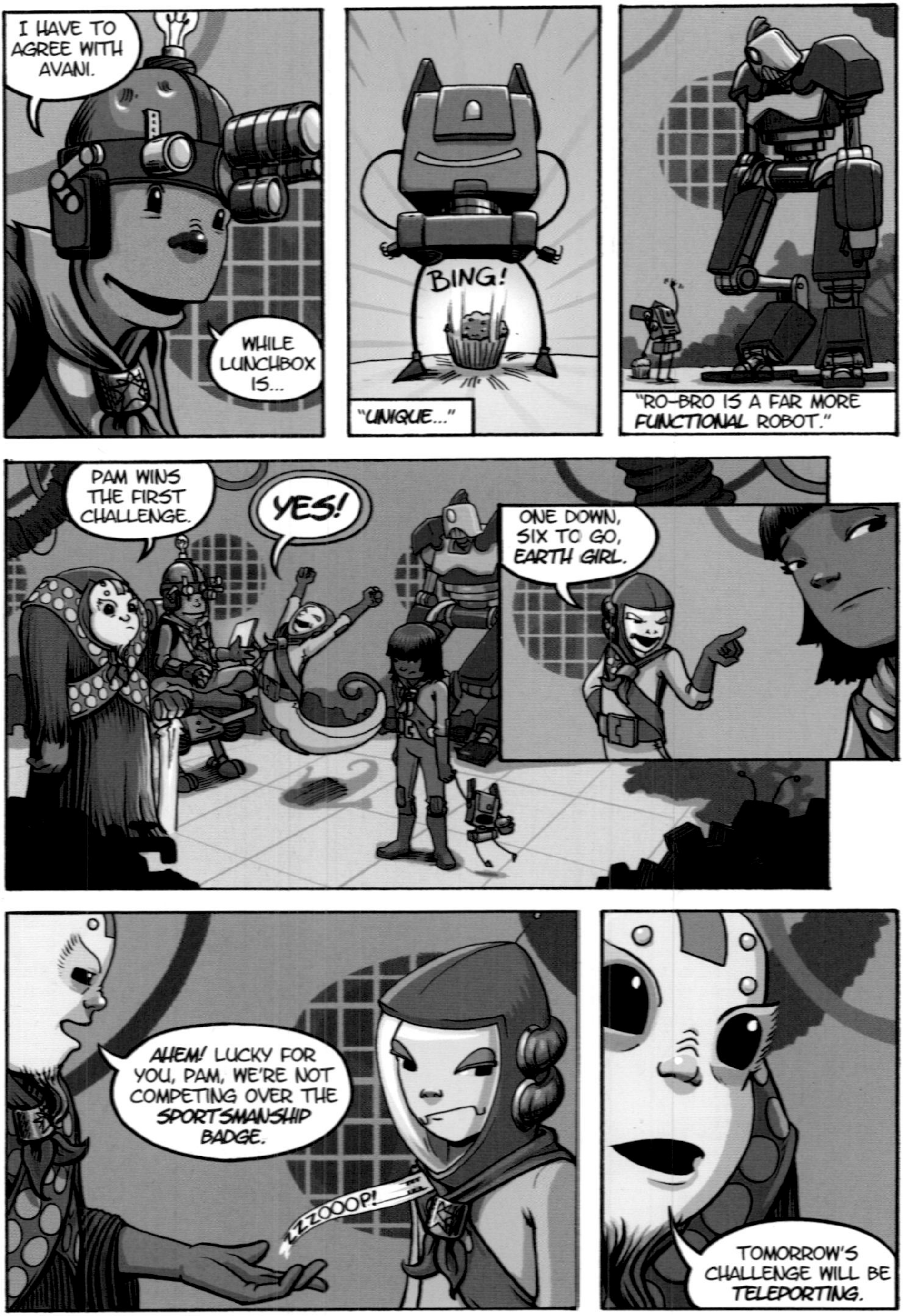
I HAVE TO AGREE WITH AVANI.
WHILE LUNCHBOX IS...
BING!
"UNIQUE..."
"RO-BRO IS A FAR MORE FUNCTIONAL ROBOT."
PAM WINS THE FIRST CHALLENGE.
YES!
ONE DOWN, SIX TO GO, EARTH GIRL.
AHEM! LUCKY FOR YOU, PAM, WE'RE NOT COMPETING OVER THE SPORTSMANSHIP BADGE.
ZZZOOOP!
TOMORROW'S CHALLENGE WILL BE TELEPORTING.

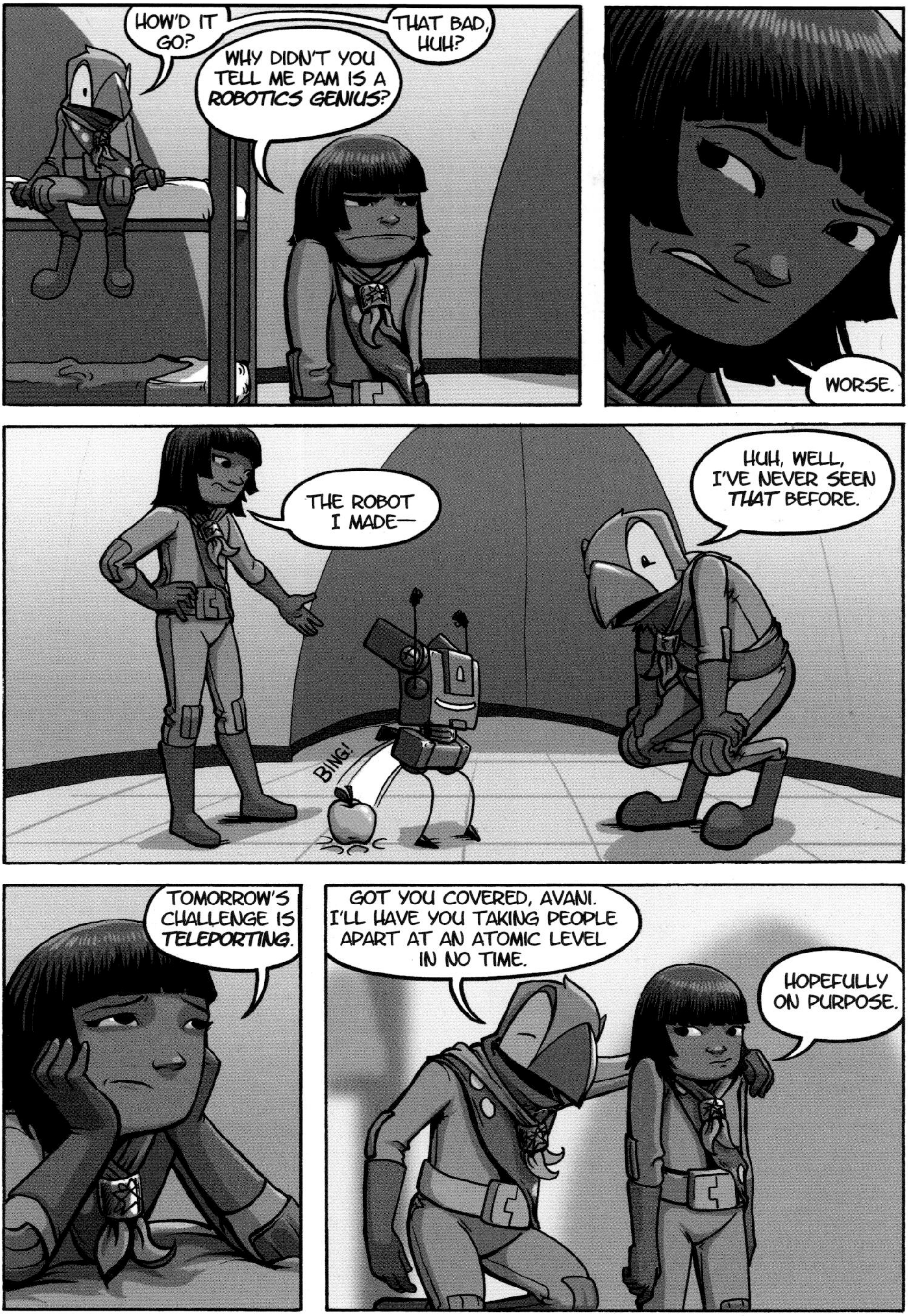
HOW'D IT GO?
THAT BAD, HUH?
WHY DIDN'T YOU TELL ME PAM IS A ROBOTICS GENIUS?
WORSE.
THE ROBOT I MADE—
HUH, WELL, I'VE NEVER SEEN THAT BEFORE.
BING!
TOMORROW'S CHALLENGE IS TELEPORTING.
GOT YOU COVERED, AVANI. I'LL HAVE YOU TAKING PEOPLE APART AT AN ATOMIC LEVEL IN NO TIME.
HOPEFULLY ON PURPOSE.

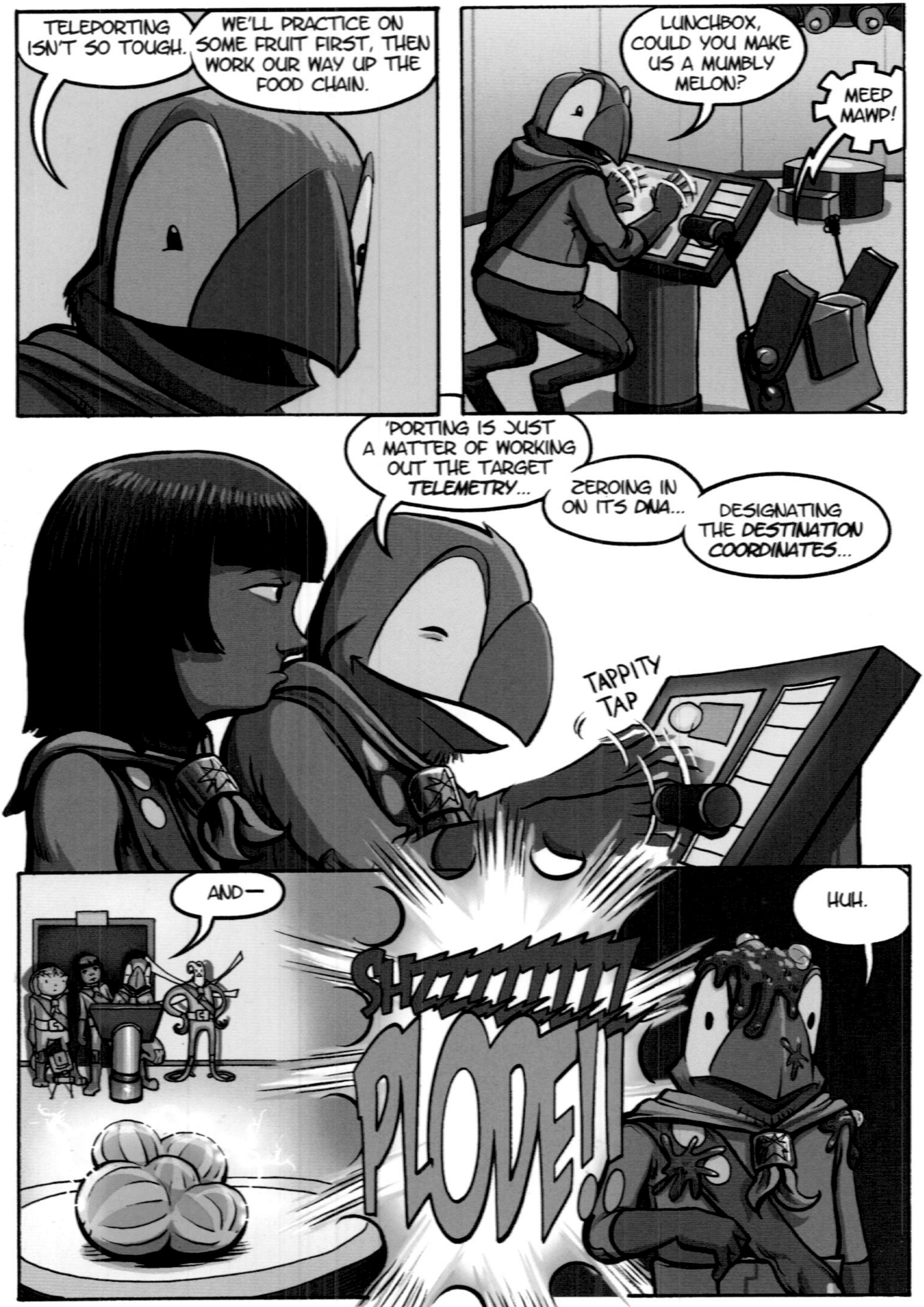
TELEPORTING ISN'T SO TOUGH.
WE'LL PRACTICE ON SOME FRUIT FIRST, THEN WORK OUR WAY UP THE FOOD CHAIN.
LUNCHBOX, COULD YOU MAKE US A MUMBLY MELON?
MEEP MAWP!
'PORTING IS JUST A MATTER OF WORKING OUT THE TARGET TELEMETRY...
ZEROING IN ON IT'S DNA...
DESIGNATING THE DESTINATION COORDINATES...
TAPPITY TAP
AND—
SHZZZZZZZ
PLODE!!
HUH.

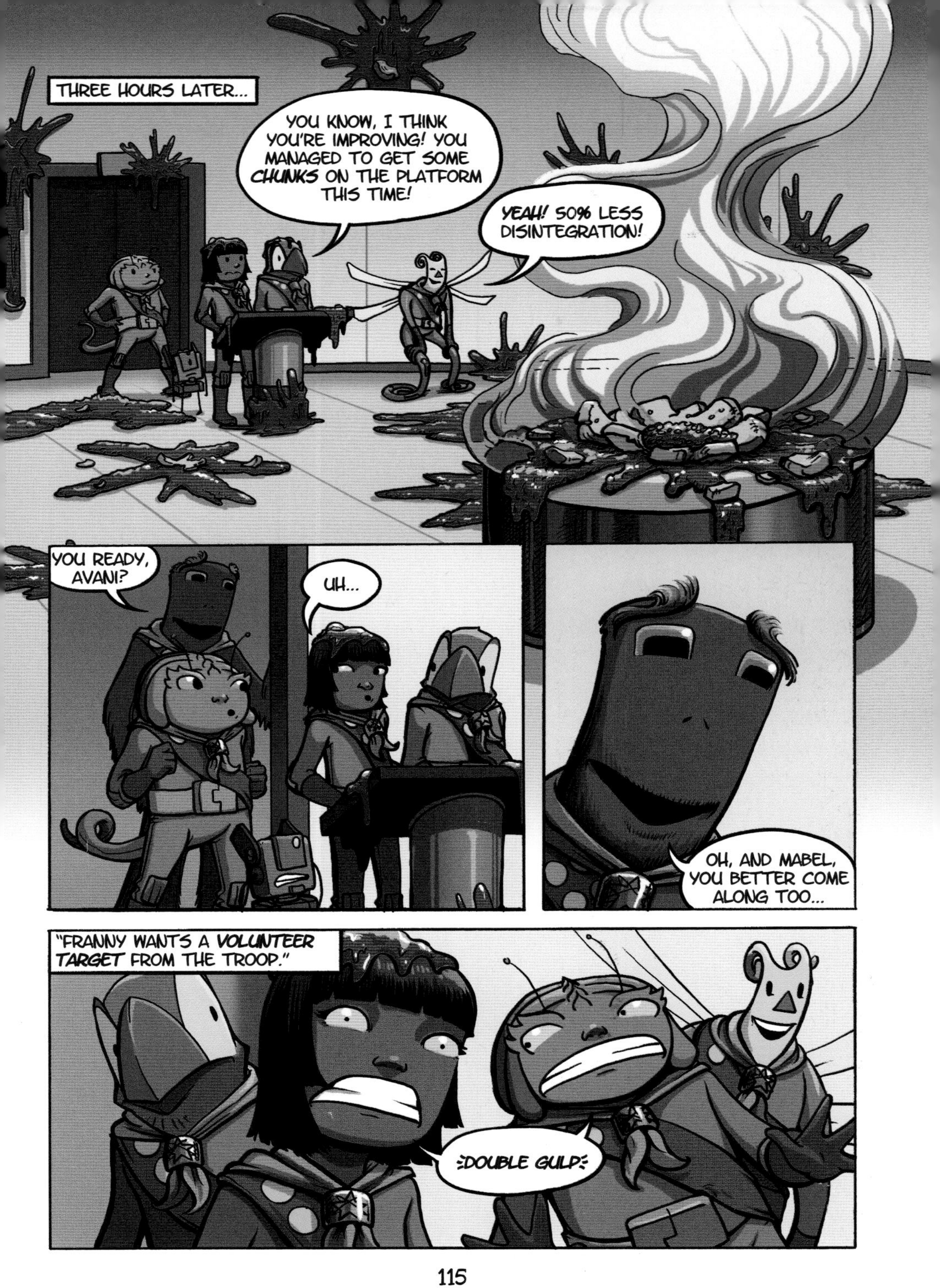
THREE HOURS LATER...
YOU KNOW, I THINK YOU'RE IMPROVING! YOU MANAGED TO GET SOME CHUNKS ON THE PLATFORM THIS TIME!
YEAH! 50% LESS DISINTEGRATION!
YOU READY, AVANI?
UH...
OH, AND MABEL, YOU BETTER COME ALONG TOO...
"FRANNY WANTS A VOLUNTEER TARGET FROM THE TROOP."
DOUBLE GULP

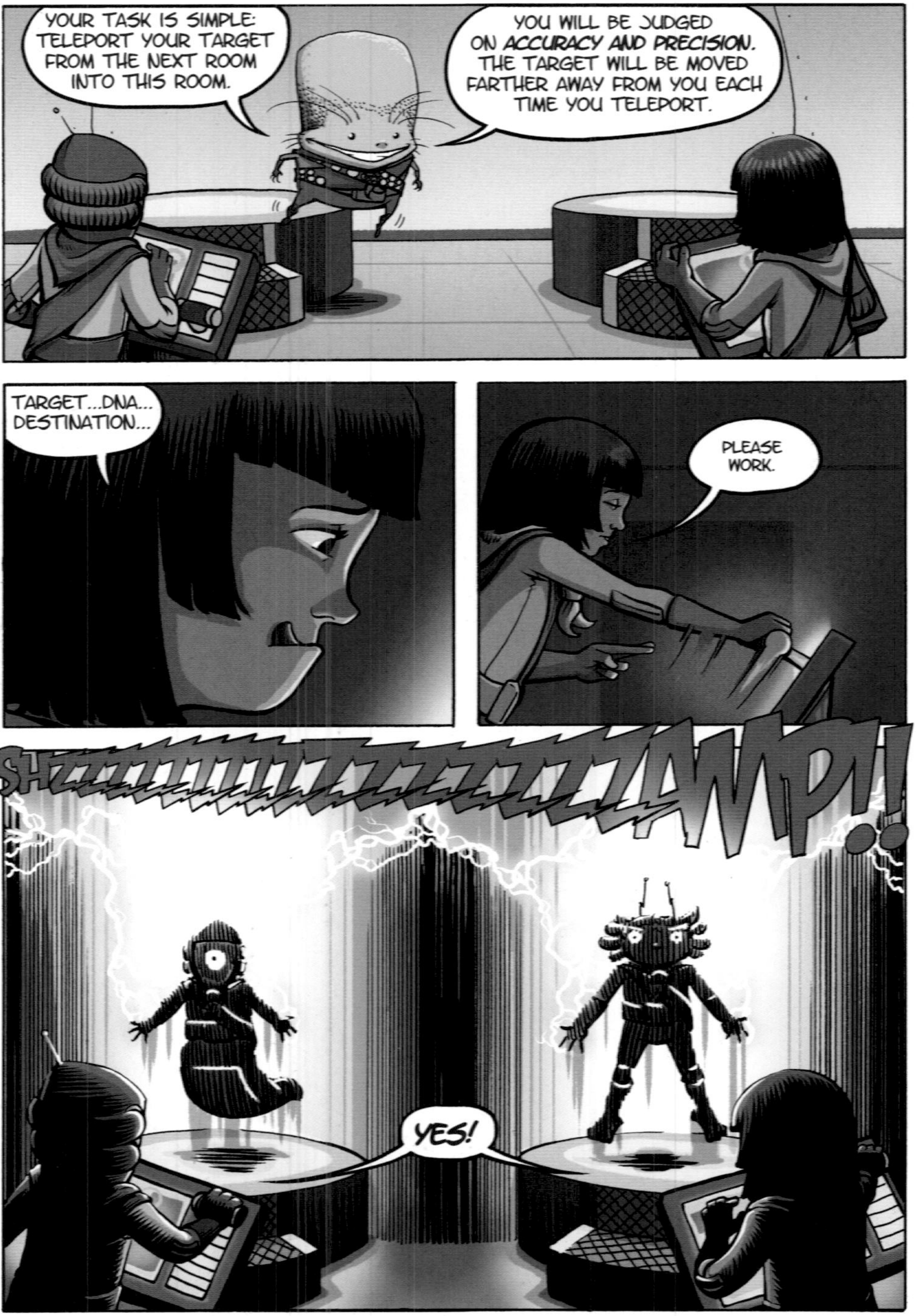
YOUR TASK IS SIMPLE: TELEPORT YOUR TARGET FROM THE NEXT ROOM INTO THIS ROOM.
YOU WILL BE JUDGED ON *ACCURACY AND PRECISION*. THE TARGET WILL BE MOVED FARTHER AWAY FROM YOU EACH TIME YOU TELEPORT.
TARGET...DNA... DESTINATION...
PLEASE WORK.
SHZZZTTTTTZZZZZZZZZZZZZAWP!!
YES!

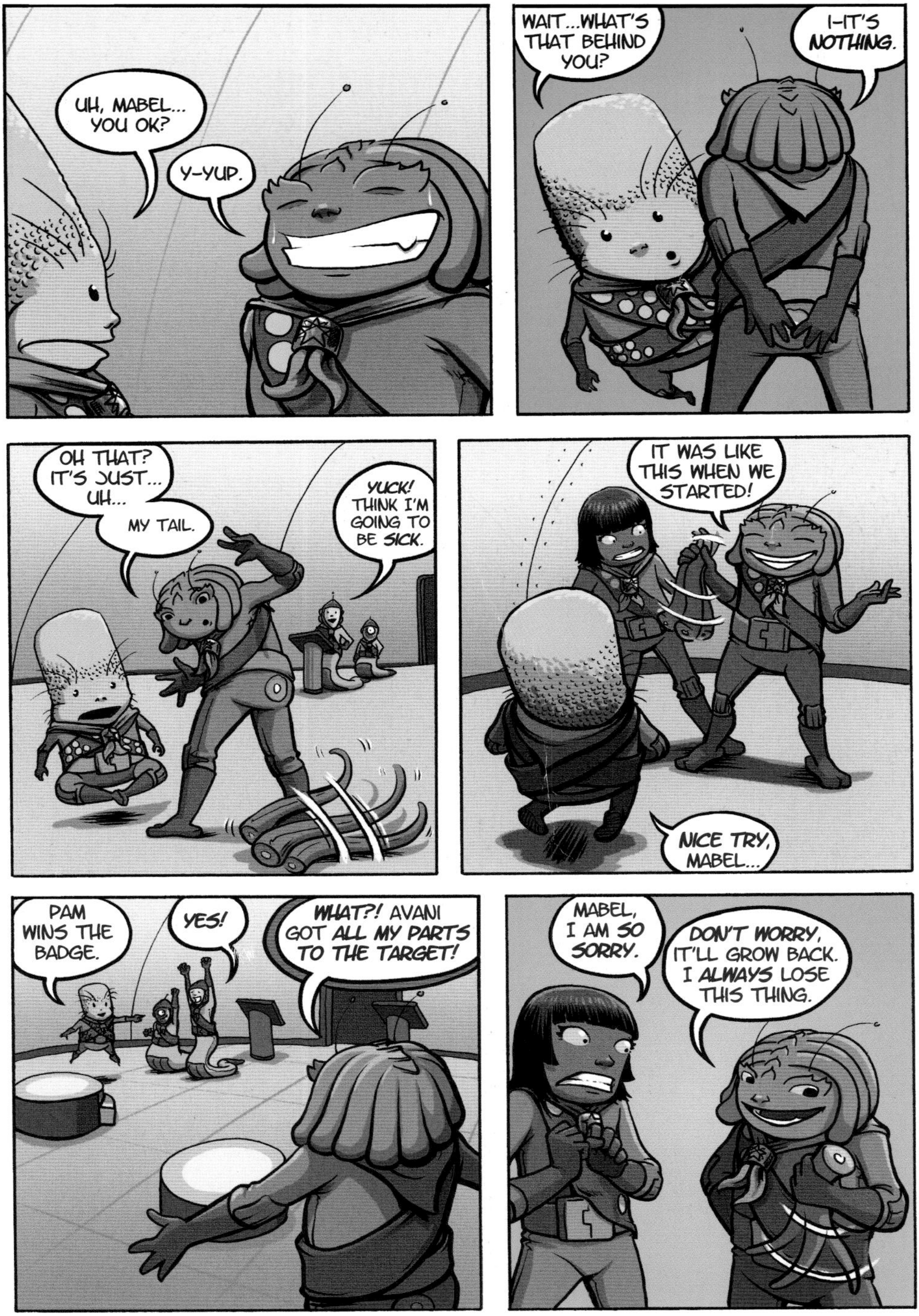
UH, MABEL... YOU OK?
Y-YUP.
WAIT...WHAT'S THAT BEHIND YOU?
I-IT'S NOTHING.
OH THAT? IT'S JUST... UH...
MY TAIL.
YUCK! THINK I'M GOING TO BE SICK.
IT WAS LIKE THIS WHEN WE STARTED!
NICE TRY, MABEL...
PAM WINS THE BADGE.
YES!
WHAT?! AVANI GOT ALL MY PARTS TO THE TARGET!
MABEL, I AM SO SORRY.
DON'T WORRY, IT'LL GROW BACK. I ALWAYS LOSE THIS THING.

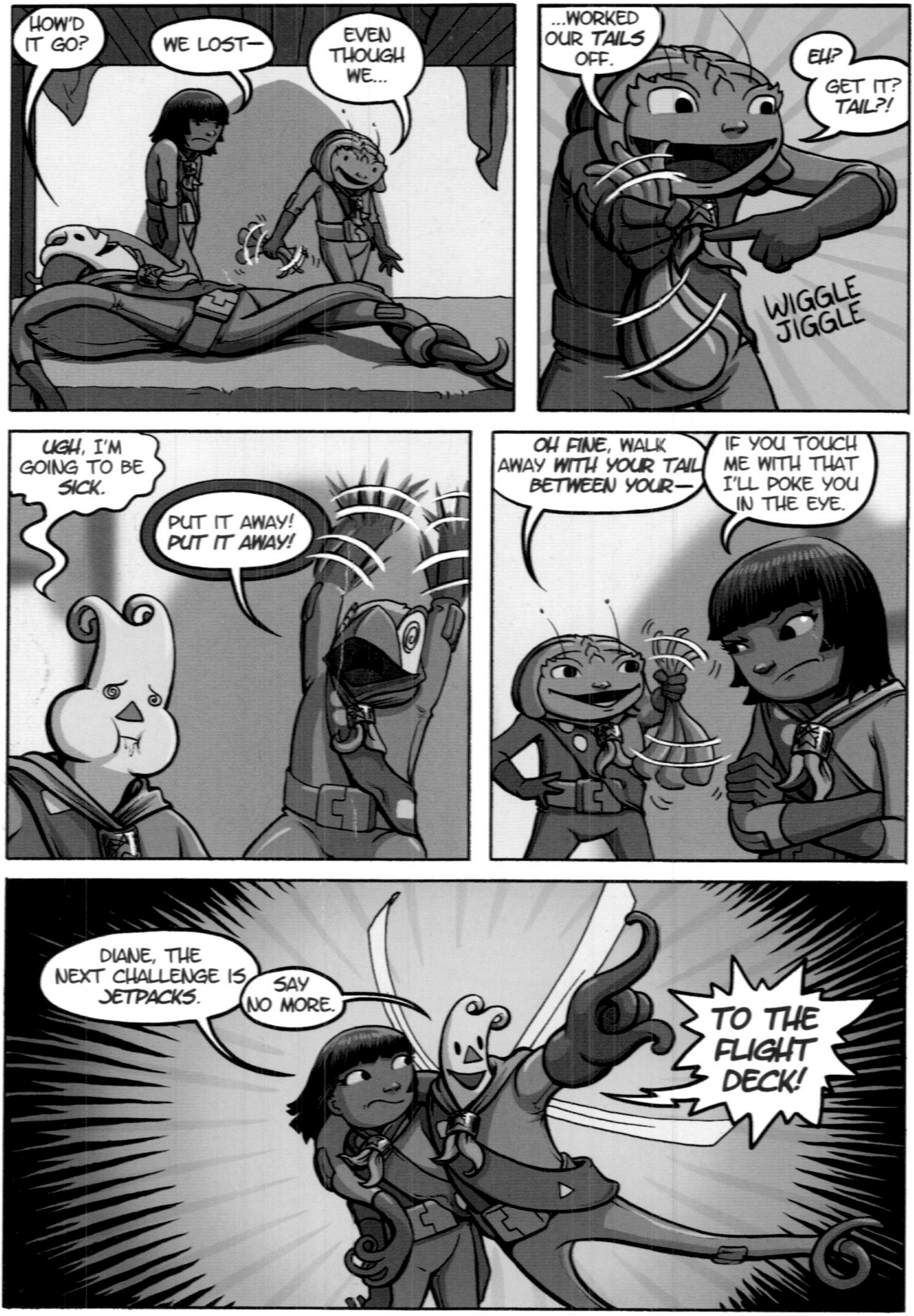
HOW'D IT GO?
WE LOST—
EVEN THOUGH WE...
...WORKED OUR TAILS OFF.
EH?
GET IT? TAIL?!
WIGGLE JIGGLE
UGH, I'M GOING TO BE SICK.
PUT IT AWAY! PUT IT AWAY!
OH FINE, WALK AWAY WITH YOUR TAIL BETWEEN YOUR—
IF YOU TOUCH ME WITH THAT I'LL POKE YOU IN THE EYE.
DIANE, THE NEXT CHALLENGE IS JETPACKS.
SAY NO MORE.
TO THE FLIGHT DECK!

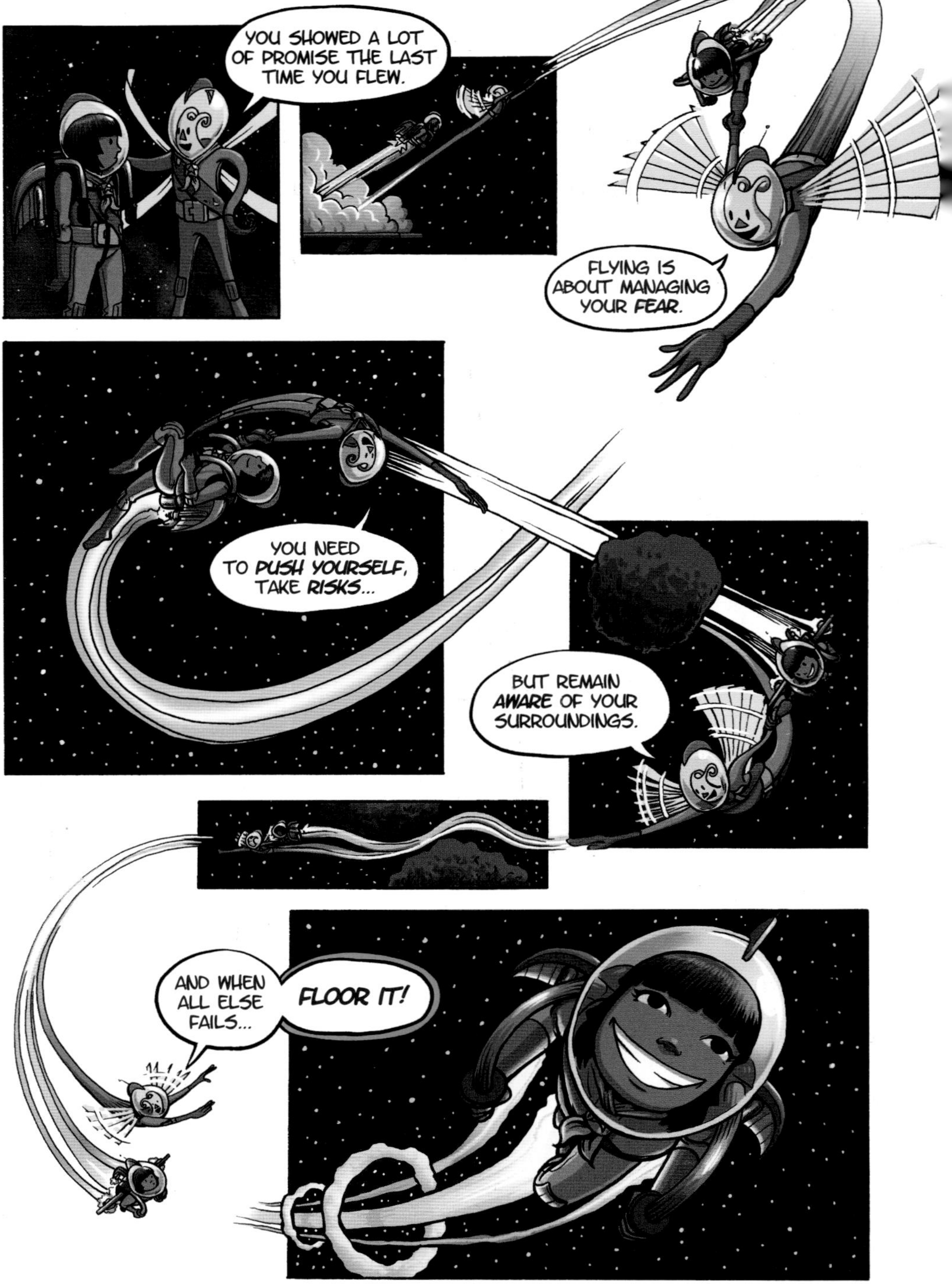
YOU SHOWED A LOT OF PROMISE THE LAST TIME YOU FLEW.
FLYING IS ABOUT MANAGING YOUR FEAR.
YOU NEED TO PUSH YOURSELF, TAKE RISKS...
BUT REMAIN AWARE OF YOUR SURROUNDINGS.
AND WHEN ALL ELSE FAILS...
FLOOR IT!

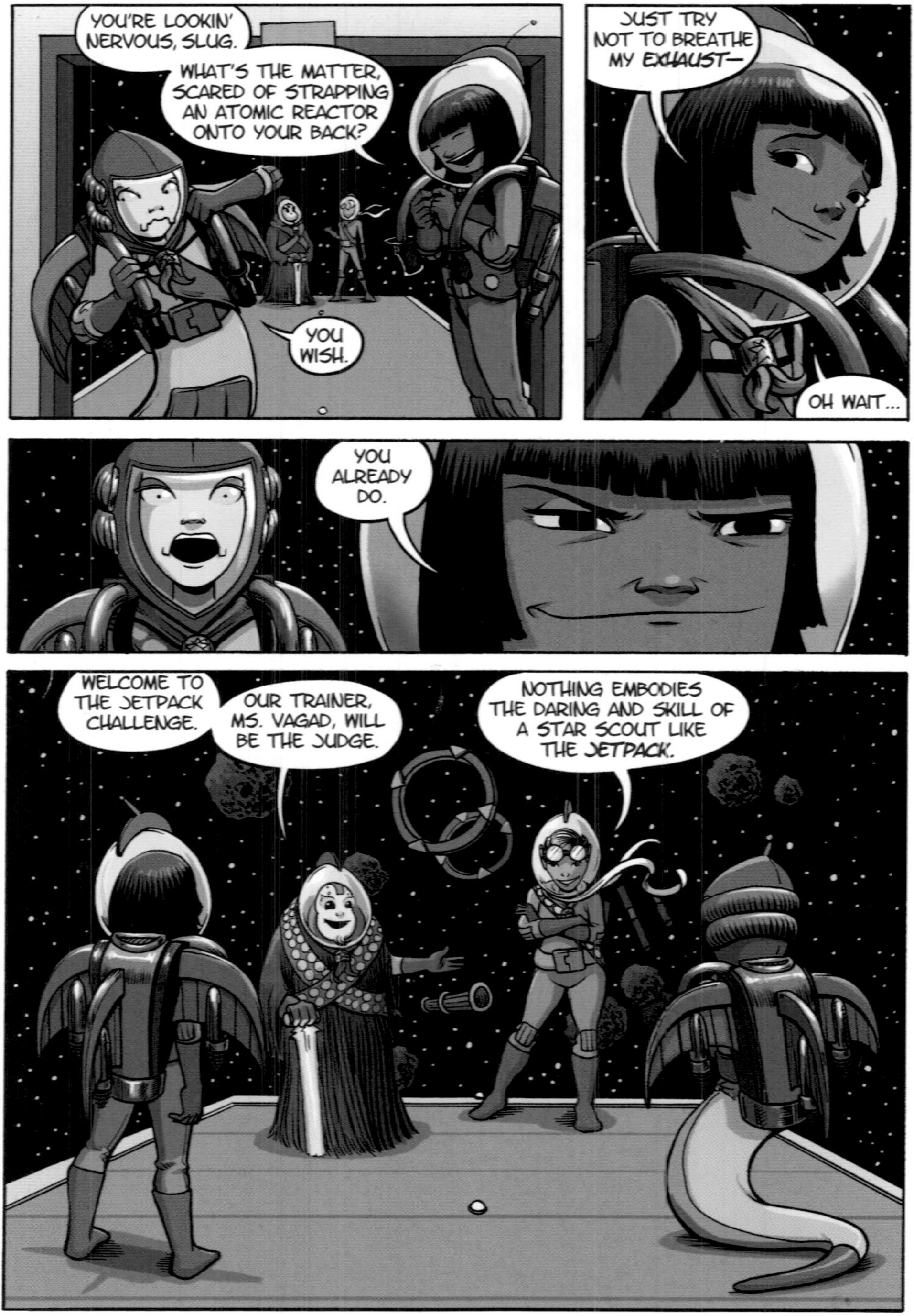
YOU'RE LOOKIN' NERVOUS, SLUG.
WHAT'S THE MATTER, SCARED OF STRAPPING AN ATOMIC REACTOR ONTO YOUR BACK?
YOU WISH.
JUST TRY NOT TO BREATHE MY EXHAUST—
OH WAIT...
YOU ALREADY DO.
WELCOME TO THE JETPACK CHALLENGE.
OUR TRAINER, MS. VAGAD, WILL BE THE JUDGE.
NOTHING EMBODIES THE DARING AND SKILL OF A STAR SCOUT LIKE THE JETPACK.

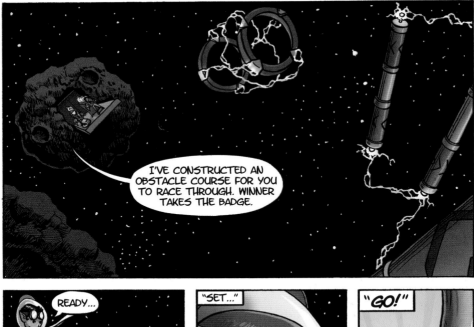

I'VE CONSTRUCTED AN OBSTACLE COURSE FOR YOU TO RACE THROUGH. WINNER TAKES THE BADGE.

READY...

"SET..."

"GO!"

CLICK!

FWOOSH!!

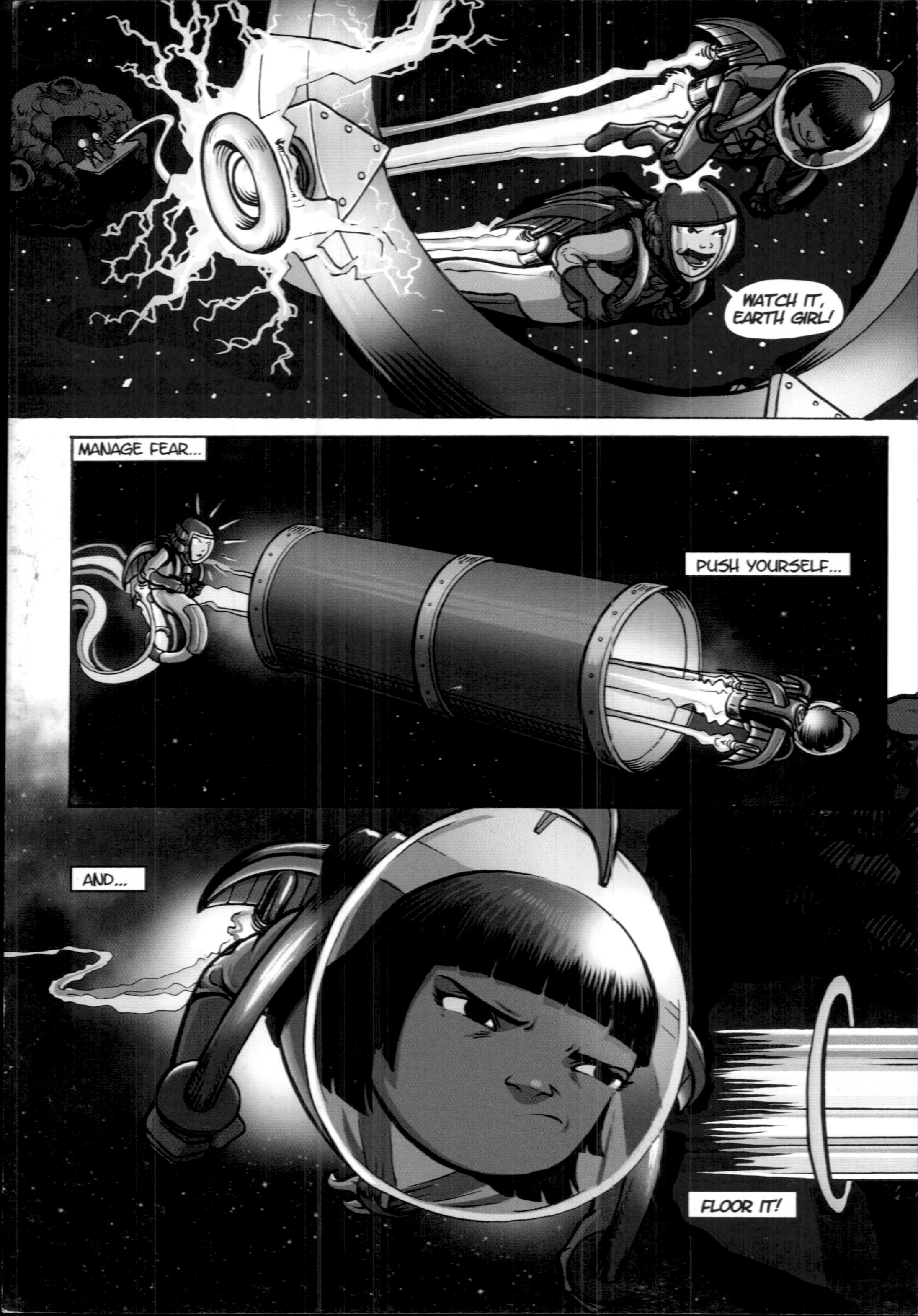
WATCH IT, EARTH GIRL!
MANAGE FEAR...
PUSH YOURSELF...
AND...
FLOOR IT!

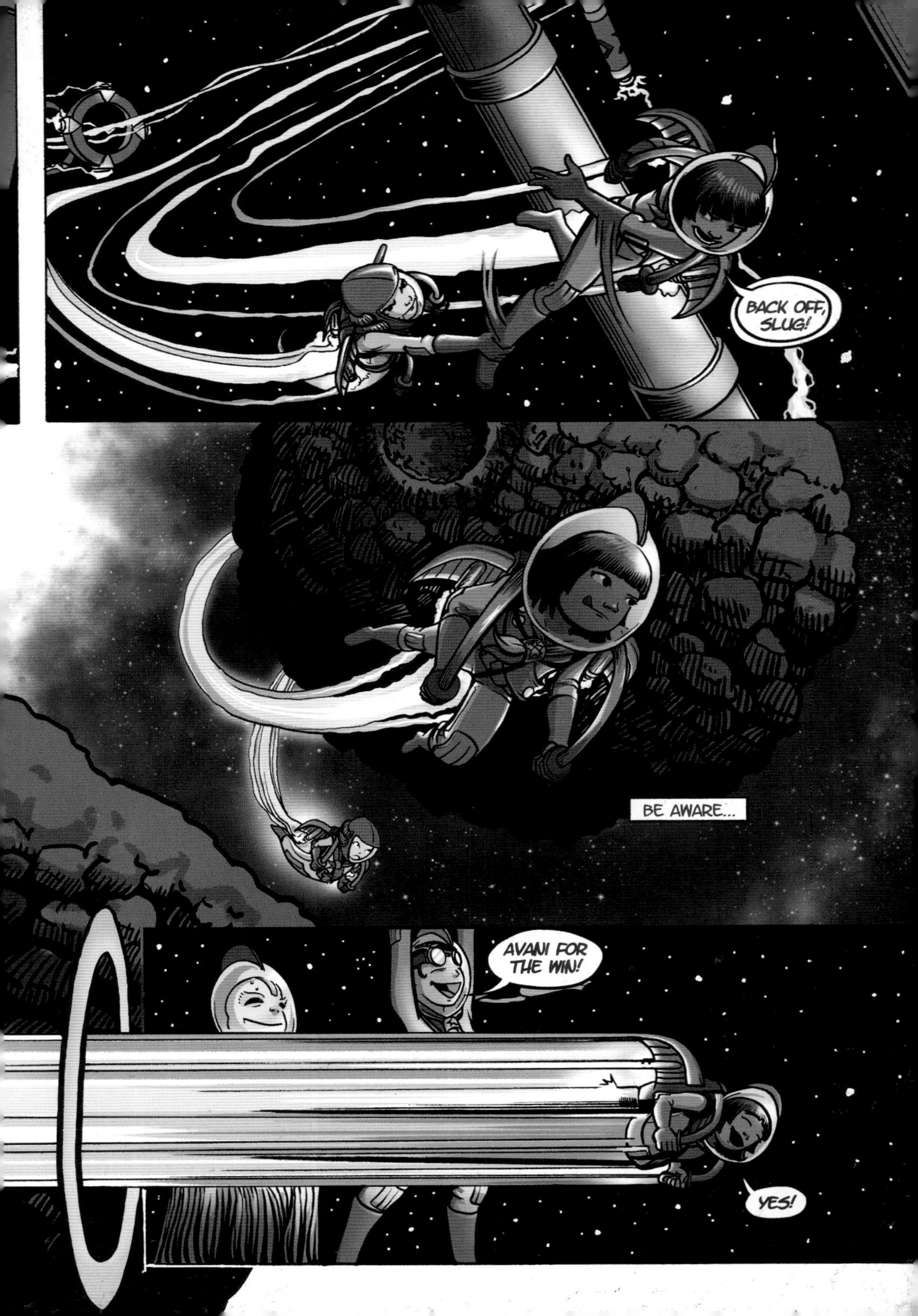
BACK OFF, SLUG!
BE AWARE...
AVANI FOR THE WIN!
YES!

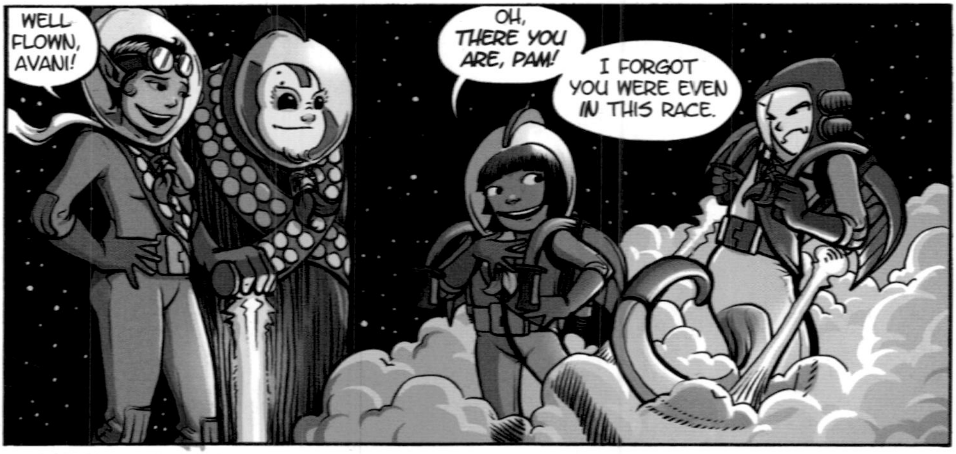
WELL FLOWN, AVANI!
OH, THERE YOU ARE, PAM!
I FORGOT YOU WERE EVEN IN THIS RACE.

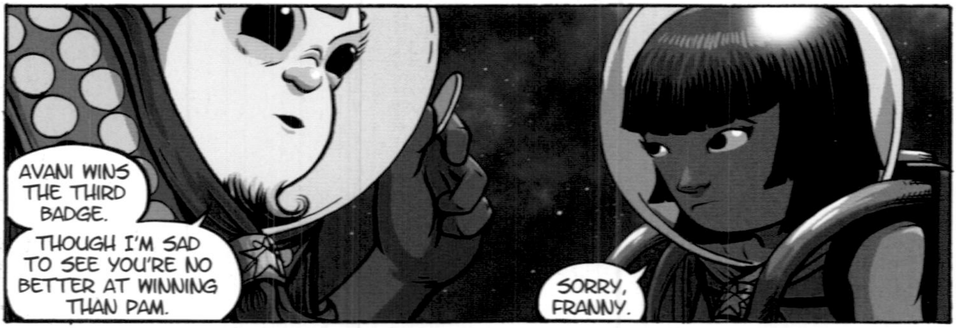
AVANI WINS THE THIRD BADGE.
THOUGH I'M SAD TO SEE YOU'RE NO BETTER AT WINNING THAN PAM.
SORRY, FRANNY.

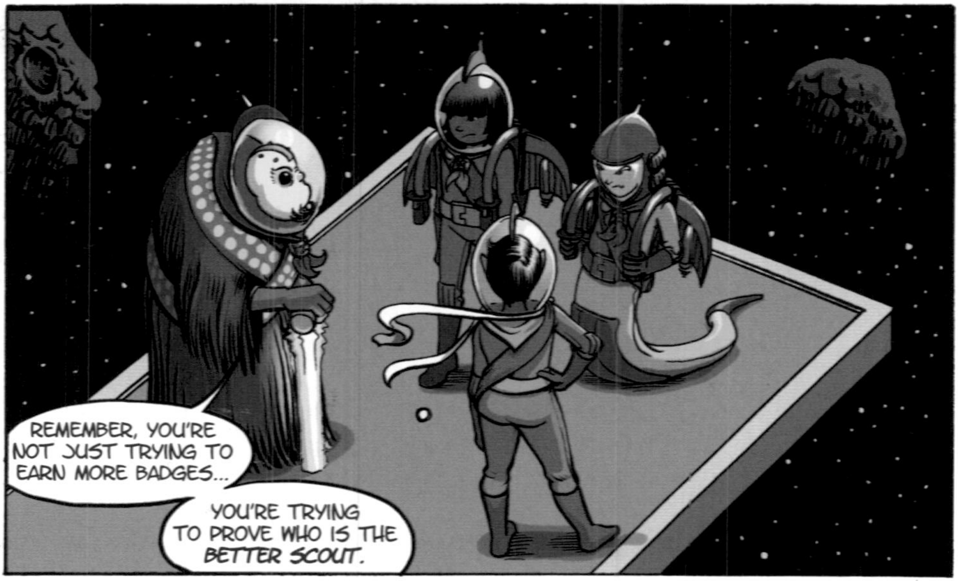
REMEMBER, YOU'RE NOT JUST TRYING TO EARN MORE BADGES...
YOU'RE TRYING TO PROVE WHO IS THE BETTER SCOUT.

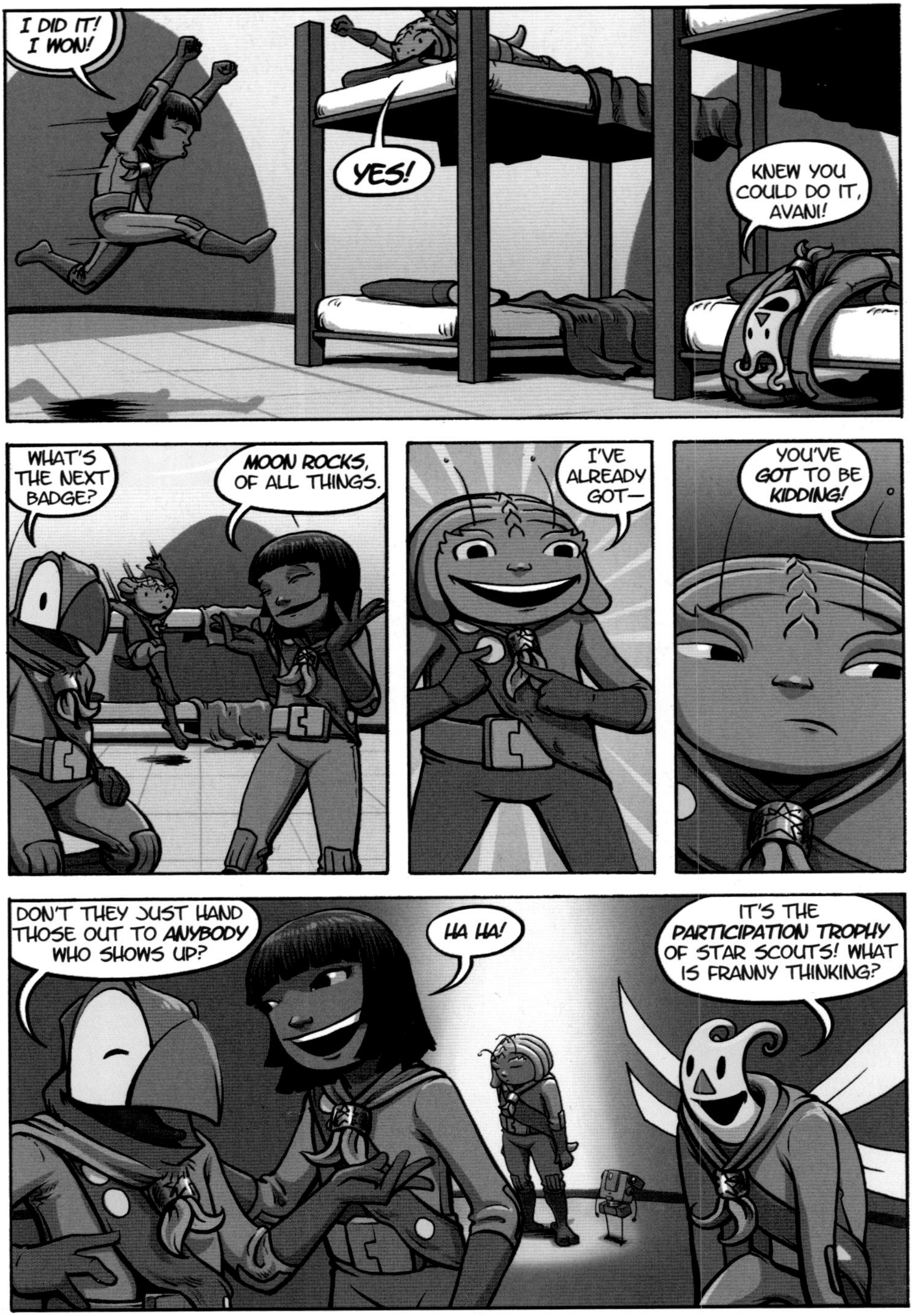
I DID IT! I WON!
YES!
KNEW YOU COULD DO IT, AVANI!
WHAT'S THE NEXT BADGE?
MOON ROCKS, OF ALL THINGS.
I'VE ALREADY GOT—
YOU'VE GOT TO BE KIDDING!
DON'T THEY JUST HAND THOSE OUT TO ANYBODY WHO SHOWS UP?
HA HA!
IT'S THE PARTICIPATION TROPHY OF STAR SCOUTS! WHAT IS FRANNY THINKING?

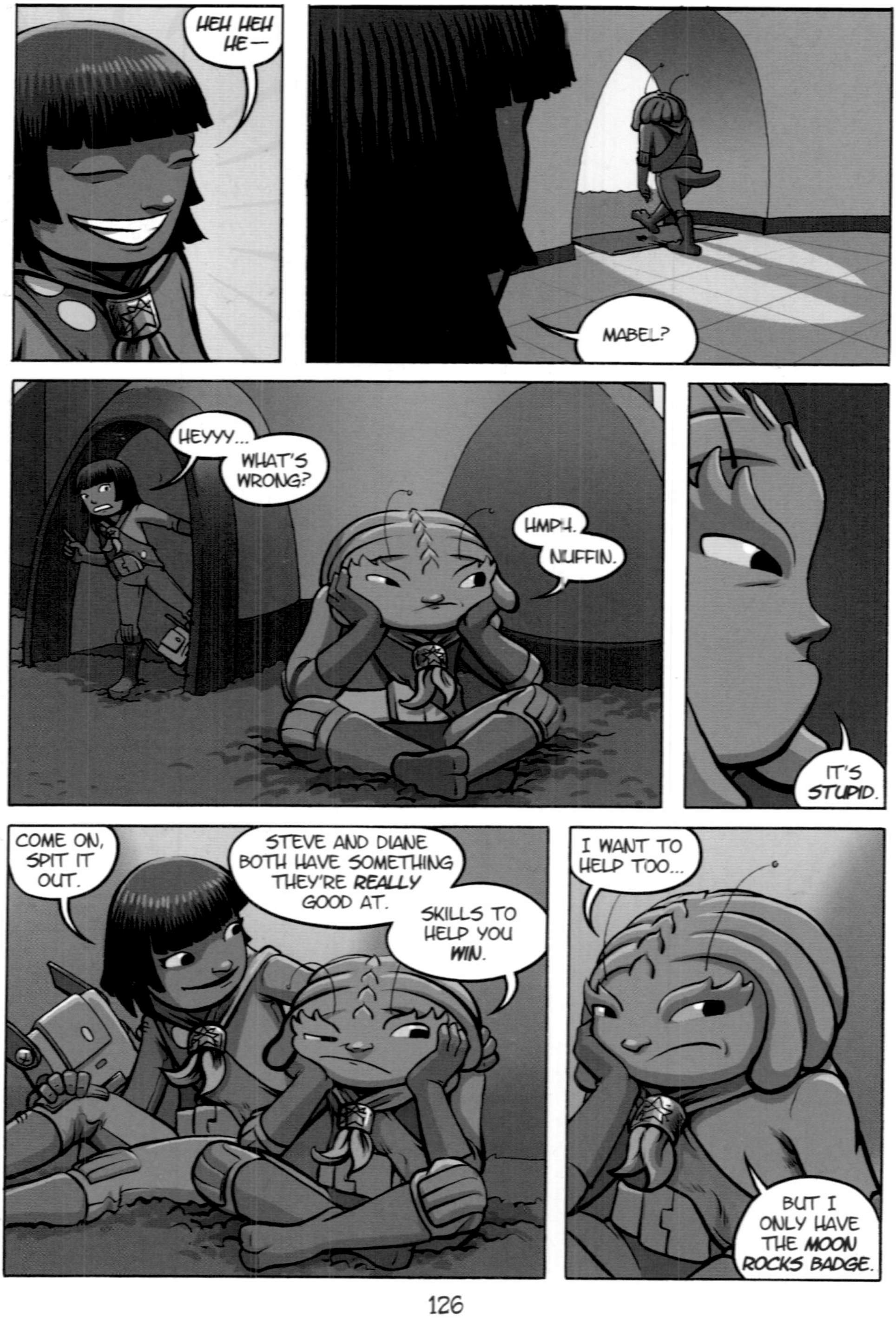
HEH HEH HE—
MABEL?
HEYYY... WHAT'S WRONG?
HMPH. NUFFIN.
IT'S STUPID.
COME ON, SPIT IT OUT.
STEVE AND DIANE BOTH HAVE SOMETHING THEY'RE REALLY GOOD AT.
SKILLS TO HELP YOU WIN.
I WANT TO HELP TOO...
BUT I ONLY HAVE THE MOON ROCKS BADGE.

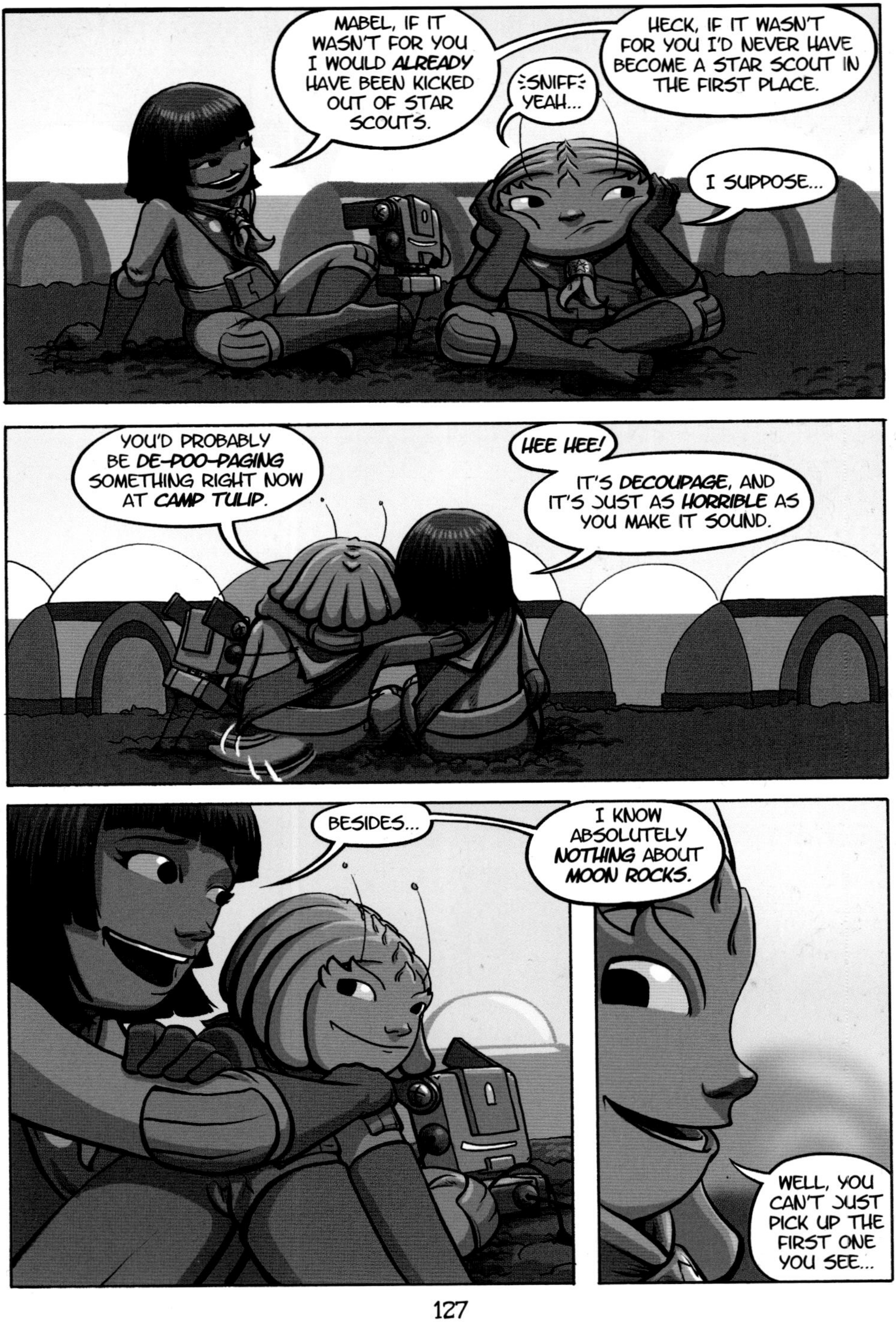
MABEL, IF IT WASN'T FOR YOU I WOULD ALREADY HAVE BEEN KICKED OUT OF STAR SCOUTS.
HECK, IF IT WASN'T FOR YOU I'D NEVER HAVE BECOME A STAR SCOUT IN THE FIRST PLACE.
SNIFF YEAH...
I SUPPOSE...
YOU'D PROBABLY BE DE-POO-PAGING SOMETHING RIGHT NOW AT CAMP TULIP.
HEE HEE!
IT'S DECOUPAGE, AND IT'S JUST AS HORRIBLE AS YOU MAKE IT SOUND.
BESIDES...
I KNOW ABSOLUTELY NOTHING ABOUT MOON ROCKS.
WELL, YOU CAN'T JUST PICK UP THE FIRST ONE YOU SEE...

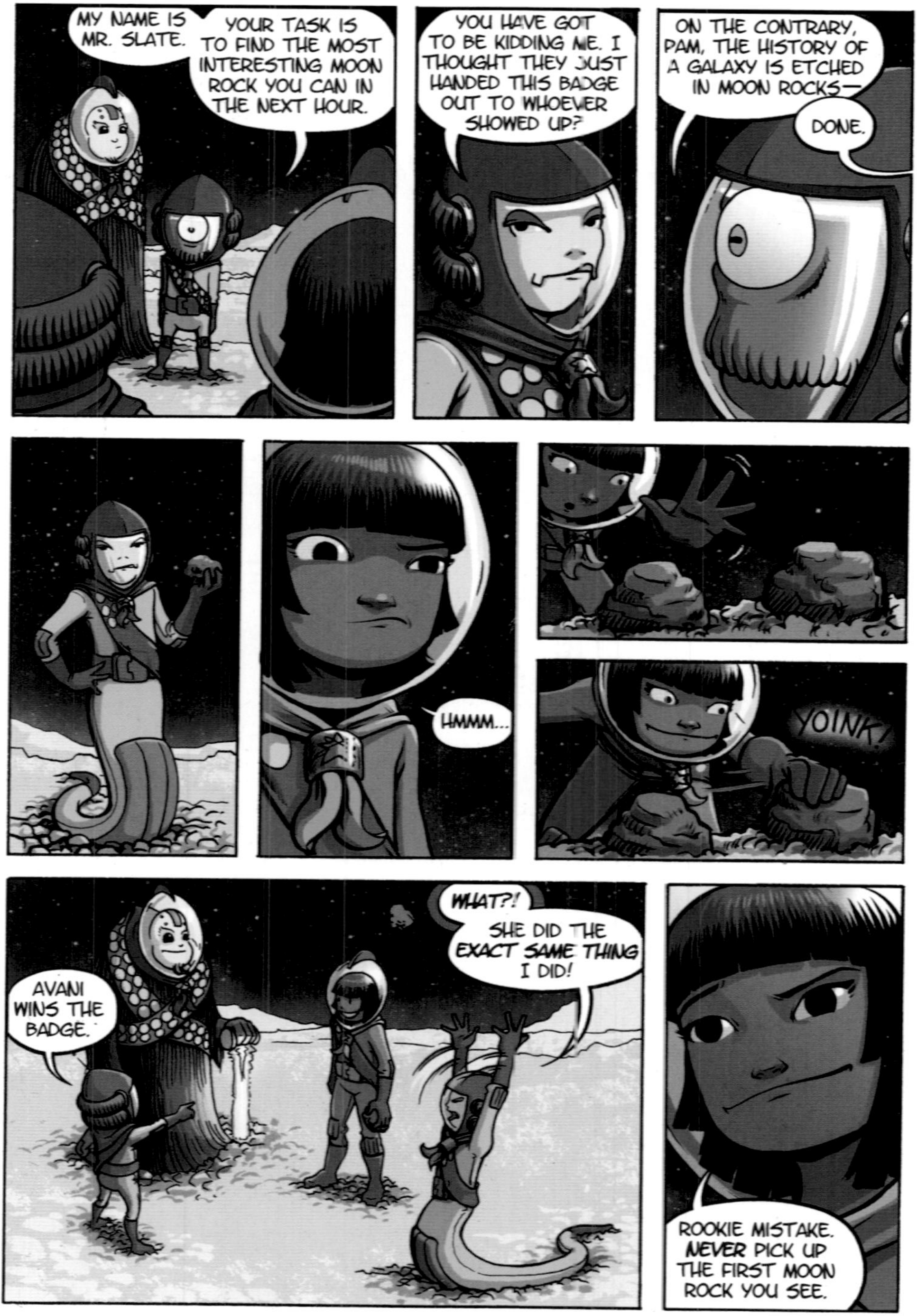
MY NAME IS MR. SLATE.
YOUR TASK IS TO FIND THE MOST INTERESTING MOON ROCK YOU CAN IN THE NEXT HOUR.
YOU HAVE GOT TO BE KIDDING ME. I THOUGHT THEY JUST HANDED THIS BADGE OUT TO WHOEVER SHOWED UP?
ON THE CONTRARY, PAM, THE HISTORY OF A GALAXY IS ETCHED IN MOON ROCKS—
DONE.
HMMM...
YOINK!
AVANI WINS THE BADGE.
WHAT?!
SHE DID THE **EXACT SAME THING** I DID!
ROOKIE MISTAKE. **NEVER** PICK UP THE FIRST MOON ROCK YOU SEE.

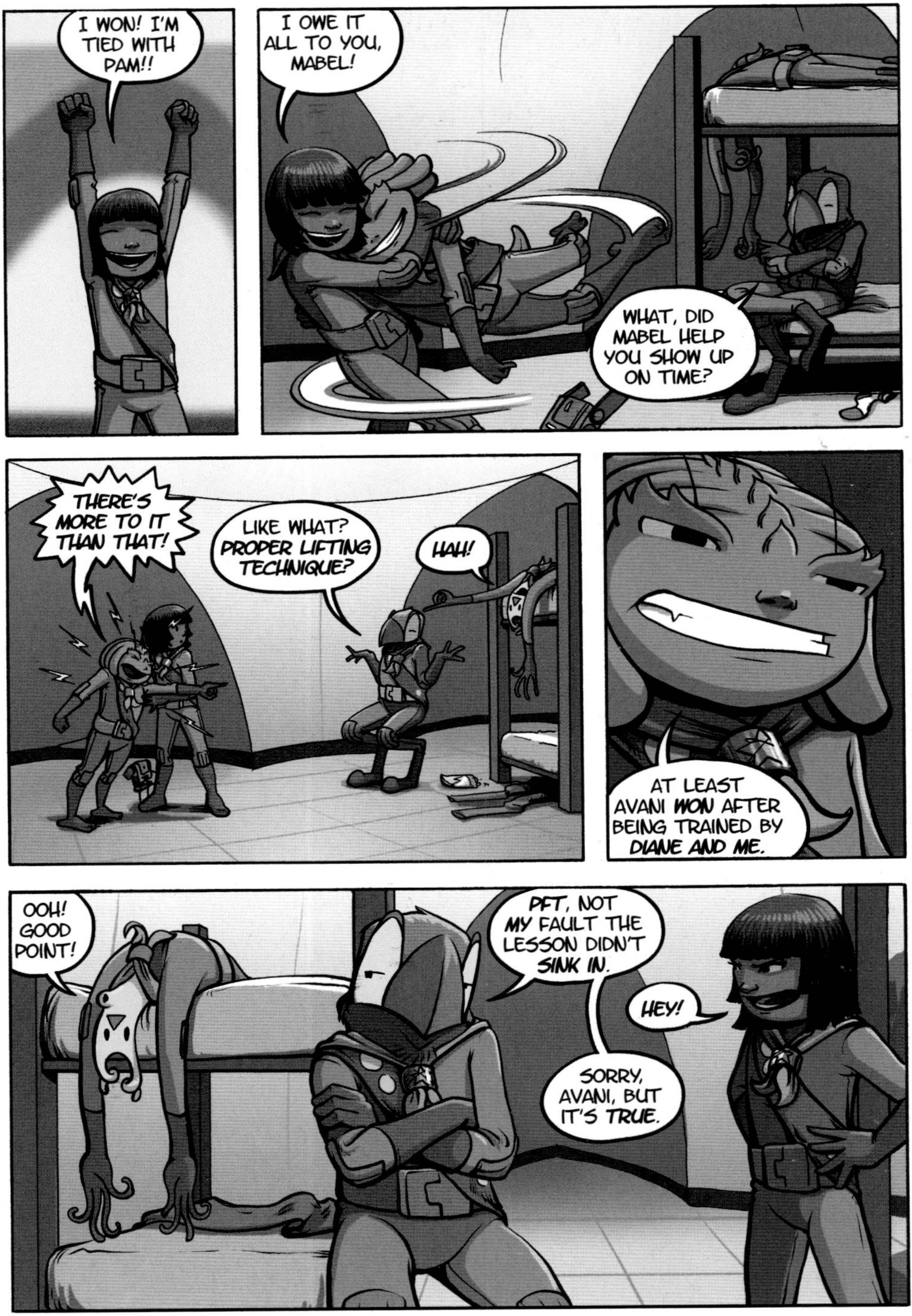
I WON! I'M TIED WITH PAM!!
I OWE IT ALL TO YOU, MABEL!
WHAT, DID MABEL HELP YOU SHOW UP ON TIME?
THERE'S MORE TO IT THAN THAT!
LIKE WHAT? PROPER LIFTING TECHNIQUE?
HAH!
AT LEAST AVANI WON AFTER BEING TRAINED BY DIANE AND ME.
OOH! GOOD POINT!
PFT, NOT MY FAULT THE LESSON DIDN'T SINK IN.
HEY!
SORRY, AVANI, BUT IT'S TRUE.

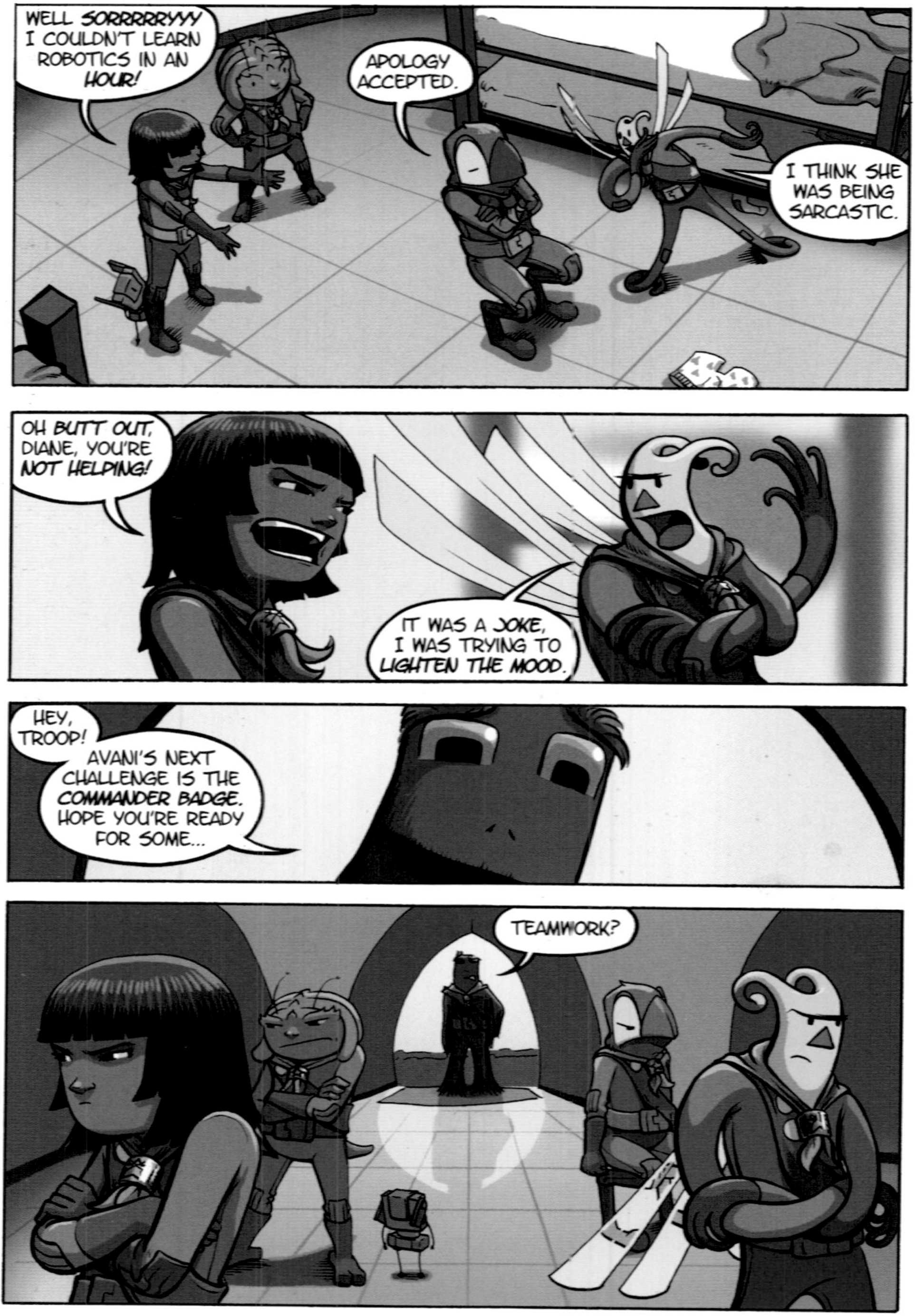
WELL SORRRRRYYY I COULDN'T LEARN ROBOTICS IN AN HOUR!
APOLOGY ACCEPTED.
I THINK SHE WAS BEING SARCASTIC.
OH BUTT OUT, DIANE, YOU'RE NOT HELPING!
IT WAS A JOKE, I WAS TRYING TO LIGHTEN THE MOOD.
HEY, TROOP!
AVANI'S NEXT CHALLENGE IS THE COMMANDER BADGE. HOPE YOU'RE READY FOR SOME...
TEAMWORK?

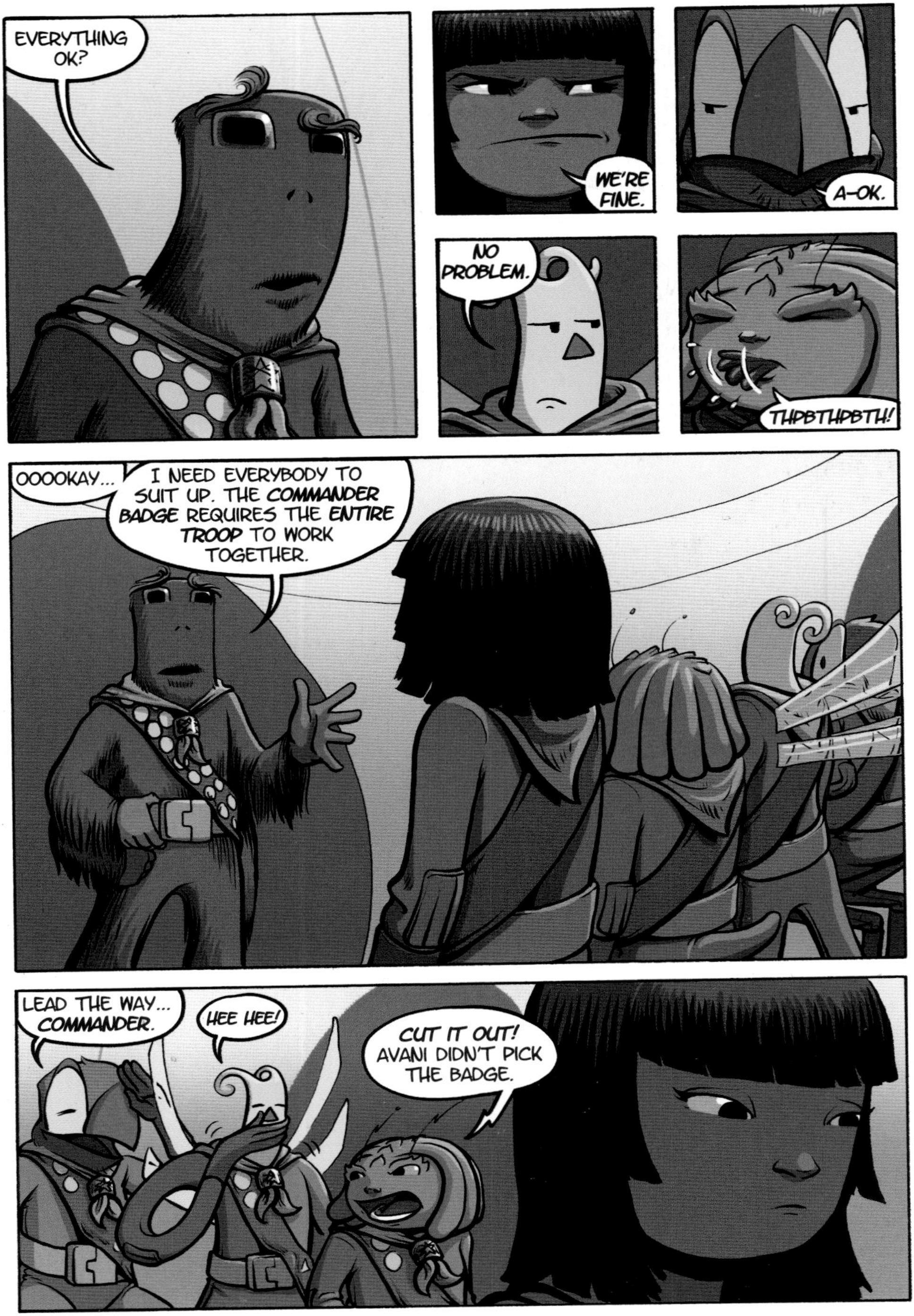
EVERYTHING OK?
WE'RE FINE.
A-OK.
NO PROBLEM.
THPBTHPBTH!
OOOOKAY...
I NEED EVERYBODY TO SUIT UP. THE COMMANDER BADGE REQUIRES THE ENTIRE TROOP TO WORK TOGETHER.
LEAD THE WAY... COMMANDER.
HEE HEE!
CUT IT OUT! AVANI DIDN'T PICK THE BADGE.

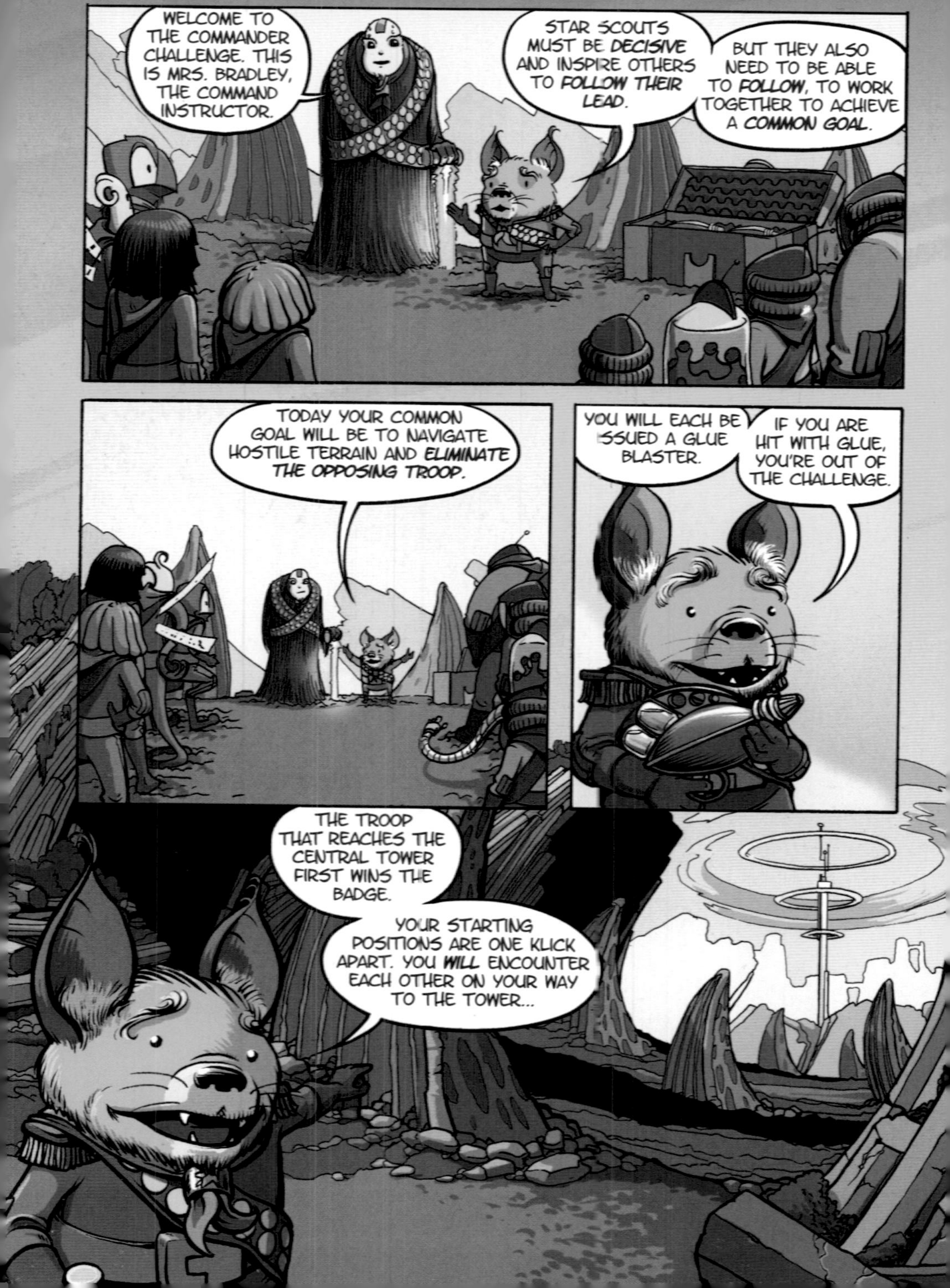
WELCOME TO THE COMMANDER CHALLENGE. THIS IS MRS. BRADLEY, THE COMMAND INSTRUCTOR.
STAR SCOUTS MUST BE *DECISIVE* AND INSPIRE OTHERS TO *FOLLOW THEIR LEAD*.
BUT THEY ALSO NEED TO BE ABLE TO *FOLLOW*, TO WORK TOGETHER TO ACHIEVE A *COMMON GOAL*.
TODAY YOUR COMMON GOAL WILL BE TO NAVIGATE HOSTILE TERRAIN AND *ELIMINATE THE OPPOSING TROOP*.
YOU WILL EACH BE ISSUED A GLUE BLASTER.
IF YOU ARE HIT WITH GLUE, YOU'RE OUT OF THE CHALLENGE.
THE TROOP THAT REACHES THE CENTRAL TOWER FIRST WINS THE BADGE.
YOUR STARTING POSITIONS ARE ONE KLICK APART. YOU *WILL* ENCOUNTER EACH OTHER ON YOUR WAY TO THE TOWER...

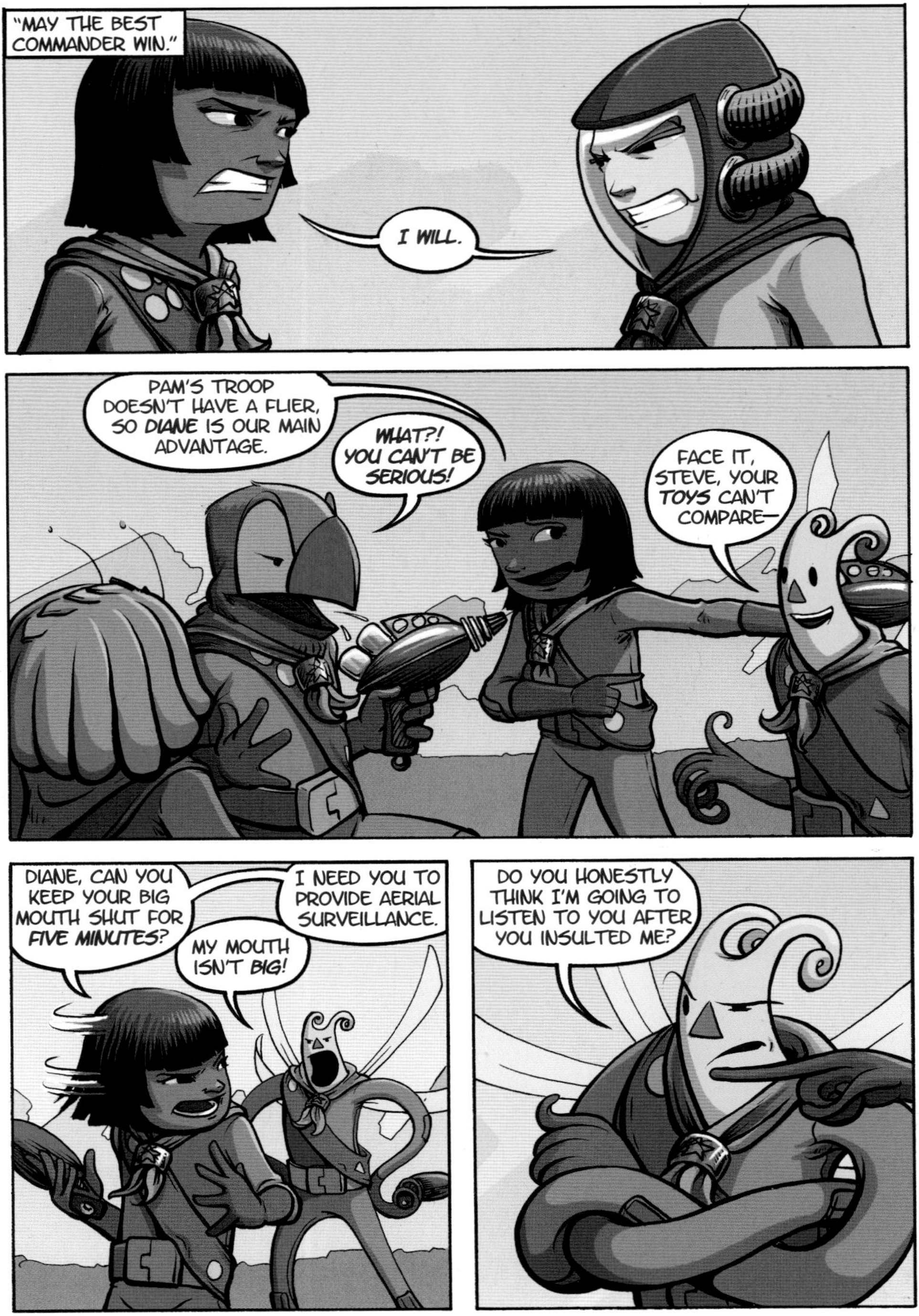
"MAY THE BEST COMMANDER WIN."
I WILL.
PAM'S TROOP DOESN'T HAVE A FLIER, SO DIANE IS OUR MAIN ADVANTAGE.
WHAT?! YOU CAN'T BE SERIOUS!
FACE IT, STEVE, YOUR TOYS CAN'T COMPARE—
DIANE, CAN YOU KEEP YOUR BIG MOUTH SHUT FOR FIVE MINUTES?
I NEED YOU TO PROVIDE AERIAL SURVEILLANCE.
MY MOUTH ISN'T BIG!
DO YOU HONESTLY THINK I'M GOING TO LISTEN TO YOU AFTER YOU INSULTED ME?

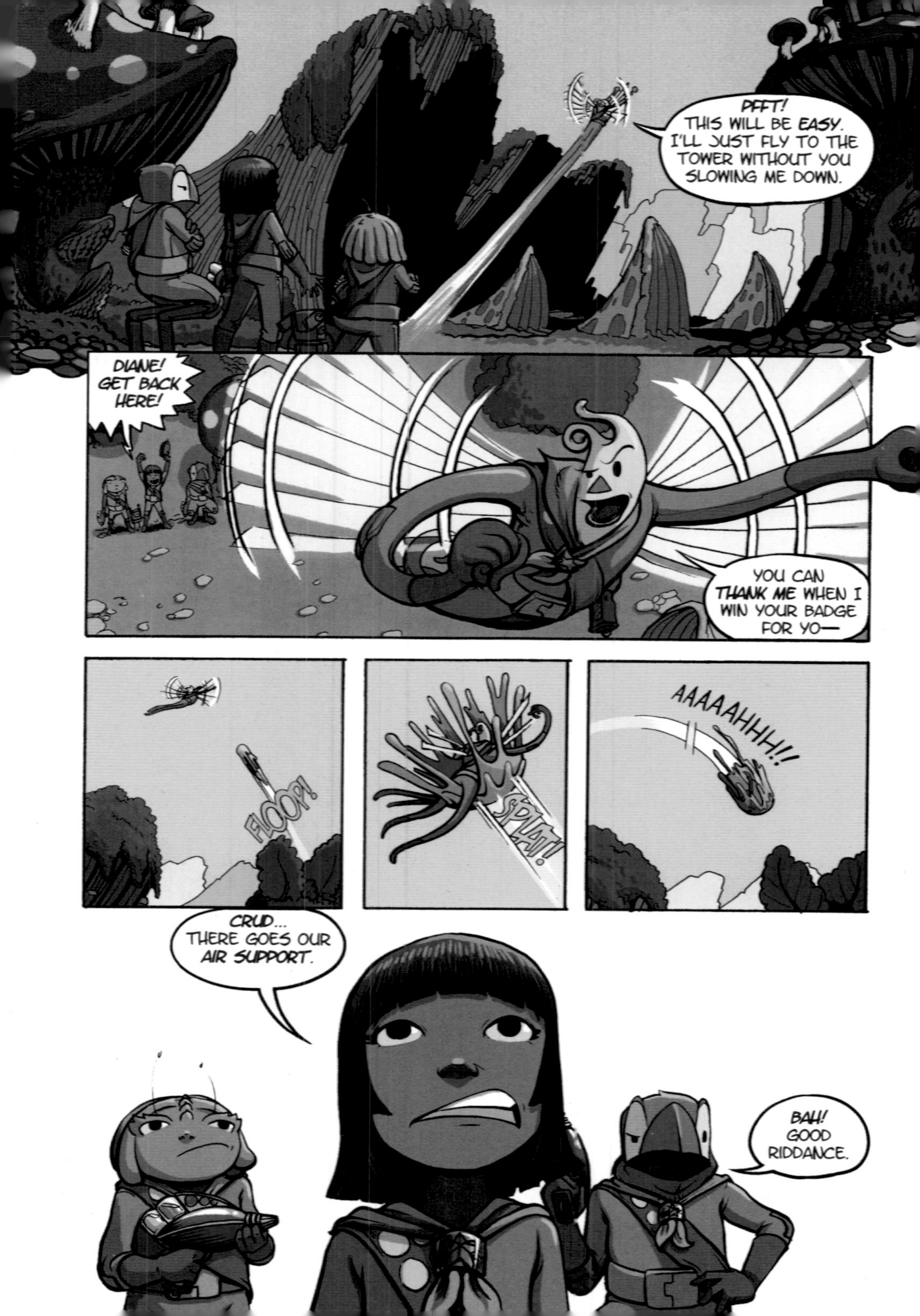
PFFT!
THIS WILL BE EASY. I'LL JUST FLY TO THE TOWER WITHOUT YOU SLOWING ME DOWN.
DIANE! GET BACK HERE!
YOU CAN THANK ME WHEN I WIN YOUR BADGE FOR YO—
FLOOP!
SPLAT!
AAAAAHHH!!
CRUD... THERE GOES OUR AIR SUPPORT.
BAH! GOOD RIDDANCE.

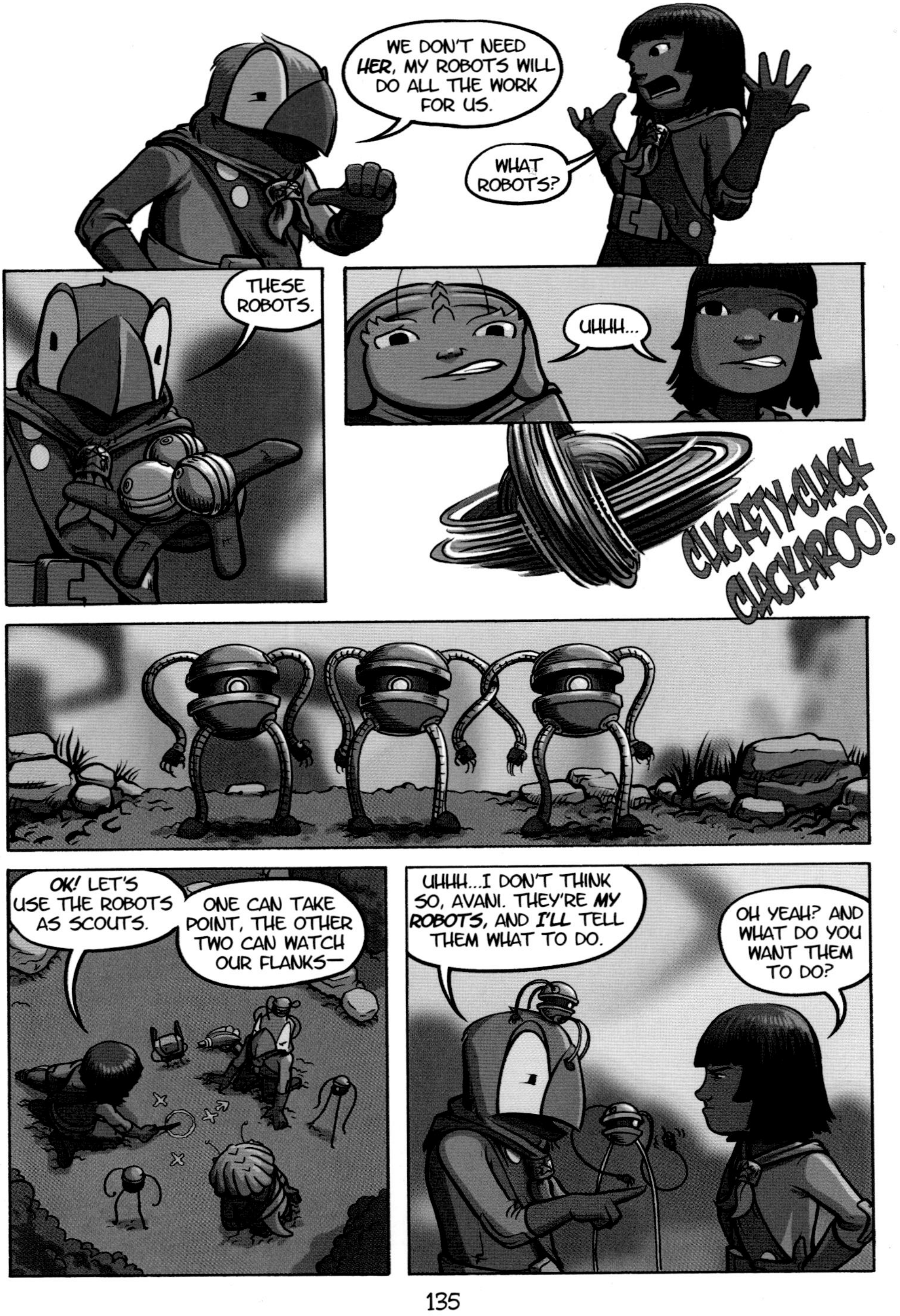
WE DON'T NEED HER, MY ROBOTS WILL DO ALL THE WORK FOR US.
WHAT ROBOTS?
THESE ROBOTS.
UHHH...
CLICKETY-CLACK CLACKAROO!
OK! LET'S USE THE ROBOTS AS SCOUTS.
ONE CAN TAKE POINT, THE OTHER TWO CAN WATCH OUR FLANKS—
UHHH...I DON'T THINK SO, AVANI. THEY'RE MY ROBOTS, AND I'LL TELL THEM WHAT TO DO.
OH YEAH? AND WHAT DO YOU WANT THEM TO DO?

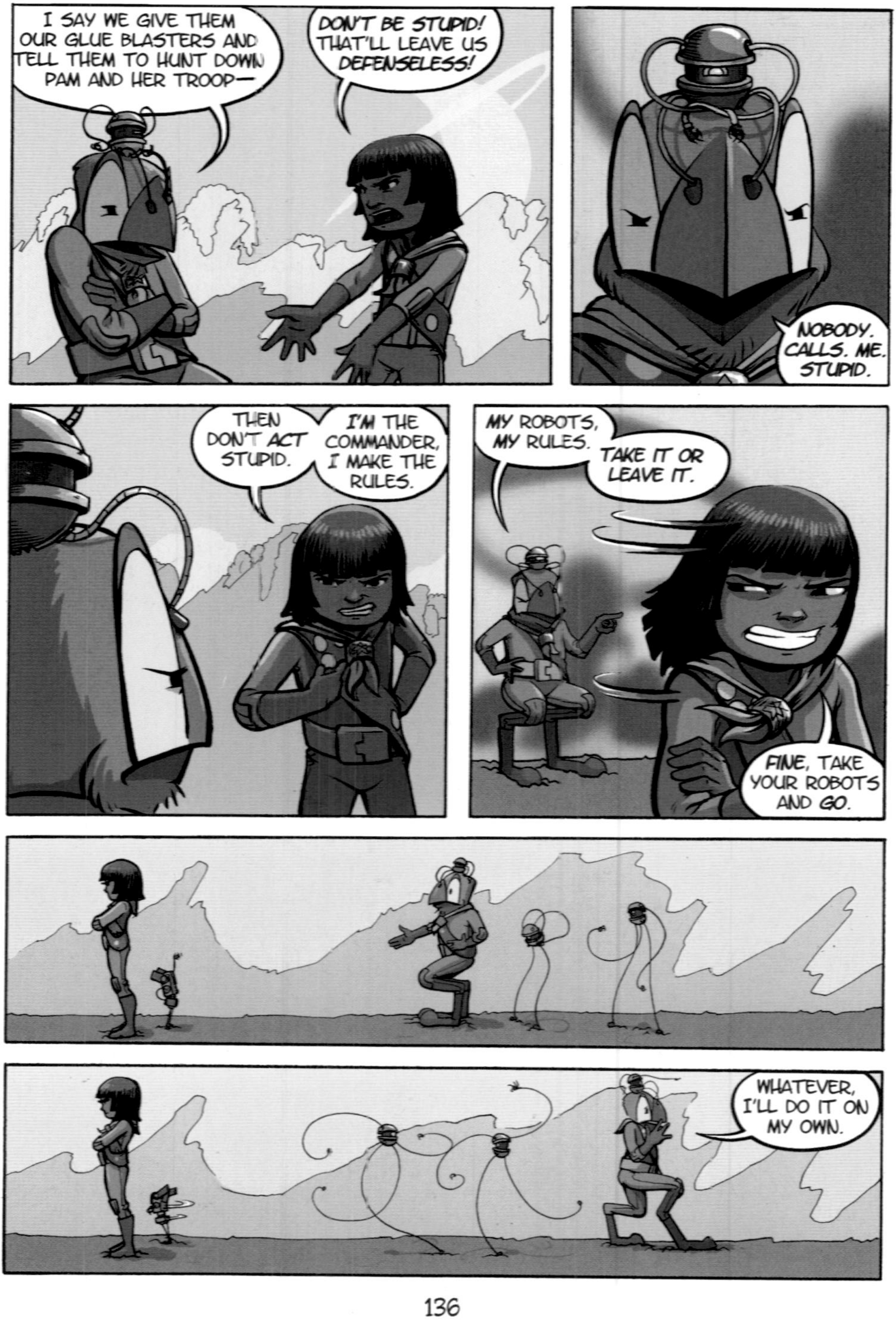
I SAY WE GIVE THEM OUR GLUE BLASTERS AND TELL THEM TO HUNT DOWN PAM AND HER TROOP—
DON'T BE STUPID! THAT'LL LEAVE US DEFENSELESS!
NOBODY. CALLS. ME. STUPID.
THEN DON'T ACT STUPID.
I'M THE COMMANDER, I MAKE THE RULES.
MY ROBOTS, MY RULES.
TAKE IT OR LEAVE IT.
FINE, TAKE YOUR ROBOTS AND GO.
WHATEVER, I'LL DO IT ON MY OWN.

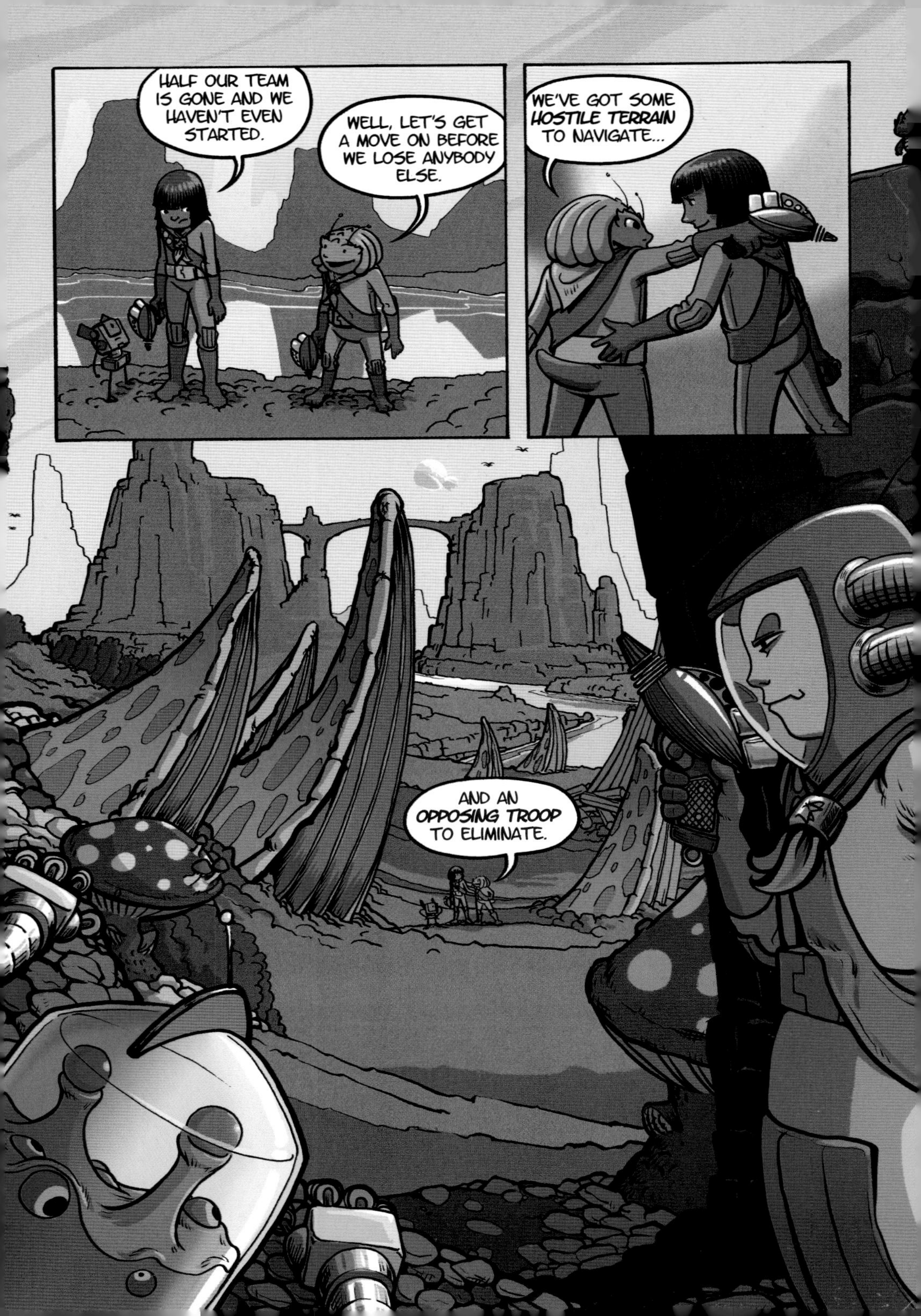
HALF OUR TEAM IS GONE AND WE HAVEN'T EVEN STARTED.
WELL, LET'S GET A MOVE ON BEFORE WE LOSE ANYBODY ELSE.
WE'VE GOT SOME **HOSTILE TERRAIN** TO NAVIGATE...
AND AN **OPPOSING TROOP** TO ELIMINATE.

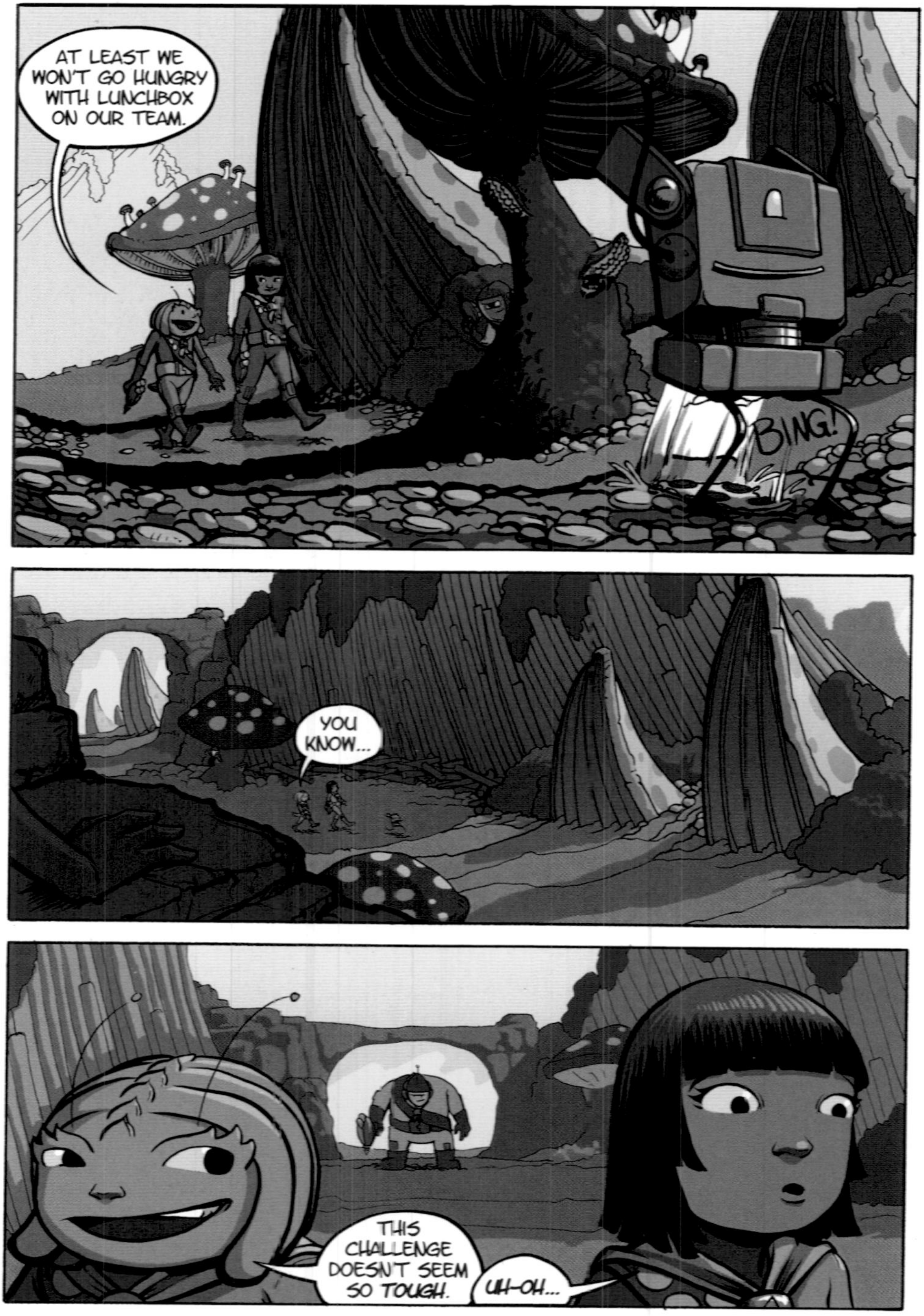
AT LEAST WE WON'T GO HUNGRY WITH LUNCHBOX ON OUR TEAM.
BING!
YOU KNOW...
THIS CHALLENGE DOESN'T SEEM SO TOUGH.
UH-OH...

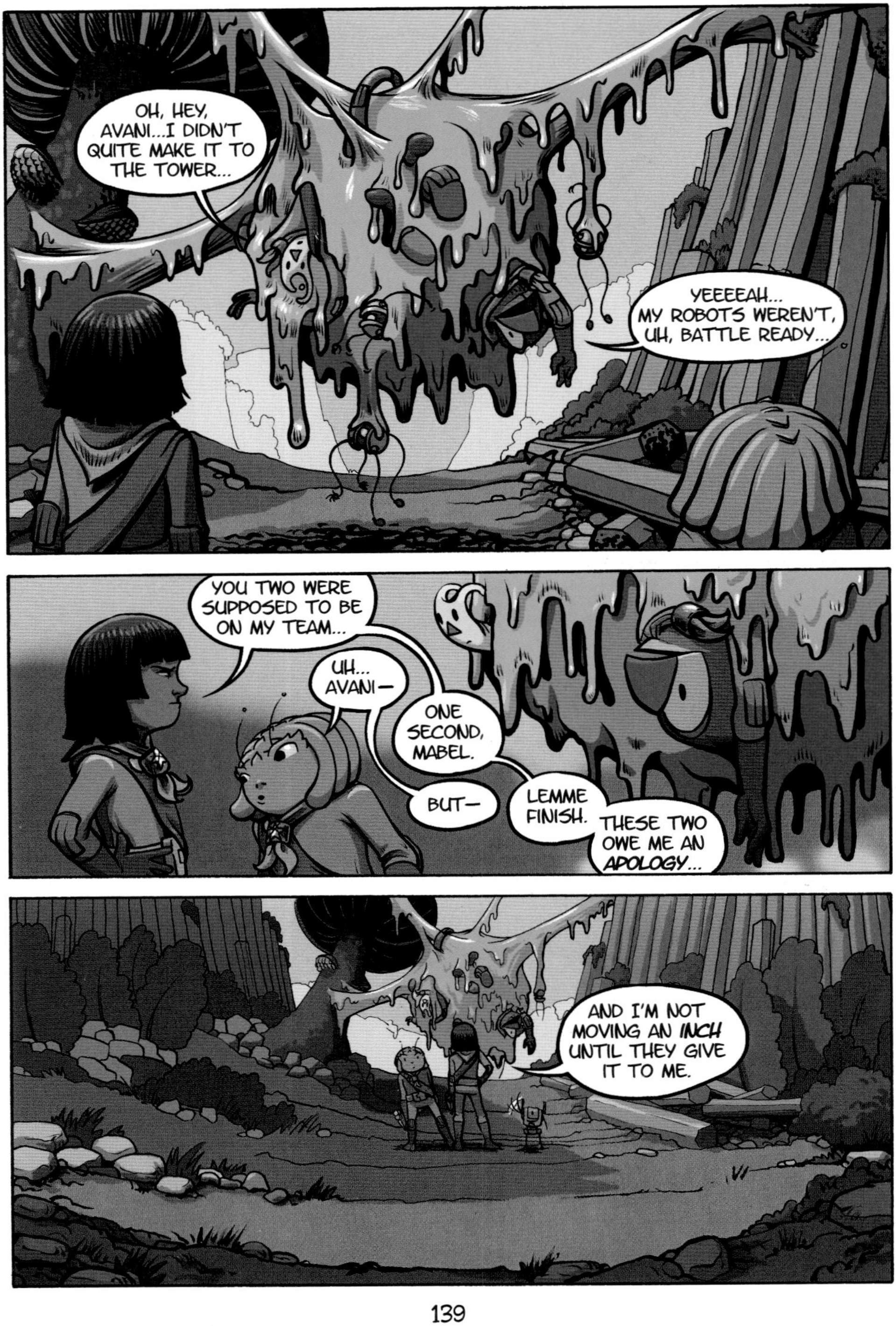
OH, HEY, AVANI...I DIDN'T QUITE MAKE IT TO THE TOWER...
YEEEEAH... MY ROBOTS WEREN'T, UH, BATTLE READY...
YOU TWO WERE SUPPOSED TO BE ON MY TEAM...
UH... AVANI—
ONE SECOND, MABEL.
BUT—
LEMME FINISH.
THESE TWO OWE ME AN *APOLOGY*...
AND I'M NOT MOVING AN *INCH* UNTIL THEY GIVE IT TO ME.

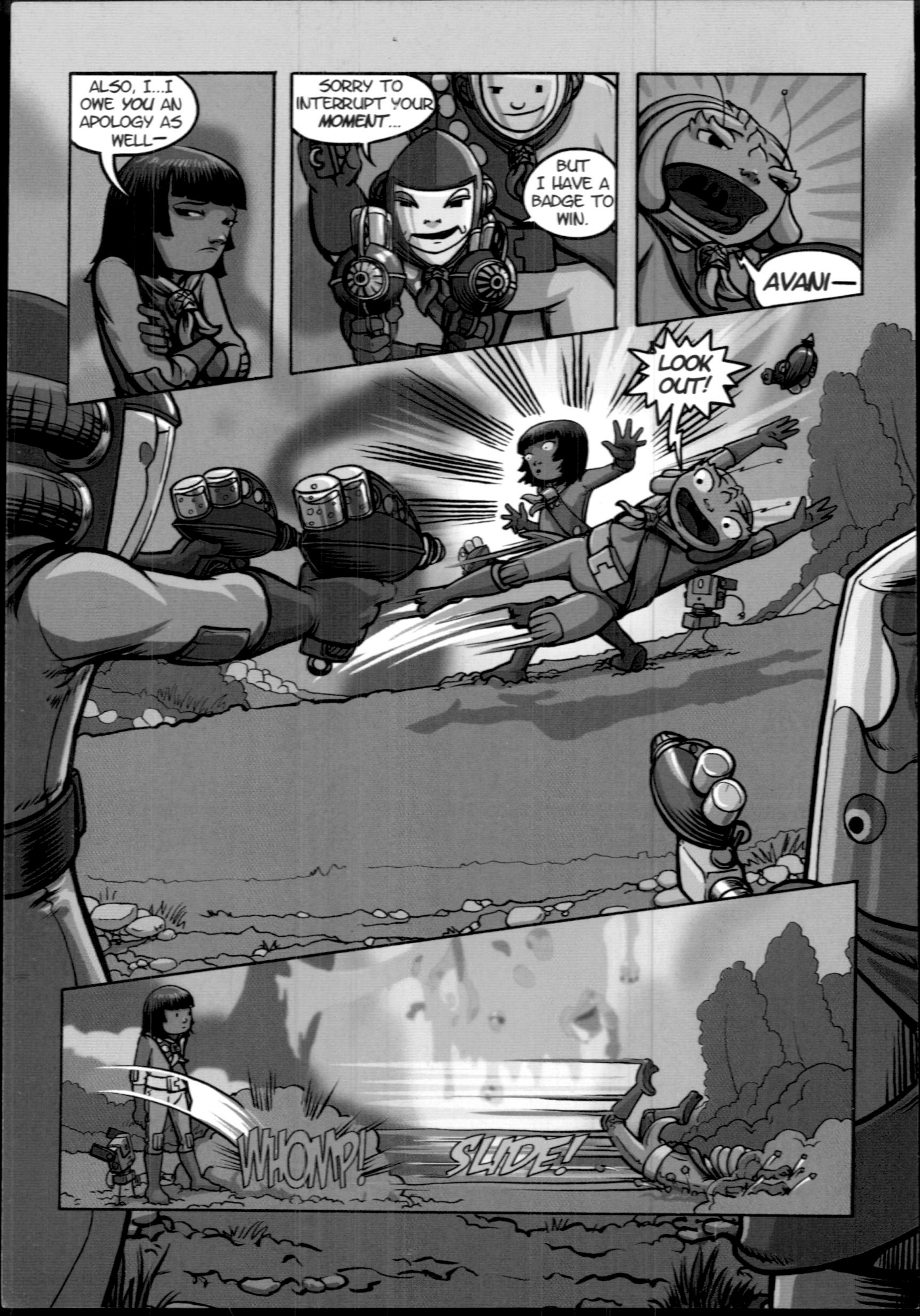
ALSO, I...I OWE YOU AN APOLOGY AS WELL—
SORRY TO INTERRUPT YOUR MOMENT...
BUT I HAVE A BADGE TO WIN.
AVANI—
LOOK OUT!
WHOMP!
SLIDE!

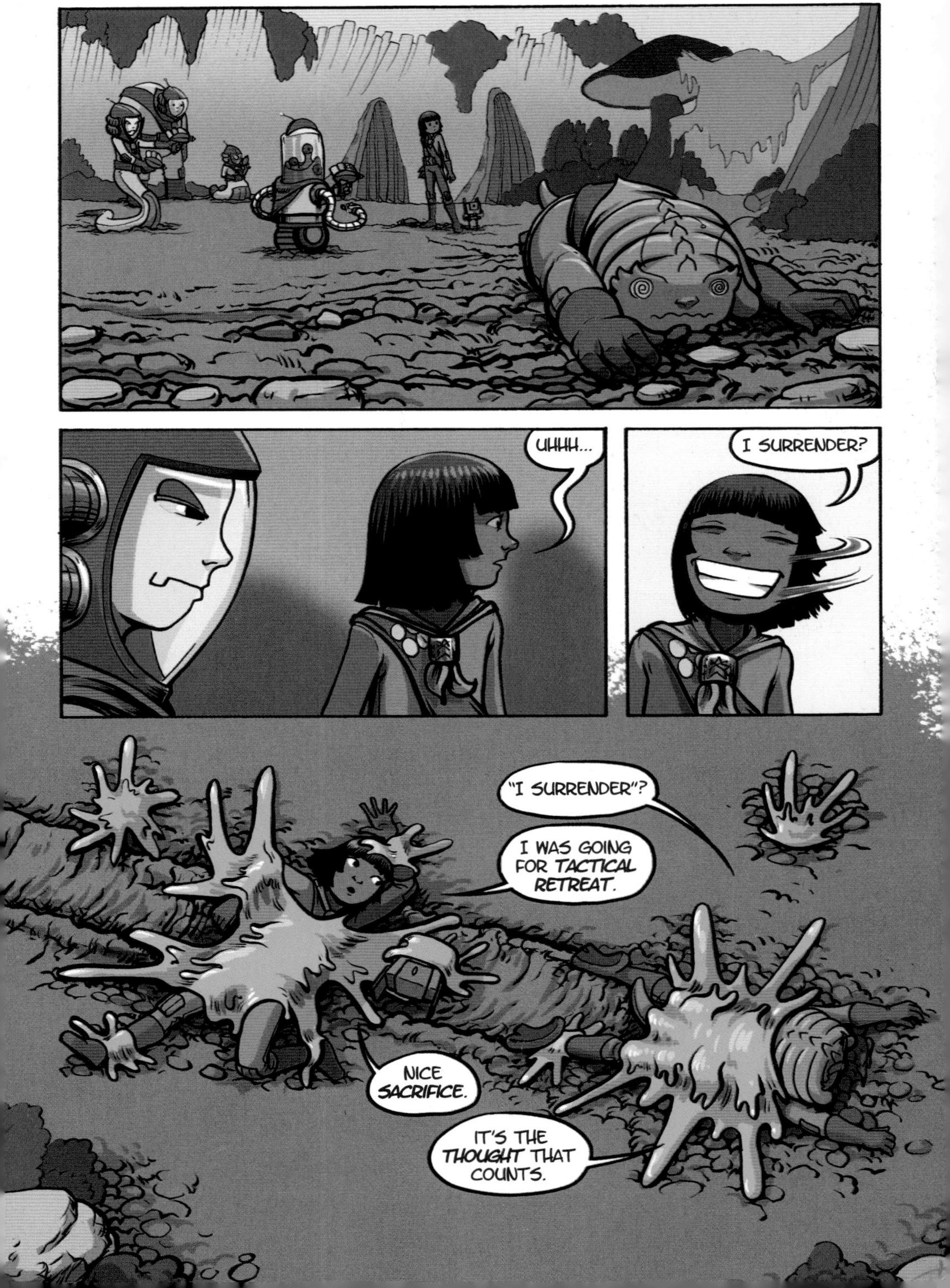
UHHH...
I SURRENDER?
"I SURRENDER"?
I WAS GOING FOR TACTICAL RETREAT.
NICE SACRIFICE.
IT'S THE THOUGHT THAT COUNTS.

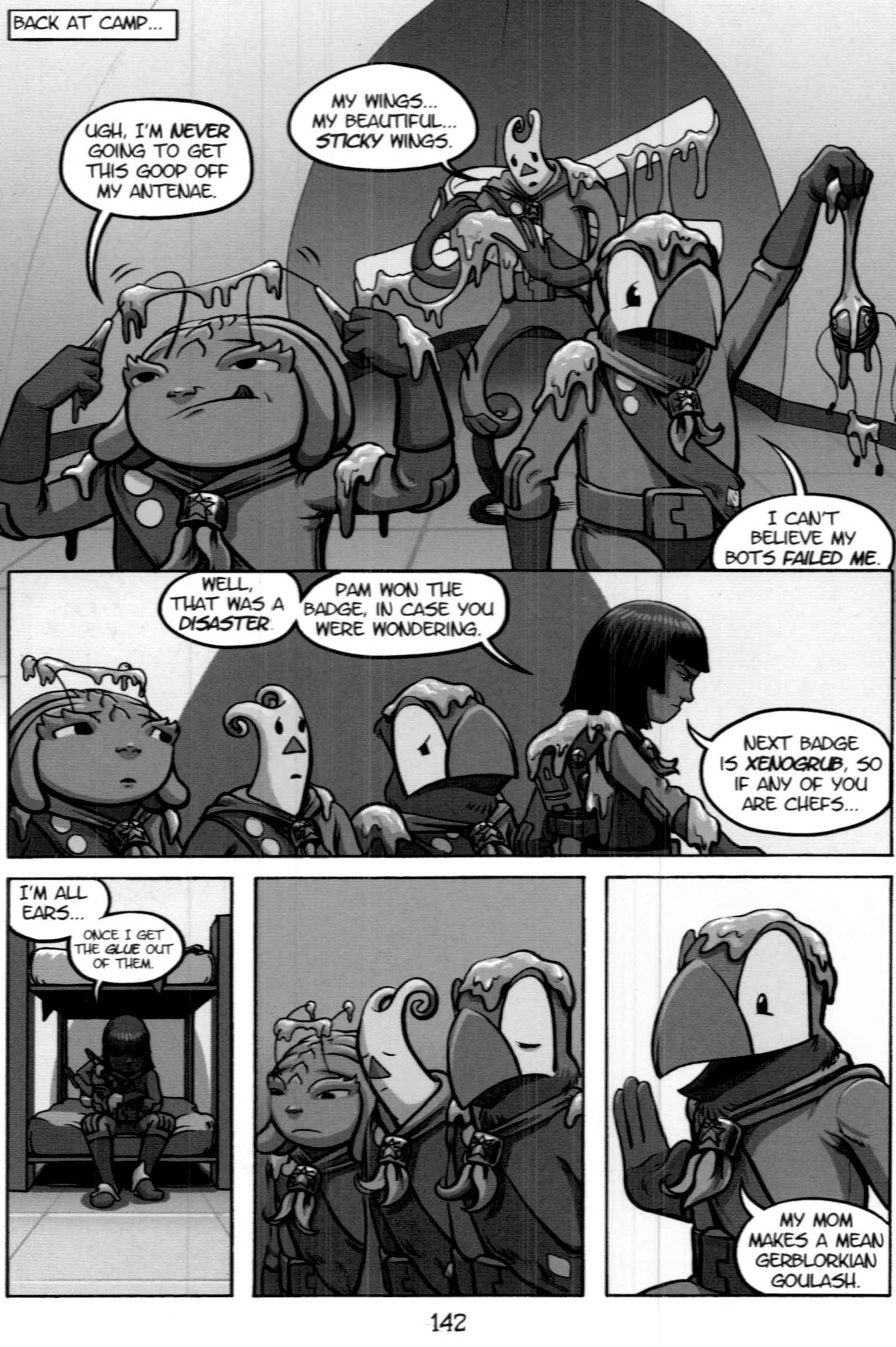
BACK AT CAMP...
UGH, I'M NEVER GOING TO GET THIS GOOP OFF MY ANTENAE.
MY WINGS... MY BEAUTIFUL... STICKY WINGS.
I CAN'T BELIEVE MY BOTS FAILED ME.
WELL, THAT WAS A DISASTER.
PAM WON THE BADGE, IN CASE YOU WERE WONDERING.
NEXT BADGE IS XENOGRUB, SO IF ANY OF YOU ARE CHEFS...
I'M ALL EARS...
ONCE I GET THE GLUE OUT OF THEM.
MY MOM MAKES A MEAN GERBLORKIAN GOULASH.

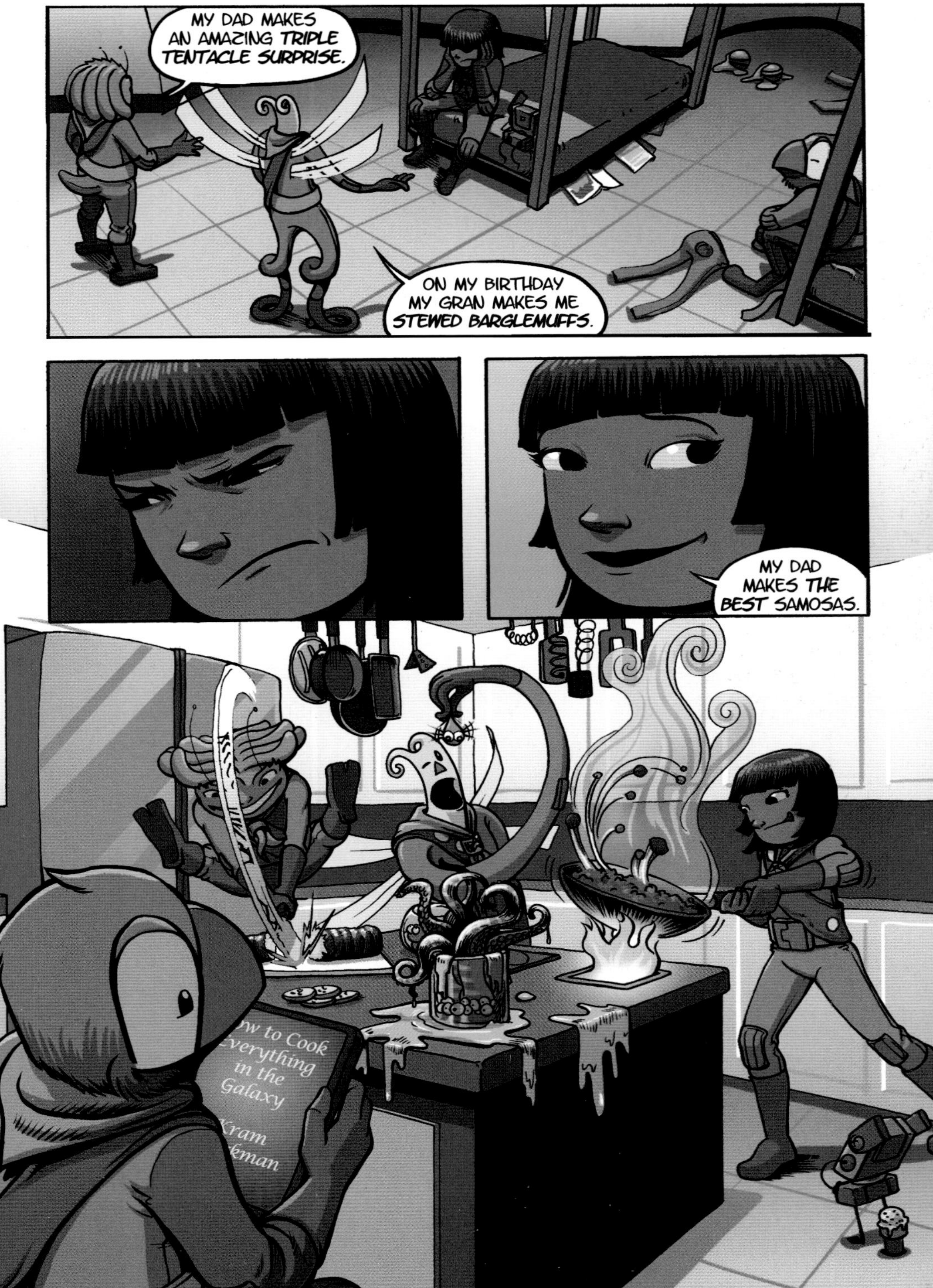
MY DAD MAKES AN AMAZING TRIPLE TENTACLE SURPRISE.
ON MY BIRTHDAY MY GRAN MAKES ME STEWED BARGLEMUFFS.
MY DAD MAKES THE BEST SAMOSAS.
ow to Cook
Everything
in the
Galaxy
Kram
kman

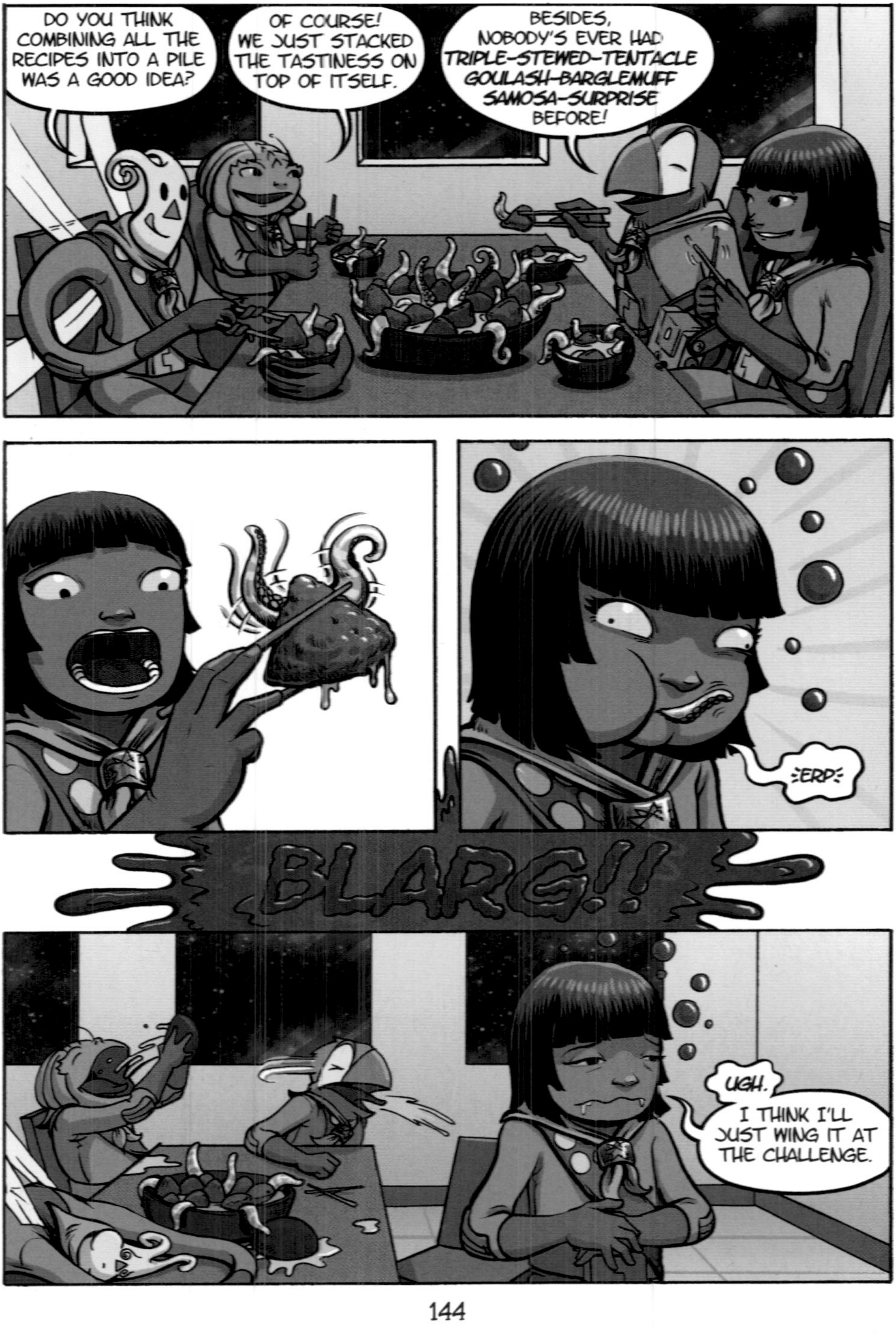
DO YOU THINK COMBINING ALL THE RECIPES INTO A PILE WAS A GOOD IDEA?
OF COURSE! WE JUST STACKED THE TASTINESS ON TOP OF ITSELF.
BESIDES, NOBODY'S EVER HAD **TRIPLE-STEWED-TENTACLE GOULASH-BARGLEMUFF SAMOSA-SURPRISE** BEFORE!
ERP
BLARG!!
UGH.
I THINK I'LL JUST WING IT AT THE CHALLENGE.

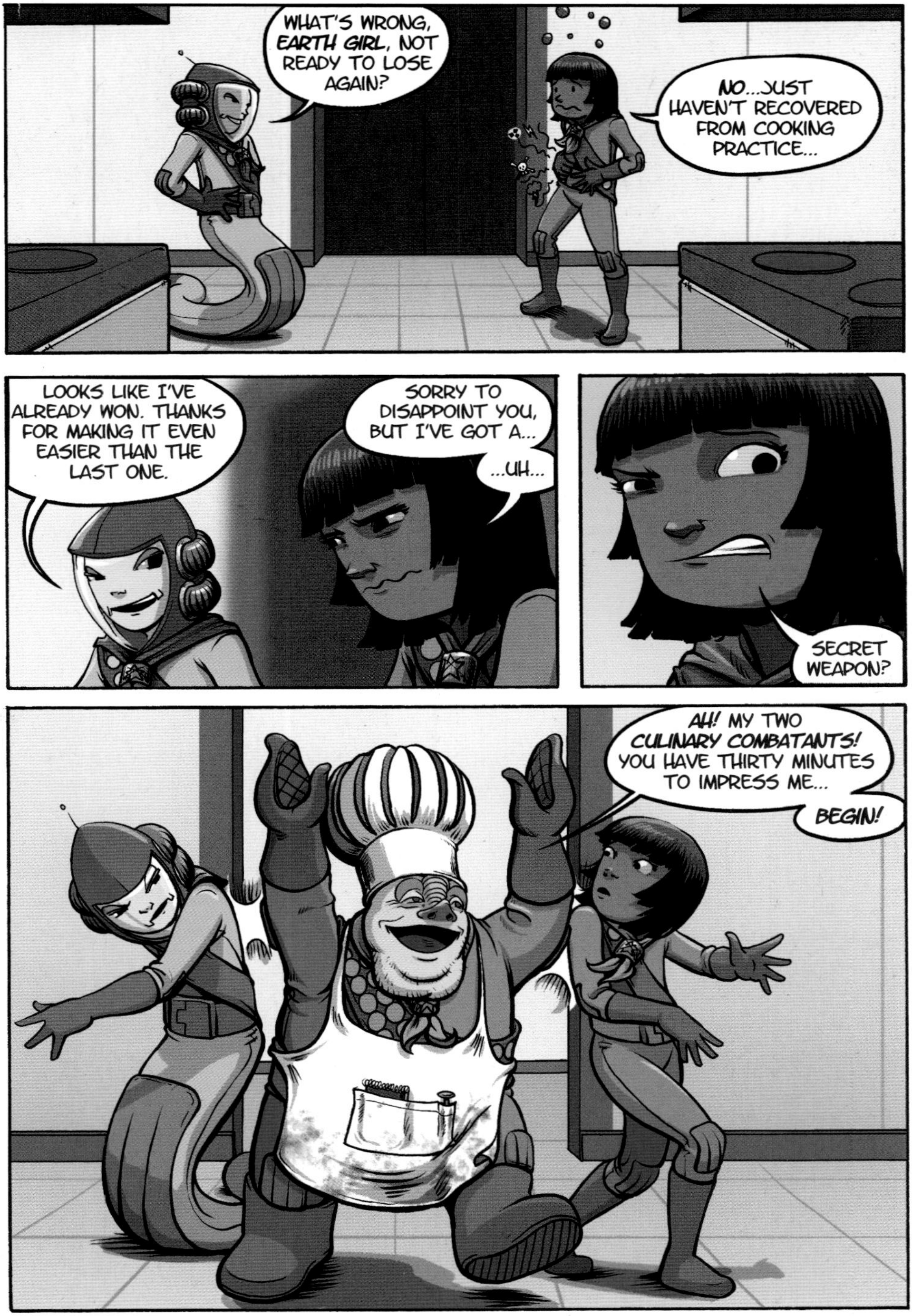
WHAT'S WRONG, EARTH GIRL, NOT READY TO LOSE AGAIN?
NO...JUST HAVEN'T RECOVERED FROM COOKING PRACTICE...
LOOKS LIKE I'VE ALREADY WON. THANKS FOR MAKING IT EVEN EASIER THAN THE LAST ONE.
SORRY TO DISAPPOINT YOU, BUT I'VE GOT A...
...UH...
SECRET WEAPON?
AH! MY TWO CULINARY COMBATANTS! YOU HAVE THIRTY MINUTES TO IMPRESS ME...
BEGIN!

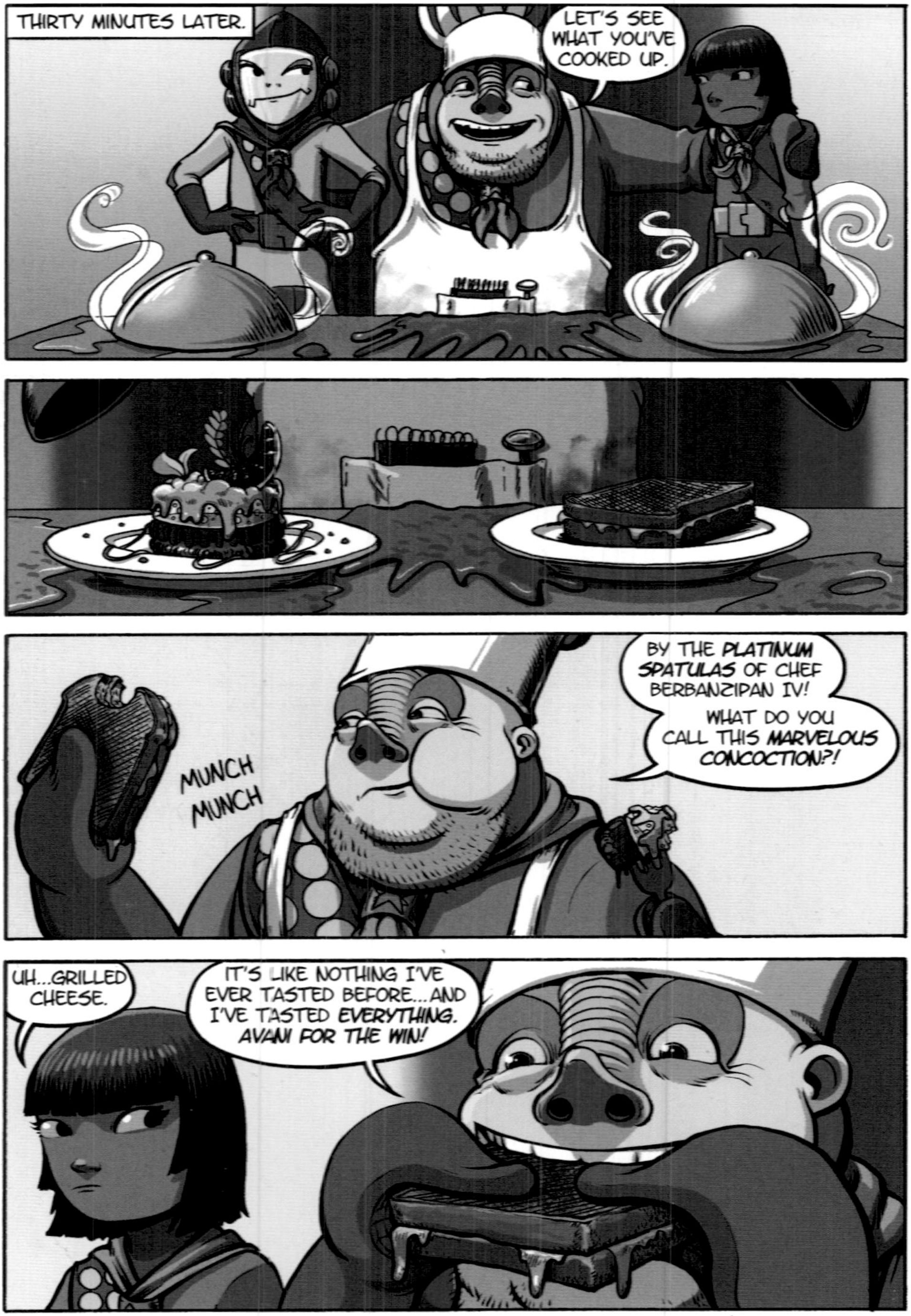
THIRTY MINUTES LATER.
LET'S SEE WHAT YOU'VE COOKED UP.
BY THE PLATINUM SPATULAS OF CHEF BERBANZIPAN IV!
WHAT DO YOU CALL THIS MARVELOUS CONCOCTION?!
MUNCH MUNCH
UH...GRILLED CHEESE.
IT'S LIKE NOTHING I'VE EVER TASTED BEFORE...AND I'VE TASTED EVERYTHING. AVANI FOR THE WIN!

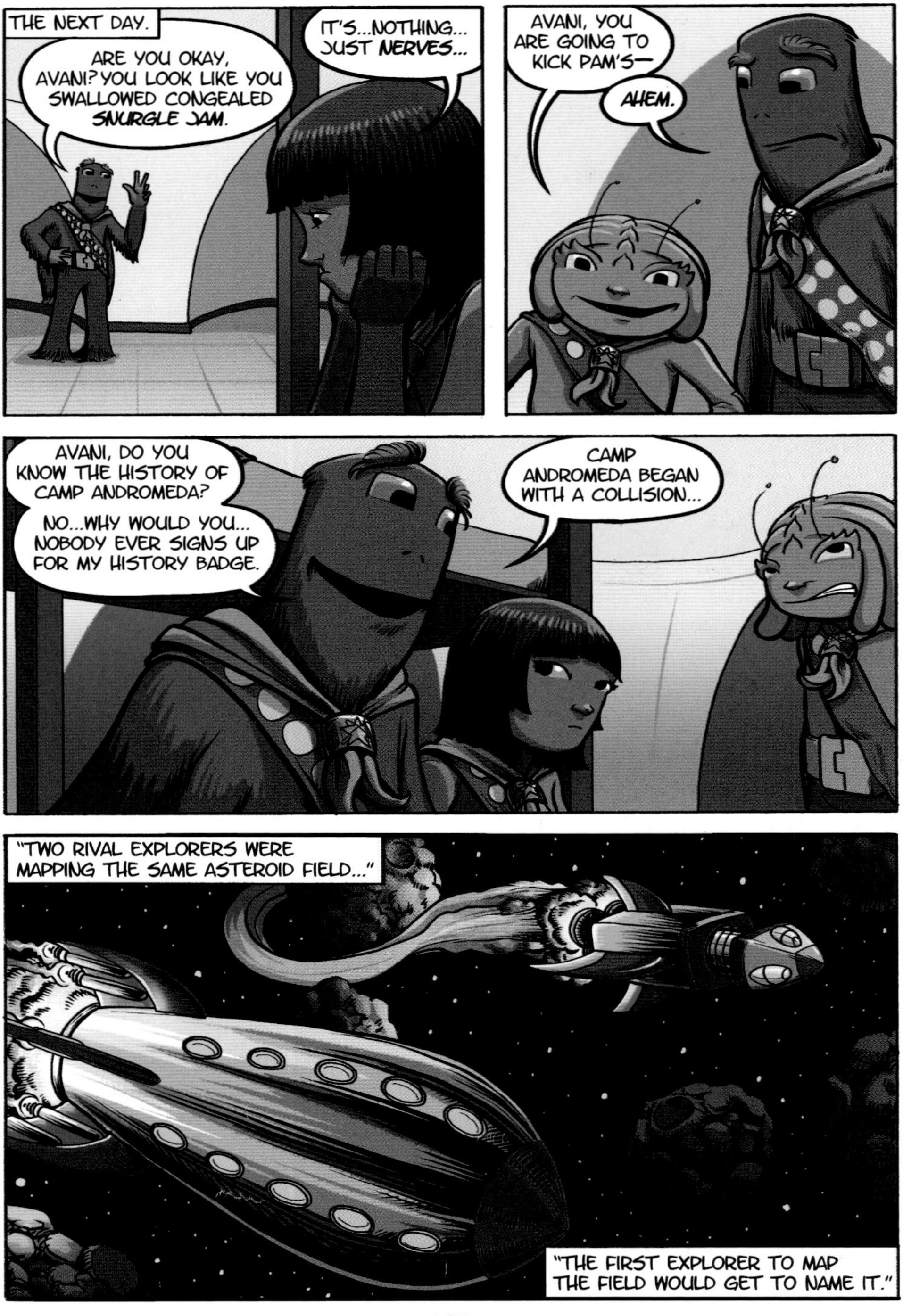
THE NEXT DAY.
ARE YOU OKAY, AVANI? YOU LOOK LIKE YOU SWALLOWED CONGEALED SNURGLE JAM.
IT'S...NOTHING... JUST NERVES...
AVANI, YOU ARE GOING TO KICK PAM'S—
AHEM.
AVANI, DO YOU KNOW THE HISTORY OF CAMP ANDROMEDA?
NO...WHY WOULD YOU... NOBODY EVER SIGNS UP FOR MY HISTORY BADGE.
CAMP ANDROMEDA BEGAN WITH A COLLISION...
"TWO RIVAL EXPLORERS WERE MAPPING THE SAME ASTEROID FIELD..."
"THE FIRST EXPLORER TO MAP THE FIELD WOULD GET TO NAME IT."

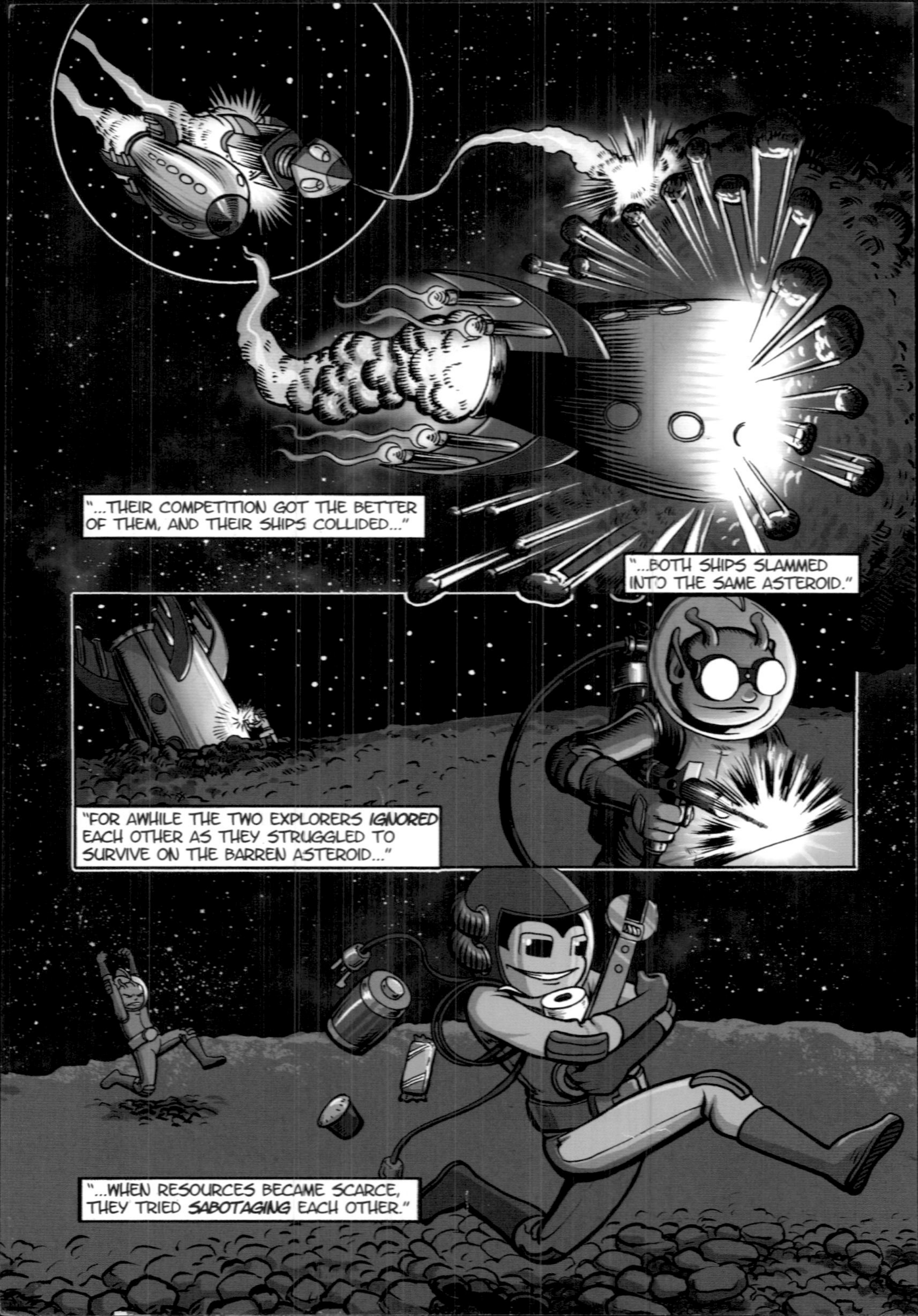
"...THEIR COMPETITION GOT THE BETTER OF THEM, AND THEIR SHIPS COLLIDED..."
"...BOTH SHIPS SLAMMED INTO THE SAME ASTEROID."
"FOR AWHILE THE TWO EXPLORERS IGNORED EACH OTHER AS THEY STRUGGLED TO SURVIVE ON THE BARREN ASTEROID..."
"...WHEN RESOURCES BECAME SCARCE, THEY TRIED SABOTAGING EACH OTHER."

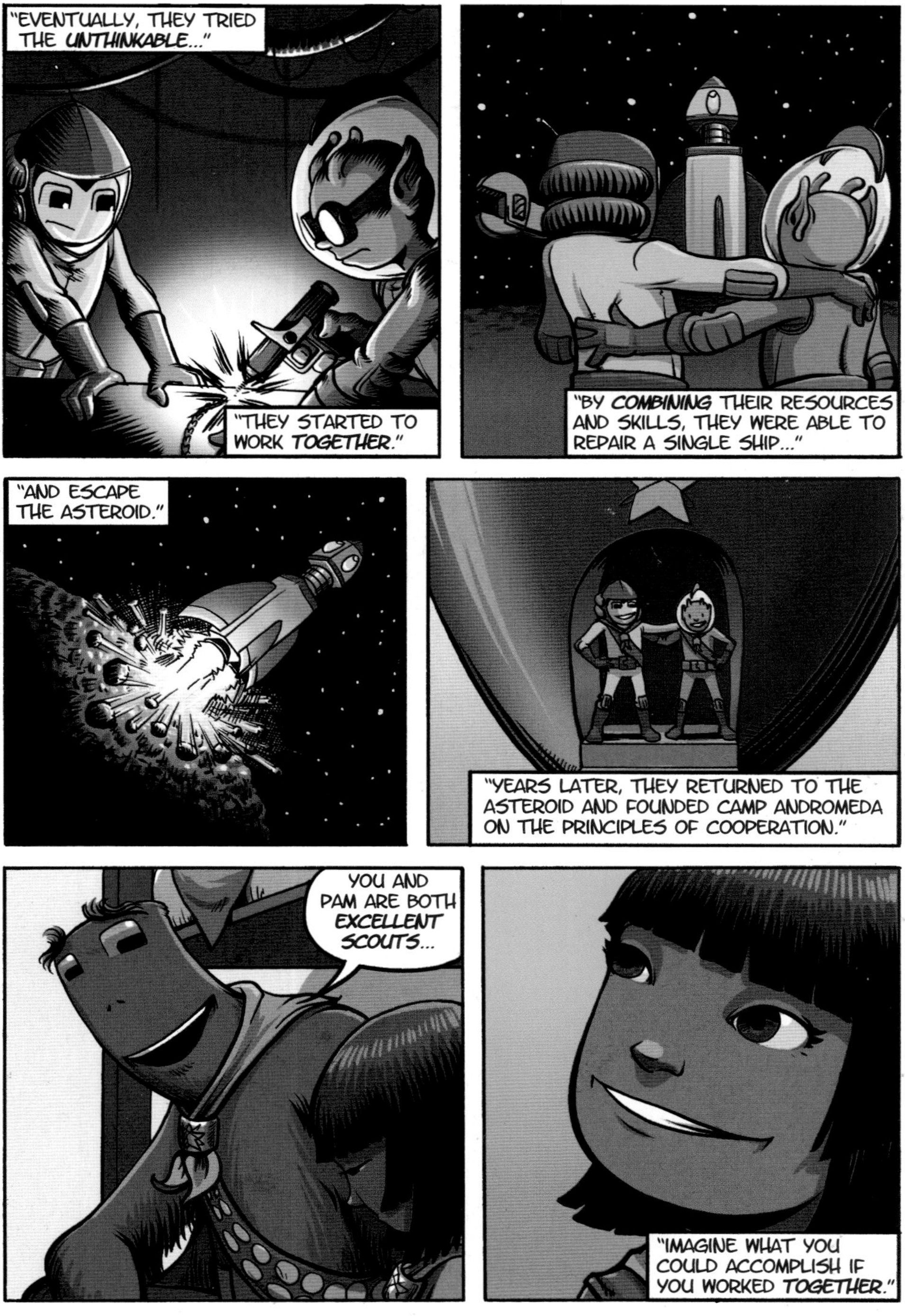
"EVENTUALLY, THEY TRIED THE UNTHINKABLE..."
"THEY STARTED TO WORK TOGETHER."
"BY COMBINING THEIR RESOURCES AND SKILLS, THEY WERE ABLE TO REPAIR A SINGLE SHIP..."
"AND ESCAPE THE ASTEROID."
"YEARS LATER, THEY RETURNED TO THE ASTEROID AND FOUNDED CAMP ANDROMEDA ON THE PRINCIPLES OF COOPERATION."
YOU AND PAM ARE BOTH EXCELLENT SCOUTS...
"IMAGINE WHAT YOU COULD ACCOMPLISH IF YOU WORKED TOGETHER."

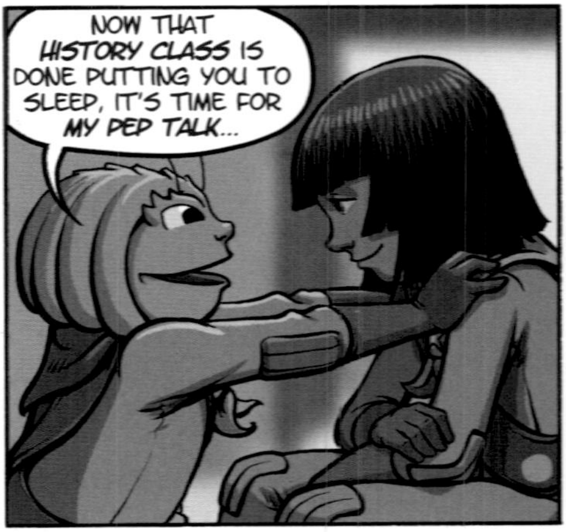
NOW THAT HISTORY CLASS IS DONE PUTTING YOU TO SLEEP, IT'S TIME FOR MY PEP TALK...

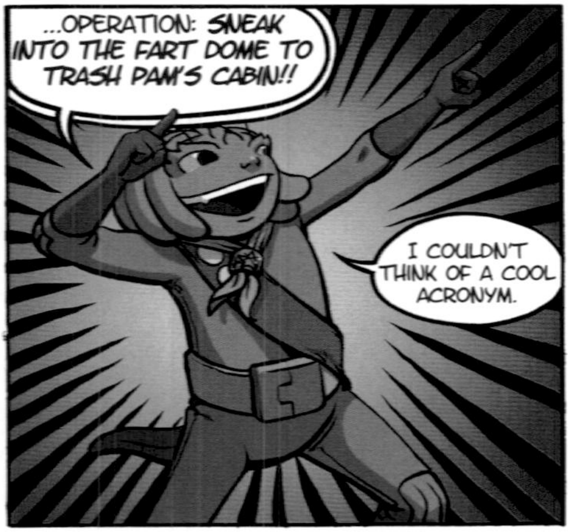
...OPERATION: SNEAK INTO THE FART DOME TO TRASH PAM'S CABIN!!
I COULDN'T THINK OF A COOL ACRONYM.

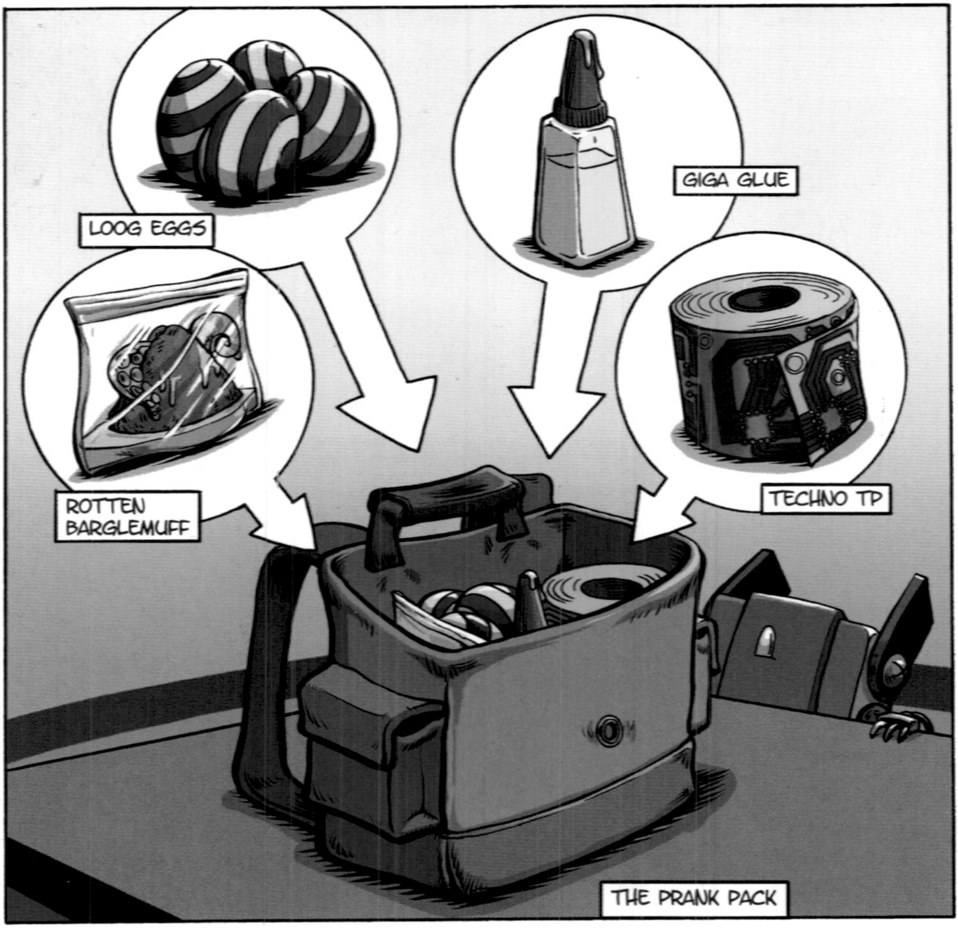
LOOG EGGS
GIGA GLUE
ROTTEN BARGLEMUFF
TECHNO TP
THE PRANK PACK

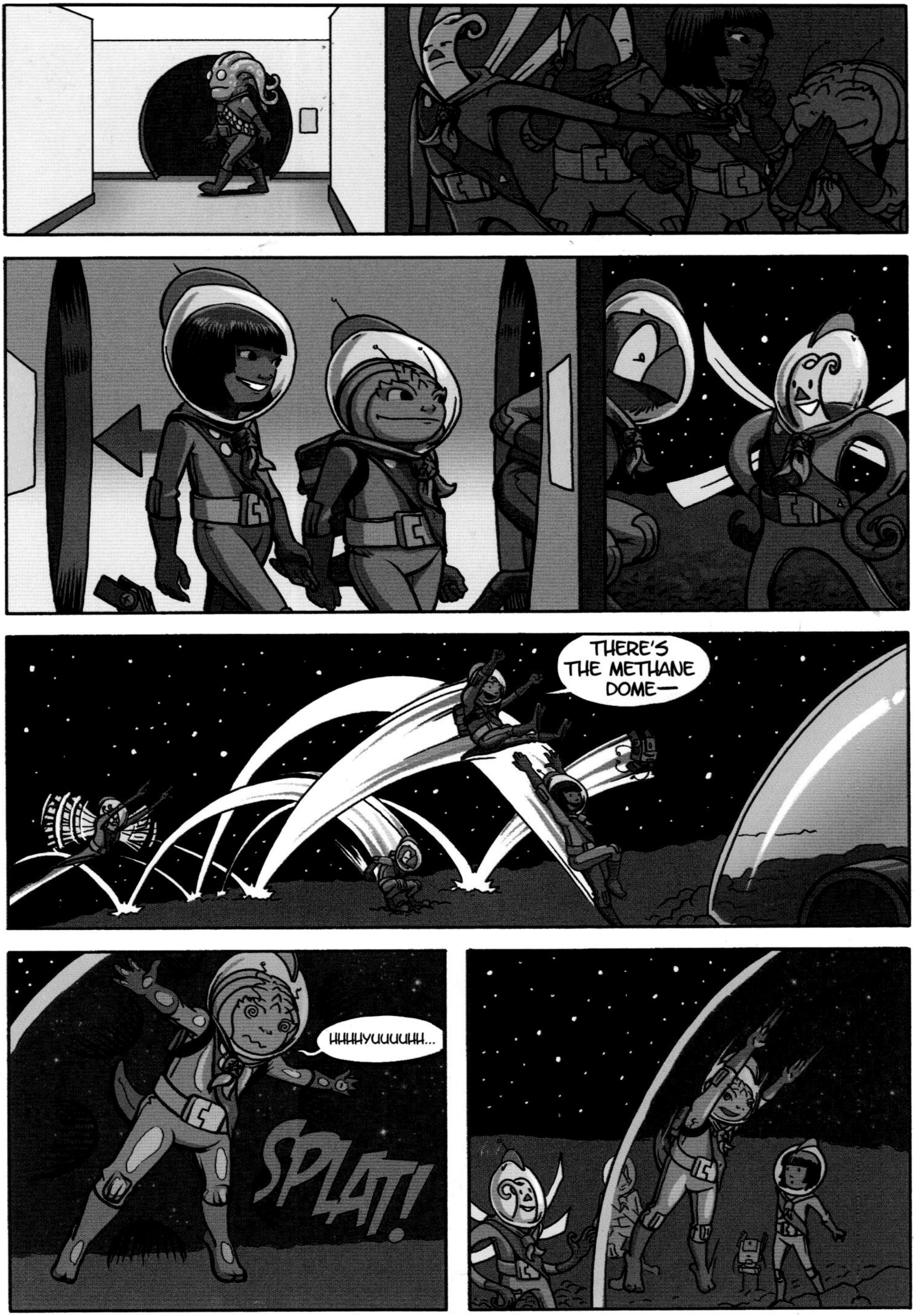
THERE'S THE METHANE DOME—
HHHHYUUUUHH...
SPLAT!

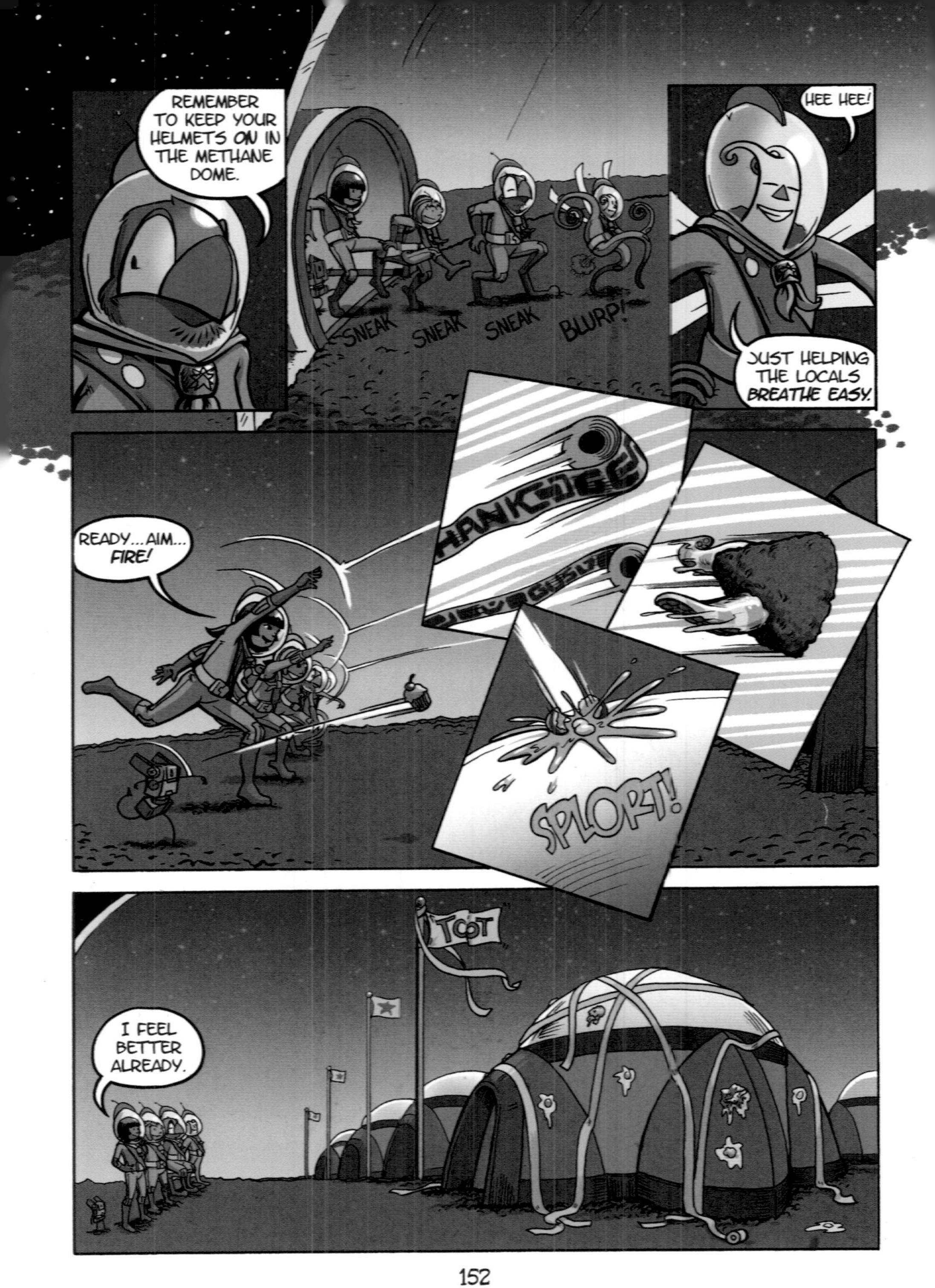
REMEMBER TO KEEP YOUR HELMETS ON IN THE METHANE DOME.
SNEAK
SNEAK
SNEAK
BLURP!
HEE HEE!
JUST HELPING THE LOCALS BREATHE EASY.
READY... AIM... FIRE!
SPLORT!
TOOT
I FEEL BETTER ALREADY.

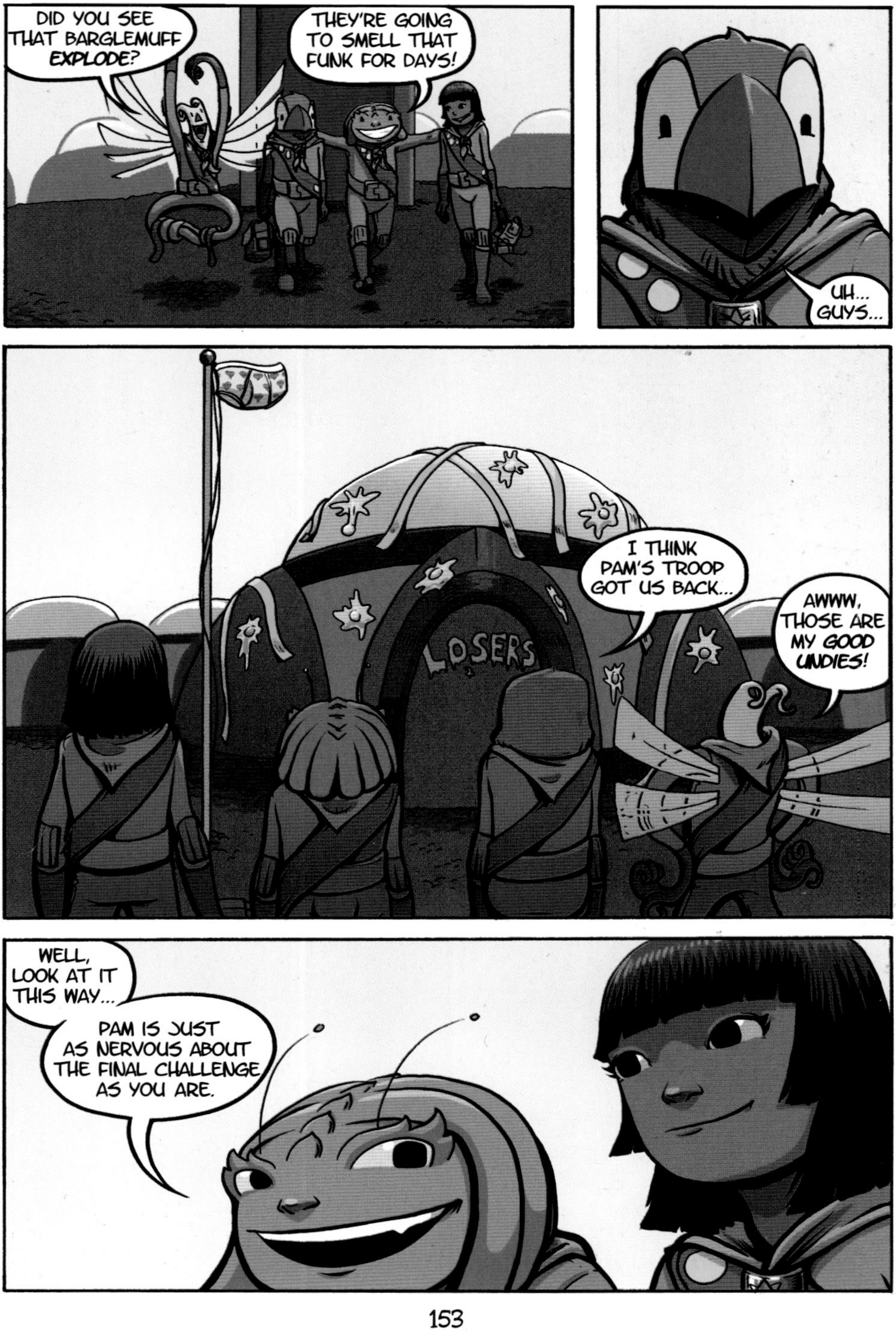
DID YOU SEE THAT BARGLEMUFF EXPLODE?
THEY'RE GOING TO SMELL THAT FUNK FOR DAYS!
UH... GUYS...
LOSERS
I THINK PAM'S TROOP GOT US BACK...
AWWW, THOSE ARE MY GOOD UNDIES!
WELL, LOOK AT IT THIS WAY...
PAM IS JUST AS NERVOUS ABOUT THE FINAL CHALLENGE AS YOU ARE.

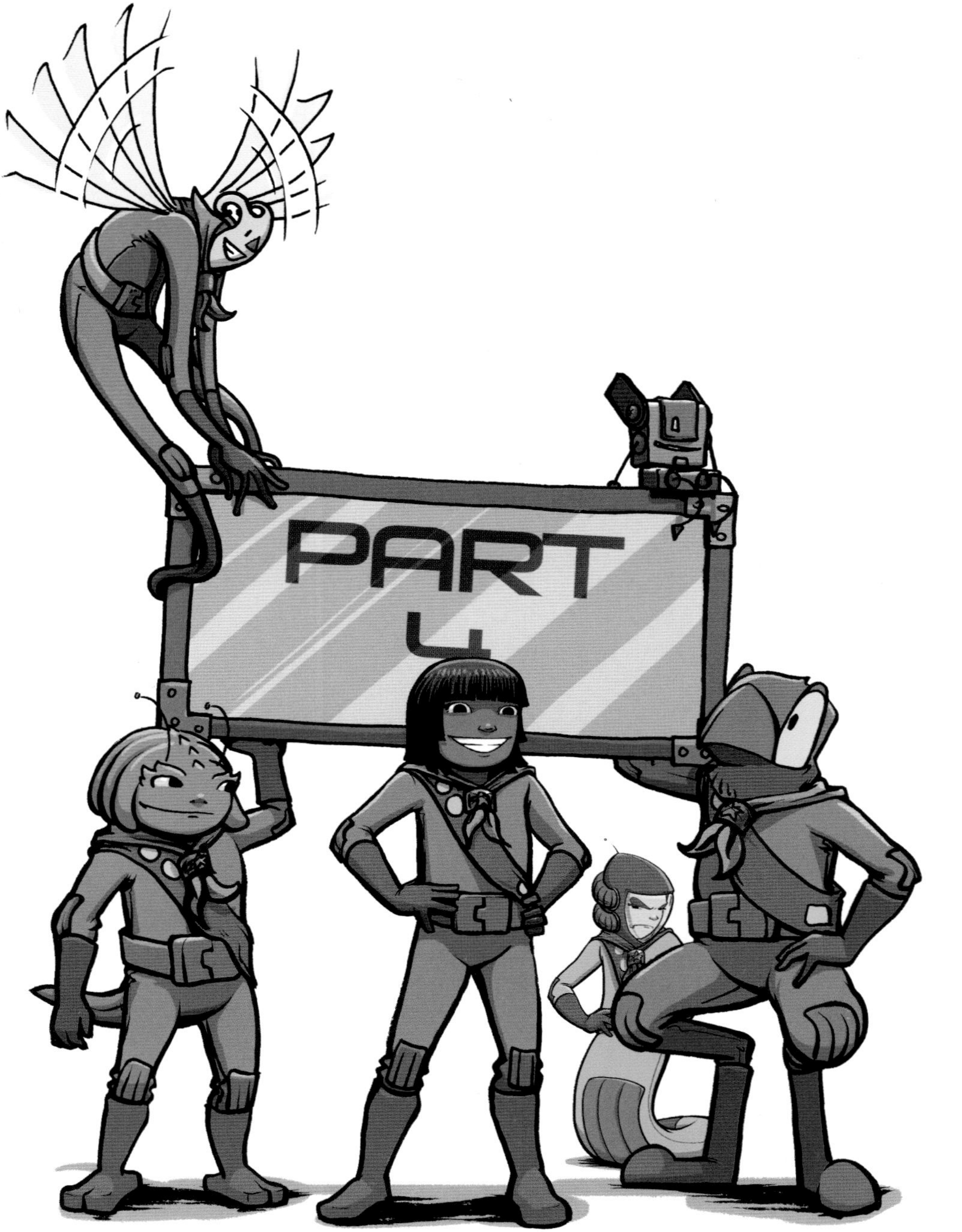
PART
4

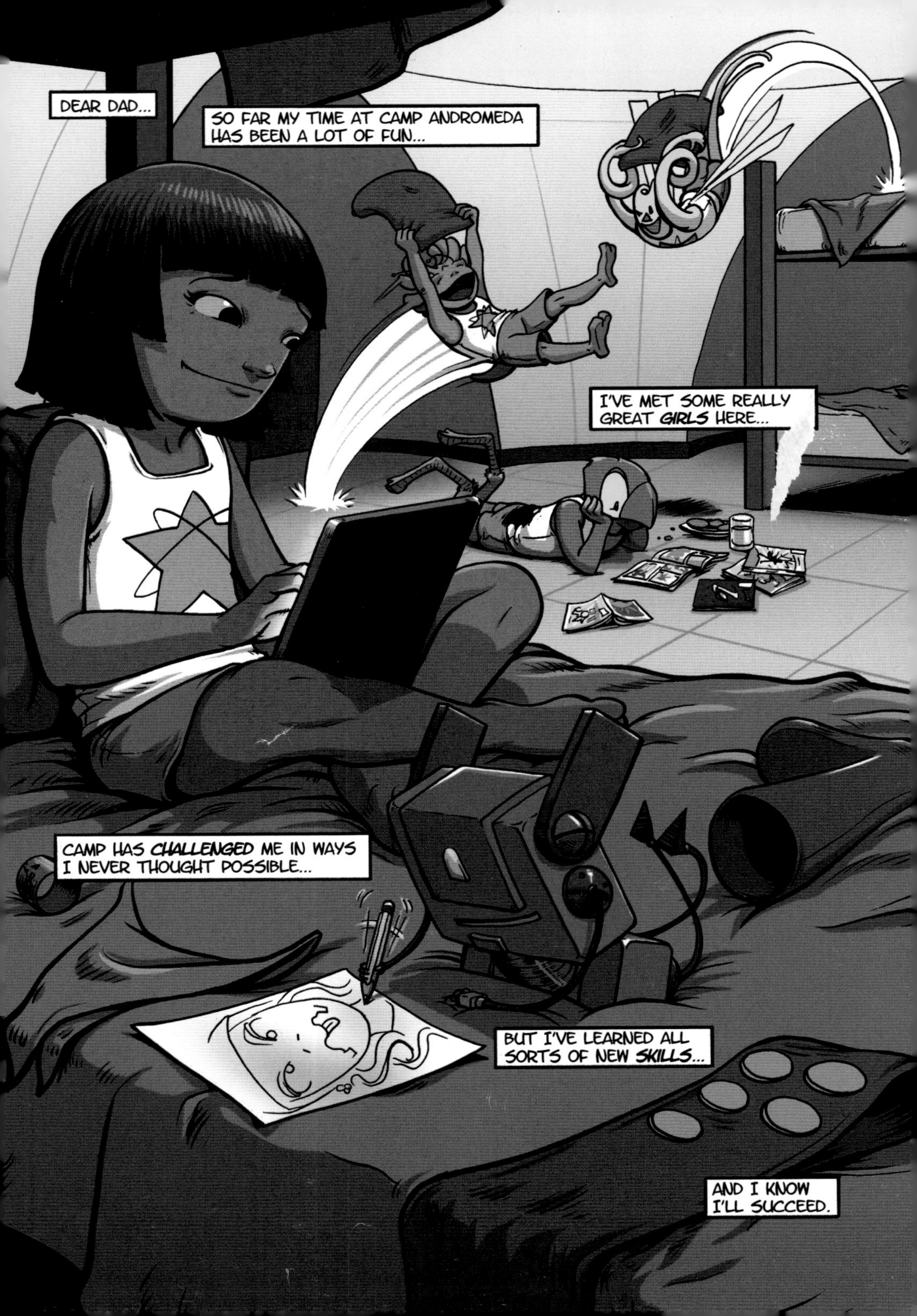
DEAR DAD...
SO FAR MY TIME AT CAMP ANDROMEDA HAS BEEN A LOT OF FUN...
I'VE MET SOME REALLY GREAT GIRLS HERE...
CAMP HAS CHALLENGED ME IN WAYS I NEVER THOUGHT POSSIBLE...
BUT I'VE LEARNED ALL SORTS OF NEW SKILLS...
AND I KNOW I'LL SUCCEED.

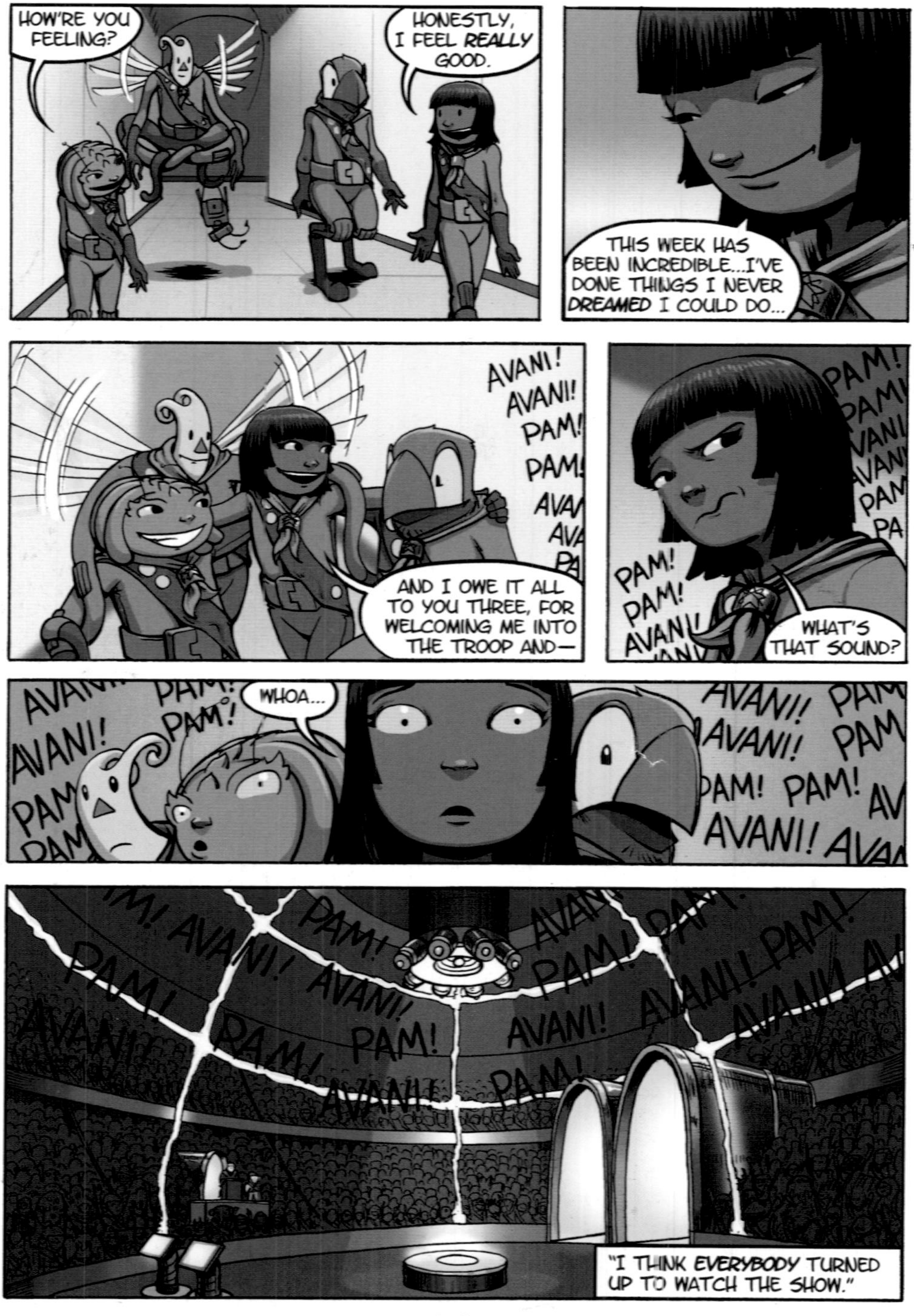
HOW'RE YOU FEELING?
HONESTLY, I FEEL REALLY GOOD.
THIS WEEK HAS BEEN INCREDIBLE...I'VE DONE THINGS I NEVER DREAMED I COULD DO...
AVANI! AVANI! PAM! PAM!
AND I OWE IT ALL TO YOU THREE, FOR WELCOMING ME INTO THE TROOP AND—
PAM! PAM! AVANI!
WHAT'S THAT SOUND?
AVANI! PAM! PAM!
WHOA...
AVANI!! PAM! AVANI!! PAM! PAM! PAM! AVANI!
PAM! AVANI! AVANI! PAM!
"I THINK EVERYBODY TURNED UP TO WATCH THE SHOW."

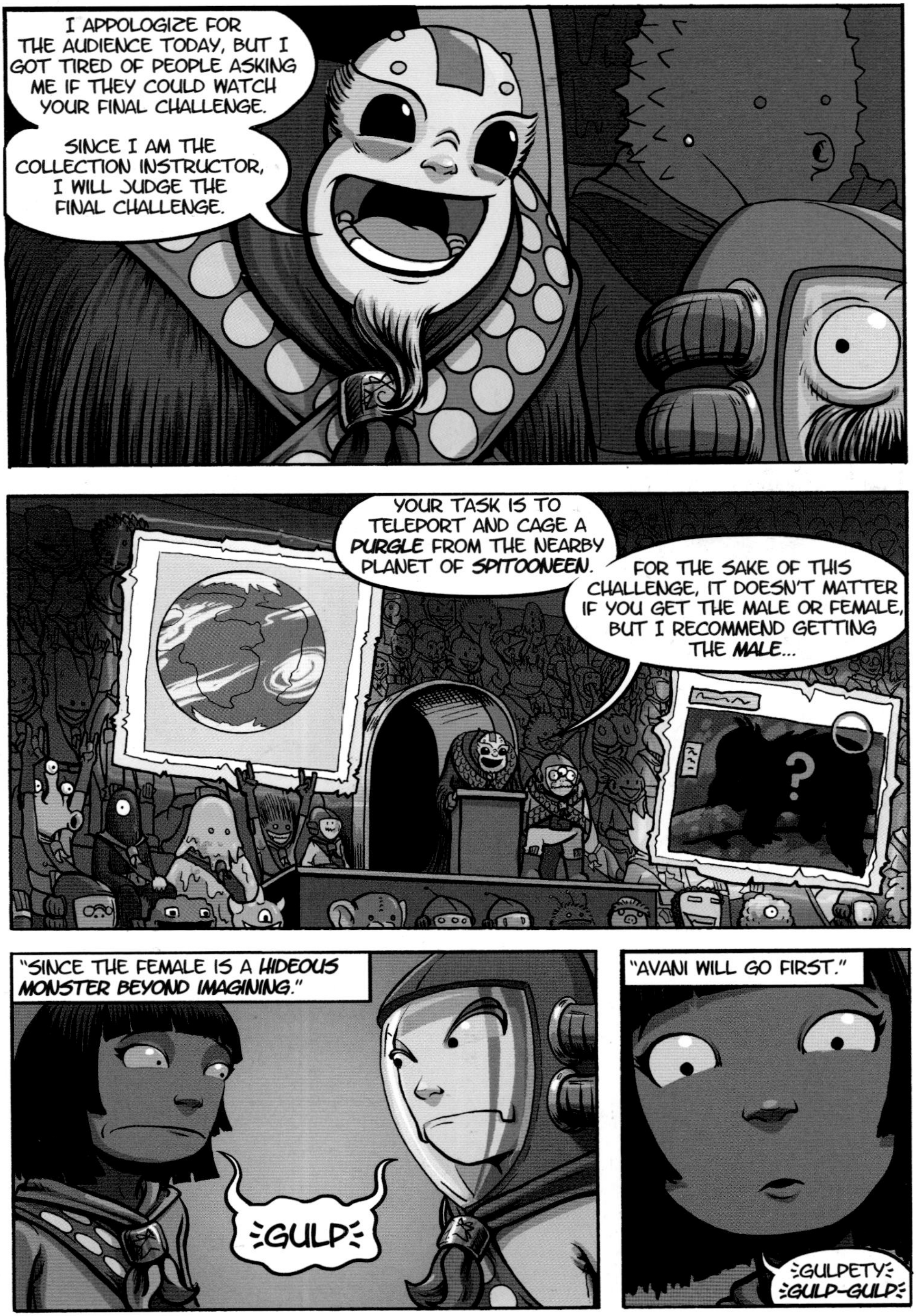
I APPOLOGIZE FOR THE AUDIENCE TODAY, BUT I GOT TIRED OF PEOPLE ASKING ME IF THEY COULD WATCH YOUR FINAL CHALLENGE.
SINCE I AM THE COLLECTION INSTRUCTOR, I WILL JUDGE THE FINAL CHALLENGE.
YOUR TASK IS TO TELEPORT AND CAGE A PURGLE FROM THE NEARBY PLANET OF SPITOONEEN.
FOR THE SAKE OF THIS CHALLENGE, IT DOESN'T MATTER IF YOU GET THE MALE OR FEMALE, BUT I RECOMMEND GETTING THE MALE...
?
"SINCE THE FEMALE IS A HIDEOUS MONSTER BEYOND IMAGINING."
GULP
"AVANI WILL GO FIRST."
GULPETY GULP-GULP

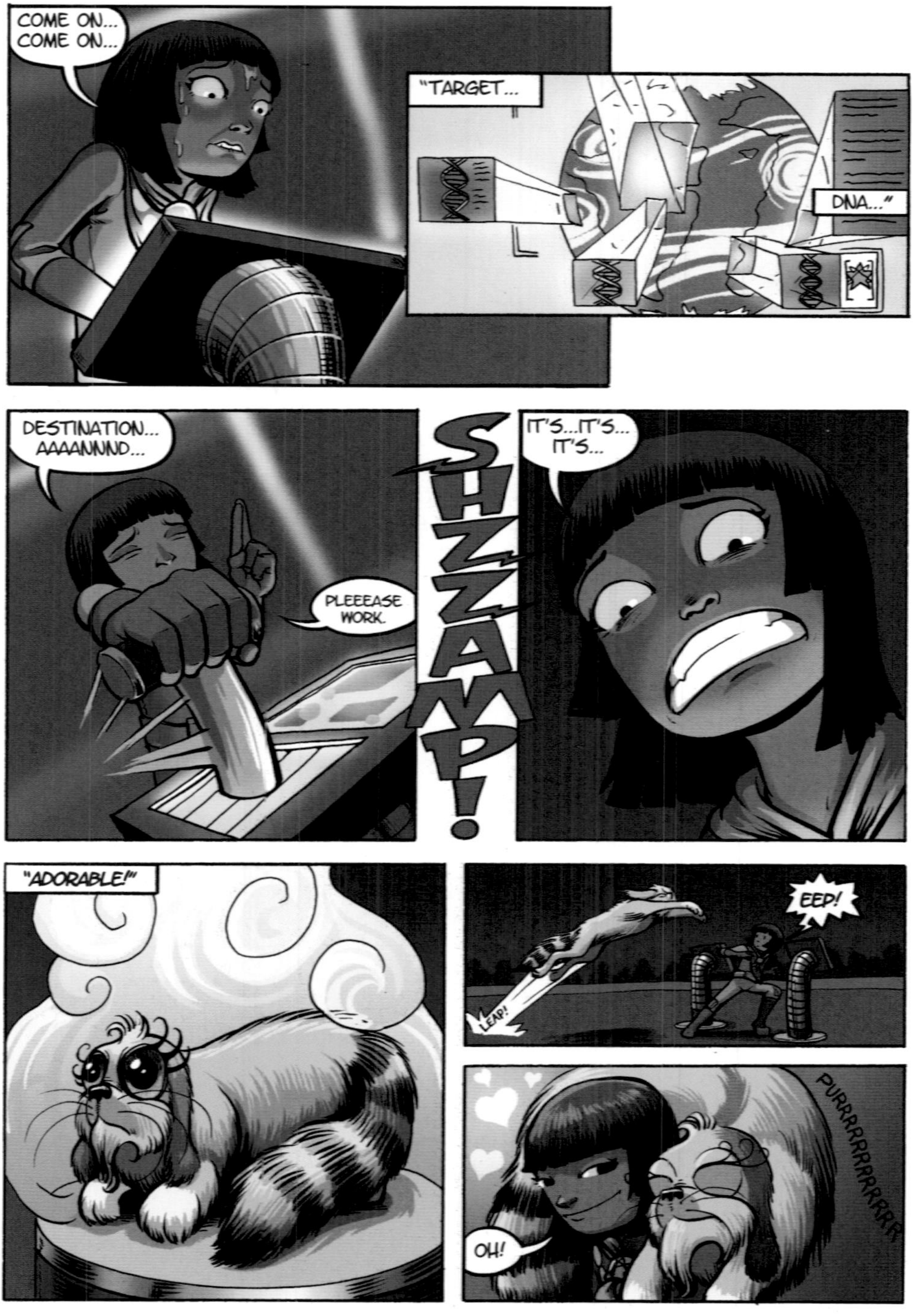
COME ON... COME ON...
"TARGET...
DNA..."
DESTINATION... AAAANNND...
PLEEEASE WORK.
SHZZAMP!
IT'S...IT'S... IT'S...
"ADORABLE!"
LEAP!
EEP!
PURRRRRRRRRRR
OH!

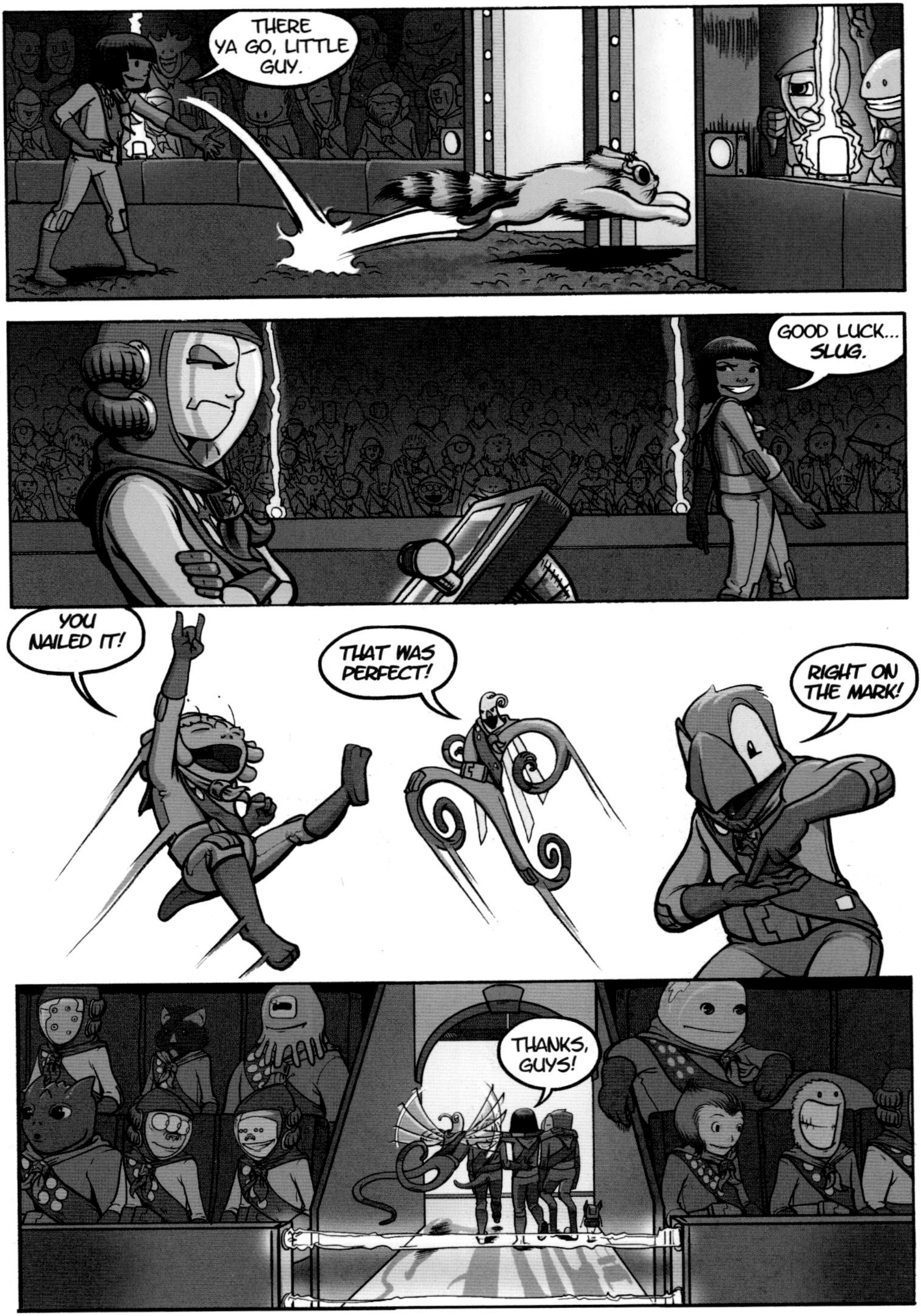
THERE YA GO, LITTLE GUY.
GOOD LUCK... SLUG.
YOU NAILED IT!
THAT WAS PERFECT!
RIGHT ON THE MARK!
THANKS, GUYS!

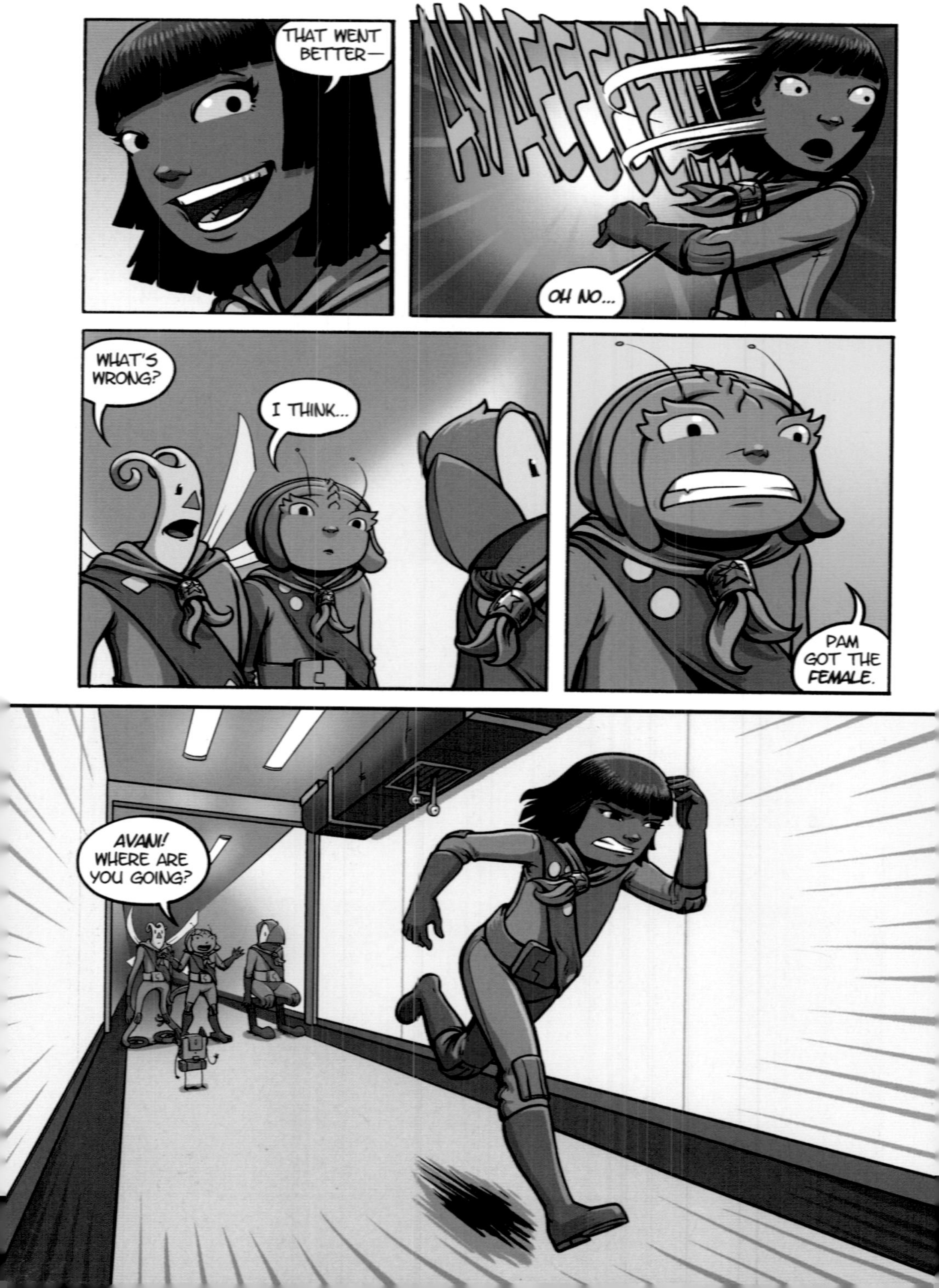
THAT WENT BETTER—
OH NO...
WHAT'S WRONG?
I THINK...
PAM GOT THE FEMALE.
AVANI! WHERE ARE YOU GOING?

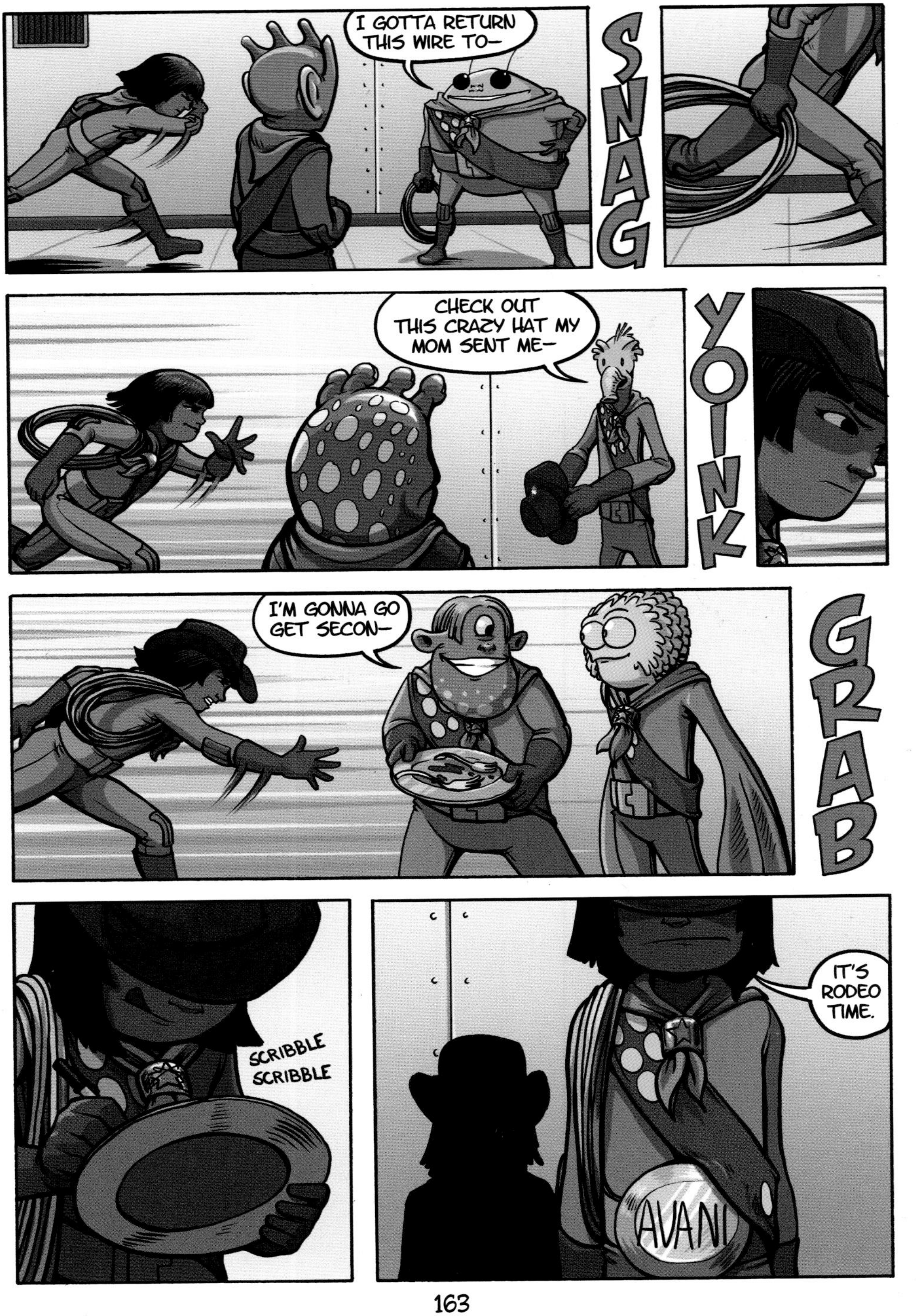
I GOTTA RETURN THIS WIRE TO—
SNAG
CHECK OUT THIS CRAZY HAT MY MOM SENT ME—
YOINK
I'M GONNA GO GET SECON—
GRAB
SCRIBBLE SCRIBBLE
IT'S RODEO TIME.
AVANI

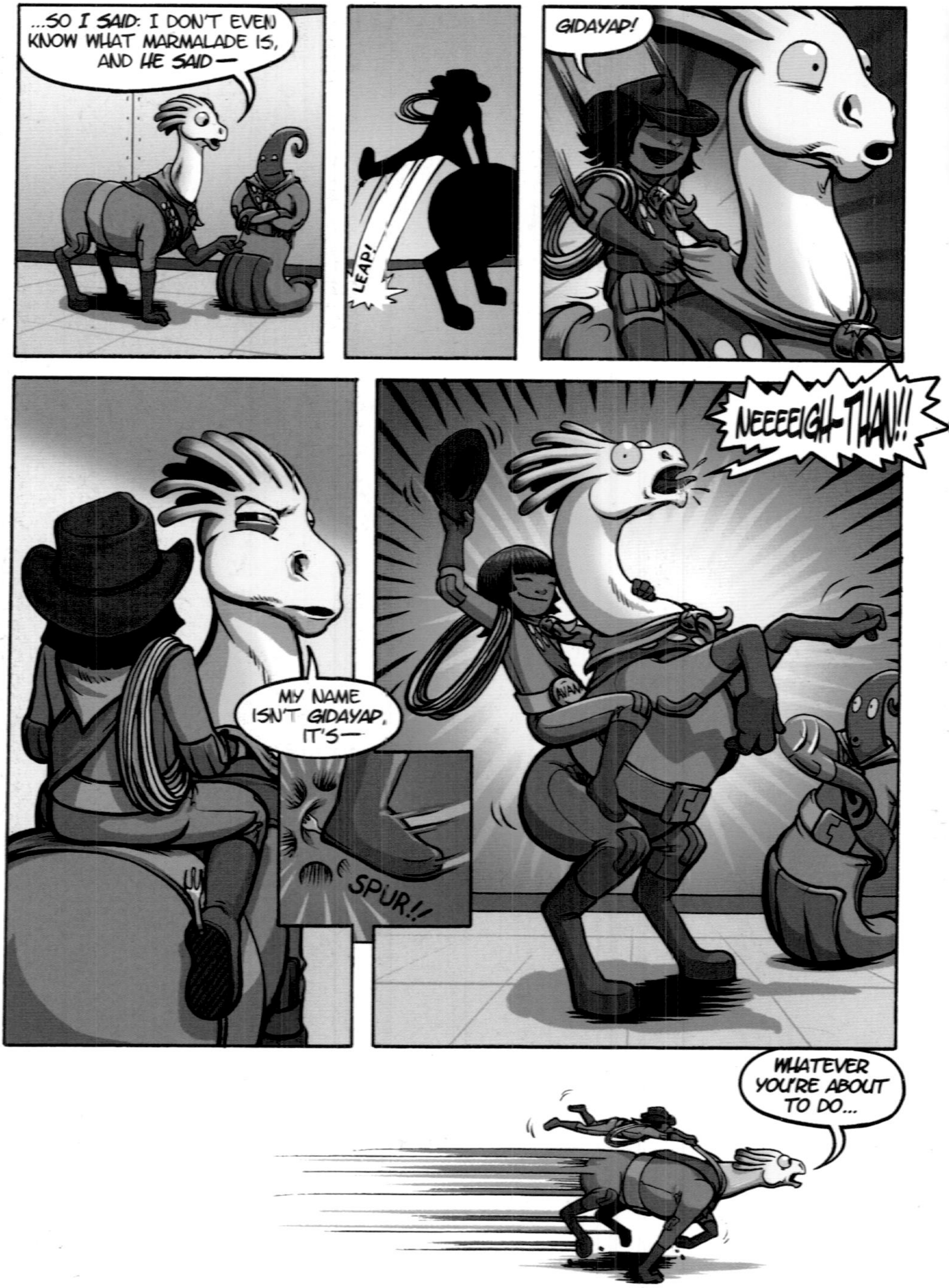
...SO I SAID: I DON'T EVEN KNOW WHAT MARMALADE IS, AND HE SAID—
LEAP!
GIDAYAP!
MY NAME ISN'T GIDAYAP, IT'S—
SPUR!!
NEEEEIGH-THAN!!
WHATEVER YOU'RE ABOUT TO DO...

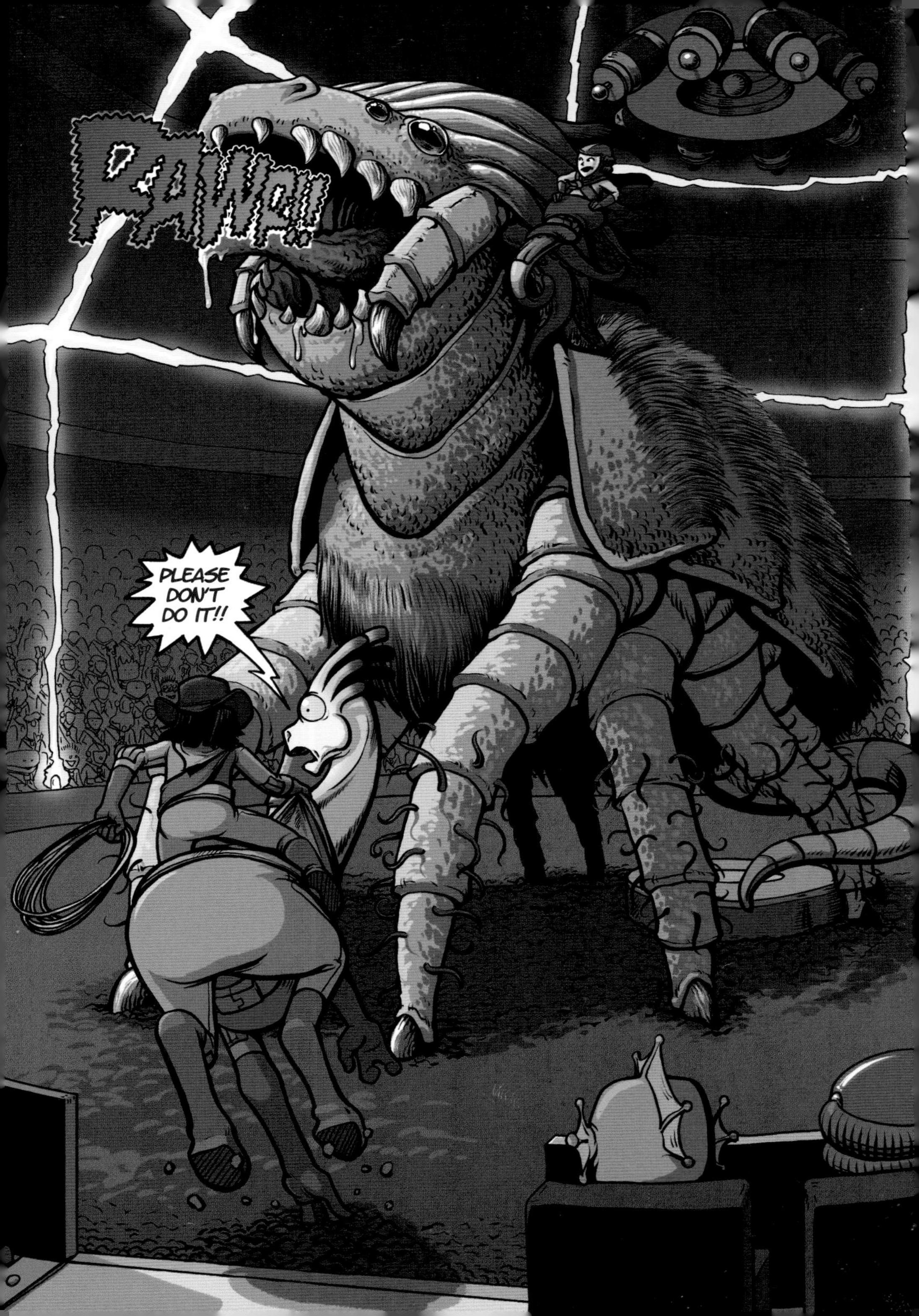
PLEASE DON'T DO IT!!

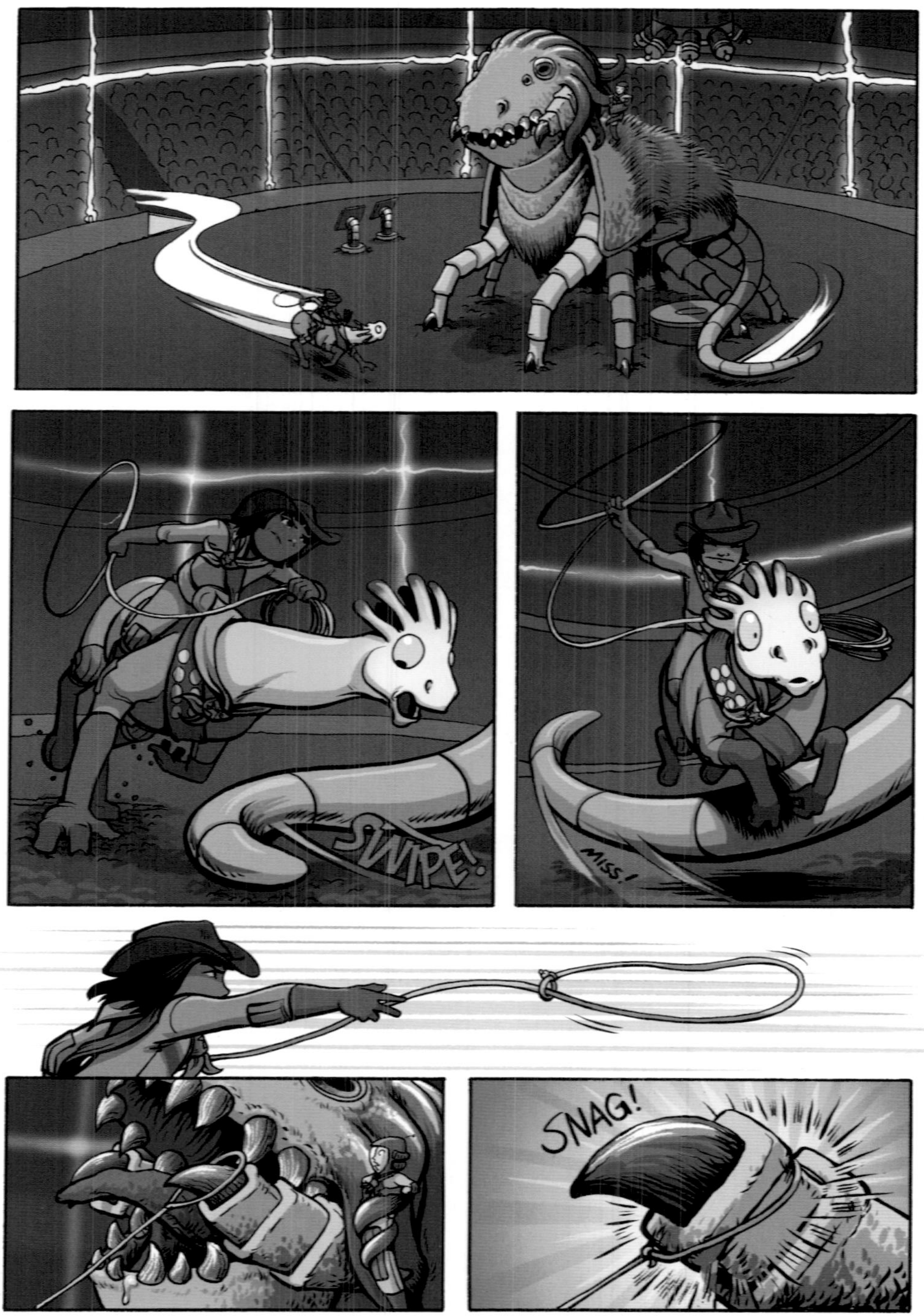
SWIPE!
MISS!
SNAG!

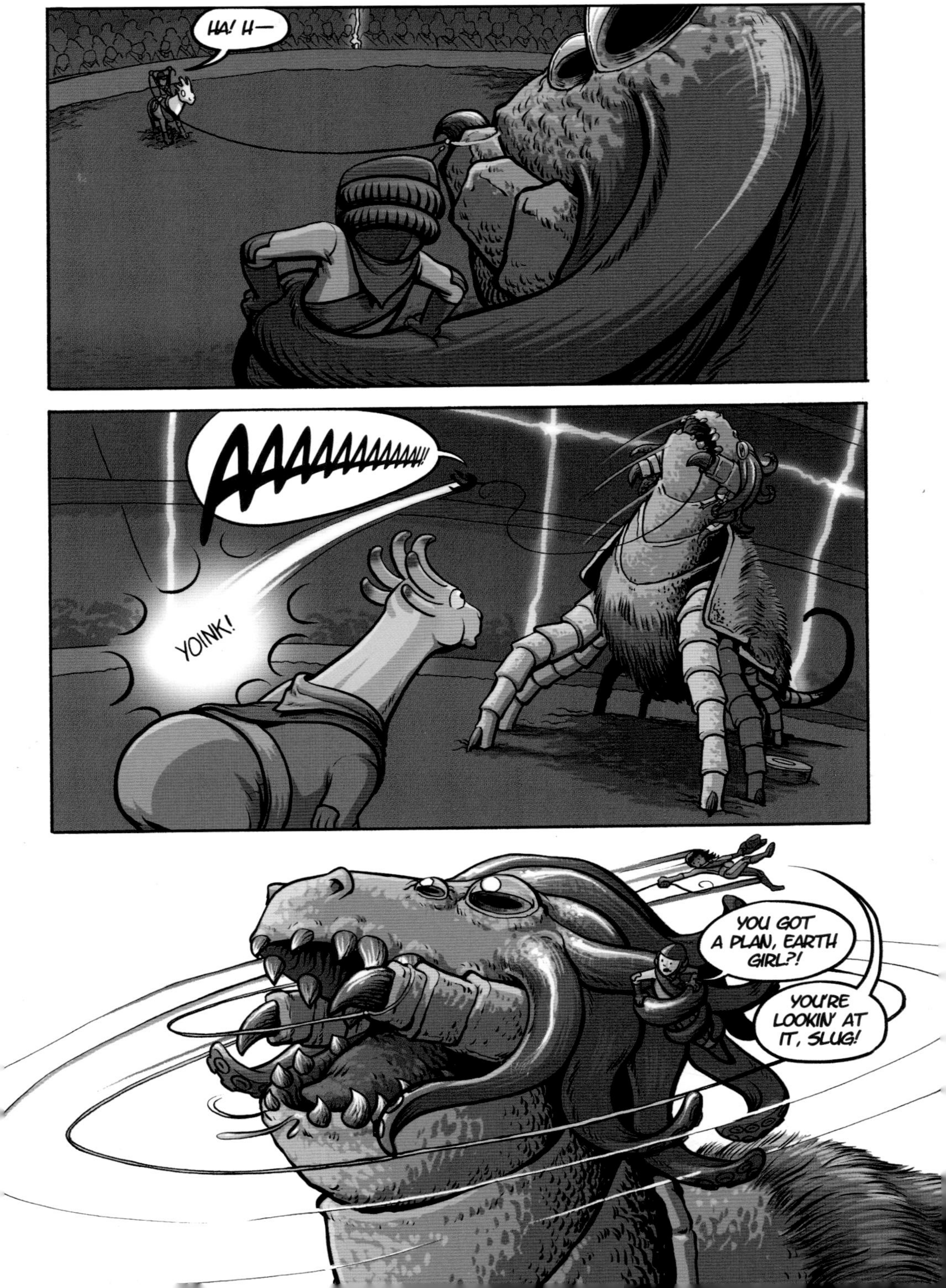
HA! H—
AAAAAAAAAAAH!!
YOINK!
YOU GOT A PLAN, EARTH GIRL?!
YOU'RE LOOKIN' AT IT, SLUG!

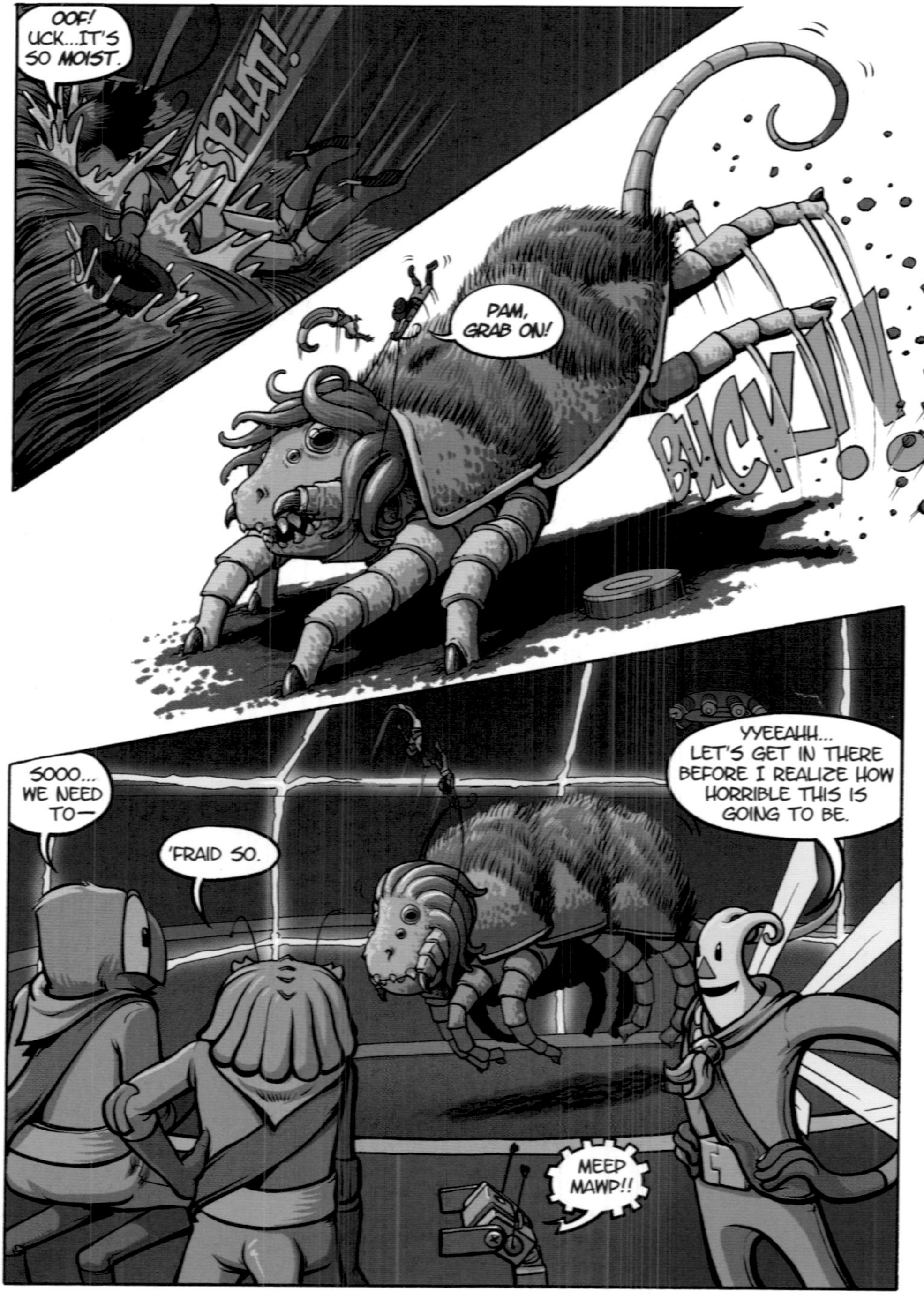
OOF! UCK...IT'S SO MOIST.
SPLAT!
PAM, GRAB ON!
BUCK!!!
SOOO... WE NEED TO—
'FRAID SO.
YYEEAHH... LET'S GET IN THERE BEFORE I REALIZE HOW HORRIBLE THIS IS GOING TO BE.
MEEP MAWP!!

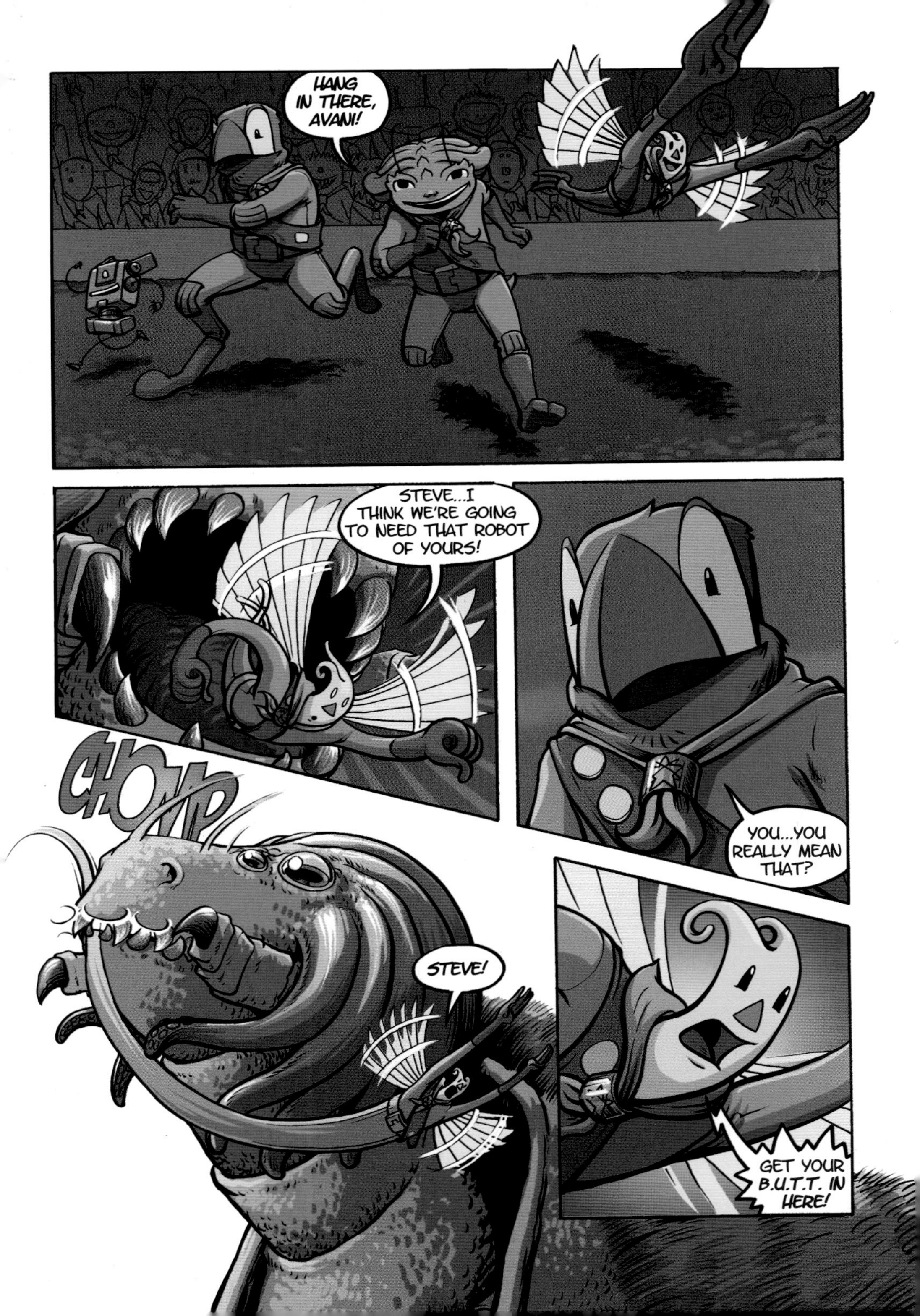
HANG IN THERE, AVANI!
STEVE...I THINK WE'RE GOING TO NEED THAT ROBOT OF YOURS!
CHOMP
YOU...YOU REALLY MEAN THAT?
STEVE!
GET YOUR B.U.T.T. IN HERE!

C'MON BIG GUY, PAPA NEEDS YOU!
VAROOOOM!!
WHAM!
POP!
RAWR!

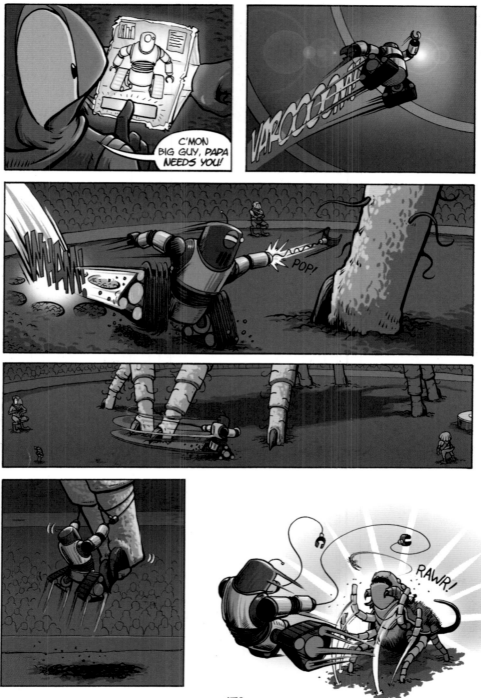

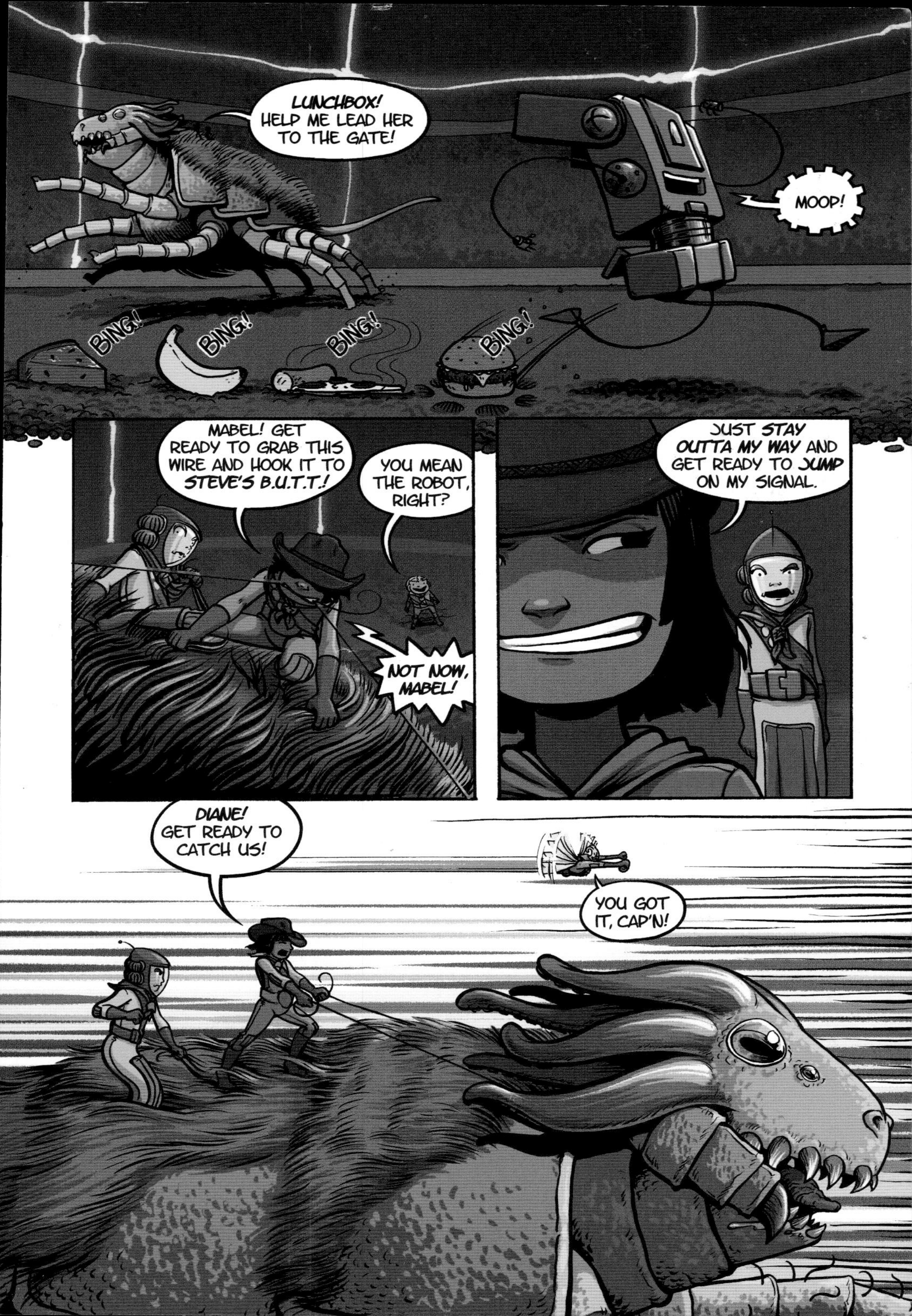
LUNCHBOX! HELP ME LEAD HER TO THE GATE!
MOOP!
BING!
BING!
BING!
BING!
MABEL! GET READY TO GRAB THIS WIRE AND HOOK IT TO STEVE'S B.U.T.T.!
YOU MEAN THE ROBOT, RIGHT?
NOT NOW, MABEL!
JUST STAY OUTTA MY WAY AND GET READY TO JUMP ON MY SIGNAL.
DIANE! GET READY TO CATCH US!
YOU GOT IT, CAP'N!

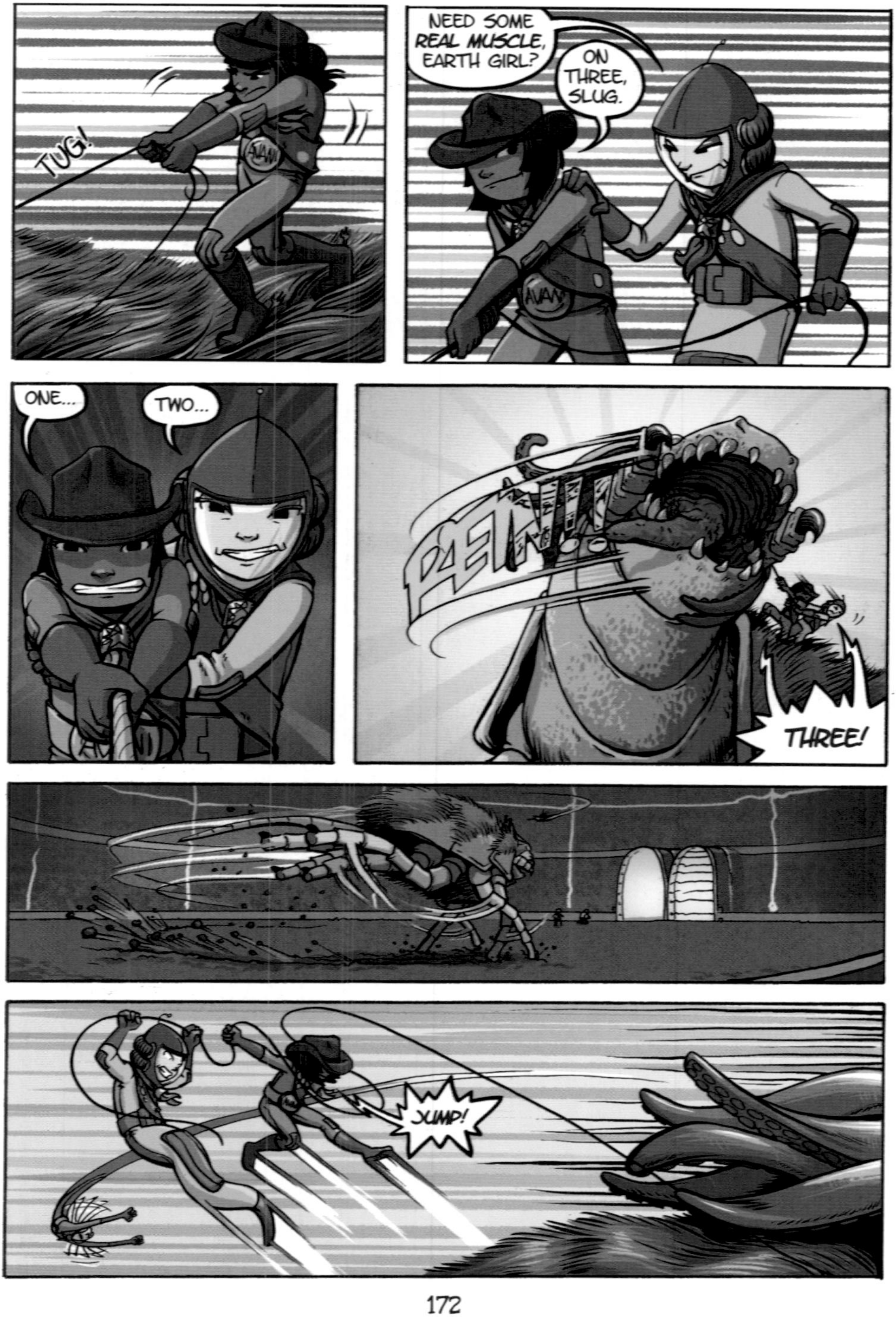
TUG!
NEED SOME REAL MUSCLE, EARTH GIRL?
ON THREE, SLUG.
ONE...
TWO...
THREE!
JUMP!

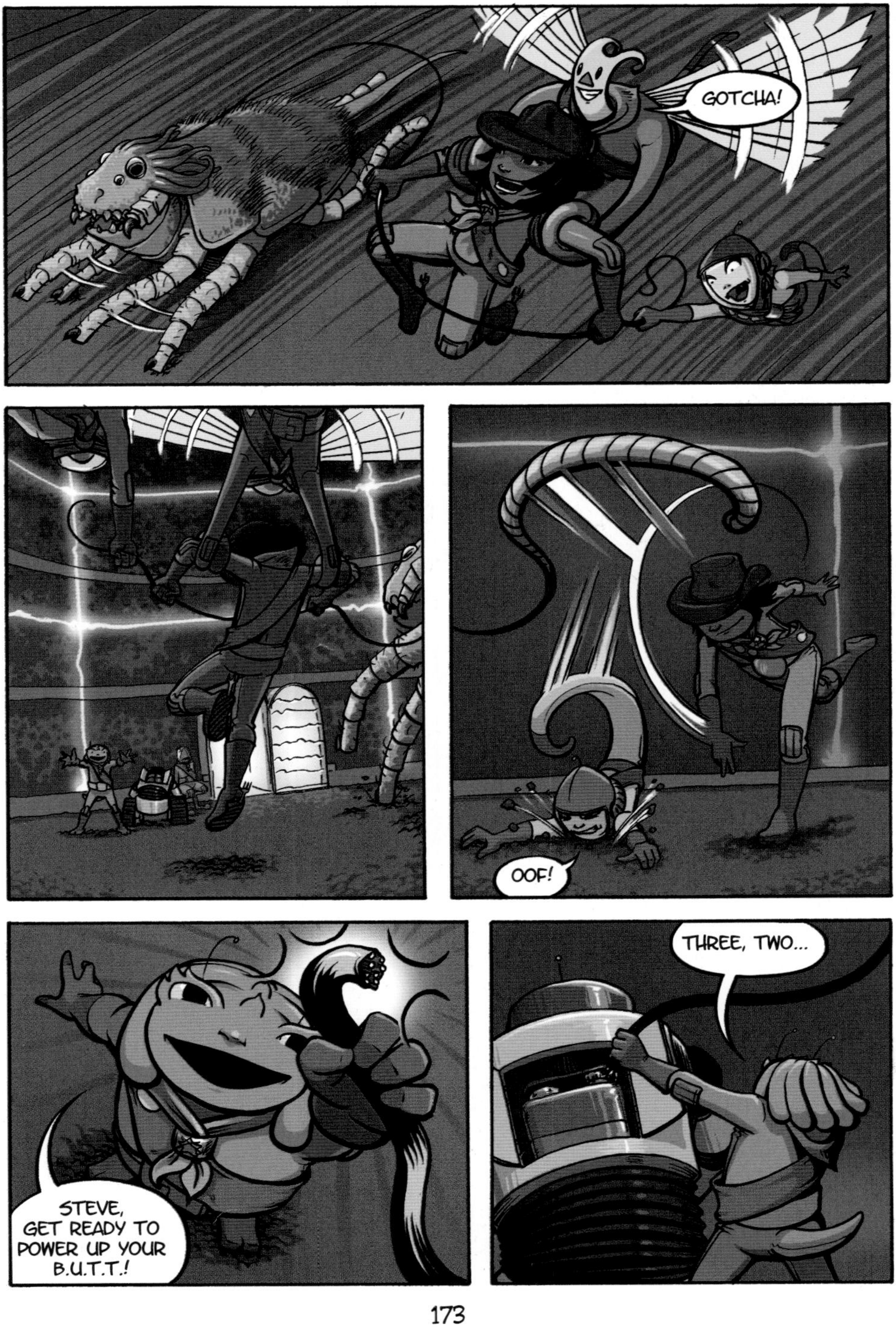
GOTCHA!
OOF!
STEVE, GET READY TO POWER UP YOUR B.U.T.T.!
THREE, TWO...

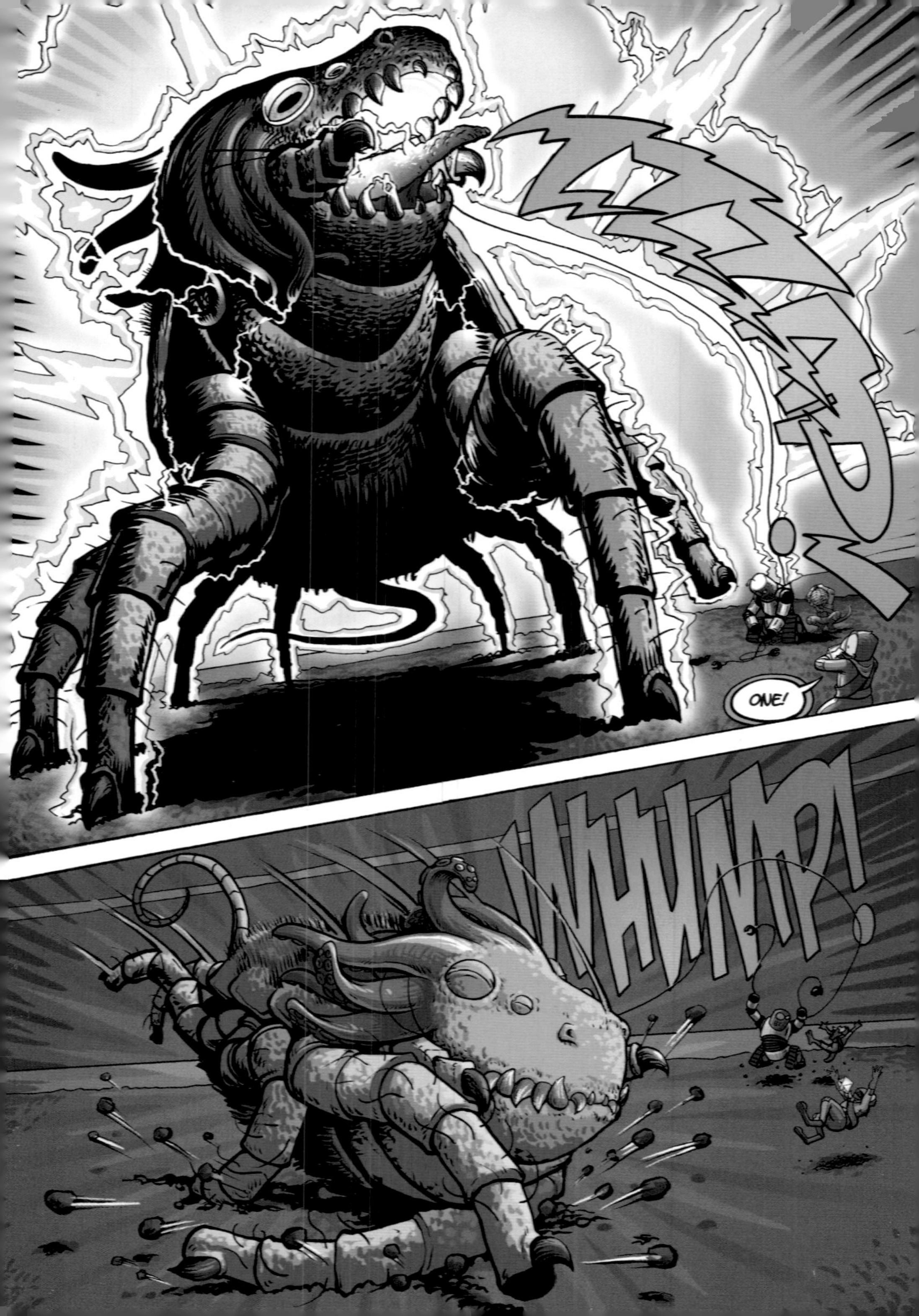
ZZZAP!
ONE!
WHHUMP!

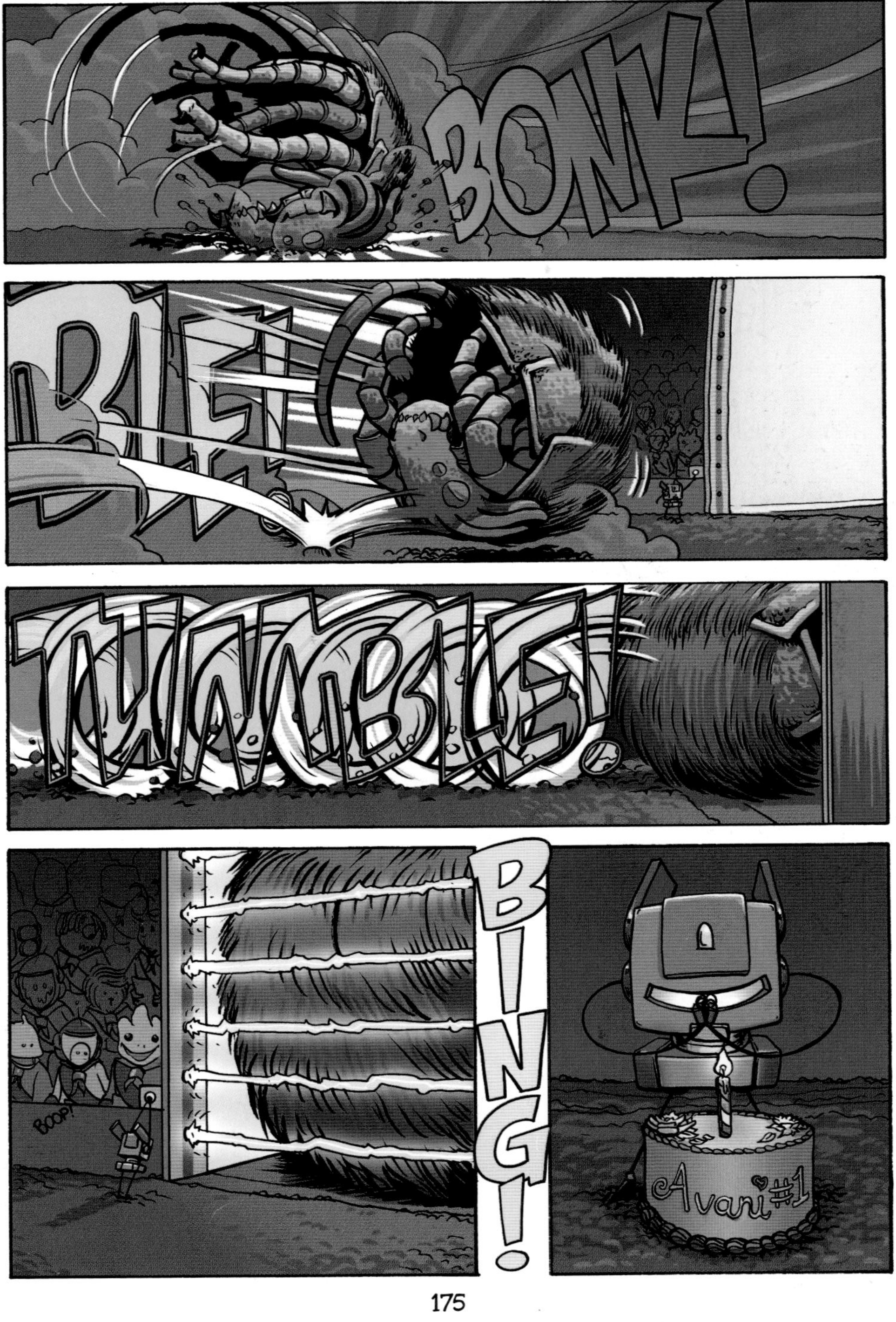
BONK!
TUMBLE!
BOOP!
BING!
Avani #1

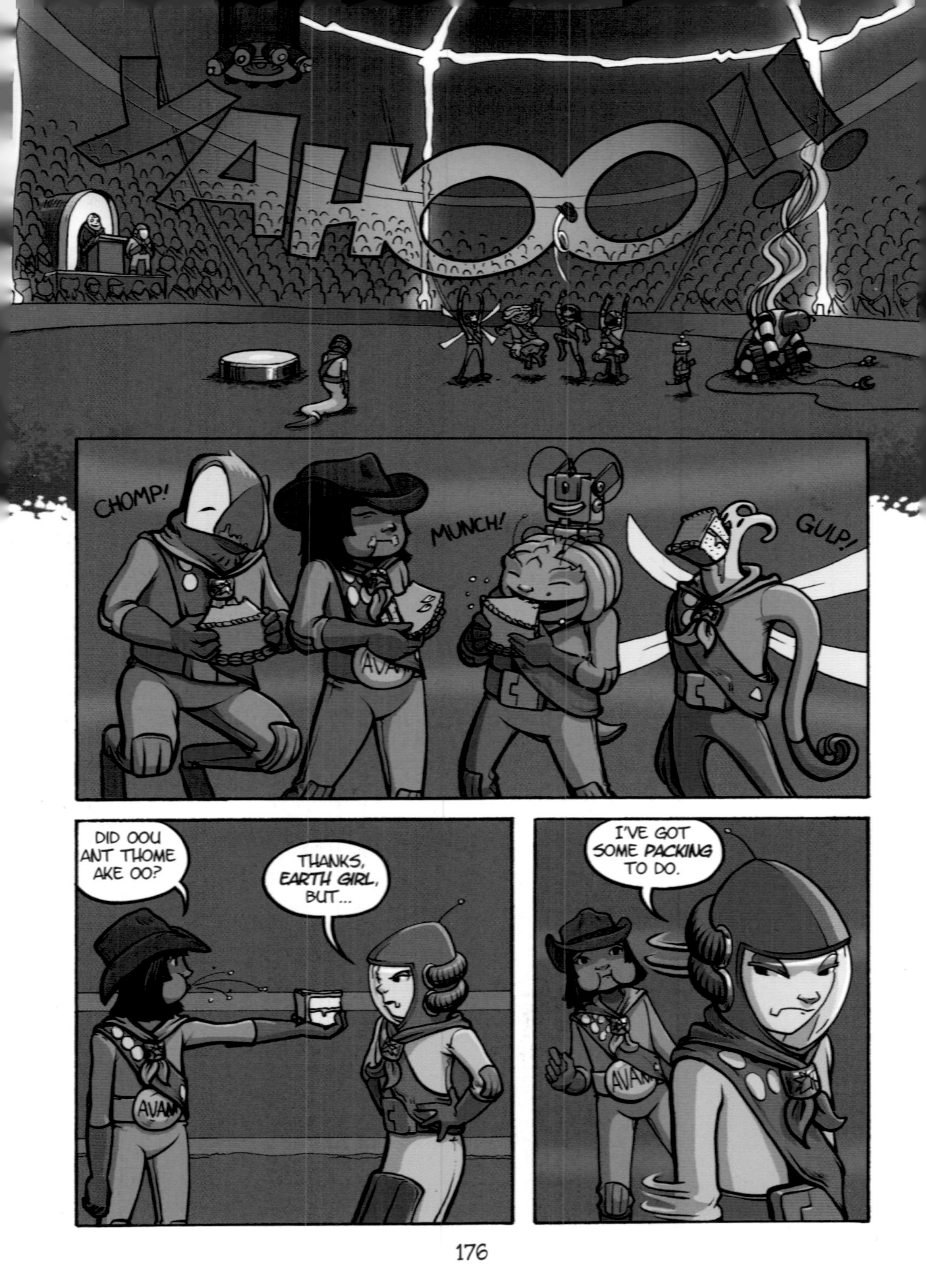
YAHOO!!
CHOMP!
MUNCH!
GULP!
DID OOU ANT THOME AKE OO?
AVAM
THANKS, EARTH GIRL, BUT...
I'VE GOT SOME PACKING TO DO.

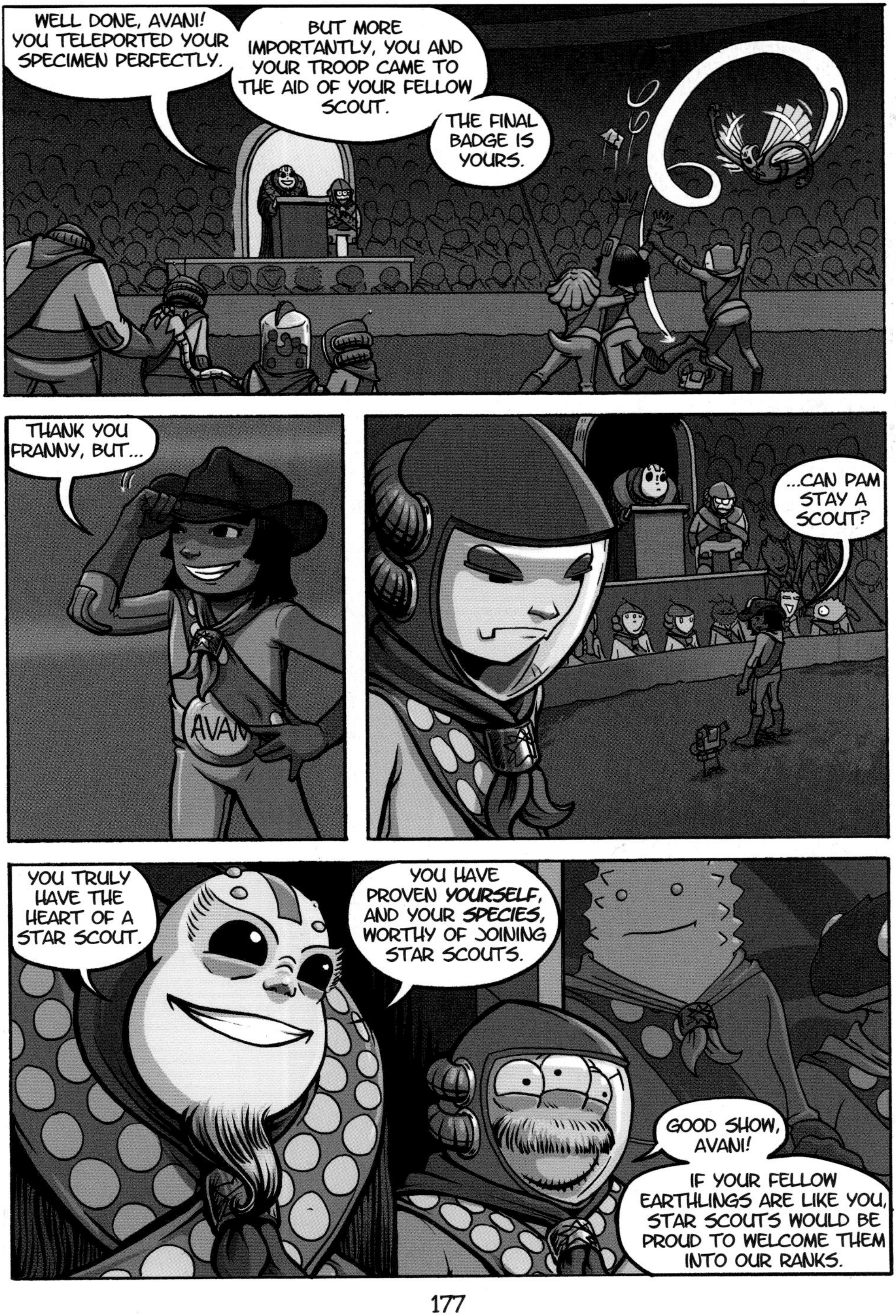
WELL DONE, AVANI! YOU TELEPORTED YOUR SPECIMEN PERFECTLY.
BUT MORE IMPORTANTLY, YOU AND YOUR TROOP CAME TO THE AID OF YOUR FELLOW SCOUT.
THE FINAL BADGE IS YOURS.
THANK YOU FRANNY, BUT...
AVANI
...CAN PAM STAY A SCOUT?
YOU TRULY HAVE THE HEART OF A STAR SCOUT.
YOU HAVE PROVEN *YOURSELF*, AND YOUR *SPECIES*, WORTHY OF JOINING STAR SCOUTS.
GOOD SHOW, AVANI!
IF YOUR FELLOW EARTHLINGS ARE LIKE YOU, STAR SCOUTS WOULD BE PROUD TO WELCOME THEM INTO OUR RANKS.

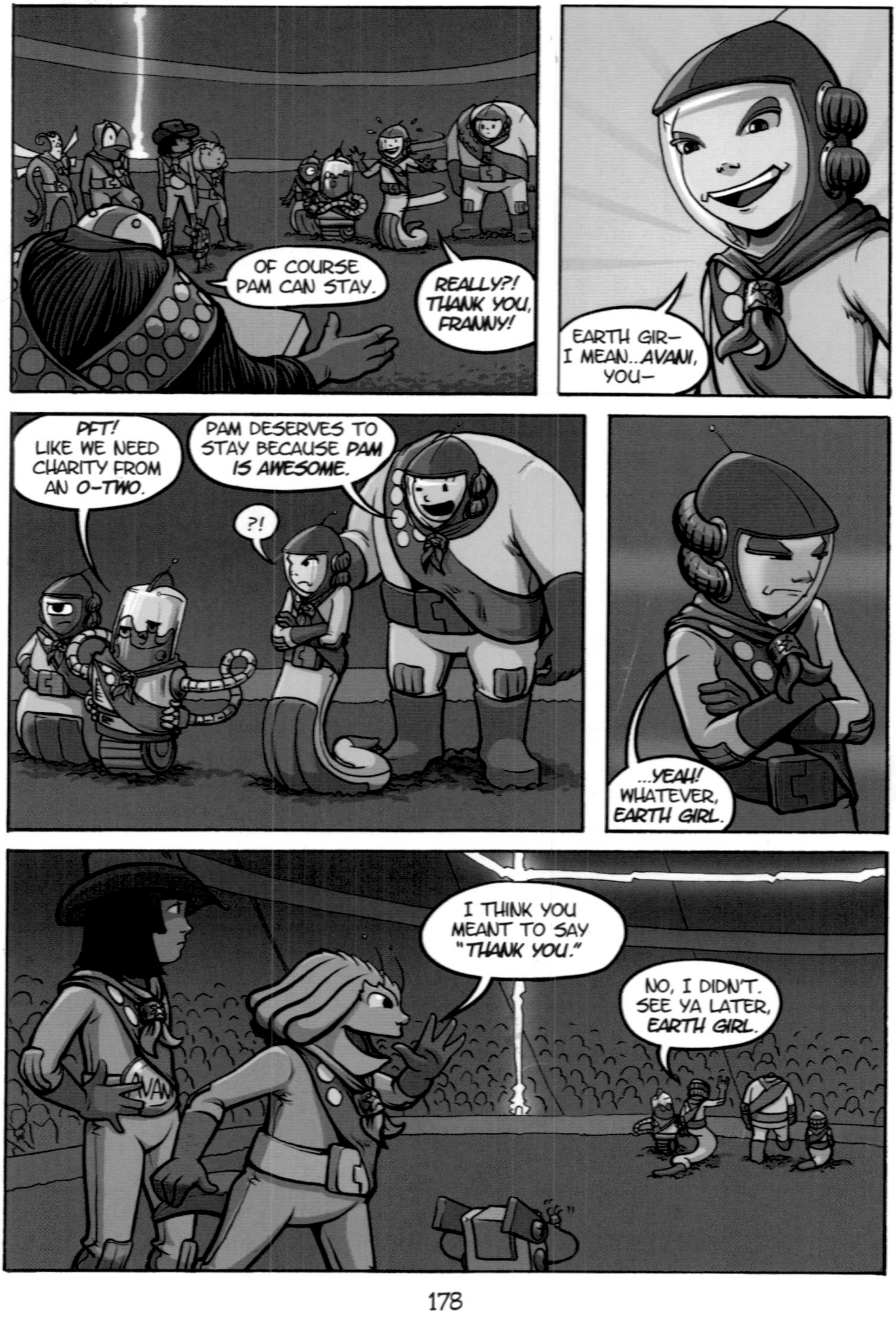
OF COURSE PAM CAN STAY.
REALLY?! THANK YOU, FRANNY!
EARTH GIR— I MEAN...AVANI, YOU—
PFT! LIKE WE NEED CHARITY FROM AN O-TWO.
PAM DESERVES TO STAY BECAUSE PAM IS AWESOME.
?!
...YEAH! WHATEVER, EARTH GIRL.
I THINK YOU MEANT TO SAY "THANK YOU."
NO, I DIDN'T. SEE YA LATER, EARTH GIRL.
AVANI

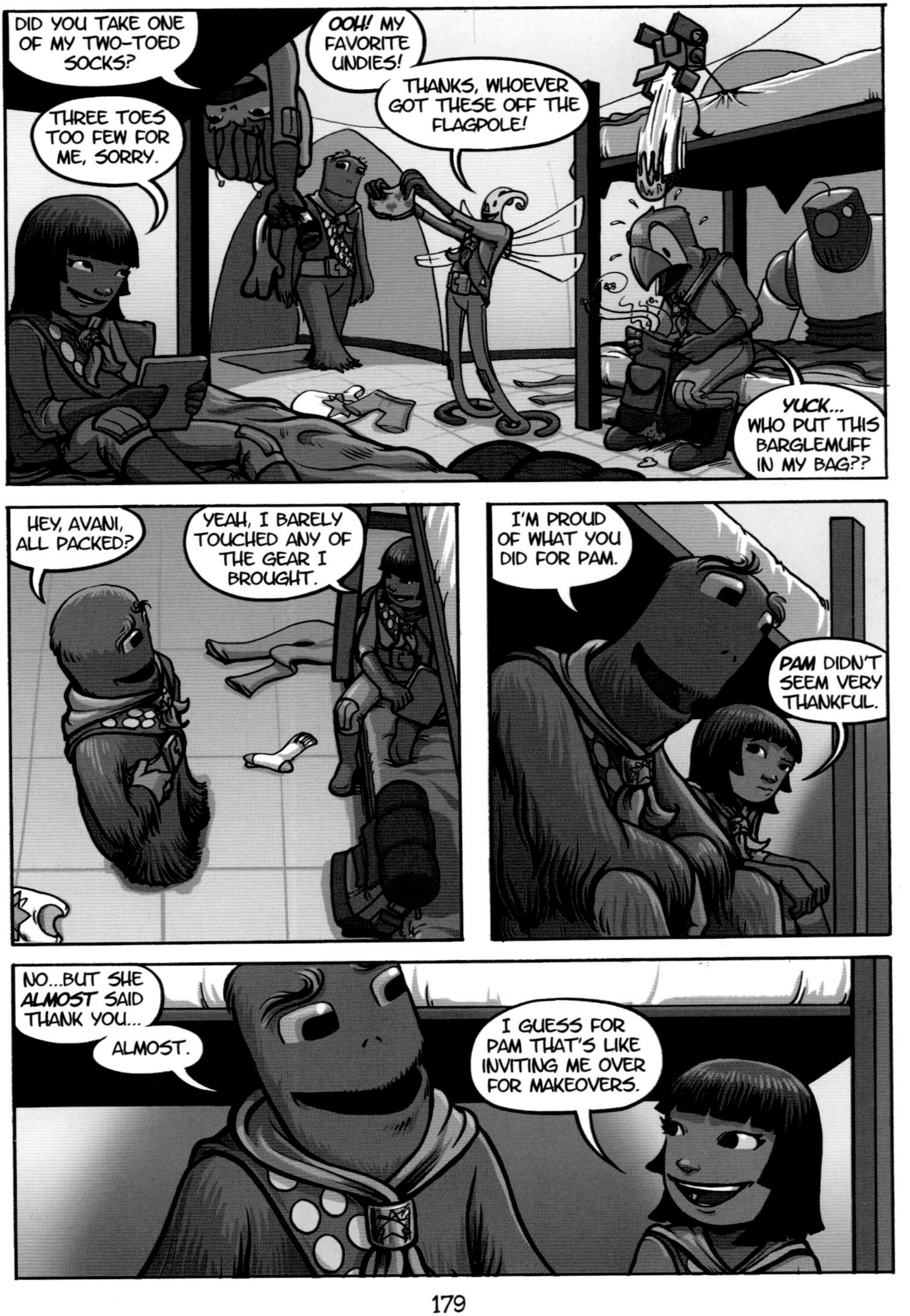
DID YOU TAKE ONE OF MY TWO-TOED SOCKS?
THREE TOES TOO FEW FOR ME, SORRY.
OOH! MY FAVORITE UNDIES!
THANKS, WHOEVER GOT THESE OFF THE FLAGPOLE!
YUCK... WHO PUT THIS BARGLEMUFF IN MY BAG??
HEY, AVANI, ALL PACKED?
YEAH, I BARELY TOUCHED ANY OF THE GEAR I BROUGHT.
I'M PROUD OF WHAT YOU DID FOR PAM.
PAM DIDN'T SEEM VERY THANKFUL.
NO...BUT SHE ALMOST SAID THANK YOU...
ALMOST.
I GUESS FOR PAM THAT'S LIKE INVITING ME OVER FOR MAKEOVERS.

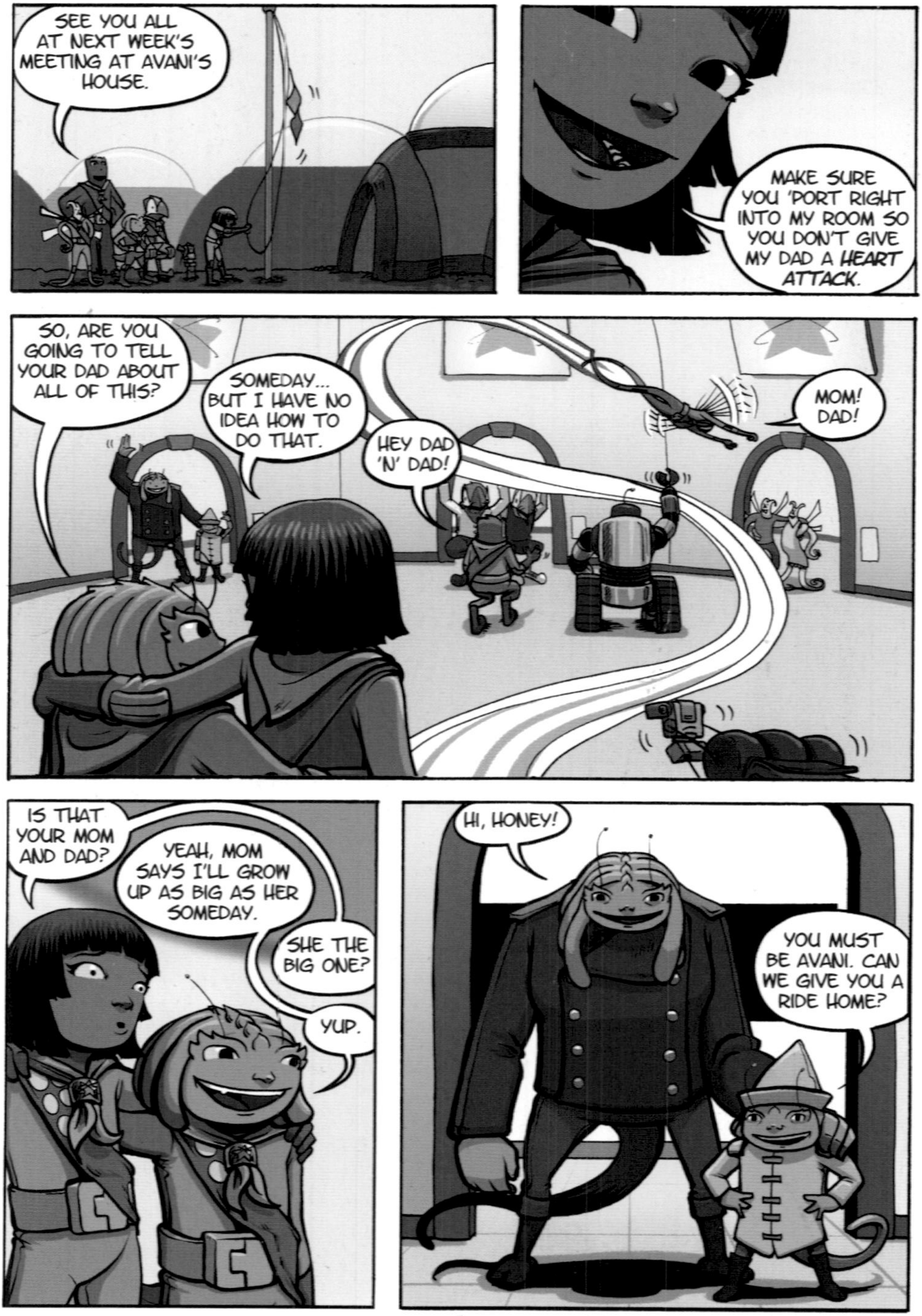
SEE YOU ALL AT NEXT WEEK'S MEETING AT AVANI'S HOUSE.
MAKE SURE YOU 'PORT RIGHT INTO MY ROOM SO YOU DON'T GIVE MY DAD A HEART ATTACK.
SO, ARE YOU GOING TO TELL YOUR DAD ABOUT ALL OF THIS?
SOMEDAY... BUT I HAVE NO IDEA HOW TO DO THAT.
HEY DAD 'N' DAD!
MOM! DAD!
IS THAT YOUR MOM AND DAD?
YEAH, MOM SAYS I'LL GROW UP AS BIG AS HER SOMEDAY.
SHE THE BIG ONE?
YUP.
HI, HONEY!
YOU MUST BE AVANI. CAN WE GIVE YOU A RIDE HOME?

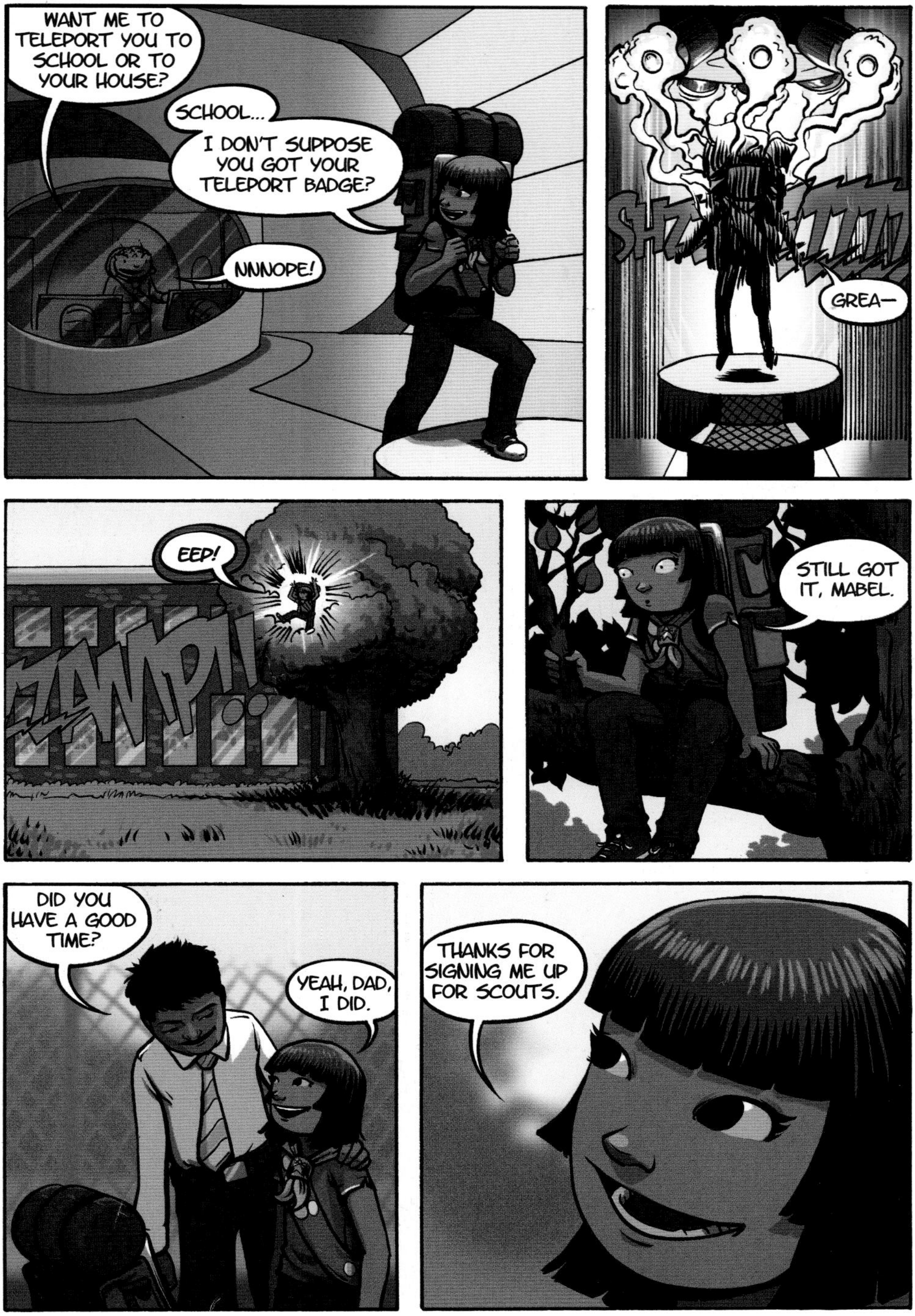
WANT ME TO TELEPORT YOU TO SCHOOL OR TO YOUR HOUSE?
SCHOOL...
I DON'T SUPPOSE YOU GOT YOUR TELEPORT BADGE?
NNNOPE!
GREA—
EEP!
STILL GOT IT, MABEL.
DID YOU HAVE A GOOD TIME?
YEAH, DAD, I DID.
THANKS FOR SIGNING ME UP FOR SCOUTS.

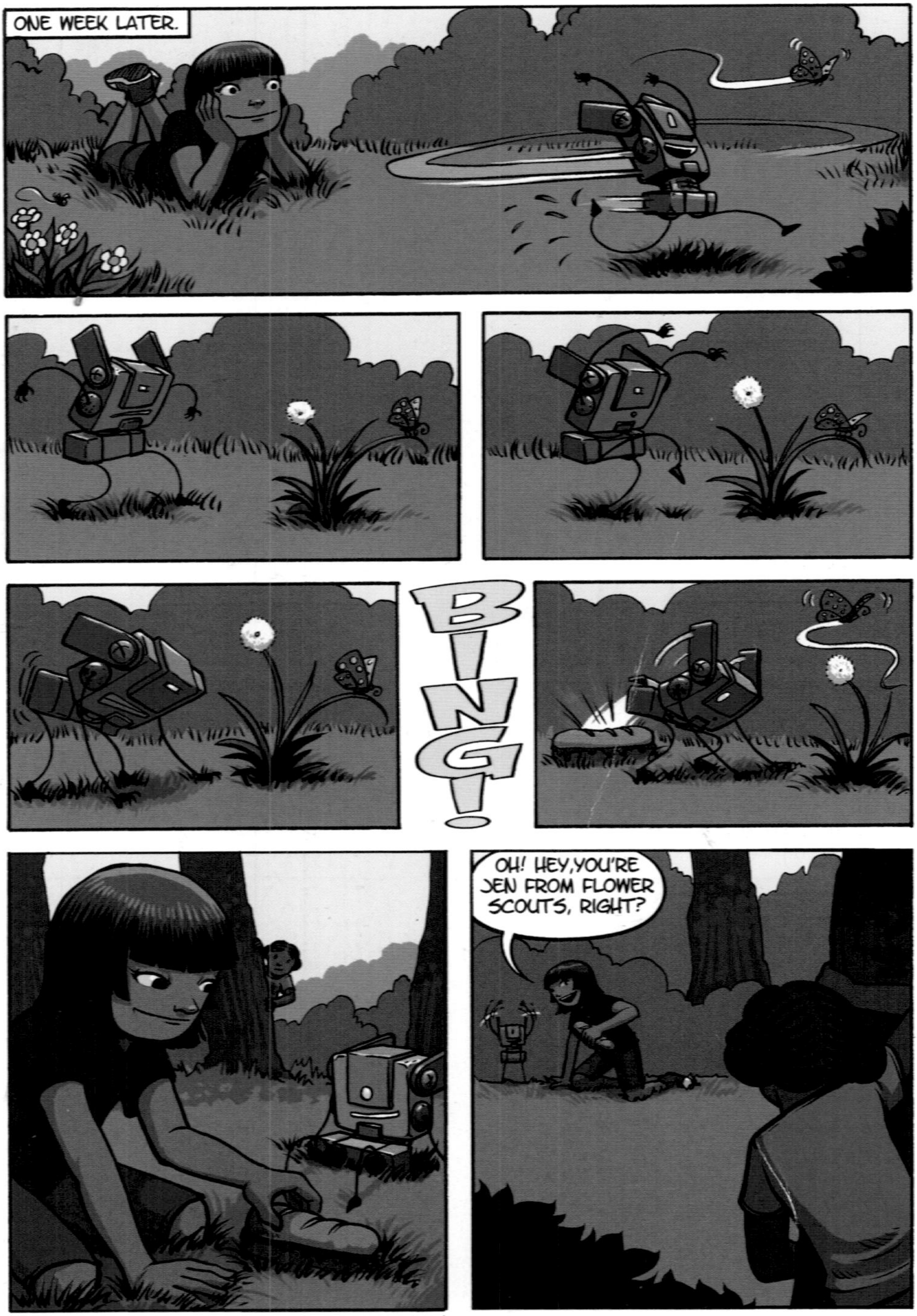
ONE WEEK LATER.
BING!
OH! HEY, YOU'RE JEN FROM FLOWER SCOUTS, RIGHT?

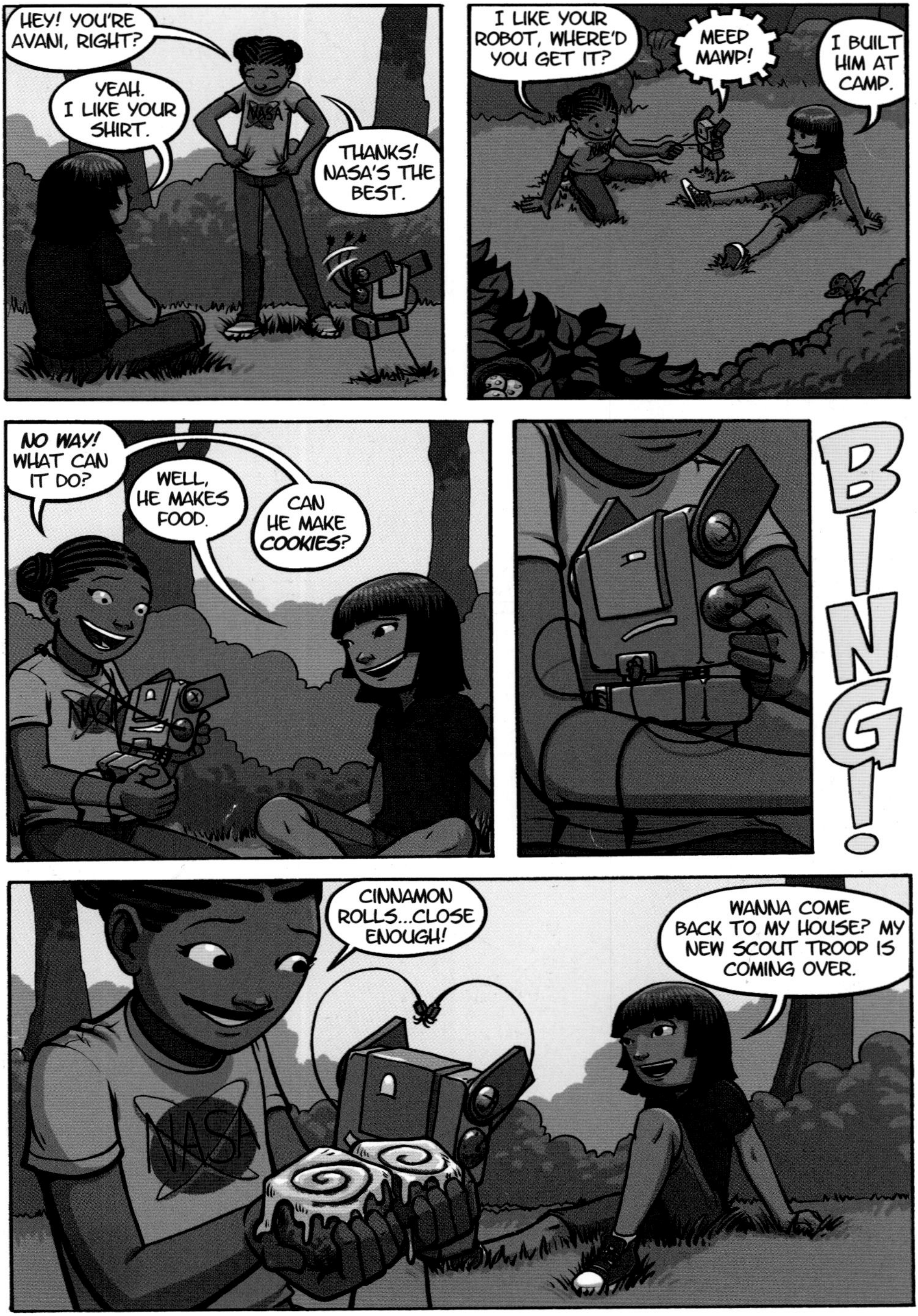
HEY! YOU'RE AVANI, RIGHT?
YEAH. I LIKE YOUR SHIRT.
THANKS! NASA'S THE BEST.
NASA
I LIKE YOUR ROBOT, WHERE'D YOU GET IT?
MEEP MAWP!
I BUILT HIM AT CAMP.
NO WAY! WHAT CAN IT DO?
WELL, HE MAKES FOOD.
CAN HE MAKE COOKIES?
BING!
CINNAMON ROLLS...CLOSE ENOUGH!
WANNA COME BACK TO MY HOUSE? MY NEW SCOUT TROOP IS COMING OVER.

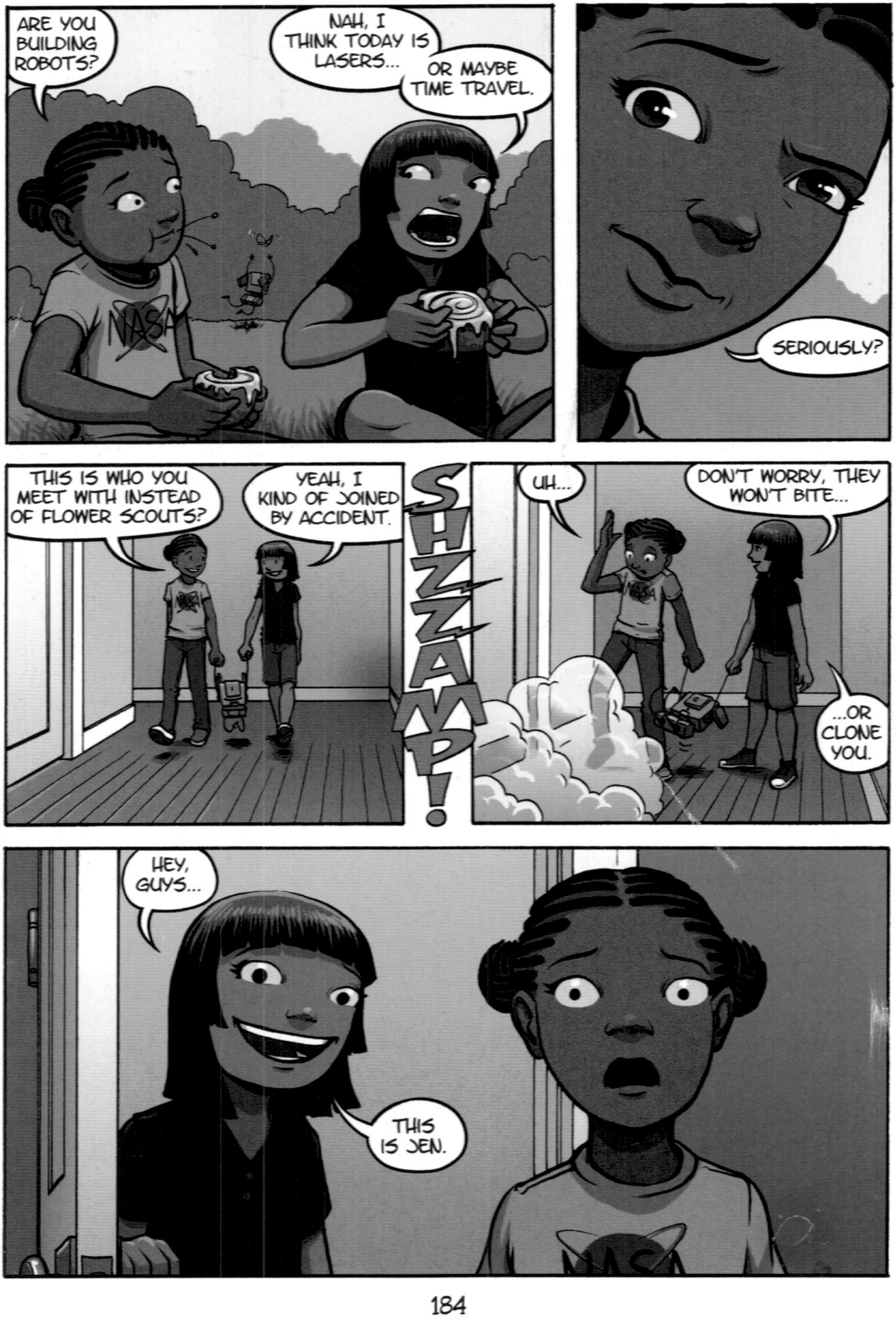
ARE YOU BUILDING ROBOTS?
NAH, I THINK TODAY IS LASERS...
OR MAYBE TIME TRAVEL.
SERIOUSLY?
THIS IS WHO YOU MEET WITH INSTEAD OF FLOWER SCOUTS?
YEAH, I KIND OF JOINED BY ACCIDENT.
SHZZAMP!
UH...
DON'T WORRY, THEY WON'T BITE...
...OR CLONE YOU.
HEY, GUYS...
THIS IS JEN.

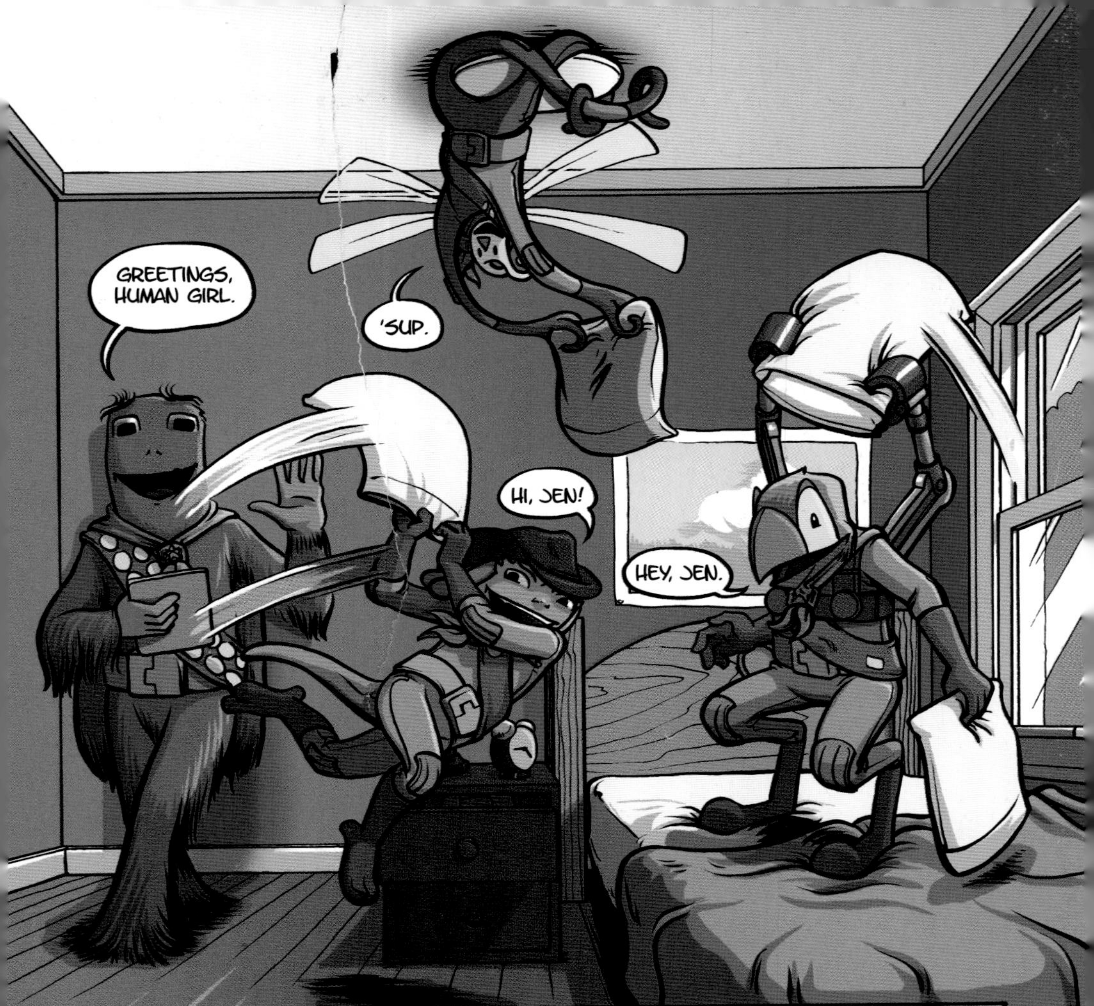
GREETINGS, HUMAN GIRL.
'SUP.
HI, JEN!
HEY, JEN.

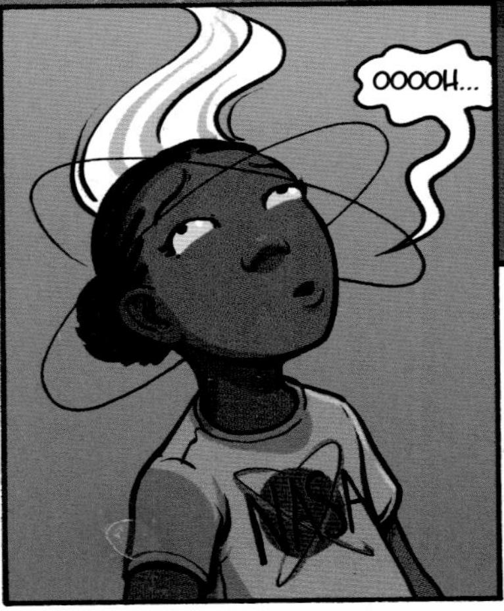
OOOOH...

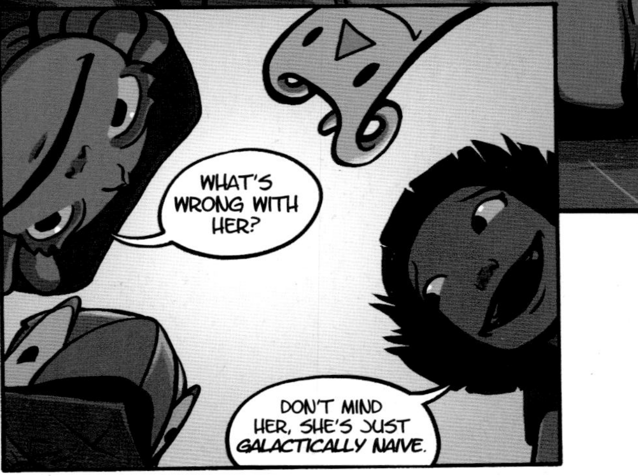
WHAT'S WRONG WITH HER?
DON'T MIND HER, SHE'S JUST GALACTICALLY NAIVE.